the Enigma Source

Breakfield and Burkey

BOOK 10: Award Winning Techno-Thriller Series

Published by

ICABOD Press

ISBN: 978-1-946858-39-9 (Paperback)
ISBN: 978-1-946858-37-5 (eBook)
ISBN: 978-1-946858-38-2 (Audible)

Library of Congress Control Number: 2018948921
Cover Design by Rebecca Finkel

2nd edition

Printed in the USA
TECHNO-THRILLER | SUSPENSE

Acknowledgments

We are grateful for the support of our friends and family while we work on these stories. During the writing ideas and thoughts are gathered from multiple places to weave into a story we hope you find as much fun to read as we do to write.

Specialized Terms are available beginning 391 if needed for readers' reference.

The irony of paper money in the digital age.
How long will it take governments to realize
that hard currency, with its analog tangibility,
can be displaced overnight by a cryptocurrency
from a rival nation? Savings simply erased,
commerce turned off, and whole populations
in economic suspended animation. Bold
predictions, but in hindsight how could we
not have foreseen the inevitable outcome?

...The Enigma Chronicles

Greed, Power, and Corruption: What's New

Poland, 80 years ago

Military troops all had their favorite places to blow off steam. This one was large, with areas for local musicians, reasonable food, a range of alcoholic beverages and a few private rooms available for a price to indulge in other refreshment fare. Only those from money or with high rank could afford them. In this case, the man waiting for someone had both.

Kondrat Mickelowski was of the older, more honorable, wealthy families that struggled with the constant regional conflicts that had been brewing for almost 20 years. His commanding presence was complimented by his height, speech, and impeccable grooming, all of which spoke to his status. His jacket was of the finest wool, cut in line with the fashionably rich of the times. Though his family indeed had position, money, and property, the values of education, human kindness, and a logical view of cause and effect had been instilled from birth. These are the values he imparted to his only son.

Life in this place in any position, he believed, was short lived while the maniac in Germany gained ground. That lunatic, in the opinion of many across Europe, surrounded himself with cruel and greedy men without conscience. Reflecting on the various recent conflicts, negotiations, treaties, and shifts in political power, he realized things were coming to a head. Hence the request for this meeting with his son, the Wolfgang.

Lively noise and revelry from the soldiers coming in for a start to the weekend spilled into the private dining area. Dark beers were flowing, in line with the weekly pay vouchers delivered earlier in the day. Military units from all sides were doing exactly as the strategy planners intended. Here's the target, the reasons are above your pay grade, and when these invaders evacuate this place, all will be well. Warsaw political leaders felt the annexation of the railway junction at the City of Bohumin was the only stop gap to German invasion.

Noise levels increased in the private room as the door opened and his son entered. He cut a fine figure in his uniform and had earned the rank of lieutenant, even at his very young age. With his education and training, he had entered service at 16. Tall and commanding like his father, he strode to the table, and as his father rose they embraced. They sat in adjacent chairs and the barmaid brought in steaming plates of food and two brimming steins.

Kondrat looked up graciously after she had set the provisions down and said, "Madam, thank you. That's all for now."

The barmaid was taken aback, as she'd expected his customary scowl, rather than a kind word.

The Wolfgang, who added a small smile and a twinkle in his blue eyes, also voiced, "Yes, thank you, madam."

Uncertain but pleased, she grinned, curtseyed and left without a word.

"My son, how was your travel? Any issues?"

"No, Father, though the rumors swirling about the New Order and what they plan are everywhere. It seems to be inevitable, regardless of the negotiations by our leaders."

"Agreed. It seems that the mandate is for a total Germanisation of Europe, one territory at a time. Without the intervention of the west, it is only a matter of time. The various delay tactics are just that. Our families, languages, traditions, religions, and associations will be wiped out if the lunatic is not stopped."

"How can I help, Father? What can I do? I am rising in the ranks and gaining ground from those currently in power, though I sense some reluctance to share information. Officers are having sidebar correspondence with those outside of Poland. With the latest border change negotiation, it seems we are being painted as a German annexation. Is that how you view it?"

"Exactly, and it will only get worse. I have a unit I would like you to request transfer into, though it will appear to be a demotion. Meanwhile, I am going to try to liquidate some of our assets and place them outside of our country. I will let you know where and the details for access. It won't be as much as I would like, because I want to make certain that our staff and the surrounding community have a share to help overcome what I feel certain is going to be devastating to everything you know and how you were raised.

"Men who get addicted to power, especially over other people and land, stop at nothing to gain what they want. This is one of mankind's biggest failings. There always seems to be some narcissistic psychopath who quietly rises up with the right message to gain his or her agenda. With education or the right influential circle, they often further their power addiction by military means. But you should know that our threat from the Nationalists in Germany is not the only consideration. The Soviets to the East are uncommonly quiet in this theater of aggression, and that is just as troubling."

The young lieutenant nodded and stated, "Father, how do you stop someone like Hitler, or is it even possible? The old wounds from the Great War have left many feeling guilty and ready to acquiesce to calls for repatriating lost territories, regardless of new national identities. Poland finally pulled away from the Kingdom of Prussia after the Treaty of Versailles set the stage for our independence. Now here we are again, being looked at as another territory to be annexed by Germany."

"Honestly, my son, I sadly think that a bullet to the head would be the most effective. However, it is morally wrong, period! The best way to stay ahead of the interlopers is to stay ahead of them and not let them get a foothold. Vigilance, coupled with better information and methods to apply the information, is the right solution, though it is the most elusive. As an example, if you can watch all the pieces on the chessboard during the entire game, you can know the traps in advance to know what to avoid. It is a skill that few possess."

The lieutenant was lost in thought about the commentary as he finished his food. This logic flow was not a new concept to him. However the current world situation was much closer to home. "I will make arrangements for the transfer, Father, when I return to Command. Do you think it will be enough to make a difference?"

Kondrat emphatically stated, "It always makes a difference to do the right thing, especially against tyrannical maniacs. Thank you, my son. You are the hope of the future. Stay safe. God speed."

CHAPTER 1

Did You Really Need a Different Introduction?

Present Day

In his cheeriest voice, Otto greeted, "Bruno! How are you, friend? It's been ages since we've spoken! I was beginning to think that our last round of business was the end of our interactions, but I am delighted to see I was mistaken. How can I help you and your associate? It is not often that I am approached by one of Interpol's finest cyber detectives and one of the directors of the Global Bank. May I assume that this has something to do with the latest developments in the cryptocurrency markets and the ensuing theft that occurred?"

Bruno sat dumbfounded for a moment, unable to respond. In his Instant Message window on his PC, he was alerted to a new message.

> How does this man know that I'm on the call?

Bruno, somewhat dazed, responded:

> You said you wanted the best... no one sneaks up on these people...

Otto puzzled a moment, then asked, "Bruno, are you still there? Are you okay? Can you hear me?"

Finally Bruno cleared his throat and responded, "Otto, this is my anonymous calling line that goes through a bank of anonymizing servers just so I can have a completely cloaked conversation with people demanding extreme security. How did you know it was me? And, furthermore, how could you possibly have guessed who was on the call with me? Finally, why do you suspect we are calling about cryptocurrency matters?"

Otto suppressed a smile and innocently replied, "Oh, pardon me, Bruno. Have I made some misstatements to your distinguished guest?"

Bruno clucked his tongue in annoyance and continued, "On second thought, I don't really want to know all the tricks of the magician. Allow me to introduce Tonya Van Den Berghe from the Global Bank.

"Otto, I was asked to make introductions, but as you can see, Tonya, these are the people we call on when we need that which cannot be done. I'll leave you two to talk in private. I assume that the voice tunnel is encrypted, Otto, after my initial but naïve outreach to you. Good day to you both."

Otto didn't have time to reply to Bruno's hasty departure, so he offered, "Tonya, apologies if your call didn't catch me unawares. We work very hard at being informed. That way when we are called upon to help we can take up the assignment quickly. How may I be of service to you and your organization?"

Tonya, relatively young but well-educated and informed about the world stage, quickly moved past her initial surprise, almost smiled, and acknowledged, "Otto, I believe your demonstration clearly proved your point about your organization's effectiveness. You are correct, I am calling with regards to cryptocurrency matters and some very high-profile thefts that lead us to believe the Global Bank has been compromised.

"To that end, I would like to meet and discuss the contents of a package I need to provide you. It will give you all the details we have so far, but there are some things that I cannot discuss over the phone, even though I rather believe that the line is certainly encrypted. Would that be possible?"

Otto nodded and answered, "Understood. In a chat window that I'm opening up on your computer, I will place the location of a cyber-Drop Vault. We use this with special customers for secure document and data sharing. It will help us to begin work immediately with current information. When and where would you like to meet? I presume that time is of the essence."

Tonya smirked as she replied, "You know it, Mr. Magician!

"I will upload the information within the hour. I would like to meet with you or possibly your right hand designate the day after tomorrow in Paris. I would prefer that we keep discussions on this topic out of our headquarters in New York City, though I assure you I have the support of our Managing Director in this matter. I can, of course, provide credentials."

Otto reviewed the background information on Tonya, including several photos provided by ICABOD, the team's Artificial Intelligence Supercomputer. The young woman had graduated in the top of her class from Harvard Business with a focus in International Finance, with no extraordinarily high financial portfolio and her remaining two years of education debt being paid monthly. The photographs provided included professional headshots of her even smile, her heart-shaped face framed by shiny chestnut colored waves that just reached her shoulders. The photo date was three months ago and included her physical attributes of height at almost 1.8 meters and a lean 59 kilograms. It struck Otto that her facial lines were very sophisticated, yet she seemed approachable.

He commented, "Based on the nature of the discussion, credentials will be necessary. I will have you meet with Wolfgang Mickelowski, our Financial Director in Paris, at noon on Wednesday. Unless you have an objection, we will arrange for the meeting to take place in a secure conference room at Regal Financial in La Défense, just west of the Paris city limits. I have an associate on the Board of Directors of the main branch of the institution's headquarters in Zürich."

Tonya replied, "That is very agreeable. Thank you, Otto, I look forward to meeting with Mr. Mickelowski."

The call was disconnected and Otto called Wolfgang. They chatted for a few moments and decided the best course of action was to assemble the team. They agreed to a time, and Otto waited for the package upload from Tonya to read en route.

Tonya Van Den Berghe studied the desk phone, then reached for her personal cell phone that was still capable of making an encrypted call, and dialed a familiar number from her contact list identified by only an icon. Once the encrypted call was launched, she steeled herself for the pending conversation.

It seemed like an eternity before the call connected, and a pleasant voice answered, "How did the call go with Bruno's recommendation? Do we have the services of this unbiased group in Switzerland?"

Tonya replied, "Yes, Madam Director, we have their services, but, boy, what a creepy call! I mean, the man Bruno connected us to, Otto, knew right away who we were and almost to the letter of what we wanted. It was almost like he knew the work to be done and we would only need to verify the terms and conditions. Bruno seemed uncomfortable and bailed from the call. I finished the negotiations.

"Madam Director, I'm not completely comfortable with this type of contact, no matter how highly your Interpol contact, Bruno, recommended them."

The smirking voice on the other end of the call asked, "Do you feel we are on the right trajectory?"

Tonya had some trouble reeling in her irked state of mind but offered all the professionalism she could muster.

"Yes, Madam Director, we are on the right trajectory with these people. Not only did they know exactly who was calling over a supposedly anonymized voice channel, but they picked up on my presence, while correctly surmising the nature of the call. I've not witnessed this kind of digital sleight-of-hand before, and, well, it made me feel like I was right out of the University again.

"Since I took this job with your organization, I've only been embarrassed and humiliated twice during my tenure. The time you first pulled me aside and suggested that I not dress like a low class/no class call girl, and now this time with Otto the Magician."

The Director chuckled and gently reminded, "Oh, so not the time I stumbled into your office after hours and almost interrupted you with, what's his name? Though we were peers at our previous job, you do work for me know. Well, never mind. What are our next steps with the Magician? I assume they took the project, but what fee did you settle on?"

Tonya swallowed hard and admitted, "I…we didn't discuss a fee, only a meeting place and where to ship the advance materials so his team could begin work."

The Director sighed like someone ready to chastise an underling and then commented, "I'm glad your taste in men has improved over the years, but remember that even a low class/ no class call girl discusses price before putting the goods on the table. This is most unlike you. You need to take charge and not get rattled when you are in charge of an assignment."

Now mortified, Tonya stammered, "I didn't get rattled. Okay, I got a bit rattled, but when we meet in Paris I can…"

Thoroughly enjoying the teasing she was delivering to her associate, the Director soothed, "Tonya, it is a part of working in this field.

"I can tell you that because he did the same thing to me many years ago. I was an up-and-coming professional who thought she could hold her own in a male dominated world of high finance. My ego had to be ambulanced off the premises the first time I encountered him. I thought he might help you adapt more readily."

Tonya was stunned at the admission. But before she could say anything the Director responded, "That encounter helped me to get to this position. I'm hoping that someday it will help you get here too."

Tonya, somewhat chastened, quietly offered, "Thank you, Ingrid. I will try and be that person you believe I am."

Ingrid stepped back into her hard-edged Director role as she sharply reminded, "Understand, we need all the resources we can muster to intercept these disruptive cryptocurrency Johnnies and their cottage industry before one of these products catches on. We need time to get ours to market before we lose control of global finance. We don't want to be caught making buggy whips while the internal combustion automobile is being rolled off mass-production lines. Time is not on our side in this matter, so whatever Mr. Magician wants to charge is fine. If he and his organization can help us hold our position until we are ready, then his price is chump change compared to what our next position will be. If he doesn't, then he will be paid with useless currency, and none of it will matter anyway."

Tonya swallowed hard and stated, "Yes, Madam Director. I understand."

CHAPTER 2

It Looked Good on Paper
...The Enigma Chronicles

The panic and tension thickened throughout the building as each person entered, then frantically pushed and shoved those ahead of them to gain the front spot to demand their funds. The directors watched the increased madness through the glass walls of the meeting room, yet were powerless to stop the ever-growing chaos. It was a classic run-on-the-bank scenario like the old films and photos portrayed from the 1920s in the U.S. There was no shortage of desperate people having an anxiety attack concerning their funds. No one wanted to wait patiently in line for their money. The pushing and shoving continued to escalate within the line but did not quite reach the head of the line. Police were there to try and keep order, but most of them ended up joining the human tidal wave of desperation. This was just one frightened mob in one location in this small struggling country oppressed by debt. Some of the other banks in this impoverished country had wisely refused to open until communication avenues with the panic stricken improved.

In this formerly thriving city, the military, which was really only a volunteer militia, was called out to assist when martial law was declared. Its lack of success in controlling the crowds added to the chaos. Comprised primarily of weekend warriors, the militia had never been trained to be a true peacekeeping force. Friends and family begged and cried to them for personal support efforts, and the militia members' subsequently weakened resolve was like accelerant on the crazed population. The police began to exit once they received their funds, leaving only the privately hired mercenaries, politely called internal security, to protect the banking institutions.

Here, inside the country's central bank, Mathias wondered how long he and his directors would be safe behind the internal security force and bulletproof glass. The images from the outside cameras convinced him that trying to go out to his favorite restaurant for lunch would be insanely unwise. It occurred to him that if this mob scene couldn't be brought under control, he and the other directors would be trapped here. He began to feel queasy at the thought of surviving on vending machine food until the mob was contained and under control, which might take days.

Mathias had a way of working with any group due to his ability to appear like those around him. He could be imposing if he rose to his nearly two meters and 90 kilograms, with his broad shoulders, squared facial structure and dark well-groomed hair. His suits were custom made in Hong Kong of the finest materials, and they suited the part he was playing in this scenario. As Mathias watched the chaos surrounding him, he had to admit this experiment had failed, not because the technology didn't work, but because people believed they were being swindled out of their money. What Mathias and the other directors had failed to realize was that in order for the regular population to make ends meet, they had to operate in or with the underground economy. To function in the underground economy, cynically called the EU, one needed hard currency for conducting business, which was highly mobile even if it was fiat money. Yes, several European governments had declared fiat money to be legal tender, but historically, money was backed by physical commodities such as gold and silver. They lacked understanding of the continual devaluation as those resources dwindled.

With his British accent, Mathias captured the ear of the authorities. His sales pitch suggested that by shifting everything to digital currency, the government could put an end to the EU. Then they would finally get the tax revenue they'd been missing. The powers-that-be had completely missed the fact that the loss of mobile hard currency would simply drive the entire population, heavily dependent upon the EU, into a subterranean-subsistence level of poverty. The governments involved in this joint experiment had made the classic mistake of pushing the population into a position where they now had nothing left to lose. Now, with the poorly trained but armed militia joining the frightened mob, and no police willing to defend the new world order, things could not have been blacker for the digital currency plan.

One of the larger, well-fed directors meekly asked, "Did the specialty donuts get delivered this morning? Can you ask the private security persons if they are on their way up?"

At that same moment, gunfire cracked several corners of vertical glass panes in the directors' meeting room. The eminent threat of the collapse of the fractured glass walls was immediately on the minds of the directors at the table.

Alois Dutch, who was always addressed as Dutch, entered through the lavatory door adjacent to the boardroom. He was imposing in his loose suit, which obviously concealed his holstered handgun. His gravelly voice barked, "The donuts are here, but the coffee is still brewing! Who wants to wait, and who wants to go? The chopper is on the roof, but there is only room for three!"

Mathias frowned and retrieved his own personal 9mm semi-automatic. He promptly made the selecting votes. All the frightened directors stared in shocked disbelief as Mathias shot them all in rapid succession. After one shot each to the head, Mathias turned to Dutch and calmly stated, "We now have room for the donuts, but let's pick up coffee along the way. I would like to have room for the cream and sugar to be added."

As a seasoned mercenary, Dutch wasn't surprised at the efficiency of the meeting's abrupt ending, so he responded, "Good by me. I've always thought the coffee here isn't strong enough for my tastes." Dutch was about the same size as Mathias, but his blue eyes and blond hair echoed his German heritage. The lines of his face, permanently turned down mouth, and haphazard scars spoke to his uncompromised lifestyle filled with brutality.

They both got low as they exited out the back door, away from the disastrous scene, and quickly moved toward the stairwell that would take them to the helipad on the roof. Mathias had snatched his ever-close metal briefcase, containing his standard escape materials, after eliminating the competition for seats in the helicopter. The special purpose briefcase was also bullet-proof. With its side sling, it made for a perfect shield should any more stray rounds head his way. As they climbed higher in the stairwell, the noise from the lower floors receded, and it was almost quiet as they got to the last door leading directly to the roof.

Dutch did a quick spot check from out in front and then motioned to Mathias to follow. They both swung quickly into the helicopter. Once the door closed, Dutch pounded on the glass behind the pilot and with a thumbs up indicated it was time to go. The pilot pulled the helicopter up to clear the building edge then smartly pushed the craft forward, gaining speed as quickly as he could.

Dutch smirked as he commented, "Maybe we need a new line of work. I mean, there must be something wrong with getting your whole agenda adopted by the Finance Minister, rubber stamped by the governing body of this backwater country, only to have to escape with our donuts, yet leave the coffee behind as we run for our lives."

Mathias ground his teeth in anger and remarked, "You know, I can ask the pilot to take you back and drop you off if you prefer."

Dutch knew he was on thin ice. "Alright, I'm fine here." Then he shifted the discussion as he added, "I have to admit, we almost pulled this one off by the numbers. But just like my CO used to say after a failed operation, *it sure looked good on paper!*"

Mathias stewed a moment as he mentally reviewed the carefully laid plan. "I know this model will work, Dutch! I just need a larger target audience! This one was just too small and too prone to backward superstitions. If they accepted my financial model…"

Dutch cut him off as he questioned, "We're going to try it again, huh? Now, you can always count on me for another turn at the roulette wheel, but I maintain we don't try this again without our trusty contingency plan in place! By the way, what is our plan B?"

Mathias offered a chilling smile and responded, "We will do a larger country where they have more to lose and more for me to gain! We hunt where there is lots of financial turmoil already present, because it will hide our footprints."

Dutch, now in something of a humoring mood, asked, "You don't think someone will notice that you're pitching a distributed digital currency to displace a centralized paper currency? It seems a lot like being out on a first date, where you're staring down the front of your lady's low cut evening dress and humbly proclaiming you admire her for her mind! She ain't buying it, and they won't buy it!"

A wry smile crossed Mathias's face as he admonished, "Dutch, your problem is that all the time you spent in the Deutsches Heer made you too cynical. You know what they say in marketing financial concepts: packaging, packaging, and packaging!"

"Yeah, but they also say that in taxidermy work!" Dutch couldn't contain his sour look.

Redefining What a Long Day Means

It was late in the day, and Su Lin had just finished tending her animals, in particular her favorite pig, Franklin. At 160 kilograms, Franklin could have been a formidable adversary to her slight Asian build, being less than half his weight. Over the years of their friendship and her training, he'd become more of a barnyard pet and confidant. As she tidied her long silky black hair into her typical braid halfway down her back, she mused about how thankful she was that Franklin had outgrown his tendency to want to sit in her lap, as he had done when he was just an armful.

Franklin was a very bright hog who took everything in stride, and he showed a genuine affection for Su Lin. However, today Su Lin was distracted. Every unusual noise seemed to pull her attention in a different direction. Ever in tune with his human companion, Franklin stopped to test the air with his extremely sensitive nose. Su Lin halted her activities to study the surroundings of the familiar Georgia farm, but nothing looked wrong. Except that something seemed wrong. A most unsettling feeling came over her as she walked back from the pens to the house.

Andy's hound dog, Wrinkles, was fast asleep and didn't bother to raise his head up to watch Su Lin trudge back from the pens as he usually did at this time of day. Wrinkles' afternoon siesta was always secondary to the kitchen snacks that he got when Su Lin began to cook supper.

Su Lin studied the large hound as she approached and remarked, "I must agree with Andy's assessment of you, Wrinkles. If you were any more laid back, you would be constantly slipping into a coma. You must have played pretty hard today, to not even get up to begin pestering for snacks."

Su Lin stopped just outside the door and looked around the property one more time, hoping to alleviate her unsettled feelings, but the well-kept Georgia farm with its large welcoming home was perfectly in place. They had recently repainted the home in brick red with white trim, giving the house a certain quaint elegance without pretension. She shrugged her shoulders to loosen the cloud of doubt she felt and went inside. Su Lin paused at the mirror in the mud room, verifying that her hair was in place, and no dirt was apparent on her ivory skin. Even though she'd had servants for much of her adult life, she enjoyed her work with the animals.

As she closed the screen door, it flashed through her mind that locking the door would be a good idea, even though they never did. Andy always wanted folks to be able to drop in. He'd insisted you couldn't be neighborly if the door was locked. However, she decidedly wasn't in the mood to discuss how southern folks in the country always left the doors unlocked, and she went on in to check on Andy and see if he was ready for dinner.

Andy's office was a cross between a high tech server room, operations area, office area, and something of an electrical power drain on the grid. If he wasn't wearing his headset while talking to one of his many customers, or signed into a high tech webinar, he was building something for testing or trialing in his operational headquarters known as the Rock-n-Roll Domain. It wasn't uncommon for Su Lin to check on him, only to find him totally absorbed in some new technical project with some rock music playing at varying decibels in the background.

As she wandered closer to Andy, she noted that his white hair was a bit long, but nice with waves, offsetting his broad shoulders which suited his big hands. When he hugged her close it was like being wrapped in a cocoon of gentle protection. He was by all standards a big man, just shy of two meters and nearly 90 kilos. She smiled with fondness, until she drew closer and noted with dismay all the high-caloric junk food packages strewn around, mostly empty.

She immediately fussed, "Andrew! We've talked about this! Your heart attack was supposed to be a wakeup call for your poor eating habits! The doctor said if we cut back on all the junk food, you could lead a normal life. Honey, you promised!"

Andy sheepishly offered, "Aw, sweetheart, I have turned over a new leaf. You notice that I no longer have that big salt block used for cattle on the table at suppertime. Now, doesn't that count for something? Besides, all the healthy cooking you have been doing should make up for some of the small splurges I have now and again."

Su Lin retorted, "That's because I feed all the fat trimmings to Wrinkles, who by all accounts likes your new diet. And say, what's wrong with him today? Usually he is all over me when I come back in the afternoon from the pens. Have you been feeding him your favorite concoction of cheese puffs dipped in melted fudge ice cream again?"

Andy rather soberly remarked, "Nope! Not since that last time when we had to clean up after his bazooka-barfing-from-both-ends episode. Not me, ma'am."

Before she could admonish him further, she heard something in the front room area and cast a quizzical look to Andy before she went to investigate. When she walked into the front room, she saw a Chinese man, with the bearing of a military type, complete with his short cropped black hair and sinewy arms, sitting way too comfortably in one of the over-sized leather chairs, casually waiting.

Su Lin didn't recognize the man, only the type, and she immediately disliked him. Trying to keep the alarm out of her voice, she called to Andy without taking her eyes off of the stranger. He was neither menacing nor friendly in his presentation to her, but he said nothing.

Andy barged into the room and stopped short upon seeing the stranger. He sized up the situation quickly and demanded, "Who the hell are you, and what the hell are you doing here?"

Andy, being ex-military police, always carried his 1911 Colt 45 in a holster at the small of his back and quickly reached for it. At almost the same time, he felt two cold weapons on either side of his neck. Then some very cautious, practiced hands carefully confiscated his weapon. Andy froze but still rotated his eyes from one side to the other to take in the two Chinese enforcer types holding guns at his neck.

Once the disarming process was completed, the seated man looked toward Su Lin, "Ah, Colonel Ling Po, how nice to see you again. It's been a long time. Apologies for the surveillance you apparently noticed and the intrusion, but you have been extremely difficult to find.

"Please, don't worry about the enormous dog out front; he is merely sedated. I didn't want to risk an unpleasant encounter with him while we …um…talked."

Andy, trying to reconcile why this man called Su Lin by the name from her former life attempted a bluff as he bellowed,

"No one barges into my farm house and pulls a gun on us. It's even worse when that uninvited stranger speaks to my wife, Su Lin, using an incorrect name and sedates my animal without any idea of who we are! You boneheads have come to the wrong place, so git out!"

Completely oblivious to Andy's rant, the intruder continued, "I don't expect you to remember me, but certainly I remember you, Colonel Po. When you were put in charge of the Cyber Warfare College in China, all of your adversaries thought you had been neutralized. It is obvious that they were wrong. You managed to build an excellent power base, then crush your opposition quite completely. I believe the Khan incident that you engineered was probably the best example of assassinating someone using cyber means."

Su Lin swallowed hard and sternly replied, "Now I remember you. Major Guano, the henchman for Chairman Lo Chang. I hardly recognized you without your smock and hypodermic needle."

The intruder almost smirked as he confirmed, "How nice of you to remember. However, I must point out that I am now a full Colonel, and Lo Chang is no longer Chairman in this world."

As usual, Su Lin's intelligence launched her response, dripping in sarcasm. "I understand. One criminal out and another one in his place. Some things never change, do they?"

Colonel Guano tightened up somewhat and continued, "It seems you had some highly motivated help in leaving our, uh… facilities in China. It has taken some time to find you again."

Andy was trying to mentally find a way out of the situation. He did not like being in this position especially with Su Lin the target. He was not happy with the ongoing conversation and the familiarity that Colonel Guano was showing toward Su Lin. But Su Lin motioned to him to stand down during the ongoing banter, like she had a better understanding of their capabilities. Cutting her eyes between the two henchmen and back to Andy helped remind him not to attempt anything foolish.

Guano, still seated yet certain he dominated the conversation, continued, "Your vanishing act from China was most impressive and, I must say, a little vexing for us. As usual though, you couldn't stay hidden for long. Your brilliant research that coupled nanotechnology and genetic engineering helped cast a bright light on your trail. Of course, the shabby incident with that crazed Doctor Pekoni helped us to zero in on your current location.

"Oh, and congratulations on your marriage to Mr. Greenwood. We know you tried to keep the ceremony small and quiet, but the blood tests did help to confirm that you are indeed Lt. Colonel Ling Po, aka Master Po of the Chinese Cyber Warfare College. My hunt is now complete."

Su Lin, afraid of what Andy would think, cast a quick glance at him before she responded, "Let's pretend, for arguments sake, that you are not an insane delusional errand monkey and that I am this Colonel Po. What possessed you to travel halfway around the world, looking for someone who obviously doesn't want to be found?"

Guano steeled himself and answered, "You built an early prototype of, um…a financial program that was demonstrated to several influential party members and left quite an impression. It had, as I recall, a remarkable security routine called the Grasshopper Loop, which made it unbreakable to even the most persistent hackers. My leadership has sent me to retrieve that code and its author, in the most discreet but expeditious manner."

Andy was nearly undone with this threat. Su Lin smirked in a mocking manner and informed him, "I don't have that program, but it is not true that it was unbreakable. The code was broken by, shall we say, a highly motivated hacker. Your quest to locate the author of the code is simply a fool's errand. The code Master Po allegedly wrote that was purported to be unbreakable is as vulnerable as any freeware, downloadable from your favorite cell phone website.

"Take you and your abhorrent henchmen out of our house and leave us alone."

Guano rose out of the chair and bluntly stated, "I was sent to retrieve it and you. And I will do exactly that, with or without your cooperation."

Before any further instructions could be issued by Guano, Andy used his huge hands to grab both henchmen's gun-wielding hands, pushed the assailants' weapons to point at the other, and using his thumbs, pulled the triggers simultaneously causing them to shoot each other. Unfortunately, the hot muzzle blast of both weapons seared Andy's eyes, instantly blinding him.

Su Lin's military training kicked in, and she dove for one of the weapons just as Guano drew his. Andy, though blinded, instinctively knew to go to ground around the dead Chinese henchman and look for his missing Colt 45. He wasn't sure what he could do once he was armed, sightless as he now was, but he wasn't going to give up as long as Su Lin was being threatened by Guano.

Just as Andy located his Colt 45, two shots rang out, and the room fell silent.

CHAPTER 4

Conservation through Conversation

Jacob and Petra lounged in their summer silk jammies at the bed and breakfast in town. Living with Wolfgang at the chateau was wonderful most of the time, but getting away for a day and an evening was an extended romantic date. Their hours of lovemaking had been all consuming, bordering on monumental, and innovatively erotic. Their openness with each other had allowed them to explore creative positions and sensations all over the flat, including the bed, floor, sofa, bathtub, and the kitchen counter. They'd even tried adding ice and fruits for some enhanced stimulation. They found the excitement and laughter simply improved each lovemaking session.

Petra's honey-colored hair tumbled over her shoulders while she tied her silk robe around her lithe frame. Her intelligent brown eyes watched Jacob moving about in his silk bottoms and bare muscular torso. She was mesmerized by the beautiful dragon tattoo Jacob had across his back. The blues and greens, lightly accented with gold, black, and silver outlines, made the whole image almost come alive. The scales looked like they could actually cut one if they were brushed the wrong way, and the malevolent look, coupled with its shimmering beauty, could not be ignored. At the same time, she felt somewhat troubled by the dragon tattoo, now called Sasha. Jacob had had it done during a black depression he had been going through, when they'd split apart for a short period of time. It was both beautiful and terrifying to recall the story behind it.

Lean and fit at just over 1.8 meters, he towered over his lovely partner who only rose to 1.5 meters, yet she could freeze him with a word or a look. Jacob stopped his activity, looked back over his shoulder and caught Petra staring dreamily at Sasha. Jacob's dark wavy hair was recently trimmed, showing his expressive blue eyes. He might have engineered some more amorous playtime if his cell phone hadn't rung. He quickly assessed the incoming number and answered, "Yes, sir?" He pictured Otto on the other end, with his white shock of well-groomed hair, a ready smile and a twinkle in his eye as if he knew something you didn't, which was typically the case.

Otto, one of the main patriarchs of the R-Group, announced when the call was connected, "Ah good, Jacob, I caught you before you began your evening. We have a situation that requires the entire team to get together and talk. While you are not a senior charter member of the R-Group, both Wolfgang and I value your input. Can you possibly help me locate Petra, so she can attend? As late as it is getting, I would like all of us to meet at Wolfgang's chateau. He has agreed to host a modest dinner while we consider this next series of issues."

Jacob offered, "Yes, of course, Otto. I'm fairly sure I can find the charming, alluring, but evasive Petra and convince her to attend," he said, smiling while trying to fish around under her silk robe. "Can you provide some framework of the nature of the discussion, sir?"

Otto smiled as he said, "I'm glad to see you haven't lost all your American upbringing with its heavy tendency for impatience. We will discuss it when all are gathered. See you both soon, Jacob."

After disconnecting from the call, Petra, smiling impishly, commented, "You didn't explain why he couldn't find me. I just love your discretion when speaking with my father. He knows we're over here buck naked, but he is too much the European gentleman to tell us to immediately put on some clothes and come to an important meeting."

Jacob chuckled. "While you are correct that your father is the quintessential gentleman, you are living proof that he is not the prude you cast him as. For that detail, I'm most grateful."

Petra smiled at Jacob and offered, "I guess I'd better shower and get ready to go. Care to join me so we can conserve water, my dear?"

Jacob smiled at her with unveiled appreciation. "Of course, my love. You do realize we actually consume a lot more water when we shower together, don't you?"

Petra's lusty look was amplified. "What's your point, my darling?"

Jacob returned her amorous look with additional heat forming in his eyes as his desire took flight, and he scooped her up in his arms. "There are some things I want to conserve with you and some things I want to lavish on you. You can decide which ones are which."

Petra was just putting on her final touches of makeup, as Jacob watched with his hands in his pockets, lest they mess her up. His cell phone received an incoming call from a familiar number in Georgia. Jacob puzzled a moment, deciding whether to allow the call to roll to voicemail. At the last moment he accepted the call and greeted, "Andy, it's been a while and I'd like to chat, but we're expected at a meeting momentarily. May I…"

The female voice cut him off. "Jacob, this is Su Lin on Andy's phone." She desperately added without taking a breath, her words running together, "We've had a little trouble. I wasn't sure who else to call, since I don't want EZ rushing here. I started with Carlos, and when I told him about the situation he told me to use Andy's phone and call you directly. He felt strongly that you should be briefed, so your extended family might be looped in. Carlos is still in Brazil working in Andy's satellite office. He indicated that he was too remote and with none of the connections you have access to, so I'm calling…"

Jacob was becoming alarmed. They worked on a few complex projects in the past and considered each other talented technology colleagues. He'd never heard this panicked or overwhelmed tone in Su Lin's voice. "Whoa-whoa, slow down, Su Lin! What is going on? You sound frantic. What happened…why are you calling from Andy's phone? Where's Andy?"

Su Lin swallowed quickly and tried to calm her breathing down before she continued, "We are at the hospital! We had, um…some intruders break in, and Andy…poor sweet Andy is…ah, resting comfortably…," but she broke down in sobs, unable to speak further.

Jacob, collecting his courage as well as his thoughts, slowly but purposefully stated, "Su Lin, everything will be fine. I suspect that there is more to this story, but let's defer any more discussion until you have had time to collect your thoughts. When you are not in a public area, call me so we can speak. Understood? Give me the hospital name so I can alert the others of the situation. Are you hurt or injured?"

Petra was becoming alarmed, even though she could only hear half of the conversation. Jacob persisted, "Su Lin, you are okay, right?"

Su Lin pulled herself together enough to respond. "The bullet only grazed my shoulder. I'm not worried about me, only Andy!"

Jacob calmly offered, "We don't have anyone close to you right now, but let me see what I can do to change that. I need you to be brave for Andy. It is time to pull that Su Lin courage to the surface until we can get help to you. Can you do that for me, please?"

Su Lin nodded and weakly replied, "It's different when you have someone's life, other than your own, in trouble. The hospital said I could stay in Andy's room tonight, so we will be alright for a while. They are bringing him into the room. Let me text you the hospital information. Thank you for your help, Jacob. Seems like I'm always needing you for my outrageous scenarios.

"One last thing, can you try to locate my old dear friend, Colonel Guano? I would like very much to know how he is getting on now, or if he isn't."

After disconnecting from the call, Jacob stared purposefully at Petra and exclaimed, "I think we have a new problem to address."

CHAPTER 5

Table Scraps

Colonel Guano grimaced as he stated, "What I wouldn't give to have something go right for a change. The small camera drones gave us perfect reconnaissance over the property. We mapped everything down to the last square meter, all the time-tables for deliveries and mail were accounted for, and my perimeter guards could have dealt with any unaccounted X-factor that might have showed up, but…oww. Easy on that wound, soldier!"

The nervous Lieutenant Quinn Lee replied, "Apologies, Colonel. I'm trying to get the bleeding to stop, and some pressure is necessary to do that. Here, keep this pad on the wound while I see to the others."

About that time the truck bounced through a hole in the road, shifting the occupants uncomfortably in their bench seats. Scowling, Guano acquiesced, "By the way, thanks for pulling us all out so quickly. I just wish you could have blocked her 911 emergency call to give us a little more time. How are the others?"

Quinn Lee dryly answered, "We have one left that still needs medical attention, if he is not to become a casualty as well. What do you wish to do with our fallen soldier? I believe we will have enough time to bury him at our rendezvous point in another 20 minutes."

The truck lurched again, aggravating both Guano's wound and his mood. Angry but also in pain, he tried to bellow but merely stated, "We take him with us! We don't leave our people on this soil after they have fallen in battle. Say that again and I'll make an exception in your case!"

Quinn Lee returned to tending the wounded man. Guano mumbled, "I'm certain no one at headquarters will like my update report. According to their timetables for this exercise, we should be well on our way back with the high-value target, Colonel Po. Now that she has been alerted to our presence and interest in capturing her, I am quite certain our next effort will be far more difficult."

A rather somber Quinn Lee returned his attention to Guano and stated, "Colonel, it is now just you needing medical attention. I will arrange for our two fallen soldiers to return to our homeland with us for a proper burial."

Frustrated and in much pain, Guano barked, "You understand that we can't return now, right? Our mission to return with Master Po is above all else. We can't risk transport just for two dead men. If they were discovered before we can conclude our assignment, it would be impossible to explain them to the local authorities. Since we don't know how long this operation is going to take, what do you think we should do, Lieutenant?"

Somewhat incensed himself, Quinn Lee sarcastically replied, "I believe we should keep them frozen in cryogenic cylinders and then take them back to our home planet, near the Horsehead Nebula in the constellation Orion, in our spaceship."

Guano, not accustomed to such insubordination, simply couldn't respond to the outrageous statement.

Quinn Lee realized he had greatly overstepped the boundary of military courtesies and quietly offered, "Or, we can bury them at the rendezvous as I originally suggested, since we don't know how long it will take us to reach our target goal. That way we can avoid having to explain their terminated condition to anyone in this foreign land."

Guano studied his lieutenant and softly replied, "Deep graves with no markers, please. I'll try not to get anyone else killed, but we must have Master Po."

Lieutenant Quinn Lee looked back at the two dead operatives and only nodded.

The nurses struggled to hold Andy still but they would have had better luck holding down a wounded bear while hauling her cubs away.

Andy bellowed, "I can't see. I've got people with clammy hands touching me all over. Stop the endless beep, beep. Where is my wife? I just want to go home with my wife!"

At that moment Andy wrenched his left hand free and grabbed at the closest person. It was a burly male nurse who had been summoned to subdue Andy. While the pair were evenly matched in size, the male nurse was no match for the terror and anger Andy had coursing through his system. Andy's grip on the nurse's throat could have been fatal, except Su Lin intervened as she threw herself on top of Andy, crying and begging him to stop.

Andy immediately changed gears and released his captive to sooth Su Lin with his free hand. He quieted. The male nurse backed away from the deadly encounter and collapsed into a chair parked close to the hospital bed, focused on restoring his normal breathing and slowing his heartbeat.

Su Lin's old adversaries might have classified the scene as simply one of her better performances in a high stress situation. Truth was, she wasn't acting out a carefully rehearsed role. She hadn't slept or eaten anything for the last 48 hours, and the gun-shot wound she suffered had required drugs be added to prevent infection. Now her system was experiencing some consequences no one could have anticipated. The near disastrous encounter from an old enemy of her past, coupled with the medications she was taking, had boosted her fear and anxiety levels to an alarming level and threatened her mental stability. Because everyone was focused on Andy, no one spotted her potential meltdown.

At first Andy struggled to get his fear and anger under control, to help calm his wife. When he sensed the soothing touches and soft words seemed to have no effect on Su Lin, he began to fear for her. It was as if he could feel the old demons inside of her and that actually gave him the strength he needed for both of them.

While not quite a bark, his tone with her was sharp and direct as he instructed, "Su Lin! I need you to calm down! Right now, my dear. You are better than this. I need you to be my eyes and probably my ears too since I can't get this damn ringing out of my ears!

"I want you to listen to me! Listen! You pull yourself together, because I'm depending on you! Now make sure you apologize to these nice folks for us and make sure that nurse that I was choking is alright. Tell the nurse that I'm sorry my temper got away from me."

Still working the kinks out of his throat, the nurse offered, "I'm a little worse for wear, but I'll…" the nurse paused in his speaking to cough, then finished, "take your apology." And with more sarcasm than the situation warranted, he added, "But just let that be a lesson to you."

Andy smirked slightly but continued to soothe Su Lin who kept repeating, "Don't wanna go back. I don't wanna go back…"

Her lack of responsiveness convinced Andy that Su Lin needed help more than he did. He asked aloud, "Now, since I can't rightly see any goings-on here, can I get someone to have a look-see at my bride? I don't want to let her go in this state, and well, I want to hear what the doctor thinks about her condition. I may not have known her all my life, but I'm pretty sure there is something wrong with her upstairs thinking mechanism. Can we work on that angle for a while?"

The head nurse had just returned to the room. She was a bit skeptical and asked, "Are we going to have any more outbursts?"

Andy shook his bandaged head and replied, "I know you folks are here to help, but the last 48 hours has been hell on us. Please help us, and I promise no more 'Naughty Andy.'"

The nurse nodded her head and almost smiled as she snapped, "Alright, people! Let's get moving! Let's update her vitals and get a doc in here.

"John, bring in an extra gurney, and we will lay her here so Andy can stay close."

CHAPTER 6

Crypto Research by the Powers That Want to Be

Ingrid smiled and responded to Tonya, "Thank you for calling me back on this other detail I indicated. We need people with references, but that doesn't mean they will be the only ones we contract with. Now that we are in contact with the Magician at the R-Group, I want you to discreetly reach out to another person that I want to have a separate contract with to verify some of the results from the one you just negotiated. Her name is Petra Rancowski."

Tonya wrinkled her nose and asked, "Who is she? I've never heard of her."

Ingrid, playing the patient parent with her protégé, stated, "My dear Tonya, the reason you have never heard of her is because she doesn't hang out on social media or have a website that advertises the services of a gifted encryptionist. I have done the homework here, and for every bank that has had a problem with data confidentiality or discovered a cyber breach in their supposedly bullet-proof encryption infrastructure, she has been brought in to harden the bank's attack surfaces and establish solid encryption practices. You can believe that she is known in all the right circles for the flawless work she does, building unbreakable encryption algorithms that secure financial institutions' assets."

Tonya, a bit astonished, then asked, "Okay, so how do we get ahold of her? Does she have any accessible contact information?"

Ingrid, enjoying the new task assignment, said, "She begins every new banking assignment with a burner phone, and once the assignment is complete, you can no longer reach her through that number. There is no known method of contact that I have discovered, and I only recently discovered her last name. It is also known that she only uses aliases when on the Internet so for the most part she is untraceable. In fact her modus operandi is almost identical to the cyber thugs from the Darknet."

Tonya, feeling irked by the assignment, tersely asked, "You want me to hunt down another magician? Then my question still stands, how do I even reach her to offer her this assignment?"

Ingrid, sensing the frustration rising in Tonya's voice, retorted, "My dear, unless you are one of her established customers, you must phish for her. I will send you the information of her favorite chat room where she has been known to appear if something interests her. There you must pose a unique but interesting encryption puzzle piece and wait for her to bite on the bait. Then you cautiously reel her into the assignment with more tidbits of information until she commits. She will ask for your references and where you located her name. I have sent you the names of three people that were willing to trust me with her name and to whom she can go to verify that you are genuine. Oh, don't bother to negotiate with her. Whatever fee she wants, simply agree to pay it. She is a highly prized professional, and she does not haggle. You can barter with Arabian street vendors but not this type of cyber professional."

Tonya sourly retorted, "I don't know why we are even in this exercise if there is no appetite for digital currency. Nobody wants to honestly explore the next generation of currency. As far as the U.S. is concerned, cryptocurrency doesn't exist!"

Ingrid, tiring of the tantrum from her protégé, sternly admonished, "Young lady, command yourself! Legacy currency, and in particular the U.S. greenback, is the world's reserve currency. You cannot simply allow the digital thugs of the planet to launch a digital currency that might destroy world financial order overnight. I know you think we here at the Global Bank are only trying to preserve the status quo and keep the U.S. dollar as the world reserve currency, but that just isn't true.

"I have told you more than once, digital currency is the wave of the future, but it must be introduced carefully so as to not derail economic civilization as we know it. Our Global Bank, along with all the other sovereign countries, cannot sit idly by during this transition. We must be in control of this coming financial disruption, and for that I need every computer genius I can get my hands on. Now go find my encryptionist!"

Although annoyed, Tonya obediently acknowledged her new assignment and disconnected from the call.

Quip was munching on a tart green apple as he strolled into the operations area where he normally worked in the R-Group data center.

He was about half done with it when his A.I. Supercomputer ICABOD queried, "Dr. Quip, you had asked for all related search items on launches of all new cryptocurrencies with any common threads to each other. I believe you were specifically looking for groups that had fragmented, thus spawning competing C-Cs looking for market dominance. However, the underlying fundamentals have proved to be a little more challenging than our original search."

Quip puzzled a moment, and after setting his unfinished fruit with a mess of other half-eaten items, stated, "I believe we determined that anything that was built upon the Blockchain technology would be a fair starting point for hunting the many derivations that C-Cs we're now launching with."

ICABOD responded, "That was certainly true until someone, actually several someones, figured out that Blockchain technology could be used in manufacturing supply chains, food production tracking, and generally securing a myriad of Internet of Things, or IoT, components. Our beginning assumption of using Blockchain as the starting point has become like searching the Internet for something digital; Blockchain is penetrating basically everything, rendering our search criteria useless."

Quip sat blinking, then stated, "Alright, let's go back to our original premise of cryptocurrencies built upon Blockchain technology. Will that narrow our returning data sets?"

ICABOD responded, "I anticipated your request and have already done so. The results clearly show a highly fragmented array of cryptocurrency launches and some very spectacular failures with some jail time awarded to several entrepreneurs. What I find curious is that the competing C-Cs are remarkably untraceable even though they are digital in origin. They tend to be more analog and untraceable even though they are actually electronic. An interesting dichotomy, in that we have great tracking ability for analog currency but little to none for digital currency."

Quip puzzled and offered, "That does suggest we need new tools to track digital currency if we want to stay in the information brokering business. Add to that all the 21st century manufacturers and producers baking Blockchain technology into their distribution processes and our task is being made nearly impossible. Hmmm…maybe we are looking at this all wrong."

ICABOD queried, "Dr. Quip, I have registered that contemplative look on your face before. Does this mean you are going to remove the half-eaten food items that seem to collect next to your work station? I admit there is quite an impressive collection of mold and fungi being harbored there with some color hues not normally associated with edible food, but I only mention it since Mistress Eilla-Zan threatened me the last time she found the area in this state. She reprimanded me for allowing you to, as she said, soil the nest, as it were."

Quip raised his eyebrows and asked, "She threatened you?"

ICABOD admitted, "She promised to bring Mistress Julie with her to completely trash the Feng Shui of our data center by moving server blades from their normal clusters to the wrong areas, leaving cables hanging out of their normal tray routes, and even pulling some blade servers out to stick in the aisles."

Quip now quickly grabbed a trash can and hastily scooped up the offending items, and after taking the can outside, came back with lemon-scented counter cleaners to freshen up the entire surface area.

ICABOD noted the effort. "Good."

CHAPTER 7

The Risk or The Request, Which Weighs Heavier?
...The Enigma Chronicles

When Bowen directed them to the conference room in the chateau rather than the comfort of the library, they realized that the cocktail hour and supper might be delayed. The table was set with note pads and a wireless keyboard that was connected to the full screen on the wall. The scene on the screen at present was of a lovely scrolling garden in downtown Zürich, which Wolfgang was quite fond of for walking. Fresh coffee and a small tray of biscotti were available on the side table.

Quip, with his unruly hair tied back with a leather tie and generally casual attire, had come directly from the office with Otto. As the chief technology leader of the team, he often worked many hours inside the data center, so casual worked. Though slightly taller than Jacob, they both had similar builds. He kept ICABOD, their Immersive Collaborative Associative Binary Override Deterministic supercomputer, on the bleeding edge of AI capabilities. This allowed him to help effectively lead multiple projects.

Quip had driven Otto to the chateau as both his new bride, Eilla-Zan, and Otto's wife, Haddy, had a prior commitment they could not alter. This allowed Jacob to brief Quip on the call he'd received. Quip stared and listened intently as Jacob sketched out what he had gotten from Su Lin. Petra, still stunned at the seriousness of the situation, listened intently with concern for their friends.

Finally Quip asked, "What do we need to do? Sounds like we need some more background info on the situation. I don't think that we need to loop in Eric from our favorite three letter agency, but it does sound like we need someone at ground zero to assess the situation."

Jacob nodded and agreed, "Based on the dialogue I had with Su Lin, I believe we should try to get someone there who they have high confidence in, like a family member. I don't see just anyone from Julie's team being quite the right choice. What about EZ?"

Quip, wanting to quickly kill that approach, responded, "I don't see EZ as being the right person without me being along. If this was just standard family illness stuff, I wouldn't be so hesitant. However, with forced entry from intruders and then bullets flying as a result, I don't agree with using EZ by herself. I'm sorry, but there it is."

Petra observed, "Are you suggesting that since Jacob got the call, it probably ought to be him to go see what is going on? Is it better to put him at risk? Is that it? What if I say no?"

The awkward conversation ceased as Otto and Wolfgang entered the room. They each took a seat at opposite ends of the elegant table. By silent agreement, Petra and Quip stopped the discussion. Wolfgang looked between the two of them as if feeling the unspoken tension. Jacob schooled his face into no commitment.

Sensing that an important conversation had been interrupted, Otto stated, "Good evening, all. Sounds like we might have a full agenda, since I suspect you have an additional item to add to our discussions. Let me recommend that everyone secure some of the high octane coffee before starting the cocktail hour. Let's get to it."

Wolfgang sensed the tenseness of Petra and Quip, and noted his grandson Jacob was the calmest of the three. He picked up his coffee, and a wry smile came over his face as he stated, "Otto, I don't believe we will get everyone's full attention if we begin with the digital currency topic we need to work. Why don't we lead with what is chafing at our protégés?"

Otto, somewhat annoyed with the agenda being altered before they even got started, loudly commented, "ICABOD, are you okay with deferring the briefing until we get this new issue on the table? It appears that what is on Quip, Petra, and Jacob's mind is highly charged emotionally and therefore cannot be addressed as our second agenda item."

The even-toned software-generated voice of ICABOD offered, "I do sense the urgency of their issue in their voice intonations, so I quite agree, Otto.

"Allow me to state that I captured all their relevant dialogue before you and Wolfgang joined the meeting. I have already begun to sift through the events that has Andy and Su Lin in the hospital in Georgia."

Both Otto and Wolfgang were startled by the statement. Otto pressed, "Alright then, let's get to it! What do we know so far?"

After all the facts had been related to the team, Quip solemnly added, "I'm not quite sure what to do at this point. I mean, EZ needs to know about this situation, but I confess that I don't want her dashing in there to find the same kind of confrontation Andy and Su Lin experienced.

"If I tell her, she will want to go, and I wouldn't feel right about not going too. Kind of gives the shop here a vacant look, when we have the current Blockchain Project we need to be working on."

Petra commented, "Let's face it, Quip, we are not the right people to dispatch to a situation like this. We're computer geeks, not ex-military combatants. I know Su Lin called Jacob, which kind of puts the onus on him, but that is not a good use of this team's resources. I have the same reluctance of having him go as you do about EZ. Would it make better sense to loop in someone from Julie's team? They're better suited for this level of work with their background and military experiences."

Jacob added, "I considered that, except Su Lin called me for help. This suggests that a certain knowledge base might be needed. I don't feel right about hiding here and letting her expectations go unaddressed. I am also not certain what her comment on Colonel Guano was related to. It is uncharacteristic of her to look to her past, isn't it?

"What if we could get someone from Julie's team to go with me?"

Petra tersely stated, "This is about sizing up the situation and approaching the problem correctly. I don't believe for a minute that you are guilty of hiding here, Mr. Jacob Michaels!"

Before the conversation could proceed further, ICABOD interjected, "I took the liberty of contacting Miss Julie. She will be dialing into this meeting shortly to provide her perspective on this matter."

A few moments later ICABOD routed Julie's call into the meeting room conference phone.

Julie greeted, "Hi, all. Apologies for not invoking the video portion for the call, but I'm still a little, um…rough looking from my abduction. It will all heal soon, but, well, you know how vain females can be.

"ICABOD provided only sparse details for me, other than it was most urgent that I attend, if at all possible. What's up?"

Otto began, "Julie, this is one of those situations where we don't know what we don't know. Andy and Su Lin were apparently wounded during a break-in at their farm. It sounds as if there is possibly some involvement somewhere from an old adversary, Colonel Guano. No luck yet locating him, though we are checking all avenues in and out of Georgia.

"Jacob received the call and feels a moral obligation to be on site. Petra has voiced her objection. EZ is unaware of the situation currently but will undoubtedly insist on being there to care for her father once she finds out. Quip will not let her leave without him, but until EZ is told that is an unknown.

"Wolfgang and I are being pulled into a new issue of focus arising from a breach in security at the Global Bank, for which Interpol called a short time ago requesting our help. We still need to brief Quip, Petra, and Jacob further on this issue, but Su Lin was the initial topic."

Otto when on to brief Julie on the details they had learned regarding the armed intruders, Andy's wounds, and the latest from the local authorities in Georgia they had acquired.

"I hesitate to ask you to go to Georgia yourself, based on your ordeal with those Muslim extremists. Possibly one of your team could be used to insure Andy and Su Lin are safe when they leave the hospital. That's all I've got at this point. I would like your thoughts, realizing this is a lot to digest on such short notice."

Julie chuckled and responded, "Well, Otto, you certainly netted out THAT situation quickly."

Jacob then added, "Julie, Su Lin was quite rattled when I spoke with her, which is why she probably started with me. My thinking is that she will want some level of comfort with the person or people we dispatch to see what is going on.

"We all know historically when things go wrong for Su Lin, she seems to always need a fully armed extraction team to get her out. In her life, there are no small troubles."

Julie sighed and agreed, "Boy, you got that right! I thought we had her well stashed after getting her out of that dungeon, but then she…oh, never mind!

"Let me see who I have available. I have to ask, Jacob, since she has a high affinity for you, are you agreeable to partner with someone from my CATS team? Petra, would you be okay with that? We are only talking about a few days it sounds like, and by then the situation should be under control. If it's nothing, then we all disengage. If it becomes an ongoing problem, then we pull everyone out and enact Plan B. We can make a Plan B, right?"

CHAPTER 8

What Are the Odds?
...The Enigma Chronicles

Julie smiled as she recalled the fun Juan had with the twins all day. They'd built forts, he told stories, and had a loud game of chase, until Julie insisted the twins take a short nap before supper. The playroom looked like a tornado had entered rather than two children, aged three, and one father, close to the same age. Juan bounded out of the shower after his playing, scoping out Julie with pure lust. His longish ebony hair curled slightly when wet, giving him a roguish appeal. He had recently shaved, likely because his daughter always rubbed his face and frowned if it was scratchy. The towel he wore hung snug at his hips, offering a clear view of his muscular torso Julie so obviously admired.

Juan caught her look and raised his eyebrow in hope. "It's a shame, my love, you didn't volunteer to wash my back," commented Juan.

Julie laughed and replied, "We'd still be in that shower, and besides, I had a call I really needed to take. Come sit, we need to talk about it."

She took his hand and gently guided him to the table and chairs in the sitting area of their lavish bedroom. The enormous suite had a private bath, separate room for visitors and access to the stairs to the children's room and play area on the floor above.

Julie's family home in Luxemburg was their permanent residence. It was spacious, to say the least, yet still had all the wonderful homey qualities they'd agreed were right for the children. Like many European homes, it had multiple floors, guest and resident rooms, designated dining, and a full ballroom which opened onto a lovely garden. It was furnished with care and painted in brighter colors than were typical of the era in which the home was built, thanks to Julie's mother, Haddy. The staff maintained it as if it were their own. Most of the staff had indeed lived there for the majority of their adult lives.

Maude Matthews, their full time nanny for the twins, Gracie and Juan Jr., was like extended family. Haddy had located Maude just before Julie delivered the twins, and everyone fell in love with her quick wit, pretty smile and lovely face framed by blonde hair. Even though she was a bit older than Julie, she handily kept up with the twins. Whenever Julie or Juan had to travel, she was ever vigilant with her charges. The twins played hard but were well-behaved and learned very quickly. As was Julie's family tradition, education started very early and covered a wide range of subjects, including their current focus on Spanish and English. Maude was as diligent about the children's education as Julie and Juan. She was adept at offering ideas to help the twins consider learning more of a game and less like a chore.

Before sitting, Juan grinned as he gathered his lovely wife into his arms and replied, "I would rather we take our conversation to bed. I worry that you aren't getting enough rest to recover from your London ordeal."

Julie melted into him, then pulled back slightly as she flashed her special grin, chuckling as she answered, "I am recovering just fine, and I promise we can play later. This is really important, honey!"

Juan released his hold and pulled out her chair. After she was seated, he took his seat and saw she had several scraps of paper with various notations. He glanced at them and picked up a few words, including the name of his brother Carlos. Carlos was the older of the two brothers who both sported similar black hair, a mustache, powerful build, and darker complexion, in line with their Mexican heritage. Carlos was the taller of the two, but when they were together it was difficult not to notice they were related. "Alright, my darling, what is going on? Are you just doodling my brother's name or working on a new problem? Start at the beginning, please."

Julie nodded and calmly related the information she'd learned during the call. "Su Lin and Andy had intruders, apparently with weapons. Shots were fired, and Su Lin was grazed by a bullet. Andy suffered some blindness from being too close to one or more muzzles when the shots were fired. They are both at the hospital. Andy is currently having his heart monitored as well.

"The latest information I have is that the intruders got away. This in itself presents a bit of a mystery since Su Lin was certain at least one person was shot. The police are investigating, and we are trying to make certain we stay up-to-date on the latest findings. Law enforcement is suggesting it was a robbery gone badly.

"Not surprisingly, Quip doesn't want EZ going to the farm in case the thugs are still around. Su Lin did not indicate that Andy was asking for EZ, but as you know she is devoted to her father."

Juan looked at the sadness in the eyes of his darling wife. Her bruises were healing, but it would take time for her to reconcile being taken and beaten, even though she ultimately escaped by damaging her captors on the way out. He fully admitted that each minute together seemed so much more precious than before that fateful London assignment. "Honey, I'm glad they are being treated and we can monitor their progress from here. I know how much you respect and care for Su Lin, especially after your history together." He reached for her hand, enclosing it into his and gently added, "You can't travel right now and, to be honest, I would like to stay together here for a little longer."

Julie agreed with a weak smile and stated, "I know. I'm not up to going. It is EZ who will want to get to her father. Quip hasn't told her yet, but he needs to hurry. She will want to be there as quickly as possible. How could she not? Since she works for us, Quip was hoping we might delay her making the trip until more investigating is done.

"Added to this, Su Lin originally called Jacob with news of the ordeal. Petra doesn't want him going because of the uncertainty of the intruders. The family called me to see if our team could help. I have been running over all the team members and their current assignments to decide who could go. I simply can't decide who I would risk, if these thugs are still about. Also, Su Lin's request of the state of health of a person she knew in China whom she has never mention before is out of character. That said it may actually mean something but I'm not sure what."

Juan thought about her comment and decided she was still too vulnerable to even go to the office. He feared her current state would make her second guess her typically logical, deductive, reasoning skills. As soon as she recovered enough physically, he'd make certain they resumed their sparing and workouts to improve her self-confidence. His beautiful wife, mother of his children and the most fearsome badass female he'd ever met, would recover. It would just take time. When they had returned from London, he'd promised to work with her and support her while she recovered. He was somewhat uncertain as to how, and he had no clue or experience with being that kind of person.

"Julie, in what capacity was our team asked to help?"

"It was suggested that keeping a watchful eye and checking out the farm thoroughly was the initial request. With Su Lin, though, it must be someone she trusts, and her list of trusted people is fairly short. Jacob, Petra, and Otto are the top people, and they lack bodyguard capabilities. She trusts me, of course, but to be honest I am not ready for that sort of effort. Carlos is too far away, and he is actually in a better position in Brazil to keep Andy's business rolling along. Quip knows Su Lin, and they get along well. But you know from working with him that technology and analysis are more his strengths.

"None of our team has really been around or worked with Su Lin."

Juan chuckled, "Right, besides if Quip wouldn't permit EZ to go, I'm fairly certain she would protest his going. What about Mercedes? Didn't Mercedes help out when someone tried to nab Su Lin?"

Julie thought for a moment, and a small, genuine smile appeared. Her light brown wavy hair, now a bit longer, bounced a bit as she agreed, "You're right, she did. I guess I'm a little muddled not to have recalled that. Mercedes has the right background to bodyguard. If we send her in first then Jacob wouldn't need to go along for Su Lin's comfort factor. With her lithe form and curly brown hair, no one ever suspects she could kill you in any number of ways with her bare hands and flush the body parts down the toilet." Julie paused and said, "We were lucky to get her on our team."

Juan mused, "I'd forgotten that part on her resume under

special skills. Let's tell her to catch the next flight, but please don't offer to watch her cat."

"Oh, Juan, the twins just love her cat. She is hardly any trouble at all, and don't do that other white meat routine again."

"Nope, that cat drives me crazy and makes me sneeze. The twins can visit and keep her food filled. A little responsibility wouldn't hurt them."

Julie flashed another smile reserved for Juan and raised her right eyebrow in total appreciation of her man. "Can you please call her while I just slip out of these clothes and into something skimpy? Meet you in the middle!"

Juan nodded and then realized what she'd actually said and replied, "You tempt me, woman."

"Oh, I hope so!"

CHAPTER 9

A New Target on the Horizon

Staring into his computer screen, Mathias nodded his head as if making up his mind on a topic. Without moving his gaze from the screen he announced, "And there's our next target: Venezuela. They've hosed up their economy so badly that their current inflation rate is 180%. The Global Bank is predicting this year's inflation rate to be over 700% and likely to soar to 2,068% in the next year."

Dutch smirked while he commented, "Boy, talk about your over-achievers!"

Mathias gave his henchman a disapproving glance, then returned his gaze to the screen while he continued, "Maduro is the current economic barbarian in a distinguished line of socialists who all believed more socialism would fix their situation. He subscribes to the classic definition of insanity. You know, doing the same thing over and over but expecting different results."

Dutch rolled his eyes, shrugged and agreed, "Sounds like a textbook example of insanity to me."

Mathias ignored the comment as he continued, "His plan was to make life as wonderful as it was at the end of World War II." Mathias looked disgusted as he insisted, "Look at this! In the mid-1900s, Venezuela was an economically developed country with a stable democracy. In 1944, the purchasing power of the average Venezuelan was more than 10 times the current one. By 1950, Venezuela boasted South America's second largest GDP per capita and seventh largest in the world. The wages of her workers were higher than those of most Western European wages.

"Hell, now they've gone from barely any inflation, at their peak in the 1940s, with their Bolívar currency one of the world's most stable, to stratospheric inflation. They boasted a free market economy that grew 10% per year, to this near hopeless mess of a centralized government that believes confiscating and owning everything is the only solution.

"Ah good, they have done everything wrong they possibly could. This makes the timing perfect for us to intercede. Their centrally planned economy is imploding. The fools are drinking their own Kool aid and believe suspending private ownership due to temporary emergencies is perfectly justified and helpful."

Dutch puzzled a moment before he asked, "There's also some corrupt cronyism inside this government that we can exploit, right? We're not just going in as caped-crusaders to help the poor downtrodden, are we? You know I hate that sort of role!"

Mathias shot Dutch another disapproving glance before he continued, "This is exactly what I was looking for. Another failing socialistic government where we can make a grand entrance and solve their economic issues.

"My cryptocurrency solution will be easier to introduce here than that last backwater country we tried, because there's nothing for these poor fools to go back to. They can only go forward with our solution.

"Now, all I need is some corrupt high ranking official who wants in on the ground floor with us to launch the project."

Dutch smirked and with a sarcastic overtone asked, "Gee, do you really think we will be able to find someone in this Venezuelan soup with the weak moral fiber required to support your plan?"

Mathias grinned as he reassured, "It's what I'm counting on. I'm making the calls and setting up a meet based on a contact I just received. It feels like the perfect storm."

Later that evening, Mathias was struggling to keep his annoyance in check during the conference call. Several times he muted his cell phone so he could vent his irritation. In his mind's eye he pictured the tall, lanky geek on the other end. Though the coder kept his head nearly shaved, his beard was unruly and offset his dark eyes that hid behind reading glasses, which tended to slide constantly toward the end of his nose.

Dr. Halvorson was their resident mathematician who always seemed to be thinking while everyone was speaking. The pale yellow eyes, blank expression, and droopy mustache of his companion gave the impression he was a raging forest fire gone out due to heavy rains, but you couldn't be more wrong about his abilities. It was his theories and Cody's software coding that had brought them this far. Sometimes, Halvorson just listened and said nothing.

Fed up, Mathias flatly stated, "Cody, this is all swell thinking, but I'm not up for product enhancements at this stage of the project! What we have already is perfectly suited for what I have in mind for this customer. Even if this is a 1.0 release, I don't want to have you add a bunch of junk that won't be online for six months! I'm heading there next week with our cryptocurrency, and it must be solid."

Cody bristled, shooting an irritated glance at Halvorson, and coolly responded, "Our C-C product is solid, Mathias. What I am suggesting is that it can do more than simply displace a paper currency.

"Look, you forget what money's designed for! It's not just a medium to transact business between two entities. We're talking about lending, writing contracts, loans for infrastructure building, and everything else that money enables while building an economy! If all you think about is using C-C to buy groceries or petro then you're leaving money on the table!"

Dutch lowered his head so that he could give Mathias that raised-eyebrow stare to silently reinforce Cody's position in the discussion. Mathias ground his teeth in irritation at the prospect of being too short-sighted in their product offering.

As a final point, Mathias demanded, "How much time are we talking about here? Hours? Days? Weeks? I have a meeting with these people next week so you better be able to work on this in background mode, Cody. Halvorson, make sure Cody doesn't over-rotate on my deliverables!"

Cody, sensing a thawing in Mathias's attitude, brightly promised, "Hey, no problemo! We need the cryptocurrency as the foundation. Everything else depends upon it. So you offer the C-C with all its stellar attributes like we've always done, but then you launch into phase II where we layer the additional benefits they can gain from C-C as a part of their economic expansion. That will give us some time to build and test the peer-to-peer lending attributes, along with the commercializa-tion of the lending features that the banks and other financial institutions will need to embrace the new technology."

Dutch cynically asked, "You will, of course, leave a little wedge in there for our cut of the action, right? I'm not going into this cesspool wearing a good guy halo, hoping they build a statue for me somewhere that pigeons can poop on."

Mathias glared at Dutch. Cody cheerfully responded, "Of course, my man! We make sure we get some of the initial issue. We control the digital coin supply so it appreciates in value. Then, we quietly sell our initial investment at a pace no one will get alarmed about. Lastly, we take our earnings and retire on a nice beach somewhere that has top heavy waitresses who love to serve fruity chick drinks."

Mathias drolly replied, "That was our plan on the last go 'round, but instead, we had to run for our lives. Maybe you two ought to join us when we go to Venezuela in case the project goes sideways again!"

Dutch chuckled and sarcastically inserted, "Oh wow, you mean have 'Codan the Economic Barbarian' around to help with our extraction? Gosh, I feel safer already!"

Cody brightly responded, "'Codan the Economic Barbarian', I like the sound of that!"

Mathias rolled his eyes and openly remarked, "Nothing like being trapped in a situation with a comic duo who isn't the least bit humorous.

"Alright, Cody, begin the programming on phase II and let me know if you need to alter the base C-C to support the lending piece. I don't want any surprises that will delay or derail the plan."

Cody, oblivious to the question being posed, asked, "Can I have a gun, like Dutch? I wanna look cool too!"

Mathias stated, "Why, of course you can, just no bullets! Now get coding!"

After they disconnected from the call, Dutch stared at Mathias and bluntly stated, "A water pistol for him, maybe. But not a gun. He's no good with anything mechanical, or anything that doesn't support a keyboard."

Mathias frowned as he nodded. "Agreed."

CHAPTER 10

Any Plan is Subject to Change
...The Enigma Chronicles

Mercedes arrived at Julie and Juan's place in time for breakfast. Being a true early riser, she loved the early morning meetings at their home. It seemed a little strange that she was requested to bring a suitcase with four days of casual clothing and Tiger along. Fortunately, her marmalade-colored cat did well in the carrier, meowing the entire time in pure delight. She preferred Tiger be with the twins if she was going on a short trip.

Her brown hair was a mess of curls, almost dry following her quick shower, but with no time to add makeup, her green eyes weren't as highlighted as her norm. The casual jeans and top she threw on after completing her morning workout hugged her trim figure. Jim, her lover, had left on assignment two days before, so she had worked out alone. They had met when they worked on the same team at the U.S. agency where Jim was also known as Stalker. Mercedes was a first-rate, multilingual operator who always seemed too sweet to hurt someone, but she was quick-witted, sure-footed, and an excellent shot with any kind of weapon at any distance.

Seconds after she knocked, the door was opened by Maude, the good natured nanny to the twins.

"Good morning, Mercedes! They are waiting for you in the dining room. The twins and I just finished our breakfast in order to leave you in peace. Set your suitcase down and come on in."

Gracie spotted her from the hallway and squealed, "Juan, she's here and she brought Tiger. Come on, help me."

Little Juan appeared as if by magic, and ever the little gentleman, tried to take the burden of the cat carrier from Mercedes. "Aunty Mercedes, I help with that. I need to take him upstairs before Papa sees he is here."

He flashed a little smile at her, and both of the twins started racing up the stairs with Maude close behind them.

Mercedes was still chuckling as she entered the dining room, grateful that she was a morning person and enjoyed the excitement of little ones. She wasn't ready for any of her own, so she happily lived vicariously through the antics of the twins.

They greeted one another as Mercedes found a chair, and fresh coffee immediately appeared. "Thank you, Gwen, I needed this." She smiled at the housekeeper with sincere appreciation. Gwen took her food order and vanished out the door nearest the kitchen. Even with the sun only just up, the dining room appeared bright and cheerful. The splashes of color everywhere Julie attributed to her mother, Haddy, currently at the house in Zürich.

Juan warmly greeted, "Hey, Mercedes, thanks for coming over. Were the twins successful in thinking they could quietly spirit the cat to their room?"

Julie laughed and flashed her trademark smile. "'Quietly' and 'your children' can't possibly be in the same sentence. Gracie yelled for Juan, and they giggled up the stairs like a herd of inebriated elephants. Even as well-built as this home is, they can make the old floors creak as if we had a hundred guests!"

"But Juan Jr. was so cute trying to hold up the carrier by himself. I'm not sure how Maude keeps up with those two free spirits," said Mercedes.

"How are you feeling, boss? I used to hate when I would get banged up on a job, but you've really cultivated some amazing rainbow coloring. Sorry, you know me, I always say things straight out."

"Mercedes, we all know that self-expression is not one of your weak points. I am feeling better," Julie stated, "though not ready for any field assignments yet. That's why we wanted to get you involved in a trip to the states. Georgia in fact.

"You recall Andy's farm in Georgia, right? It's where we girls decided that you liked your Jim a lot. Like we expected you to jump him in the pool. Oops, sorry, that may have been a bit too straightforward as well."

Mercedes chuckled and said, "Nah, that's fine. True too. What about the farm? I know Su Lin and Andy recently ran off and got married, without even the benefit of our having a party. Boy, was EZ steamed about that. I thought she said she was planning a big get together for later in the summer. Is that what this is about?"

Julie's face clouded as she somberly replied, "No, not yet. But I do expect EZ to get steamed when we call her in a bit."

"Ah, good! Thanks, Gwen, for the wonderful food," Julie exclaimed as Gwen set down Mercedes' plate and some extra toast. Gwen grinned and quickly left.

"Now let's eat up, form our plan, and then call EZ. I'm hoping you can help us shape the right message for her. Quip will be on the call for support as well. He understands the delicacy of the situation."

Julie placed the call from their office inside their suite. She had thought about all of them going to the office, but it seemed unnecessary. They had a great set up and access to all the information they needed.

EZ and Quip appeared on the monitor. EZ's red mane of curls was resting over her shoulders. Her heart-shaped face highlighted her startling sea-green eyes and long lashes against her peaches and cream skin. She announced, "Hi. We're here. What's up, guys?"

Julie reported, "EZ, you need to take a breath and listen to everything, please."

EZ nodded, but her face looked anxious as they saw Quip's arm pull EZ a bit closer.

Julie continued, "Alright, now remember we are all here for you. Mercedes, Juan, and I are on this end, and because my face is still healing, I am off camera, but I can move closer if you wish.

"Jacob received a call yesterday from Su Lin that she and your dad were attacked at the farm. The dog had been given some sort of tainted meat which caused him to sleep through the attack. Your dad has some temporary blindness due to being too close to one or more gun barrels when they were discharged. He's resting well but under observation for at least three more days, per the doctor this morning. Su Lin is having some adverse reaction to medications they gave her after they dressed a wound to her shoulder."

EZ interrupted, "Quip, did you know about this and not wake me up last night? Why wouldn't you tell me immediately?"

Knowing he was in trouble, he somberly responded, "Sweetheart, I did avoid telling you, but only until we could get a plan together. Jacob, Petra, and I discussed that we were not equipped to possibly fight intruders if they were still about. We suspect they may be gone, but possibly only temporarily if they weren't finished. Su Lin was vague on that point when she spoke to Jacob, and we are madly researching some of the information she did offer to see if we can close the loop."

Julie cautioned, "EZ, let me tell you what we have planned so far.

"Mercedes will be going to Georgia to check out the farm and take care of the rest of the investigation. The local authorities were unable to find any shells or casings, which suggests a professional hit of some sort. Once she has checked it out and looked in on your dad and Su Lin, she will coordinate your coming in to help."

EZ looked ready to kill Quip as she raged, "I want to go to my dad now. You had no right to keep this from me. Not any of you."

Juan interjected, "EZ, we need you to run some cell signals for us, which you can't do on a flight to the states. That's a part of your specialized job, to help us get to the facts of the case. You are the most qualified for this portion. Let Mercedes check things out. Su Lin and your dad both know her. Help us find out who broke in and why, please?"

Mercedes added, "I promise, I'm on a flight in an hour and I'll see them first thing. I listened while Julie spoke to the doctor. They'll not be released for several days. We explained who you are so now the doctor will keep you directly informed. We provided your direct number and information. Let me do my job, and you do yours!"

EZ nodded with tears clearly filling her eyes. She pushed Quip's arm away, then disconnected the call.

CHAPTER 11

Perhaps a Gift From God

Genesis smiled seductively at the two men as she announced, "Gentlemen, Director Noya will receive you now." It irked Mathias that he had to pull Dutch's arm to distract him from the buxom office manager's impressive cleavage and refocus on walking towards the manager's door without stumbling.

Genesis had trouble suppressing her smile and at the last moment distracted Dutch further, as she reminded, "Oh, wait! You forgot your visitor badges! Here, let me pin them on you." Mathias watched with disgust as Genesis fumbled expertly with the clip-on badge for maximum distraction for Dutch.

Mathias snatched his badge and quickly clipped it on to his shirt while Dutch got the full treatment of his badge being attached to his first belt loop. The only consolation for the episode for Mathias was that he got to watch Dutch turn and walk straight into the open door because he was staring down the front of her blouse.

Genesis was about to rush over to comfort Dutch when Director Alejandro Noya stepped into the room and intercepted the situation. "Gentlemen, please come in. Thank you, Genesis. That will be all for now."

Mathias walked into the office ready to do business, while Dutch kept watching in both directions, one, to make sure he missed the door this time, and two, in case he got more encouragement from Genesis.

Alejandro closed the door behind them so they could not only talk in private, but so that he could get their full attention, particularly from Dutch.

Alejandro smiled politely and began, "You would understand that my office manager has many skills, but she excels at her namesake. Genesis not only translates into the beginning, but you will regret it forever if you bring her into your life. You would understand that her skills are useful, but not for you and not for today."

Mathias fidgeted with Alejandro's recounting of their clumsy entrance, but Dutch just blushed at being so distracted by feminine charms.

Alejandro suppressed his smile and sensed that the conversation needed to move forward. He offered, "Gentlemen, let's progress to the business at hand, shall we? Mr. Petersen, you indicated that you had what you considered to be our economic salvation but failed to provide much more than that statement as a proof point."

Mathias replied as politely as possible, "Apologies, but I was under the impression that the upfront fund transfer provided most of the proof points to further our discussion. And please, call me Mathias, Director."

Alejandro, mildly annoyed at the inference, stiffly rebuked, "The funds transfer provided an introduction, not the substance of your claim. You have your introduction and now I want the details, Mr. Petersen."

Mathias quickly reeled in his initial irritation from the meetings' opening farce and replied, "Director Noya, forgive me if I choose words that seem too blunt. To the outside world, Venezuela appears to be collapsing, and frankly, no one seems to be willing to lend a hand. Yes, I know the Russians will sell you their castoff weapons, but there is no corporate or private investment being directed to this country.

"Venezuela is being circled by the investment vultures, waiting for her to expire so they can swoop in and dine on the carcass. Using our economic model on your current circumstances, we are predicting a 20% chance of economic survival as a country. I am afraid our modeling for your personal circumstances is not that high."

Alejandro's nostrils flared, and with some difficulty, he managed to maintain a civil tone as he responded, "You're not the first person to sit in that chair to predict my government's demise!

"Venezuela has had adversity before, but we will survive it and on our terms. Make no mistake on this accord. Why don't you tell me what you're selling, so I can tell you why we don't need it?"

In a quiet reserved tone, Mathias politely offered, "We don't doubt your resolve to persevere in your economic plight. However, Director, with hard currency flowing out, economic inflation skyrocketing, and with little food and no medicines to offer your people, your time is limited. The problem, as we see it, is that you are trying to build a new economic model but are using outdated financial tools.

"Your government is trying to re-write the Venezuela economy after a socialist model, but the fundamental flaw with your approach is that you are trying to use Capitalist tools that depend upon a centralized banking model. As we see it, your currency, the Bolívar, is evaporating faster than you can print it. On top of that, U.S. dollars as the world reserve currency is being exported through any means possible, and your only asset on the world stage is oil. The problem gets back to paying to extract, move, and store it while there is no reliable transaction medium. I am sure it hasn't escaped your attention that Venezuelan oil prices are less than everyone else's?"

Dutch could see Alejandro's jaw muscles tensing with anger, but he was recognizing everything being said was true. Dutch was impressed, yet again, at the way his partner could weave a story.

Alejandro collected himself mentally and finally asked, "Then what precisely do you propose to help our situation? Of course, the follow-on question we will ask after the first is, how much is your help going to cost?"

Mathias paused a moment for dramatic effect, then said, "Take your country to the 21st century with an economic model built upon digital or cryptocurrency. Our company already has the computer algorithms to launch and control a state-issued digital currency for your government. You, Director, control the sale blocks of the digital currency initially at a value close to the U.S. dollar. You use the U.S. dollars to pay off back debt and to get your coinage into the hands of your buyers. You eliminate your government-issued currency overnight, which has little to no value in foreign markets, and replace it with the new digital currency.

"With the chance at a vibrant market, your black market disappears overnight as well. Because the e-currency is very easily monitored, tax evasion is a thing of the past. Stability returns to your Venezuelan markets along with confidence in fair value exchange when trading.

"I'm sure you recognize, with your expertise in world economics, this same model has already been deployed in Estonia when they faced the Soviet fallout in 1989. They were simply cut off from the Soviets and had to begin from scratch. They turned to the digital age and walked away from the old Soviet model of analog anything. That includes digital currency. Why, you can even become an e-Citizen of that country and never even live there! Imagine getting tax revenues from your citizens without having to provide physical infrastructure for them to live!"

Alejandro studied Mathias and Dutch a moment. He almost smiled before saying, "You know how we translate the name Mathias here in Venezuela? It means, Gift from God."

CHAPTER 12

Don't Tell Anyone
if You Feel Sad...

Mercedes strode purposefully away from the baggage carousel with her roller-board bag in tow and her cell phone pressed to her ear waiting for the call to connect. It irritated her to have the call roll to voicemail...again.

She mumbled as she groused, "It's been three days and no word, dammit! He knows better than to go off on one of his dark ops assignments without checking in first! I don't care if he is saving the world from the bad guys. I just want to hear his voice!"

She tucked her phone away just as she reached the passenger pickup area. Mercedes scanned the area looking for her ride when her phone chirped with a text message from her ride service that read:

> Your HOMBRE ride service is here, Ms. Field. Please look for us on the West side of the terminal, in the gray minivan.

Mercedes rolled her eyes and shot back a text that read:

> Listen, HOMBRE, Ms. Field is on the East side of the terminal so get your buns over here pronto!

A few minutes later a late model minivan, covered in layers of gray dirt and dust, screeched to a halt in front of Mercedes, and the driver got out to assist with her bags. The flowing robes of the driver swirled around the end of the minivan, and she fully expected him to be antagonistic toward her. In a faulty broken English he pleaded, "Don't be anger with me, Madam Sahib! This is only my day 2 on the job as an HOMBRE driver, and the app sent me to the wrong side of the airport! I proud to be in this country and work for HOMBRE as a driver. Please do not give me a poor rating! Five star ratings are critical for advancement. I need to earn enough to buy driver's license and insurance. Punish me with less tip but your rating, if it is poor, will cost me my job! I beg you!" He then dropped to his knees and held his cupped hands to his chest.

Mercedes was taken aback by the prostration of the HOMBRE driver at the curb and embarrassed by the display. She scanned the immediate area and quietly asked, "You got a name?"

The man lifted his head and wiped an invisible tear from his eye and stated, "My name is Khalid Effendi."

Not wishing to spend any more time on the incident, Mercedes asked, "Khalid, can we just go now, please? Get me to where I need to go and we'll see about your rating."

Khalid brightened up quickly and promptly loaded both Mercedes and her bag with no wasted effort.

As they pushed through the airport gate and onto the highway, Mercedes smirked slightly and offered, "Khalid, an excellent performance. The robes and the broken English with the tears… well, very nice touch. Couldn't Jim just have called me himself rather than use this bogus clumsy contact?"

Khalid chuckled and in perfect English replied, "He asked me to get a message to you so you would stop worrying. He can't interrupt his unplanned assignment and is engaged in some heavy stuff. So heavy, they confiscated his phones, identities, and I think his service weapon."

A little alarmed, Mercedes asked, "Isn't that a little unorthodox? I mean, with all his tools gone, what's he supposed to do, shout and gesture at the bad guys?"

Khalid tugged at his chin in thought. "They are holding him incommunicado for now. And no, I don't know why. If you ask any of your old contacts, they'll know you're on our soil, which may not be in his or your best interest.

"My advice? Get your business done quietly and get out, back to your European home. We're operating in a class 5 storm right now, and Jim doesn't want you caught up in it."

Mercedes' mind raced with all the new information, coupled with her intimate knowledge of clandestine operations. She was unable to decide the right next step. The mission she was on paled against her concern.

Finally she grumbled, "This just sucks! He probably knew this was in the works, which explains why he was so quiet before he left. I wish he had told me why he was sad. Why do men do that?"

Khalid smiled wistfully and offered, "Perhaps it is because they care so much, ma'am."

Mercedes spent several hours with Andy and Su Lin at the hospital. The staff had cautioned her that it might be premature to bring them home. EZ had spoken to her dad, who said he wanted his own bed. This request had been stated with a high level of insistence in a call they'd just concluded.

Andy's eyes had been covered for days from the flash burns he suffered during the attack. The doctors were taking a wait-and-see attitude to his recovery. Since the human eye is remarkably adept at healing from these type of wounds, they wanted to keep the bandages in place for at least two more days. Andy was terrified at the prospect of being permanently blind, and this fear made his behavior and his mood swings erratic. When the nurse was showing Mercedes how to change the bandages as well as clean and dress the wounds, he became combative, regardless of her coddling.

Su Lin's trauma was no less difficult with her unexpected reactions to the medications. Her IV drip of fluids was critical for nourishment. When she tried to help sooth Andy during the dressing changes, his hands would get caught in Su Lin's lines, raising her anxiety and resulting in her crying out. This naturally caused Andy to overreact because he could see he was the cause. It took Mercedes and two of the staff to normalize the situation enough to complete the treatment.

After the struggle, Mercedes valiantly attempted to secure their discharge, but she faced repeated temper tantrums, by one or both of them, amounting to a total refusal to cooperate. Mercedes threw up her hands and proclaimed, "No, we are not doing this, children! You two will stay here where there are trained professionals to deal with your aberrant behavior! You should both be ashamed of yourself when all any of us want to do is help. I will go by myself, since you have both ticked me off for the last time, and scope out the farm alone!

"I'll keep in contact with the staff here and be here for the bandage removal, Andy. I will call with any important status changes! I will make certain your foreman is aware and taking care of the animals, but you two need to clean up your act! If you behave for the staff, I will give good reports back to EZ and keep this between us."

The room fell silent while Mercedes seethed, then the head nurse quietly offered, "She's right, you two are not ready for unassisted care at this time. I'm going to put you back into your beds while you heal a bit more under supervised care.

"I know you're anxious to resume your regular lives, but in my professional opinion, you're not ready to leave here yet. And since we don't have someone to discharge you to …well, we all need to work a little longer."

Andy bristled slightly, then contritely replied, "Y'all are probably right. Nurse, discharging us to Miss 'Grumpy Britches' here is probably a poor idea. Let's try it your way for a while.

"Su Lin, you get settled first, honey, while I sit here."

CHAPTER 13

The Prize, Alive...

Guano, trying to sound as upbeat as possible, greeted, "Ah, Finance Minister Kuan-Chun, I trust I am not interrupting your busy day. I thought I might check in and provide an update on my progress..."

The minister angrily interrupted, "We already know your first attempt failed, Guano. Our monitoring stations were already keyed into the operations, but the press coverage your failed mission received filled in most of the missing details." He snidely added, "Far quicker than this call. I believe you promised this committee stealth and finesse in a very important clandestine operation. When do you propose to begin implementing those attributes? You will be happy to know that when the whole incident was posted on social media, we quickly got the event classified as fake news so the trusting fools would remove the incident and provide some air cover to you and your team. It would be far more amusing if it wasn't your poorly orchestrated kidnapping attempt all over social media."

Guano ground his teeth as he slowly closed his eyes in an effort to dissipate his irritation at being dressed down by a party member. Once Guano got his temper under control, he asked, "Since you are already aware of our circumstances here, you would understand that we now need some replacements to carry on with this operation. I trust you are still willing to invest in this operation to achieve success?"

Now it was the Finance Minister's turn to be irked at the conversation tone. "Yes, we have a couple of replacements en route to you. You will find them well versed in that cultural desert of America. You are getting them because they know how to blend into the insanity of America to get the job done. We wanted someone who could continue the mission in case you should end up dead. But don't worry, their instructions are to follow your orders. Unless, of course, they are foolish orders like the ones issued on your first attempt to secure our prize!

"I understand you are quite familiar with them already. We are sending you Won and Ton. Do not fail again, Guano, but bring us Master Po, or you will become the subject of more fake news on social media."

Unable to digest the new personnel assignment to his team, Guano closed his eyes and let his head limply fall forward in hopes that he could have unheard who was being sent to him. After a moment of ghastly reflection, he finally asked, "Tell me this is some cruel hoax and that you are not really sending those two imps of Satan!

"Those henchmen of Chairman Lo Chang are not soldiers. They are singularly unqualified to be on an assignment like this! Don't you think Won with his slashed face and missing tongue might be a little too noticeable? And with Ton doing all the talking for both of them, it is easy to see how stupidity can be doubled! Those two have bungled more ops than anyone still left alive. I thought we were talking about investing in this operation, not derailing it!"

The Finance Minister smirked, "That's what I like to hear! A properly motivated leader enthusiastically receiving his new assets. Don't call again, unless you secure our prize. That had better be soon, Guano."

Guano barked, "Lieutenant, get in here now! We need to do some planning before the replacements arrive."

Lieutenant Quinn Lee scurried in from the outer room with a surprised look on his face. "Wow! That was fast! You only just got off the call a few minutes ago and…"

Guano, annoyed that their operations had been reported on social media, cut off his speech. "The two individuals they are sending are not soldiers trained for this kind of military operation but a couple of leftover henchmen from the old Chairman Lo Chang criminal faction. The individuals, Won and Ton, are to be our replacements. Doubtless they are being sent to retrieve the package we have to surgically remove from this continent. Understand, they are not to be trusted. I expect when we get Lt. Colonel Po, we will no longer be valued assets and will be terminated as liabilities."

Lieutenant Lee swallowed hard and said, "I know of them and their reputation for cruelty. But why hit us? What did you and the minister discuss?"

Guano ground his teeth and snarled, "They were chosen because they have a blood feud with me. I was the one sent to bring the Chairman for trial, but gave him my pistol so he could go without losing face. They threatened me with retribution someday, and it looks like this is that day. It would have been easier for the minister and his group to hide their intentions if they had sent two military grade replacements. After the dressing down I received, and news of the replacements being sent, Lieutenant, let's just say the sword of Damocles is hanging over our heads."

After a long sobering silence from both men, Lieutenant Lee offered, "Sir, that being the case, we need to engineer our success and their tragedy, so we don't become fatalities. Being something of a practical engineer, I have what may be a workable idea.

"Do you remember the old fable about the two adventurers and the Treasure of the Dragon? They both arrived at the lair of the dragon and fought a duel for the right to enter first. The crafty adventurer threw the match and let the brawny adventurer go first. Once the crafty adventurer was inside, he made a great ruckus that insured that the dragon would be annoyed at the intrusion and destroy his competitor. Then the crafty adventurer snuck in while the fight ensued and gathered up all the treasure he could and promptly left. I propose that we let the adventurers, Won and Ton in this case, be the first ones in with this dragon."

Guano clucked his tongue and dryly stated, "You know, of course, that I've heard this tale too. In the telling I heard, the dragon whacked both of them because he was listening and knew there were two of them to destroy."

After a sobering moment, Guano continued, "But I rather like your telling, so let's figure out how to make good our escape with the treasure."

CHAPTER 14

Finding the Right Lead is an Art

Petra and Jacob decided to leave early and work from the chateau. They were frustrated that they had not found a clear lead on the currency that had gone missing before the demise of Stuart Chesterfield, aka Steven Christopher. Wolfgang had begged off going to work for the last few days, claiming he felt he was getting a cold and wanted to stay close to home. He indicated he would rest as needed, but he could work there if required. The discussion could wait until dinner, but Jacob wanted to run some ideas by him as the eldest member of the core team and the finance wizard.

Wolfgang was a strong, dignified gentleman with graying hair that was always groomed perfectly, not too long nor too short. Up until the last few days, he typically dressed early in well-fitted suits that enhanced his tall well- balanced physique. Lately, he remained in his dressing gown following breakfast then often returned to his suite to read or rest. Bowen had mentioned his growing concern to Jacob and Petra that morning just as they were leaving for work. Jacob was a bit concerned with his grandfather's health as he was getting on in years, but his mind was still quick, and he was familiar with this situation.

Petra and Jacob had been singularly focused on Chesterfield, who had absconded with millions over the course of his scam. They had originally surmised Chesterfield had distributed his take to several banks, including one in Hong Kong, during his last actions in Panama before his death. As Petra and Jacob continued to hit one dead end after another with each of the banks, they decided they needed to ask the master. Along with his genius for finances, Wolfgang might be able to provide some additional direction or avenues for them to continue their pursuit of the funds. To date, they figured they had traced a mere ten percent of the funds. They hoped Wolfgang might suggest some additional avenues to check to get a better handle on the millions attributed to Chesterfield's scam.

Bowen smiled as he welcomed Petra and Jacob home. They each had assigned suites in the chateau, but tended to stay in Jacob's as the fireplace was larger. Though the furnishings in his suite were heavier and definitely more male, the rich brownish tones were to Petra like sliding into a pair of comfortable Italian loafers. Bowen had worked as the butler, valet, and companion to Wolfgang since he was a young lad. Not only did he know everything about the interworking components of the chateau, but he also managed the staff. His hair was graying, but his posture was perfect, putting him slightly taller than Petra, as he inclined his head to direct them to the library after taking their outer wraps.

"Jacob, your grandfather is in the library sipping some cabernet and reading the current newspaper. He ate very little today and didn't take his normal walk. If he doesn't shake off this cold complaint, which he voiced again during breakfast, I would appreciate a recommendation from you that he needs to see his physician.

"I have asked Cook to prepare his favorites for supper and she can serve in an hour's time, if you wish."

Jacob nodded agreement with a slight smile and a concerned look as he clasped Petra's hand and entered the library. Wolfgang was indeed sipping wine and looked up with a half-smile at their arrival.

"I could pour for you, my boy, but it would be far easier on both of you to take care of it, if you don't mind. I am a bit light-headed, perhaps too much wine with so little to eat."

Petra moved toward Wolfgang to sit as close as possible and held his hand near her cheek. "Wolfgang," she asked with some concern, "are you warm enough? Your hands feel like ice cubes."

Wolfgang nodded and replied, "It's the seasons changing, my dear. Perhaps Jacob will start a small fire to warm the room."

Jacob moved to the fireplace and lit the already set fire. Jacob brought the drinks over to them and began his request. "Grandfather, we are having a hard time tracking the funds. We used the programs you suggested ICABOD was familiar with, but we have not had any real hits at this point. Is there a special variable we should be using to increase the effectiveness?"

ICABOD had so many programs in its library and an array of data sources far superior to any other supercomputer. Quip had designed ICABOD, yet it had almost been brought down by Wolfgang as he had used ICABOD to build some complex search analytics programs which were used to grab huge amounts of data with no throttle on processing power. As a result of this almost disaster, Quip had modified the ability of ICABOD to expand space during complex routines.

Wolfgang smiled and slurred slightly as he commented, "That is one really smart system, that ICABOD.

"No special variables are needed, other than to point ICABOD to search destinations that maintain confidentiality, as well as those that are not controlled by governments. I was reading something earlier I meant to set aside for you and thought that perhaps Chesterfield had invested in some Blockchain venture. There are so many of those springing up and then failing. Perhaps Chesterfield invested in this sort of arrangement and lost everything. He would never have kept the cash in a safety deposit box or the like, so I think that avenue would be useless to focus on at this point. And precious metals for that amount would weigh far too much."

Jacob thought for a few moments and then agreed, "Wolfgang, I think you're onto something. Petra, can we do some modifications to the search for Blockchain and let ICABOD work while we have supper? I'm suddenly famished."

Petra nodded and went to access her laptop from the adjacent room.

Jacob extended his arm and said, "Grandfather, let's proceed to supper. I know that Cook was busy making your favorites. I can smell the cobbler from here, which I know comes after the roast beef, but if you want it first, I won't tell."

Wolfgang half smiled, shakily rose and latched onto Jacob's arm. Then he slowly walked toward the dining room, meeting Petra.

"I added that criteria and will check how it ran after supper." She reached for Wolfgang's other arm and leaned into him. "Wolfgang, you are so crafty! I think that will help get us to the next level."

Wolfgang started to nod his agreement, when he gasped and groaned. His knees buckled, and it took the two of them to help him to a chair.

Jacob tried not to panic as he called out confidently, "Bowen, I think we need to see that physician now. Perhaps you can call emergency services, unless you feel we can take him into town faster."

Bowen rushed around the corner, then stopped when he saw Wolfgang crumpled in the chair. Bowen walked close and took Wolfgang's pulse and stated, "Oh dear! His pulse is irregular." Bowen caught his breath and tried to remain calm as he added, "Yes, Mr. Jacob, our taking him will be faster. I'll bring the car around, if you can lift him into the car."

"I can. Petra, would you please call the hospital and alert them to his condition. I am trying to run through my mind the top symptoms of stroke and heart attack, and he appears to have some symptoms of each, though I could be wrong. Also, grab a pillow and perhaps a cover. He is still very cold."

Wolfgang looked a bit confused and replied, "Don't fuss. Alright I am. Aspirin too."

Petra looked at Jacob with concern and insisted, "You carry him out, and I will get aspirin and call Otto. I didn't know he was taking aspirin, did you?"

Jacob didn't respond. He was grateful for his daily workouts as he carefully lifted Wolfgang into his arms. Cook appeared, undoubtedly alerted by Bowen as he left to fetch the car, to help navigate the doors and patting Wolfgang as she promised to save the delicacies if he would simply get well.

They arrived safely at the hospital where Wolfgang's doctor and the staff were waiting. They rushed him away, suggesting the family wait in the room reserved for them. Updates would come in as frequently as there was news.

CHAPTER 15

Idiotic or Just Plain Inept
...The Enigma Chronicles

Petra found waiting for news in a hospital, even in such a nice waiting room, was awful. Fortunately, they could alter the music channel or even have television if they wished. Jacob seemed completely lost in thought and unwilling to talk. Once in a while he would rest his hand on her arm or knee and pat her gently. She knew that he had spent many hours in hospital waiting rooms for one reason or another, including the hours he sat by her bed when she had been beaten so badly and lay unconscious for days. Bowen had returned home to collect a few items, including their laptops in case they wanted to work and was now positioned by the door quietly reading a book so as not to disturb them. Everyone dealt with life situations in their own way.

Feeling totally at odds, Petra finally decided she would test the Wi-Fi connection. After she enabled a secured connection, she posted an update to Quip to share with the rest of the family. Jacob leaned over and looked at her wording and then kissed her cheek and murmured a quiet thank you. Then he rose and left the area without an explanation. While she suspected he would walk the hallway, possibly to find some fresher coffee, he was actually trying to see if he could gain a status on Wolfgang.

Petra took a look at her current assignments and updated the status where it made sense for a couple of the jobs. Then she wrote a summary of her findings for submission to one of her regular clients, suggesting they get together next month for some scheduled updates on their site. She provided several customers with encryption updates as well as participated in their technology refresh discussions. Customers who had her under contract expected her to take care of them regardless of her life events, though most were very tolerant if she said she had to delay for one reason or another. Many had been her customers for over five years, and she had secured their total confidence.

Finishing all the small tasks and checking that her settings were current, she exited those programs and accessed the search she had set up before Wolfgang had collapsed. Shaking her head slightly, she murmured, "Wolfgang, even when you feel lousy, you are so much smarter than any of us, it is unbelievable." The result of the change she'd made only hours early had resulted in four new leads for them to follow. One of the sourced transactions listed had a timeframe she remembered being close to when Chesterfield had left New York, but that certainly could be wishful thinking on her part. She made some notes for herself and then made a code shift for the tracking routine ICABOD controlled.

Looking around, Petra noticed Bowen had fallen asleep with his head leaned against the wall and Jacob still had not returned. She got up and walked over to Bowen. Gently tapping him on the shoulder, he roused just enough so that she was able to guide him to the couch and convinced him to lay down until there was news. Her smile reassured him that she would wake him if the doctors appeared with any updates. Petra returned to her laptop and decided to spend some time searching some of her favorite haunts online to see the current chatter.

There were four sites she frequented to get the current buzz and commentary from the hacker community. It always surprised her how transparent people were on these sites. When she first started exploring these sorts of sites, the test had been to see how fast she could locate the origin of a given comment as well as the real identity of the commenter. It was an exercise that helped her learn how to hide cyber identity and keep others from ever finding her. When Jacob had tried long ago to find her, he had to have the exact sequence Quip provided in order for her to get noticed. Of course, at that time flag and alerts were set to send notifications. Some changes had occurred since that time so that the R-Group could keep their secondary activities much more hidden as they continued to grow.

In her third stop to known locations, she was astounded beyond belief. There was a post on the wall which stated,

Petra Rancowski please call Tonya at +33 1 4075 3210

Petra stared at the screen. It was beyond odd that this would be so blatantly posted or that she had not been notified. Where were her alerts? Then she noticed the posting had been made less than five minutes ago. Suddenly her laptop and cell phone received repeated alerts to the posting along with the origin information. Checking all the origin data as well as backtracking the trail, she ended up at a laptop assigned to a Tonya Van Den Berghe at the Global Bank IT Department. There were some interesting files on the laptop which Petra found contained some very personal information, as well as passport and credit information, which she captured. She cleared the post and attributed it to a question-able hacker who no one trusted. Chuckling again at the absurdity of the message, let alone the way it had effectively worked at getting her attention, she decided to update the team on the occurrence for the project and placed the call.

"Hello," stated a suspicious lady who clearly did not see a number or identity of the caller.

Petra decided to have some fun as she responded, "Hello, is this Tonya Van Den Berghe?"

Tonya hesitated slightly then replied, "Maybe, who's calling?"

Petra smiled slightly to herself as she continued, "This is the collection agency reminding you of your past due payment on your skiing trip you are purchasing for the upcoming season. We have your credit card information, but we need your authorization to confirm the charge transaction. I can do this for you now if you like."

Tonya was immediately on alert. She had visited a couple of websites and asked for pricing information on some trips but had not set dates at all. Very concerned, she stated, "I haven't reserved a trip for this season. I have only been looking at a couple of options."

Petra smiled and replied, "Madam, I have your American Express number as 9871 2131 2220 0000 5."

Tonya screamed into her phone. "Stop, you have no right to my credit information. Where did you get that number? Who are you?"

"Why are you angry? You asked me to call your number less than ten minutes ago. Now, who told you to try to approach me in this manner? And why doesn't your organization have better security on your machine? I have some encryptions services which can help with this issue," stated Petra. "You, Miss Tonya, need to understand how the web works and how to help yourself. What are you, ten years old?"

Tonya stammered, "Oh, is this really Petra? I had no idea if such a crazy post would work. No, I'm not ten, but the cloak and dagger approach I was told to use seemed so old-fashioned."

Petra retorted, "What is it you need, little girl?"

Tonya felt confident now as she replied, "I need to set up a contact with you to check some information I will be receiving from another contractor. My boss heard you were the best at checking the results and data analysis. Would you consider working for my organization?"

Petra shook her head at the naivety of this woman and replied, "Sure, for the right amount. But I want to meet you first. One of those seeing is believing things. Since you are in Paris, how soon can you take a flight to Zürich? We can meet at the airport and establish a contract."

Tonya grinned at her good fortune and said, "I can be there tomorrow evening. How will I know you?"

Petra replied, "I will see you at the exit from security in the lounge reserved for Air France concierge customers. Your status should allow you to gain entrance easily. I will be there by 7 pm. If you arrive earlier please wait."

Tonya felt as if she had really accomplished her job in short order. "But how will I know you?"

"You won't," answered Petra. "I will recognize you from your passport photos. Safe travels, and don't do that type of posting ever again. It could get you hurt. Bring your laptop so I might fix it."

Petra disconnected the call then hunted down Jacob to fill him in on the woman they would both end up dealing with.

Tonya disconnected from the call and looked down at the PC screen to see the message being displayed that said,

> Your hard drive has been encrypted. Your PC now belongs to me. There is no ransom demand this time but heed the warning about foolish Internet postings.

CHAPTER 16

Checking Out and Checking In

Mercedes had arrived at Andy's ranch the night before. The foreman, Ernie Lee, greeted her with a firm handshake that spoke of his labors. His weathered skin was tanned and displayed the lines of years of work in the elements, especially the sun. Jeans and cotton shirt seemed to be his standard uniform. His leather boots probably hadn't seen a shine in years, but she'd bet the soles were replaced often. His hair was tied back and fading from blonde to grey, and he displayed a kind face and ready smile. Ernie recognized Mercedes from her prior visit and spent time showing her what he had discovered after Andy and Su Lin had been taken to the hospital.

The attack had occurred on his day off when he visited his mother, and after the police had finished with their investigation, he had been allowed back into the house.

Ernie explained, "Mercedes, I feel just awful about being gone that day. I go one day a week to see to some of her chores that my sister can't handle. Been doing that for a long time now, but I shoulda been here. When I came back that night, the police wouldn't let me in the house but did tell me Andy and Su Lin were injured but not critical. I fed the stock and then took Wrinkles back to my rooms behind the barn.

"It took two days for that mutt to shake off whatever he'd been fed to make him sleep. He's still plenty lethargic and seems sad. The only time he follows me out is when I go tend to Franklin. He does his business, sips a little water and eats a bit from my hands while Franklin eats. Then he just looks around for his master or Su Lin. She spoiled him, ya know, cooking treats for him every day. I am hoping with your being here, he will follow you into the house. He didn't even move when you drove up."

Mercedes empathized, "Ernie, I know that Su Lin and Andy are grateful you are here. They likely won't be ready to come home until day after tomorrow. If you need to go to your mother's, perhaps you can show me what to do to tend the stock."

"Oh, no, ma'am," replied Ernie, "I got a lad, Will, who I hired to help out until Andy and Su Lin are both back and okay. Will is staying in the bunkhouse. I will tell you if I have to leave, but Will is going to be here for at least a month. Andy and I both know his daddy, and he's good with the stock. Franklin is the most finicky critter we have right now, but he's okay with me, even though he always prefers Su Lin.

"Let me show you the house and some other things I found when I looked around. I honestly don't think the police think it was anything other than a robbery gone wrong. I didn't clean up the house since I thought someone like you might want to see it."

"That's great, Ernie. Show me everything, and your opinion is critical. Thank you."

Ernie walked her through the house and pointed out the areas of the fight while he related the story as he knew it. He pointed out the bullet holes but confirmed the police had not found any of the bullets as they had been already removed. The only slugs recovered were those that were fired from Andy's weapon, which had been confirmed as registered to him, but were in evidence at the police station. There was no forced entry into the house.

The police had found Wrinkles on the porch in a heap. They thought he was dead, but he was only sleeping, unresponsive. Ernie sadly said, "They called our vet, and he came out and kept him for a day until I returned and picked him up."

Outside they took a long walk around the house and out to the furthest fence line. It was an area of scrub brush and trees rarely used or even monitored. It was a good half mile or more from the house. There Ernie pointed out the tracks for a very large vehicle, like a Hummer maybe, which could have been there for weeks unnoticed. The tracks weren't on Andy's property, but it appeared that a portion of the barbed wire fence had been held down or covered. He pointed out some stains which he suggested could easily have been blood left by someone in a hurry to exit the area.

Mercedes gathered some soil and surrounding vegetation in hopes that some additional testing could be done to identify the stains. She found a bit of thread on the barbed wire and agreed with Ernie that something had been covering it. She gathered the evidence and took extensive photos of the tracks and even walked the trail of the treads back to the road where they vanished. The only indication was that, from the angle the vehicle exited onto the road, it appeared to go south, which was toward the airport.

Ernie and Mercedes returned to the house together and speculated on the possibilities.

"Ya know, ma'am, we haven't run the entire fence line on this property in a long time. Usually once in the spring to make certain the fencing is up, but the rest of our stock is kept east of the house and isn't like it once was. Andy likes the family farm," Ernie advised, "but he doesn't have the same time or needs of the stock for survival. He does have some breeder bulls and great horse stock, but only a fraction of what was once here. The gardens we have do allow for most of the vegetables we all consume and share with the neighbors."

Mercedes smiled and commented, "I get it. He loves to entertain and use his resources, Su Lin enjoys her studies of the animals, and EZ isn't here to ride like she once was. You are clearly a good friend, Ernie. Thank you for the update. I am going to head in and update EZ with her Dad's and Su Lin's condition. Perhaps tomorrow morning after breakfast we can clean up inside. I don't recall where everything belongs, but I would like to restore as much as possible before bringing Andy and Su Lin home."

Ernie agreed and then left. Mercedes went in and called EZ and the rest of the team with an update. She also called Khalid and asked that he pick up the samples she had gathered for some specific analysis as well as to bring her some equipment she wanted to install for some extra security. He reluctantly agreed. Khalid arrived to retrieve the samples a couple of hours later and to bring the requested supplies.

"Mercedes, does this mean you aren't leaving anytime soon?"

Mercedes smiled and replied, "I will leave when I finish securing this place and returning the owners. I asked for you to bring these items so I might keep a low profile. I will only be between here and the hospital, alright?"

Khalid nodded and said, "I get it. Thanks for at least heeding some of my warning. Let me know when you are going to the hospital, and I will do the transport for you and the home owners."

Mercedes looked a little puzzled that he would even care but decided she was too tired to fight it. She would talk to Julie about it later.

Deployment of the security cameras and sensors had taken Mercedes far longer than she had expected. They were all configured, and she leveraged some of Andy's computing power to manage the devices, with alerts directly to her cell phone. She placed the call to Julie, who then added EZ into the call.

"How is my Dad, Mercedes? The message you left me indicated the decision was they remain in the hospital for a couple more days, but is he going to be able to see?" EZ took a breath then added, "He'll be so lost if he is not able to see. It's his livelihood, you know?"

Mercedes soothed, "I honestly don't know what the results are going to be when the bandages are removed, but the doctor and nurses said it looked like he was coming along well. Though they did not say it in front of him or Su Lin, he actually flinched from the bright lights, which they suggested was a good sign.

"Su Lin has most of the medication out of her system, and they were confused with her reaction. She seems to be much better, but they wanted to watch her as she is still having crying fits, which upset Andy. They are going to try to change a bit of her food diet with some recommendations she provided and remove all the meds. They were actually open to her ideas based on some of her publications when she was a professor at Texas A&M University.

"Were you able to take a look at some of the satellite photos, from the dates and times provided, to see if we can even get the type of vehicle that may have been around? Was the source I provided to you able to help you look at those archives?"

Julie interjected, "We were able to find a record for at least 14 days prior to the attack which indicated the vehicle had been in place, but there was no focus on it for catching heat signals for the number of people in the party.

"How does the house appear? Were there any other clues that the local authorities may have overlooked?"

Mercedes clarified, "There were a couple of items we spotted when Ernie and I did the walk around, which I sent off to a lab via one of my prior contacts. I asked them for a rush return on them. We have some blood and fabric fragments that may give us some information. I also put a word in with my contact for some information on Colonel Guano to see if we can determine where he might be at present and what travel he may have undertaken over the recent weeks. You never know.

"I deployed some extra security sensors and cameras around the ranch. I have provided you with the data location for the administrative program to see if you can see it from there, as well as what I can view and administer from here. In this way we can do remote monitoring."

Mercedes provided the detailed information and after a few minutes, Quip joined the line with EZ.

"We can see the sensors easily and are receiving some very clear pictures," indicated Quip. "Nice work in getting these placed. It must have taken you a good couple of hours. But the results are good."

EZ interjected, "And no bad guys are hanging around, right? I can book out on the next flight to Atlanta, which would allow me to be there when Dad and Su Lin are ready to return home."

Quip blurted, "But I'm not certain it is safe yet, honey. We've not had time to monitor the …"

EZ interrupted and stated in no uncertain terms, "Honey, I love you. My dad is going to need some help, and I am going. I really wasn't asking for permission. I have the programs set up. I have the monitors on the telecommunications traffic with filters set up to trap the parameters you and Julie requested. Now that you have the cameras and the sensors you can monitor from here.

Are you taking me to the airport, or should I get a car? This is the only thing I am asking of you, sweetheart."

Julie cringed, knowing that Quip was going to struggle with this. She crossed her fingers and held Juan's hand, hoping he would make the right response. It was a very long, pregnant pause before Quip responded.

"EZ, you are not the kind of lady who takes no for an answer, and I'm not the kind of person who lamely goes along with risky situations, so allow me to worry about you. I cannot go with you at this point. I will follow as soon as I can. I do worry about you, but I can't leave right now. I would ask that once you get to the ranch, you stay close to Mercedes and/or Ernie. If Mercedes says there is a risk and asks you to do something, please listen to her. She's an expert. Your ticket is going to be at the airport, and I will take you once you get packed. I arranged for the charter flight tonight to be ready when you get there. Give me a hug and kiss and go pack, my love."

The enthusiastic kisses were heard by all with the whispers of thank you by EZ.

Quip returned to the call and added, "We are good here. I will call with the arrival time once she takes off. Can you arrange for her pick up, Mercedes? Promise me you will watch her closely, please."

Julie sighed, and said, "Good call, Quip. I knew you could do it."

Mercedes replied with a catch in her voice, "I promise to do my best, Quip. That was so sweet."

Quip chuckled and said, "That has to be a first, me being called sweet. I could get used to that. Thanks all."

CHAPTER 17

Time Standing Still
...The Enigma Chronicles

It had been hours since Petra had gone home to rest at Jacob's insistence after they had word that Wolfgang was out of danger. Jacob continued to pace the floor waiting for word on the room Wolfgang would be moved to so that he could see him. It looked like it would be a long haul for Wolfgang to recover, but he would soon be out of ICU and in a regular room. Doctors said he'd had a stroke, complicated by extreme dehydration, which at his advanced years was always risky. Though he was drifting in and out of consciousness, his vitals were stable. All his medicines and liquid nourishment were being delivered through intravenous means and strictly monitored. His primary care physician had assigned a nurse to be in the room at all times, except if the family wanted private time.

Jacob had only recently learned of his grandfather's existence. His mother's job and heart had taken her to America to raise him with her mother. It saddened him to recall he had only learned about R-Group after she was struck down, walking home from work, by an incompetent driver who didn't even bother to stop. Joining the family business was a choice she had wanted him to make on his own. When he finally met Wolfgang, they bonded over games of chess, talked strategy and learned about one another during these delightful exchanges. He knew Wolfgang was older, but his mind was good, and they had a mutual respect for each other. Jacob was unwilling to give up his only remaining family. It was an odd sensation to have only discovered this last remaining family in the last few years, and he would now be ferocious about keeping him in his life.

Bowen had returned with some food and to sit with him after taking Petra home, but Jacob insisted he keep the home running and get some rest. Jacob promised to call with any news or changes in Wolfgang's condition. He had called Otto and Haddy to let them know, but suggested they stay home for the time being. Once Wolfgang was in a room where they could actually see and talk to him, shifts could be coordinated to keep a watchful eye. Petra had called Quip and EZ with the same information and direction. Petra had tried to console Jacob before he asked her to get some rest. It was simply too much for him to deal with his feelings and hers until Wolfgang was in a room.

The head nurse, Sandy, finally came into the waiting room and announced, "Wolfgang is settled into his room. He has a lot of monitors connected, and I have asked Sue to take the first shift in his room. Would you like to see him? We do have him resting and would like to have him sleep through the night. Right now sleep is as good a medicine for him as the rest of the things he is getting."

Jacob nodded, feeling tongue-tied for a moment before he replied, "Yes, please, I want to see him. Thank you for helping him."

Nurse Sandy smiled and said, "Jacob, your grandfather has done a great deal for this hospital, donating supplies, equipment, and a new wing a few years ago. He also has been a huge community sponsor and supported many of us. He helped my husband and me turn around our finances, gaining our trust forever. He is like our family. Mine is not the only story of help he has given. We all adore him and want him to do better. To be honest, Sue was the first of five on shift to volunteer to sit with him. I assure you, even when you or someone in the family can't be here, we will watch him like the family he is."

Jacob followed Nurse Sandy down the hallway to the room at the end. She left as he continued toward the bed. It was a large airy room with two accent walls of taupe against the white he'd expected. There was a couch and a couple of extra chairs with a pillow and blankets. The chair closest to the bed held Nurse Sue, who stood when he came in. She was slight in stature with her brown hair tied back in a ponytail. Her gentle smile somehow made him feel better.

"Hi, Jacob," Sue quietly said. "He's resting comfortably. Would you like me to explain all the equipment?"

Jacob nodded, and Sue went through descriptions of each of the monitors and what the numbers indicated. She also provided a reference to the acceptable ranges of the numbers and other indicators. He took it all in and asked, "Would it be okay if I just sit with him for a while? I won't touch anything and I'll be quiet."

Sue smiled reassuringly and said, "You don't need to be quiet. You can talk to him or hold his hand or just sit close by. Right now he is mildly sedated so he won't wake up for several hours. A forced rest you could say, just short of him being in a coma. I know the doctor mentioned to you that he might place him in a coma, but he wanted to see if he responds to this treatment first."

"Yes, he did," Jacob acknowledged. "Okay, I want to sit with him a bit, if it is alright. You can stay or take a break, your choice."

Sue looked sympathetic and replied, "Let me get you some-thing to drink while you get used to all this. He's fighting the good fight."

Jacob looked at the room with all the equipment and his grandfather. Wolfgang looked so small in the bed, not the vibrant man that played chess with the finesse of a master. He hoped he would get a chance to play another game with Wolfgang. Gently holding his hand and speaking in low tones, Jacob related some of the things he had learned from Wolfgang since coming to live in Zürich and how very grateful he was for the time they had spent together. During his soliloquy, there were times when Jacob's voice cracked and tears flowed, but he also chuckled at some of the feelings he voiced during the emotional rollercoaster he conveyed. He talked with no response from his grandfather for over an hour before he decided it was time to go home and get some rest. He went and found Sue, explaining it was time for him to leave for a while, but that he would return in a few hours.

Jacob had small snatches of sleep before he finally decided it was a useless endeavor. He showered, dressed, and then went downstairs in search of Petra. Petra smiled as he entered the dining room.

"Oh, Jacob," Petra began, "I am so glad you came home, even if only for a few hours. How did he look when you left? I called this morning, and the reports are he is resting comfortably."

"Petra, he looks so small under the covers with all the wires attached. But he was resting with even breathing. They have set up round-the-clock nursing for him. I had no idea that he was so involved in the community. They couldn't say enough good things. I was, well…humbled, I guess. It gave me a new dimension on him.

"I want to eat something and then head back over there. The doctor said it would be late morning before they could discuss a plan moving forward. I thought it would be best to be there to hear what his doctors are planning for his recovery. You know, they discussed putting him into a coma to help recover. Sounds like a risky approach to me."

Petra looked thoughtful for a few moments then responded, "Yes, I want to go with you. I think we should inform Otto and Haddy to see if they want to also be there. Quip and I spoke earlier, and he is working on the changes to ICABOD searches I put in place last evening. The amount of information we are getting back needs some sorting to make sense of. I told him I'd be in later but wasn't sure about you."

"I'm not sure about me either. I can't just sit in that room but leaving him was really hard. Would you call Otto while I update Bowen? I know the whole household is worried. I am going to ask Bowen to stick around here until we get the doctors' plan and then make certain he gets some time with Wolfgang. I just don't want him to overextend either."

Petra smiled, squeezed his hand, and then went to call Otto while Jacob finished his meal.

CHAPTER 18

Hiding in the Herd

Mathias was annoyed to have an incoming call while trying to get ready for his next presentation with Alejandro and the Venezuelan contingent. It irritated him even more when he saw that it was Dr. Halvorson. Mathias looked to Dutch, silently hoping for a good excuse not to answer.

Dutch sourly stated, "He'll just keep calling if you don't."

Mathias ground his teeth and answered the call. "What is it now?"

Unfazed by the surly greeting, Halvorson responded, "Remember that trusted associate that tried to rip us off for all the hard stolen monies we had collected? We have some people nosing around looking for him and the money trail. You said to alert you when the dogs started sniffing or picking up on his trail. It's like what Yogi Berra used to say, 'it's Déjà vu all over again.'"

Dutch smirked, which only added to Mathias's poor mood. Mathias commented, "I'm glad that your astounding command of baseball quotes is still intact. Let's turn the conversation around. Can you get rid of these people like you did the last detectives? There are certain things I enjoy, and NOT hearing from police detectives is something that I really enjoy."

Halvorson clucked his tongue. "I don't think these are police detectives or the lost relatives to Steven Christopher's last will and testament. These new people aren't like the Global Bank or the Interpol money hunters I've hosed off either. When the bank account leads dry up, as in there ain't no money here, so do their efforts. This new bunch is now hunting in the right direction, like they're laser-focused."

Mathias, growing short on patience, asked, "Doesn't sound like you can get rid of them, is that what I'm hearing? As I recall, it was you that said hide everything in a cryptocurrency and let the trackers blow past with the wrong hunting techniques. Dribble some of the currency here and there to fund our operations and keep the rest as an insurance policy until our current project really launches.

"Now, as irritating as you are, one thing does stand out clear. I've known you to be resourceful, and I want to see it again. Get rid of these snoopers and keep our insurance policy safe, while I try to sell our new offering!"

Halvorson liked the kudos but further pressed, "Mathias, I know you are trying to sell our new offering which should make us well. But it is time to liquidate some more of our insurance policy for current operations. It will result in some visibility, but not a lot in the exchanges. My suspicious nature suggests that we take smaller amounts to several exchanges to better blend in to the background C-C noise. At the same time, we have more areas to be spotted in. What I'm going to suggest is that we don't liquidate any of our current generation of cryptocurrency funds out of our insurance policy, which should protect us from any unnecessary risk."

Dutch blanched at the statement and blurted, "What? You don't want to liquidate our nearly perfect, untraceable digital currency, extracted at great peril I might add, so you can feel safe? What are we supposed to do, clip coupons from a daily newspaper and live on berries and nuts, or worse, freeze-dried military rations?"

Mathias waved Dutch off of his rant and calmly stated, "Dr. Halvorson, I believe you may have hit a raw nerve with my associate, but I'm inclined to agree with him. Now I've been watching the cryptocurrency exchanges, and there appears to be one popping up every other day. Even the Chicago Board of Futures jumped on the bandwagon to begin trading in futures. While halting all our trading will cripple our operations, I like the idea of smaller amounts sold through more exchanges, as it gives us some anonymity and lowers our risk factor. Are we in agreement?"

Halvorson studied the situation for a long moment as Dutch began to pace.

Halvorson could hear Dutch's grumbling and, with some unnecessary hesitation, finally relented, "Oh, alright! You need to work on making the funds go a little farther, guys. Try cutting back on ridiculous events, so we don't have to keep dipping into the insurance fund."

After Halvorson disconnected from the call, Dutch was practically dancing and spiritedly stated, "This calls for a cele-bration! Shall I call in our favorite orgy caterer and her staff?"

Mathias looked over the top of his reading glasses and remarked, "We are economizing, so no."

Dutch slowed down and asked, "How about just two of them with takeout food from Jimmy's Chinese?"

Mathias smiled and agreed, "Ah, you do grasp the concept of economizing! I'll have the spicy chicken with fried rice, please."

CHAPTER 19

Looking at Options
...The Enigma Chronicles

Jacob, Petra, Otto, and Haddy were on hand for the doctors' meeting. Wolfgang's primary care physician, Dr. Roblinski, took the lead role in the discussion. Dr. Roblinski was only a few years older than Jacob, and Jacob felt he could relate to him. His blond hair was neatly styled, and he wore a kind smile accented by penetrating blue eyes and a clean-shaven face. He was tall at 1.8 meters yet lanky, weighing in at what Jacob guessed would be 73 kilograms. They moved to the sitting area of the room with Jacob positioned where he could watch the unmoving figure of Wolfgang.

"I am glad you could all be here," Dr. Roblinski said. He cleared his throat and continued, "Wolfgang has had a stroke, and the extent of damage at this point is unknown. He appears to have some numbness on his right side as his reflexes are non-existent. He has not tried to open his eyes, yet the rest of his vitals are good, considering. It could be he is simply tired and not willing to wake, or there could be some other damage. We have him on some medication to insure that any clots are broken up, and we may do another CT scan to make certain nothing was missed in the one we performed shortly after he arrived."

Otto interjected, "What might we do to help him, sir? We are, of course, willing to try anything you recommend. We know strokes are your field of expertise, but if you need anything, you have but to ask."

Dr. Roblinski smiled and affirmed, "I think we are good. Dr. Bryan and Dr. Logan have been collaborating with me on heart and other internal functions, so we have the best resources consulting on Wolfgang. At this juncture, we want to keep him quiet but ensure that he has activity around him. I have instructed the nurses to talk to him and read him stories, poetry, or even the current financial pages, as we know that is one of his passions.

"When you are here, you might consider talking to him about anything in his background. His work, family, activities, or even vacations, such that we can make certain even when he is resting his brain is getting some stimulation. We feel this is a good technique for those in coma or semi-coma situations. We are not inducing a coma state at this point, since his body is putting him in a similar state on its own."

Jacob looked concerned at the comment and asked, "Would it be better if you medically controlled that state? If I need to give permission for that I will."

Dr. Roblinski shook his head and replied, "Not at this point. We are happy with his progress, and he is making headway. It is simply slow. Reading him his favorite books or anything that he would be familiar with might help to get into his sub-conscious and promote brain stimulation. We will keep the medications and nourishment supplied intravenously, until he wakes enough to start taking food orally. Our recommendation is just to make certain and talk with him when you are here."

They all rose and shook hands with the doctors before they left.

Petra said, "We need to make a shift schedule so that someone is always here. I promised Quip I would come help with the programs, so I will volunteer for later."

Otto said, "Let Haddy and me stay a few hours with him. We'll talk about the trips we have taken and antics from the past. I have always looked up to him as a mentor in this business. The three of us have had some wonderful adventures in travel.

"Jacob, you head out with Petra and make certain Quip is handling the project in the right manner and then come back after dinner. If we get a bit tired, then I will call Bowen to come in. How does that sound?"

Jacob nodded and replied, "Alright, as long as you are here. I will look when I am at the house to see if I can find current reading materials in his suite and bring them back after dinner. Thank you for making it so easy for me."

Haddy patted his arm and gave him a slight hug. "He'll get better, Jacob. You just need to give it time and keep the faith. Don't forget we're here to support our family. You're part of that family, Jacob."

Quip asked, "Okay, what are you two thinking? And I mean for this project, not your …um, other after hours thinking."

After all the years Petra had spent growing up with Quip, she still bristled at Quip's rude insinuations. Before she could launch into Quip on his shallow remarks, Jacob gently interjected, "Quip, you still keep confusing being open and honest with being a jerk. Now, do we need to have EZ come referee your suggestive remarks, or can you leave your voyeuristic thoughts for your quiet time with her?"

Quip blinked a few times as he processed the challenge and then offered, "I guess that did come across rather boorish, didn't it? My apologies. Even though I know you can't forget my earlier statement, allow me to withdraw the crass comment and try again.

"What attack vector do we want to consider in this digital currency fight? From my point of view, there seems to be a large appetite globally for an alternative to regular sovereign-issued currency, but it appears that there is some sort of race going on to be first to market with a cryptocurrency for the masses."

Jacob nodded and replied, "It has taken centuries of trial and error to get the world to a somewhat orderly financial structure with each nation wanting to mint its own sovereign currency almost as a source of pride. Stocks and bonds are issued in practically every developed and developing country denominated in a predominantly paper currency."

Petra commented, "We've come a long way from the adoption of the Arabic numeral system that displaced the Roman Numerals in the 700's. It took several centuries to get general adoption of sovereign currency over gold and silver, but now we are seeing digital currency trying to displace our standard fiat money in just a few short years. I am concerned that a new cryptocurrency will be rushed to market for first mover advantage only to discover that several key pieces are missing, or worse, easily compromised."

Jacob observed, "Yeah, this is not the right area to adopt the practices of Silicon Valley, to fail fast then move on. Currency exchange drives finance, and finance is the backbone of our civilization. Without rules of finance to govern credit and payments in a trusted framework, global economies will become unhinged while everyone tries to do damage control."

Quip nodded and offered, "What I hear you two saying is that while we can't stop this rush to a new digital currency, we don't want just the first one on the market to win. And well, not to put too fine a point on it, how do we get in on the ground floor? Our mantra has always been for the R-Group to stay ahead of the game. Clearly, we have the potential of being left behind if we don't make some of our own bets."

Petra puzzled at the statement. "Are you suggesting we enter the cryptocurrency race with our own digital currency product? As in, download some Blockchain code and launch our own cryptocurrency?"

Jacob mused, "We do have that cryptocurrency proof of concept that we extracted from Su Lin's conspirators, when she was still operating as Master Po. Any reason we couldn't start there?"

Quip replied, "We wouldn't be starting from ground zero if we used it. From that standpoint, we could jump into the market with a semi-finished product."

Petra wrinkled her brow as she asked, "Semi-finished? I seem to remember that it had already been pilot tested and was nearly ready for market."

Jacob politely commented, "I believe Quip is suggesting that we build in trap doors for the R-Group to operate transparently when dealing with the cryptocurrency, before releasing it."

"Oh, of course!" Petra smirked and sarcastically added, "No one would think to check the code to see if there is a trap door in it! If it can't be demonstrated as completely bullet-proof, no one, and I mean no one, will want to use it.

"Dr. Naïve, what is your second plan of introduction into the cryptocurrency wars?"

Quip pouted and, with a petulant tone, quietly said, "It's no fun playing with you if you are always going to be so pragmatic. Jacob, can you build a trap door that no one can find?"

"Don't you think that before any sovereign nation or corporation were considering adopting a new cryptocurrency to build their economy on, they would first launch an army of Petras at it to see if someone had done just that?"

Quip's eyes grew very large as he asked, "You mean there are more Petras in the world than just her? Astounding!"

Tiring of the conversation with Quip, Jacob replied, "I suggest contacting Su Lin and eliciting her ideas on the cryptocurrency she built to see if it is even feasible to insert a backdoor into the programs. If it's possible, then we can jump start our project. Otherwise we won't waste any time on a dead-end effort."

"Do you think she will help us, even while she is still in the hospital?" Petra asked. "She has been quite adamant about not dredging up her old life, no matter how noble the goal."

Quip added, "She might simply tell us to go pound sand, but I think it's at least worth a try."

Petra rolled her eyes as she commented, "Thank you for that extra polished comment concerning a possible refusal. One would think that after you began married life with EZ you would have abandoned your coarse comments and speech patterns."

Quip innocently posed, "Where do you think I learned all these nifty phrases?"

Normally Jacob was willing to do verbal sparring with Quip, but he again checked his watch and, almost as if on cue, marched to the door and casually offered over his shoulder, "I need to get back to the hospital. I'll check in later."

Petra watched him leave abruptly and quietly after the door had already closed offered, "Good-bye, Jacob."

CHAPTER 20

Naughty or Nice?

Quip snarled, "Hey, look! Don't be flaring your nostrils at me because of my comment! I'm asking the obvious question here of what we're going to do with our projects, now that Jacob is camped out at the hospital. I get that Wolfgang is out of the action and Jacob is his only family. But we need to soldier on here. It seems it's down to just you and me! Just for the record, I know how you feel, Petra, because EZ took off to care for her last remaining family member too. You're not the only one drifting here!"

Petra reeled in her emotional state and quietly offered, "I'm sorry, Quip. I 'd forgotten about EZ putting everything on hold here to care for her father. You're right. We are the only ones holding down the fort and…well, I guess I feel almost abandoned, because I sense his pulling away. I'm worried about Wolfgang, but I didn't expect to lose Jacob…it's almost impossible to talk with him…," her voice trailed off as tears filled her eyes.

Quip uncharacteristically gathered her up in his arms to comfort her and softly offered, "Petra, I'm so sorry about how things are going right now. I'm sure everything that can is being done. We have two very special people in our lives, and right now they can't be here. You've always been that special sister I never had, so I want you to know I'm here for you until we get to the other side of this. Please don't despair, he'll return. He loves you too much to be gone long."

Petra's tears trailed down her cheeks as she offered haltingly, "No wonder EZ loves you so much. Before history rolls over, so do I." Petra gave Quip a small kiss on his cheek and then pulled away to collect herself.

Following a few moments of emotional downshifting, Petra finally offered, "Dr. Quip, let's get back into character and get the R-Group refocused. Let's talk about what we can do, since talking about what we can't do is ruining my makeup."

Quip absentmindedly stated, "Yes, um, my makeup is getting ruined too.

"We have two attack vectors in front of us, as I see it. ICABOD and I have been working on one of the ideas we hit on to try and find Chesterfield's money. We believe that since we can't find his money, we should coax the money to us. To that end, our new program, Non-linear Aggregation of Unrelated Galactic Heuristics with Temporal Y-axis intercepts, or NAUGHTY, should be able to lure what you and Jacob postulated was a flight to cryptocurrencies built on Blockchain technology."

In a rather deadpan way, Petra asked, "Have you been thinking naughty again?"

Quip brightened and stated, "Catchy, don't you think? Anyway, with our NAUGHTY program we want to launch a cryptocurrency brokerage/clearing house service for all the digital currency that is awash out there. We begin grooming the participants' list, looking for likely suspects that might lead us to discover where Chesterfield's money went."

Petra studied Quip a moment then said, "Are you serious? Launch our own cryptocurrency exchange? That is like saying we are setting up Adolf's Bank and Trust! You don't just launch a cryptocurrency exchange without regulatory permissions, gobs of funding, and a flock of political support that…"

Quip cut her off. "The cryptocurrency exchanges that are out there and coming online every other day are currently un-regulated. Our NAUGHTY program spotted that right away, so your first objection is irrelevant. The NAUGHTY program is designed to piece together what shouldn't be possible and to determine who has the C-Cs, which is the first step to find where they are."

Petra finally closed her mouth, swallowed and said flatly, "Boy, when EZ is gone, your view of life takes a very narrow focus. I mean really, NAUGHTY?"

ICABOD interjected, "Mistress Petra, Dr. Quip insisted on the naming convention which was over my protests. I unfortunately will have to endure the tarnish that this naming convention brings."

Seeing no point in arguing further, Petra asked, "You said two attack vectors? Please tell me the other one has less color to it?"

Quip blinked several times to collect his thoughts, then offered, "Well, actually there are three, but we discarded the third one so we could focus on the second one, which is to relaunch the cryptocurrency base code we obtained from Su Lin. We take it and add it into the cryptocurrency noise that is out there, as you suggested, to become a competitor. This also has the possibility of luring our prey into our clutches to retrieve the missing Chesterfield funds."

Unable to continue that line of thought, Petra reluctantly asked, "Alright, I have to know. What was the third one?"

Quip grinned and said, "Why, military intervention of course! I always wanted to lead an armored division into battle against incredible odds, much like Alexander the Great! The armored attack vehicles give it more panache, don't you think?"

Petra thoughtfully commented, "Perhaps we should have let you go with EZ."

Tonya sat fidgeting in the Air France concierge lounge in Zürich while she waited for Petra. Since she was an international traveler, she had access to the open bar, so to help steady her nerves she ordered a mimosa. She sat sipping it and occasionally opened her PC to see if the ransomware had vanished, but each time she tried booting it up she was rewarded with the same blocking note that stated:

Remember to follow instructions, sweet chops.

After the third steadying mimosa, she looked at her watch and sourly groused, "It's after 7:00 pm, and I'm waiting like the good little girl who can follow directions, but I wonder where Princess Petra is."

Moments later, a very well-dressed lady, with perfect hair, makeup, and manicure sat down next to Tonya. In a sarcastic tone, Petra offered, "I'm right here, dearie! You know, when I said wait for me if you got here before 7:00, I didn't mean for you to consume a whole bottle of the bubbly. It's good to know you got your vitamin C requirements for the next week all in one sitting. Now, are you too crocked to discuss what you were hounding me for, or shall I try to wade through your slurred speech to make some sense out of your request?"

It hadn't occurred to Tonya that Petra might have been there early to observe her before their meeting, and it irritated her that she had been such a novice about waiting. Unable to remove the irritation from her attitude, Tonya replied with equal sarcasm, "My, we ARE in a mood, aren't we? Does this mean you won't repair your unwarranted hacking? I still can't get past the vulgar message with your vicious ransomware program."

Petra studied Tonya a moment and then took the PC and typed in 25 alphanumeric characters, along with several punctuation marks, that released the offending program's grip on the machine. When she handed it back, Petra calmly stated, "By way of introduction and my proof point to demonstrate that I am Petra Rancowski, I encrypted your PC and now I have removed the program. Now, what did you want to talk about?"

Tonya steeled herself, and with all the professionalism she could muster, stated, "I was instructed to engage your services for our financial institution to assist us with evaluating a contractor we have engaged for a working issue. To be honest, it's not so much the contractor as the problem we want solved, and encryption is at the heart of the complication."

Petra studied Tonya a moment before she asked, "What sort of working issue are you having with this Blockchain crypto-currency? Are you looking to break into the market, looking for ways that it might be compromised, or new applications for your own Blockchain product? I'm not sure I understand the contractor statement unless you are going to fire a starting gun to see who gets to the finish line first."

Tonya began to get that same creepy feeling that she had when she spoke with Otto. Trying not to show she was a little unnerved, she innocently asked, "What makes you think that…"

Petra cut her off. "Tonya, you said your financial institution, you then asked for an encryptionist, and that suggests crypto-currency since you don't need my help with standard fiat currency. There aren't many rules yet in this space, and frankly there isn't any shortage of competitors, which also means it is difficult to pick a winning horse from the lineup. Now what exactly did Ingrid tell you that she wanted done?"

Tonya's jaw dropped at Petra's statement concerning her director. Her mind raced to try and discount Petra's assumptive statement, but before she could assemble a counter statement, Petra spoke again.

"You don't really think your people can hunt for me without me being aware of it, do you? You're in luck. The flattery being inferred from wanting me offsets the annoyance at being pestered to work on your project. Very well then." Petra handed a business card to Tonya. "Here is the secure cyber-Drop Vault where you can load all of your operational parameters. My burner phone number is on there so that you can reach me during the project. Once we are done, I will issue an invoice for my services. I am fairly certain Ingrid told you not to bother to negotiate the price with me since that will only terminate our relationship. Anything else?"

Tonya sensed the meeting was over, yet felt a little emboldened and tartly asked, "Follow the instructions, sweet chops? I assume that is a vulgar reference to…?"

Petra intercepted her and said, "Yes, it is a disparaging reference to call girls. I got that vulgar comment from someone who is no longer of this world."

Tonya repressed her smirk as she replied, "Oh, how fitting of you."

Petra rose and started to walk away, then paused, turned, and commented, "If you don't send the information, I will presume you no longer wish to work together on your project."

Left totally alone, Tonya felt a very bad headache coming on. Perhaps there had been one too many mimosas before her meeting. Rather than wait in this club, she decided to take a room at the airport hotel before her flight tomorrow evening to Paris to meet with Otto's associate, Wolfgang.

CHAPTER 21

No News Is Just That

Khalid was trying to locate the leader of the group from China. He'd been able to discover that seven had initially met up in a low-cost motel about 15 miles from the farm. They had taken two rooms and paid in advance for a week. The motel manager said they were fairly quiet, ordered food delivery, and used a lot of water. Khalid set up some listening posts and had captured some mobile phone communications. According to his translators, two men were arriving from the mainland to support their efforts the day after tomorrow.

Khalid was called by his superior. "Is there something additional we need to alert Homeland Security about, son?"

Khalid replied, "Not really, sir. Stalker asked me to keep an eye on those people Mercedes suspects caused the fuss at the Greenwood farm while she is in town. You know how trouble seems to follow that lady at times."

"I have known her to do that in the past, yes. Is Stalker still in China?"

"Yes, sir. He is still in deep cover as far as I know."

"Alright, son, let me know if you need any more help. Thanks from me as well for keeping an eye on Mercedes. She always did a great job for the agency."

The call disconnected. Khalid sat back and thought of the different options available for consideration. He organized his thoughts and placed the call.

"Madam Sahib, I have found the group, which seems to have dwindled though I am not certain as to why. Two additional men are arriving soon, so I would suggest you get ready to leave. I am happy to transport you to the airport. I think that…"

Mercedes interrupted, "Not happening, no way. EZ is arriving tonight from Zürich and likely will want to get to the hospital to see her dad. If you want to be really helpful, you can transport me to and from the airport so I can meet her flight. And please knock off the Madam Sahib routine, will ya?"

Khalid's mind raced for a good argument and failed. He wearily stated, "Yes, ma'am, I am happy to transport you and EZ. I will even do the hospital run tomorrow.

"Are all the devices active? Any problems I need to help with, I could arrive early and check on that before we go to the airport."

Mercedes grinned and replied, "They are all working just fine. I even have a way to monitor them on my smart phone app. I gave the manager here, Ernie Lee, the link as well so we could both be alerted. He was amazing as he helped me test the system. Great devices.

"EZ's flight arrives at 6:30 and then she clears customs, so pick me up at 6:00 if you don't mind. Thank you, Khalid. By the way, have you…"

Khalid interrupted, "Not a word back yet. Don't worry though. No news is good news."

EZ's flight landed in Atlanta and was taking the long way around to the terminal. She called Quip, and when the call was connected she said, "Hi, honey. I landed safely in Atlanta, though I'm not certain how long the plane will taxi."

Quip grinned as he stated, "Ever the patient one, my dear. As long as you are safe and sound, let the pilots collect their frequent ground miles. According to Julie, Mercedes will meet you on the other side of customs. She also secured a driver for you both to use while you are in town. We could extend this service for Andy and Su Lin after you feel they can be left alone, if you want.

"Did you get any rest on the long leg of your flight? I miss you already."

EZ smiled and replied, "I miss you too, honey. I know you wanted me to stay, but I honestly feel better being here, at least so I can see him for myself. Any updates from his doctor?"

Quip soothingly commented, "Not yet. The doctor said it could take days or weeks. Patience is what is needed. Once I wrap up this current job, if he is not recovered fully, I will join you there, alright? I should have told you that before you left, while I was holding you, but you distracted me. You always distract me.

"Please take direction from Mercedes, and stay out of trouble."

"Yes, dear."

The plane finally parked, and they deplaned. EZ collected her baggage and made her way through customs. It was fast, easy, and nearly painless.

As she walked through the secure door, she saw the friendly face of Mercedes. They hugged like best friends and made their way to the outside. Their car waited with a driver in a sensational Prince Ali look-a-like outfit, turban and all. She caught herself as she looked around for the rug.

He bowed and announced, "Madam Sahib, so glad you arrived safely. You and Mistress Mercedes sit in the back. I will load the luggage. Here at HOMBRE ride service you are to be spoiled and pampered."

EZ giggled, but Mercedes just rolled her eyes. After they were settled, Mercedes leaned over and said, "He just does that to show off. His name is Khalid, and he is a friend of Jim's. We can make him quit it if you like."

EZ replied, "Oh no, I'm going with the spoiled and pampered part. How are Dad and Su Lin?"

Mercedes briefed her on the latest and let her know they would arrive early in the morning at the hospital to speak to the doctor. She went through the tirades they both had, of which a good portion was directed at the medicine Su Lin was taking. Once the doctors had stopped that medication, Su Lin seemed to dramatically improve, even asking for her laptop to record some of her findings.

Mercedes then explained what she had done to safeguard the property and had elicited Ernie Lee's help. It was the first time she had spent any amount of time with Ernie Lee and commented on how critical he was to the farm and helping her. She asked how he was compensated as she wanted to add a bonus or something for the extra effort. EZ smiled and made light of it, noting that she and Andy took great care of Ernie Lee.

CHAPTER 22

All Communications are a Form of Code
...The Enigma Chronicles

Jacob finished up the first round in creating the trap door and provided the code to Quip and Petra, then went to the chateau to change. He had his laptop, which he would take along to the hospital in case the team needed some remote support, but he was most interested in finding materials he might discuss with Wolfgang. The earlier call to the hospital had reported no change in Wolfgang's condition, and that Haddy and Otto left when Bowen arrived. Bowen would be returning soon. Jacob didn't want to wait to go to the hospital so he went up to Wolfgang's rooms to see if he had any current books near his sitting area or bed that he had been reading.

Jacob had never been into these rooms, and he was amazed by the artwork on the walls. This suite had three connected rooms which were somewhat old fashioned, but elegant at the same time. The artwork was a mixture of the Renaissance themes of music, religion and science. When he looked closely at a couple of pieces that caught his imagination, he discovered one painting done by a Spanish artist, El Greco, which appeared to be an original. His mother had often taken him to art galleries, and she had regaled him with her knowledge of artists who were categorized as Renaissance. She spoke with fondness of the Golden Age of Polish Culture which extended from the late 15th and to the late 16th century, commonly known as the Polish Renaissance period.

The dark wood furniture gleamed from constant care. The fabrics were clearly more modern in color and textures than the originals for the pieces, but they were lovely. In the sitting room he found a very comfortable-looking leather chair where he could almost picture Wolfgang reading. A paperback novel containing a bookmark near the end helped identify his fondness for current mystery authors. He picked up the book and moved through the arches to the bedroom. The king-sized bed had a lovely golden velvet comforter, which looked very inviting, and pillows with personalized embroidery which he presumed his granny had sewn.

There were two nightstands, one on each side. He went to one of them and opened the drawer to find several leather bound books. Picking up the one on top and opening it, he was delighted to find it was like a notebook or detailed accounting, clearly written by Wolfgang. The date on top was within the last few weeks. As he thumbed through a few pages, he found it was not a daily diary type of format, rather random notes of activities that likely captured Wolfgang's interest. Jacob located a page with some comments on his improvement with chess which made him smile. He made a mental note to bring the chess set as well so when Wolfgang woke they could play if he wanted.

Jacob removed the rest of the books he found in the drawer and was amazed at the number. There were over a dozen. When he opened the last one it was more than 30 years old. He opened the cabinet doors below and hit the mother-lode of these books. Comprehending the potential history contained within these volumes, he thumbed through and found what he suspected was the oldest. He began to read what seemed like the beginnings of a historic novel.

(June 1939, Poland)

"You say you were sent here from the Lancers? What did you do wrong, Lieutenant?"

With his shoulders aligned in perfect posture, he stood to his full 1.8 meters in height. His angular, sharp features and eyes the shade of the Mediterranean Sea showed not a hint of emotion.

The Lieutenant responded, "Sir! What makes you think I did something wrong?"

The Captain sneered and shot back, "Because everyone wants to be in the Lancers. If that is where you are from, you must have screwed up and they shipped you out!"

The Lieutenant steadfastly offered, "There is, of course, another possibility. I requested to be transferred to signals and communications. I wanted to be where the advanced thinking is going on. Of course, after our brief exchange, perhaps I was mistaken."

The Major smirked slightly, which only served to irritate the Captain. He barked, "It also says on your report that your insubordinate questioning of procedures highlights the fact that you are unsuited to be in a crack unit like the Lancers. They only want team players who can follow instructions and not over-think why something is done a certain way!

"It isn't going to be any different here, mister! Now I want to know, if you were transferred out at your request, what was the underlying reason?"

The Lieutenant stiffly asked, "Permission to speak candidly, sir?"

The Major nodded, but the Captain just stared.

The Lieutenant continued, "Sir, my statement of wanting to be in an intellectual role is still valid, but there was another reason. I uh…didn't feel comfortable parading around on a horse sporting a large phallic symbol as a weapon. You may consider me a bit too old school, but my university professor suggested that when males exhibit that kind of presentation it is because they are over-compensating for their own shortcomings. I can fairly represent that I don't have that issue."

The Captain was livid, but the Major laughed uproariously. After the Major regained his composure, he stated, "Lieutenant, we certainly don't parade around like that around here! Let me be the first to say that we do indeed need some thoughtful and observant soldiers in this outfit. Welcome aboard! Captain, see that the Lieutenant is bunked with the other two new recruits.

"Oh, and Captain, try not to ride the new recruit just because he abandoned the highly prestigious Lancers that you so dearly wanted to accept you. That is all, gentlemen."

The Captain, incensed at having his career ambitions belittled by the Major, commanded, "Alright, wonder boy, fall in with the others! Maybe we can teach you enough to make you useful to this organization."

Unflinching, the Lieutenant offered, "Yes, sir! With the state that Europe is in, and our English allies on the other side of Germany, we need to prepare for all contin-gencies."

Later on —
Once the Captain left the billeting quarters, they all breathed a sigh of relief. The Lieutenant stuck out his

powerful, strong hand, gently engulfing the hand of the Lieutenant closest to him, then smiled as he greeted, "My name is Ferdek Watcowski. I'm sorry I stirred up the Captain, but I felt compelled to tell the truth.

"This is where I want my career to go. I'm pretty sure we don't have much time before all the politics of Europe devolve into war."

At the comment, the smile on the other man's face faded. At a command- ing height of more than 1.9 meters, the man clearly emitted military in his demeanor and grooming. His jet black hair was cropped per regulations and highlighted the distinctive widows-peak of his hairline. Thick black eyebrows rose above his unreadable onyx colored eyes. His commanding figure was at full attention as he inclined his head and firmly shook Ferdek's hand. He stated, "Wolfgang Mickelowski, at your service, sir. And this delightful gentleman over here is..."

The powerfully built male with chocolate brown hair, cut a bit long by military standards, sported a dapper mustache to match the twinkle in his eyes as he grinned and stood. He was shorter than Wolfgang, at what Ferdek estimated to be just over 1.7 meters. He extended his hand and added warmth to his smile as he offered, "I'm M. Octavius Rancowski. Pleased to meet you. Permit me to say that your brief introduction, with its honest exchange of thoughts on your first day on the job, has earned you my undying friendship for thoroughly pissing off the Captain."

Ferdek raised his eyebrows and asked, "Octavius? A few more syllables than I am comfortable with. Do you have a nickname that doesn't make you sound like a Roman Emperor?"

Octavius grinned and replied, "Gosh, it doesn't sound like we are going to have any trouble getting YOU to say what's on your mind! My dad always called me Tavius. It always rankled my mother who desperately wanted more formality in our household. Besides, you both have nicknames, why not me as well?"

Ferdek grinned and asked, "I hesitate to be forward, but I cannot help but notice you seem to be in a bit of discomfort."

Tavius shrugged his shoulders in nonchalance and explained, "A minor setback with some clumsy moves on my last trip on maneuvers. My shoulders prefer moving in line with my hips for my back to ache less. I am practicing the balance of movement. Now, tell us about you and your background."

Ferdek accepted the commentary without judgement and commenced, "I think we have the start of an alliance, gentlemen.

"My father is in the diplomatic corps, and he has told me in confidence that Poland is in more trouble than anyone wants to believe. The Germans annexed Austria with no protests from anyone. Then the British and French helped the Germans retake the Sudeten land from Czechoslovakia without firing a shot. Then Hitler finished off the Czechs this past March. The Ambassador believes Poland is next."

Wolfgang mused, "The actions of the British and the French are fairly troubling. My contacts in the Czech government told me they weren't even allowed at the negotiating table in Munich while Britain and France chopped up their country for Germany. It was such a vile thing, watching the newsreels and hearing Chamberlain proclaim peace for our time while holding that flimsy piece of paper like it had saved everything."

Tavius offered, "They did that to help stop another European war."

Ferdek stated, "They didn't stop anything! They only postponed the inevitable!"

Wolfgang studied Ferdek. "We've all heard the announcement from Britain and France that they will guarantee Polish sovereignty against any German aggression. However, let me point out that they are on the other side of the continent, so it brings up the obvious question of how precisely are they going to honor that guarantee with Germany in between our countries? The logistics appear to be a little daunting, from my point of view, if Britain and France can even be trusted to honor the agreement, that is.

"The other troubling thing we've learned is that the British are only just now rebuilding their armed forces. If our information is correct, that would put them at proper strength in 1941-42. Then the French will only participate if the Brits do. In reality, we might not even have any allies to count on."

Tavius offered, "I sense you have something on your mind, Ferdek. You're not really the career-minded individual you claim, are you? What is the real motivation for you to be here?"

Ferdek flexed his jaw muscles as a sign of annoyance. "My father arranged for me to be here. The diplomatic corps is seeing a lot of German communications traffic here in the east, and a lot of it is going to the German Ambassador here in Warsaw. However, the Germans are using a cypher for their communications, making them completely undecipherable. My father is certain that if we could break the codes they are using and read their communications, we would be in a better position to deal with any treachery. I'm here to help do that."

Wolfgang commented, "We don't really know what we are up against. It is rumored that the Dutch did some pioneering work on an encryption technology that got picked up by the Germans. As usual the German engineering elements improved it, and it is apparently the communications standard that the Oberkommando der Wehrmacht ordered deployed into all the Armed Forces."

Tavius nodded and added, "Yes. We've learned it's called the Enigma Machine. With a machine on each end and identical settings, communications go in one side, are turned into something unintelligible which is telexed to an end point, at which time the reverse process is done, rendering the communication readable again."

Ferdek pondered that a moment, then responded, "With your communications encrypted, you can say or discuss anything without fear of someone else reading it. Gentlemen, we need to be able to read those encrypted messages. Do you want to help me?"

Jacob closed up the book and gathered the oldest three to take to the hospital. As he thought about what he'd just read, he wondered if it was a factual recount of the time or Wolfgang's attempt at writing a fictional novel. Regardless, it would provide some great reading material for his time with Wolfgang at the hospital. Perhaps even a new family link he could learn from.

When he arrived back at Wolfgang's bedside, he decided to begin reading the book aloud, hoping it would get a response.

CHAPTER 23

One More For The Flight, If You Please

Tonya was engrossed in flirting with the charming man who had walked into the lounge, looking like he'd stepped straight from the pages of her favorite international magazine. His natural smile seemed to radiate charm while his hair looked casual yet perfect. She was unable to hear his voice as a repetitive noise kept distracting her. Feeling like she was falling back into the world after a sensation of floating above it all, Tonya saw the stranger vanish as the noise increased in volume and insistence. In her mind the thought of opening her eyes was akin to begging for pain, as she realized it was the phone ringing.

Reaching her hand and arm from under the warm covers, she groped around for the source of the noise. About the time she located the device, the ringing ceased. Frowning, then smiling, she rolled over and searched her mind to recapture the debonair male she would love to share another cocktail with. Tonya had almost settled back into her semi-dream state, ready to search for the stranger, when the noise began anew. She flipped over, sending the covers flying, and grabbed at the annoying phone.

"Hello," she grumbled, "And thank you for the wakeup call that I didn't ask for. What is it?"

The man on the other end of the call cleared his throat and responded, "This is not the hotel, Madam Van Den Berghe. I had hoped you were still in your room, perhaps getting ready for lunch. In checking with the hotel, they indicated you had requested a mid-afternoon check out for your early evening flight."

The fog was starting to clear, and the voice was familiar, though she was not able to place it. The 'getting ready for lunch' comment caught her attention so abruptly she opened her eyes, causing an immediate throb in her inner brain. As she gathered a small portion of her wits, she realized who was on the phone. "Otto, is that you? Why are you…? I mean, how did you…? I guess you…"

"My sincere apologies, Madam, for such a poor beginning to our conversation. Yes, of course, this is Otto. I didn't wake you, did I?" Otto asked without a glimmer of sarcasm, yet with a level of consideration she'd rarely heard.

Tonya licked her lips and slowly sat up as if that would help her advantage in the discussion. "No, of course you didn't disturb me. I wasn't expecting to hear from you, but I planned to phone your associate to meet him in the morning as we had discussed."

Otto quietly replied, "Yes, of course. I appreciate your remembering. There has, however, been a development on our side that is forcing a change of plans. My associate, Mr. Mickelowski, finds himself unexpectedly delayed. I was hoping you might reconsider your travel and meet with me at your hotel, perhaps in an hour? I could make it earlier if you would rather. The Zürich Hilton has a marvelous luncheon selection, especially their desserts, and the lounge is always the perfect place to see anyone of notoriety on any given day. I would insist on this being my treat for the inconvenience."

Tonya was rapidly losing her grip on where she was, let alone him knowing where she was and that her flight was this afternoon. Rather than worry about it, she decided the food might calm her rolling stomach. "That actually sounds good, Mr. Magician. I suddenly find myself rather hungry. If they will serve us a meal in the lounge, how about one hour?"

Otto chuckled and agreed, "That works very well, Madam. Would you prefer a mimosa or bellini? You have but to say, and I will have it ready upon your arrival. They do a fine job, on both of these selections, for the weary traveler. You do sound more like a mimosa fan, however."

Tonya made a slight choking sound and offered, "I think a nice mimosa to start our breakfast, um… I mean luncheon, would be wonderful. See you in an hour."

Tonya disconnected and made her way to the bathroom. One squint in the mirror told her she should have opted for a Bloody Mary. She started a hot shower and tried to let the heat seep into her skin as she gently soaped down. When she turned off the water, she found she felt somewhat better. Drying off then letting the hairdryer do the work on her wavy hair made the most of her available time. Then some artful makeup application and she would be ready to roll. Her shaking hand guaranteed no eyeliner was applied. Gently slipping into a dress that hugged her trim shape, she slipped on her shoes and turned to appraise herself in the mirror. Tonya grinned at the reflection when she realized she looked pretty good.

As she walked into the lounge area, almost on time, the room was packed with people of all shapes and sizes, alone and with others. It dawned on her that Otto was not someone she would recognize, and they had not done the, 'I will be wearing black, and you?' routine. At a loss, she looked around for a single man at a table, when the waiter interrupted her search.

"Madam Van Den Berghe, your table is this way." He gestured for her to follow him.

Otto rose, reached for her hand and charmingly brushed her knuckles with a dry kiss. "Here you are, Madam. Thank you for joining me for luncheon. You are even lovelier than I imagined." He stepped out of the way and added, "Please have a seat, Tonya, and we will solve the problems of the world financial markets."

Sliding over on the bench to put some room between them, she ended up positioned in front of the promised mimosa. She tossed it back and grinned as she handed the glass to the waiter to refill.

The waiter responded, "Of course, Madam. I will be back shortly to take your order."

Otto grinned and replied, "Had I considered you might be thirsty, I would have had two brought over. Since you are obviously a lady of good breeding, ordering a bucket of mimosas would be out of the question. Now please take a moment to make your selections for luncheon, and we can move forward with the discussion of your dilemma."

Tonya scanned the menu and resolved to order several items to make up for her feelings of inadequacy around this man. The waiter returned, and she ordered her selections, along with an additional mimosa. Otto was older than Tonya had expected. Quite the gentleman, as well as distinguished. He did seem kind and he had ordered her drink as promised. Otto quietly watched her and waited for her to speak first.

Tonya sipped her current drink and offered a slight smile as she began, "Did you get a chance, with the change of plans, to review all the materials I had sent over? I am most interested in your findings and guidance, Sir."

Otto grinned and responded, "I did review them, along with members of my team. It seems that your organization wants to stroll down the path of cryptocurrency. Is that correct?"

Tonya bristled a bit and gruffly answered, "Stroll seems like an inappropriate term for addressing this sort of directional change. This is a major change, but being on the correct side of this is critical, so initial investments are modest, but I don't think that is equated to 'strolling.'"

Otto smiled and kindly lectured, "My dear Tonya, if I might be so bold, I don't mean to minimize your documented approach. You need to understand the current world stage for cryptocurrency. As a shift in financial handling, it has both good and bad sides.

"For example, there are several competing products for people to choose. It is a non-regulated item, so most are considering it as an investment vehicle, rather than a true replacement of hard currency. For centuries, the exchange of tangible currency for goods and services has continued because the currency, be it gold, silver, gems, or even paper, has had a form of regulation governing it. This is not really the case for cryptocurrencies. There is in fact a real issue with not only regulating but securing it to avoid modern day technology thieves."

Tonya replied, "But as long as it is digitally encrypted, it should be safe for use in paying for goods and services. It is far easier to transport over long distances when the demand for fast payments is only increasing. The immediacy of our humankind today is a well-known requirement.

"What I expect from your team is a proposed method for that immediacy as well as a transition plan to move forward toward a secure EuroBit as the universal currency in, say, five years."

Otto, well-versed in schooling his features, especially in front of clients, blanched inside. This was going to be a bit tougher to explain, especially if she kept up her steady intake of alcohol. Petra had been correct in categorizing Tonya as a bit too casual for such an important role in the world financial markets. Otto began, "Let me tell you a story of how an investor lost his major holdings with the slight shift in the view of the market only four weeks ago."

Tonya nodded, sipped her drink, and inclined her head for him to continue. She signaled for another mimosa as she half-listened to the story from the old man. Several hours later, Otto escorted her back to her room because she was so wobbly. She tried several times to get the door to open only to find she was not gauging the distance correctly. She handed Otto the key. He promptly opened the door and then held it while she oozed inside the room.

Tonya's words slurred as she attempted, "Thank you for the lunch. It was swell. We must do it again. Would you be so kind as to send me a summary of our discussion?"

Otto grinned and replied, "Of course. Now I have also helped you to change your flight home to tomorrow. There won't be a need for you to travel to Paris at all. We will talk soon. Safe travels, Madam Van Den Berghe."

Tonya wobbled into the room, kicking off her shoes. She was grinning as she relived their conversation, feeling she had held her own with Otto quite easily. She located the receipt in her pocket Otto had helped her print out in the hotel business office, showing her personal investment of ten thousand U.S. dollars in exchange for the cryptocurrency transaction she had completed online with Otto's laptop to illustrate her commitment to the emerging technology. He'd advised against making such a large personal investment without additional vetting of the provider, but she'd ignored the warning. Tonya smiled at how she had persevered, just before falling face first on to the bed, utterly passed out.

EZ and Mercedes had a brief phone consult with her dad and Su Lin's doctor. Yes, the pair could go home. For EZ, it felt like her timing to come back to help out was perfect. Khalid had been waiting at the door and bowed to EZ with an exaggerated flourish. The ride to the hospital was uneventful, with both Mercedes and Khalid scanning for any people or things out of the ordinary.

EZ almost broke when she saw that her dad was still not able to see. Su Lin leaned into EZ, and as she hugged her, Su Lin tried to apologize to her for not being enough help to keep Andy from being hurt. Andy's face lit up at the sound of EZ's voice. He seemed to calm down once he was settled into the wheelchair to leave. Su Lin wanted to refuse the ride, but the nurse was adamant about them both being escorted out in a wheelchair as a matter of policy.

Once they settled into the car for the ride to the ranch, Andy took Su Lin's hand and they both beamed with happiness.

"We'll be home soon, honey. Once we change, we can go down and look after Franklin, and I can get Ernie to give me an update.

"Now don't you fret none, little girl. The doctor said I would be seeing again anytime now."

EZ smiled and replied, "I know, Dad. You are going to be just fine. I know you can't see Su Lin right now, but she is just as pretty as ever. I am glad you are here, Dad."

Andy beamed and patted his wife's hand. "We'll be just fine together."

Su Lin leaned into Andy and sighed with pure contentment.

Ernie greeted them when they arrived and took the suitcase from Khalid as he carried it toward the door. EZ set the pace into the house with Su Lin and Andy in front of her and Ernie leading the way upstairs to their room. Su Lin suggested that EZ wait downstairs while they changed their clothes. Then they would go check out Franklin and the other barn animals.

Mercedes lingered behind the group to give an update to Khalid and asked him to pick up the prescription, which the doctor had indicated would be ready in about an hour.

Mercedes was just beginning her check of the equipment surrounding the ranch, when Ernie arrived by her side.

Ernie asked, "What's the plan, Mercedes?"

Mercedes grinned at him and replied, "You or I need to keep Su Lin and Andy in sight at all times. I suspect EZ will not stray far from her dad, but we need to watch her too.

"The equipment is all green-lit. I see you left the monitoring off from the front gate while we were at the airport. I think that is fine, but let's not do it for any extended period now that they are home. I don't see any issues outside of a fox who might be getting a bit too lazy on approaching those baby goats." She turned the video so he might see the threat coming from the west side of the property, not all that far from the ranch house.

Ernie grinned and commented, "Sounds like a plan. I can update Andy on what this equipment does for him. Heck, there looks to be some additional value for all this equipment over the long haul."

Mercedes grinned and nodded. She liked the way Ernie thought about stuff, very practical.

CHAPTER 24

The Claim of the Last Bullet

Lieutenant Quinn Lee met the two replacements at the door and uneasily admitted them. They had put on a good deal of weight in recent times, since their benefactor decided to shuffle off his mortal coils rather than face a state trial. They were no longer boyish-faced individuals who moved quickly to do the Chairman's bidding but instead moved somewhat lethargically. Their optimistic outlook on life had been replaced with cynicism and cruelty on their assignments, which tended to make them somewhat capricious in fulfilling those assignments. Won sported tiger slash marks down his face and no longer had the use of his tongue, which mandated that Ton do the talking for both of them. Since they were twins in most things, physical and mental, it was relatively easy for Ton to be the spokesperson for these brooding, angry men.

The Lieutenant stepped off to one side as he introduced them to Colonel Guano. The presentation gesture was military standard, but Lieutenant Lee was to remain vigilant in a crossfire position in case he and the Colonel needed to defend themselves.

Even to the casual observer, it was obvious that nobody liked or trusted the others. It was also true that they all had their orders to complete a job. Personal dislikes would have to wait until the assignment was over. That was exactly what Lee and Guano feared yet how the twins felt most valuable in their current work assignments.

Guano attempted a civil greeting. "Gentlemen, we were told that two seasoned pros would be joining us to help us in completing our assignment. May I introduce…"

In a surly antagonistic tone, Ton flatly stated, "Skip the pleasantries, Guano. We were told this assignment had high priority but also high incompetence in its execution. We are here to stop your sightseeing adventures in Georgia and put the project back on its original timetable. Now let's look at what you have concocted so far so we can make repairs to the time schedule. If we think there is no hope of success here, our instructions are to take over the mission and make sure you use your last bullet on yourself. Are we clear?"

Guano blanched, but Lieutenant Lee began to tremble, being at the mercy of these two cold-blooded henchmen. After a few moments of each side sizing the other up, Guano, in his characteristically expressionless way, said, "I am most gratified you haven't lost your sense of humor after all this time. I was going to ask if you needed anything to eat, but it looks like the reverse is true based on the extra muscle you gentlemen have added. That is muscle, right, and it is the reason you no longer have necks?"

Won looked ready to surge forward to avenge the taunt, but Ton held him in check. Ton cautioned, "I wouldn't aggravate him if I were you. We haven't forgotten how you coerced the Chairman to use the last bullet in his pistol, so aggravate us once more…"

Guano interrupted, "Just so you two are straight on the story, I was sent there to pick up the Chairman and take him to the People's court after an agonizing stay in prison. He knew, just as I did, that the verdict was already decided. He asked for the honorable way out, and I gave it to him. So if you want to get down to it, I actually helped him with HIS final request!"

The twins both seethed with anger, but generally accepted the new explanation, for now. Lieutenant Lee breathed a sigh of relief as tensions seemed to ease.

Feeling somewhat emboldened, Guano stated, "Let me bring you up to date on what we have done and what our next steps should be. You may not have been told that we studied the entire layout for a week before we launched our incursion, but frankly we did not count on their resourcefulness. We expected a smash and grab, but instead ended up in a firefight that was technically a draw. Since we missed our quarry, the Finance Minister branded it a total failure. We have totally lost the element of surprise, and our reconnaissance clearly shows they are prepared for our next attack. I believe our best attack vector to be a fast hard-hitting attack where we acquire a valued hostage as leverage over Su Lin to guarantee her participation. She proved that she would rather eat a bullet than help our cause. We are quite sure she will sacrifice everything for her new husband. He was responsible for killing my team members, and she managed to squeeze off the round that wounded me."

Guano sized up the twins, but they said nothing. He continued, "Her husband, Andy, has not regained his sight, so our best attack vector is to collar him, negotiate for the code that she has, and require her to return with us to China. I recommend that you two remain here with our hostage until such time as we have successfully delivered the desired code to the Finance Minister and demonstrated it to his satisfaction."

Ton smirked and replied, "Sounds like a very convenient trap for us while we wait for your successful return to China. You get your insurance policy, but what about ours? No! We take both so we are not trapped here, hoping you please the Finance Minister."

Guano managed to maintain control over his temper as he reasoned, "If we take both of them then we have no leverage over either of them. Together they have proven lethal and capable of attack. If we keep them separated, then each will fear for the other's safety and cooperate. I would point out that each team has leverage over the other by separation and threats if we don't get full cooperation. You will have the same leverage over her husband as we will over her, but only if we separate them."

Won remained motionless, and Ton grudgingly agreed, "Yes, we see the logic in the approach. What about the authorities that are invariably keeping an eye on the property? You know U.S. policy on hostage situations, right? No negotiations. So, while our hostages may be cooperative, the local and federal authorities probably won't be, and we'll still be stuck. What is your next idea?"

"We sanitize the premises as a demonstration of our seriousness, but after that I would expect you to carry out your orders. If you can disengage when we send word and leave, then you secure the hostage before your head start. If that is not possible, then simply do like you normally do. Execute Andy and everything on the farm before you leave. You are here to fulfill the role of the two fallen comrades. They were to stay here while the Lieutenant and I deliver the package to the Finance Minister. Now if you think you have all the risk, let me point out that if the package of source code and designer fail, don't you think he will take out his hostilities on whoever delivered the failed package? Which destiny do you want to bet on?"

Ton almost chuckled as he said, "Now that you mention it, Lt. Colonel Ling Po has never lost a battle on home soil before, even when it looked like she was beaten. Perhaps we might be better off taking our chances here in the U.S. They at least feed you while you're inside. And if you screw up, then we would do well to be in a U.S. prison where we will be protected from Chinese justice. Alright, when do we hit?"

Guano, now considering that perhaps the odds of survival might actually be better here in Georgia, felt a slight twinge of regret on his choice but firmly stated, "The full incursion is set for tomorrow night. I suggest you study our maps to be familiar with the terrain since we will go in at night."

CHAPTER 25

Endless Details

Jacob continued reading to Wolfgang out of the books he had brought to the hospital room. The content delighted Jacob the farther he read. He wasn't quite sure if this was material for a fictional novel or the history of the R-Group's early beginnings. With Ferdek and Tavius both gone it would be up to Wolfgang to tell him which, unless Otto had been told some detail as a child. He picked up from this point with:

Tavius quietly offered, "You know, it occurs to me that this may be hard to explain if we get caught. I might recommend…"

Ferdek cut the observation short. "IF we get caught! But, if you are going to keep running your mouth, it is exactly what will happen! Now remember, sneaky not squeaky! Let's move out!"

Wolfgang, in a low tone, cautiously asked, "You're sure we can get in past the German Ambassador's security, gain access to the upstairs communications room, map everything out and leave with our reconnaissance information, without being detected? What's our fallback position should anything go wrong or we are discovered?"

Tavius sternly added, "Hey, lighten up, Wolfpack! Didn't you just hear Ferd with his absurd statement of confidence! We're going to be fine, so long as we don't get caught!"

Wolfgang lowered his head and said, "You're right, of course. Forgive my silly caution. However, what do we want to do about the tripwire we just passed through?"

Ferdek and Tavius both looked down to see the ends of the wire just as the compound lights came on to search the area.

Tavius quickly commented, "Uh-oh! We're caught! We're in trouble! Time for plan B…oh, that's right, we didn't need a plan B because we're so sneaky, not at all squeaky! Come on, let's leg-it!"

Before they had taken two steps, the floodlights were on them, and they had two Mauser rifles leveled at them by the perimeter guards. The only thing they had going for them was that they were in civilian clothes instead of uniforms, and it gave Tavius an idea.

Before the guards could take any action, Tavius, acting half drunk, said to them so everyone could hear, "Unless her dad is really serious about his daughter's honor, I'm pretty sure she gave me the wrong address, judging from your weapons. Let me take a wild guess and say that this is probably not Rylinda's house, and there aren't any hot university babes lusting for some college hunks to drop by with a modest wine to sample!

"Boys, those girls were just shining us on! Oshifer, I'm sorry, but when they said meet them here for some hot action, we were thinking…"

Ferdek quickly picked up on the ruse and, also acting half crocked, he interrupted, "Oh, you and your raging hormones! You believed we were going to get lucky, but instead we're being held at gunpoint by two oshifers!

"I told you we should have been shuddying for our exhams. But no! You said, let's go hunt down some females and charm them! We might have, too, if you weren't so thunk as some people drink I am!"

Wolfgang too feigned an inebriated state and slurred his observations. "Bloys, bloys! Admit that those girls stole our money, as well as our hearts! Maybe these two nice oshifers will tell us how to get to the nearest toilet so we can throw up, then pee or wishever?"

One guard smirked and lowered his weapon, which signaled the other to do so as well. The guard grilled, "University students, drunk, and looking for eligible females at the German embassy. Do you clowns know this is German soil by treaty and that the ambassador has every right to shoot you for trespassing? Come on, follow me to the gate and be on your way. If you tell anyone about this episode, we will come finish the job. Understand?"

Tavius, slightly weaving back and forth, nodded solemnly, as did the others. They very quietly followed the guard to the gate and promptly left, but conducted some believable stumbling to keep up the pretense until they were far away and out of sight.

Once they had turned a distant corner, Wolfgang glared at Tavius and agitatedly questioned, "I didn't have time to bring this up before as I was focused on the trip-wire, but Wolfpack, really?"

Tavius groused, "It worked, didn't it? Sorry, but it was all adlib. Suits you though. Ferdek, can we now finish the discussion about having a plan B?"

Ferdek, quietly annoyed at the effrontery of the question, said nothing but ground his teeth at having been caught while his mates had been quick enough thinkers to get them out of the situation.

After calming down from their withdrawal, Ferdek finally managed a response. "Gentlemen, thank you for your quick thinking, and please accept my apologies for such a poorly planned mission. You were right, Wolfgang! If we'd been in uniform, we would have been shot or worse."

Tavius puzzled and asked, "What would be worse than being shot?"

Ferdek stopped then, staring directly at Tavius, said, "Being arrested and handed over to our government in complete humiliation! It would have ruined my father's career, and I would have been exiled in disgrace."

Tavius nodded and added, "Ah yes, and your disgrace would be like in Shakespeare's Macbeth, 'Get thee to a nunnery.' I can see how your future might have looked a little black, but thankfully, Wolfgang and I would have only had to write on the chalkboard 1,000 times, 'Don't screw up again, Borscht for brains!' Compared to you, our sentences would have been nothing."

Ferdek appeared chastised as he quietly offered, "Gentlemen, I'm sorry if I did not properly acknowledge your punishment as well. And yes, I appreciate the support. I must admit our first attempt was rather amateurish, but I still think it's doable."

Tavius added, "I think we need to consider more details next time. Details are everything when you play in the high stakes game of espionage."

Jacob envisioned them all nodding in agreement, and he wondered what they would do next. He closed the book and looked at his grandfather. He leaned over the sleeping form with all the beeping machines in the background and said, "This is so interesting, Wolfgang. Is it real or just a story? Wake up and tell me, please?"

CHAPTER 26

Ditch the Bits

Cody and Halvorson stared into the monitor as if they might see something different, but the website error remained unchanged.

404 Website unavailable.

After a short eternity of time, Halvorson suggested, "Try it again. If it doesn't respond, post a query on the companion website to see if we can get some comment."

Cody checked his favorite chat site in another window and, clucking his tongue in annoyance, stated, "Looks like they were a victim of a digital raid. Oh man! They got hit big time and were cleaned out by the Digital Raiders! Look at this! They are pleading with the DRs to return their inventory of digital currencies in return for no prosecution!"

Halvorson smirked and sarcastically commented, "That ranks right up there with *I'll hold my breath until I turn blue if you don't return my wealth.* Well, let us know how that works for you, buddy.

"Right now we have a bigger problem, Codan. That was our favorite cryptocurrency selling site. Not only do we need to find a replacement site, we need to find a couple of alternative sites so we can spread our sales across multiple sites to reduce our vulnerability. Who else is out there that we can look at?"

Cody wrinkled his nose as he complained, "This sucks, too! My favorite site, Crypto Currency-R-Us, just had a flash-crash!"

Halvorson asked, "Uh, flash-crash?"

Without moving his gaze from the monitor, Cody responded, "Yeah, you know. A computer glitch occurs, no transactions can occur, the day traders get their panties in a wad, and everyone wants to sell to try and get their money out. Everyone runs for the exits, except there ain't none. So as a consequence, all hell breaks loose and the exchange goes into free fall. Then everyone starts lining up outside their building window to jump, a la 1929 stock market crash."

Halvorson sarcastically remarked, "Oh my, we did remember some financial history, didn't we? Well, keep prowling for some new exchanges where we can move some of our goods. You do remember the kind of site we want, right?"

Cody turned around and innocently confirmed, "The kind that doesn't ask for our taxpayer status or government-issued ID numbers, or want our blood type, our sexual preference, to know whether we are vegans or not, if we are registered voters, or if we will sign up for their proctology newsletter,…"

Halvorson cut Cody off. "I've told you I'm not admitting to being a vegan. You need to avoid those types of exchanges, period."

Cody smirked and, as he returned to his chore, commented, "Yeah, I know the drill. Give them anything they want but not the vegan preference, got it. But it does occur to me, vegans can be just as pudgy as anyone else."

Halvorson bristled and said, "You want a hit in the head again? I'm not pudgy, mister French fry king!"

Cody, now only focused on his Darknet search engine, loudly commented, "Hey, here is something promising. I kind of like their marketing spin. Listen to this.

"Come to Our Cryptocurrency Exchange and follow our lead: Are you in the agony of a digital divorce? Ditch the Bits! Other exchanges are suffering, but not us! We deliver flash-cash, not flash-crashes! Afraid that your government will outlaw digital currency like China and South Korea? You want to take a future's position that won't have you on your hands and knees groveling? Come deal with us! We broker 1's and 0's at digital speed for peace of mind! We're unregulated, unsupervised, and unsanctioned, but we are trustworthy! Our operators are standing by now to do call backs from our off-shore facility, so leave a message!

Hmmm, kind of compelling actually…"

Halvorson, looking like he had just received a shot of Novocain, numbly asked, "Really? Does that marketing juggernaut have a name?"

With some growing conviction, Cody proudly announced, "Digital Diamonds! 'No one cares about your ones and zeroes more than us!'

"Ooo! Good copy for a tag line! Now I can get that digital divorce from that lousy site, a la ditch the bits."

They both chuckled as they made some initial exchanges.

At about the same time in Zürich, Petra and Otto both asked Quip simultaneously, "Ditch the Bits at Digital Diamonds? Are you serious?"

Quip beamed as he proudly replied, "Compelling, don't you think?"

CHAPTER 27

Assembling a Useful Plan

Petra arrived at the hospital at first light so Jacob could run home, shower, and change clothes. He took her into his arms and said there was no change in Wolfgang, but the books he had brought were very interesting, and they would discuss them in detail after Wolfgang returned home. This was code for please guard them while I am gone, but don't read them. She smiled at his retreating form and turned to fuss over Wolfgang.

After washing up Wolfgang's exposed skin, she rubbed in some moisturizer while keeping up a running monolog of how things were progressing. Once that was done, she straightened up the room and spoke to the doctor and nurse briefly when they did their early rounds. The doctor said that Wolfgang was stable and, based on some tests, they had reduced one of his medications. Petra took that as a good sign.

Setting up their connections for working had been approved by hospital security, and the medical staff deemed it not harmful to Wolfgang. She knew it would make Jacob more comfortable if they could work while he kept an eye on Wolfgang. When all was set up for their link back to their Zürich Operations Center, Petra began to review the various transactions captured in their program. Nodding her head in continued appreciation, she told the sleeping form, "Wolfgang, your thoughts on how to proceed with tracking the financial links has resulted in leads we wouldn't have considered without your insight.

"Quip has activated our digital storefront to exchange crypto-currency. As all things are for Quip, the hook is almost childish, but it appears to be working." Laughing, she added, "Who knows, this might become our next hot area of investing. We are getting several offers, two of which I think we will try to find the true origination points." She stopped talking when the door opened.

Jacob had returned, looking fresh and revitalized in fresh clothes and a smile. "I know, I stayed longer than anticipated, but the shower and the food called to me. The only thing that would have made it better was if you had been there with me."

Petra grinned and replied, "Once Wolfgang comes home, we have a date, darling.

"Now, let's see how much of this code you can get completed while I capture some of the transactions. Quip is actually getting buyers to this site. I would never have dreamed those silly tag lines would actually work."

Jacob worked on the programs to help trap the transactions as well as automatically track back to user location, physical and virtual. The addendum program was to further track the funding sources if a trader was considered worth additional consideration. Petra was tracking the sources of the trades on Quip's site and at other target sites to run the analytics on the transactions look-ing for common transaction patterns. She was also working on encrypting Jacob's programs in a new, more secure manner, while balancing this with decrypting some passwords. Crypto-currency routines protected the user, yet also had a gap in password recovery, which could be the next wave of consumer or business complaints.

Petra updated Jacob on this new customer, Tonya Van Den Berghe, and her own view of how the Global Bank should lead the charge on cryptocurrency. Jacob was stunned at the way Tonya had reached out to find Petra and the resulting meeting. They both laughed when she explained how Otto worked hard to work one angle and she the other. It was one of the strangest scenarios they had encountered since she began working with the team years ago. What made it even funnier is that this woman not only drank like a fish, but was clearly not cursed with self-awareness.

Petra yawned and Jacob announced, "Alright, sweetheart, it is time for you to go home, take your shower, and eat. We have accomplished a lot and know the direction to pick it back up tomorrow. Besides, I want to read a bit more to Wolfgang to see if he responds. I don't know why I think he hears me, but I do. Plus, it is a great story."

Petra pouted slightly before yawning again and said, "I'm tired. I apologize for not asking you earlier about the books. What do you think they are?"

Jacob cocked his head to one side, thought for a moment, and answered, "They are either some an autobiographical novel or a delightful historical novel he's been working on in his spare time. It looks like they were started after my mom left to go to America with me. I found these in his room, and it occurs to me that he might be annoyed at my reading them without his permission. They're fascinating. I am hoping he will tell me when he wakes up. Until then I want to use them as a trigger to get him back."

Petra smiled as she rose and walked to him. She grabbed him about the waist and held him tightly as she kissed him. Leaning back, she looked at him and said, "Goodnight. Enjoy the story. I can wait. If he wakes up though you need to call me."

"Yes, dear," he replied as he hugged her one more time. He turned off all of his computer equipment and settled in for the evening. He glanced at his watch and figured he could easily read for a couple of hours.

"Wolfgang, we left off at the point where you made a note that you, Ferdek and Tavius met with the Ambassador and his daughter Patrycia."

July 1939, Poland

Ambassador Watcowski frowned and crossly asked, "Can you please run your ill-conceived plans by me first, gentlemen? I would prefer to head off any more childish attempts at espionage. I've already heard from the German Ambassador about the drunk students mistakenly invading the German compound, thinking it was a brothel! I didn't research you three and bring you back here to do a clumsy breaking and entering attempt at the German embassy.

"I've been to school with these people. I've socialized with them, both personally and professionally. I can tell you from firsthand experience they are not stupid! Some of them even believe that their government is behaving badly and do not subscribe to the current fad of Nazi ideology! However they feel about their government's misguided actions, they do still serve that government. The best we are going to get is for them to look the other way for modest indiscretions. All we might get is one well-planned venture to get at that confounded encryption machine.

"Do you all understand? I know that the cheap pulp novels about American Cowboy antics are appealing to you young men, but that approach will only derail our efforts!

The Ambassador let his speech sink in, then commanded, "Now get out of my sight until I send for you.

Take heed of my warning. Dismissed."

After being dressed down by the Ambassador, they stepped out of his office and gathered in a small waiting area to discuss their next steps. Before they could start analyzing the situation, a pretty, slender young brunette strode over to them.

Her dark wavy hair hung down her back in a manner typical of a young lady from a good aristocratic family. The modest gown was fitted and of dark material, with a white collar that laid across her shoulders and closed at her throat. The length of the gown was just shy of the tops of her practical leather boots. Tensions in Europe might delay her day in the limelight of autocracy for some time. She had not yet had her presentation season to society as marriageable material.

Her smile was very gentle. Her warm, expresso-colored eyes sparkled as she casually teased, "Well, Ferdy, I heard about your escapade from the other night. Tell me, which genius was it that got you into that situation? Likely, the better question is which lightning wit got you out?"

Tavius, immediately taken by the fetching young woman, offered, "Lightning wit, huh! I think I like the sound of that! Now let me be the first to say that we need a different name for Ferdek here so we don't get him confused with the Ambassador. Madam, I sense that you know Ferdek here well enough to call him Ferdy. I'm more than agreeable to call him the same to keep the players straight. But as a corollary to that, how may I address you, my dear?"

Ferdek immediately bristled at the open conversation with the young lady and rapidly interrupted, "You will show respect, gentlemen. Patrycja is the daughter of the Ambassador, which also makes her my sister! As such, she is the ONLY human being who gets the privilege of calling me Ferdy, not you!"

Tavius recoiled in mild surprise. "Okay then, Ferd it is. Wolfpack, how do you feel about that?"

Wolfgang bristled and flatly stated, "Don't be calling me that, Tavius! Unless you want to be rebranded as Octavius the Octopus!" Then, as an afterthought, he remarked to Patrycja, "You would do well to take that open statement on his character as a warning, madam."

Patrycja smirked slightly and commented, "I can see that when all of you pool your resources you can almost assemble a whole personality. Am I to presume that Father dressed you down for a not very innovative breach in the German compound? I would bet you're now huddling out here to work out another plan."

An awkward moment passed as the men looked at one another. Patrycja's face melted into that of a composed seer as she announced, "I know everything that goes on here, so you shouldn't be surprised that your foul-up of the other night is now old news."

Tavius was not put off by her taunting. In a pleasing tone he inquired, "Perhaps Madam can suggest a better approach? I was going to suggest that since we were…ah, intercepted on the ground, perhaps we might have better luck parachuting into our target. The British have demonstrated some very promising results using that technology."

Patrycja eyed Tavius with a smile surfacing as she offered, "I'm thinking that shooting you out of a cannon will yield better results."

Tavius's laughter quickly spread to the others. Soon they were all making mock cannon fire sounds and pre-

tending to fly through the air at the German consulate. It took a moment for them to notice that the Ambassador was scowling at them all. Patrycja quickly headed for her desk, and the three males abruptly headed for the outer door of the offices.

Jacob rubbed his eyes after he'd placed a bookmark at his stopping point and stood to watch the even rise and fall of Wolfgang's chest. He quietly commented, "You know, Wolfgang, this story just gets better and better." He looked over and saw some lines on the screens which were getting feeds from the probes attached to Wolfgang. His other vitals looked good. He straightened the covers and patted his grandfather's hand and mumbled, "Good night, we'll talk more tomorrow. I miss playing chess with you."

CHAPTER 28

The Rules in a Knife Fight

The movement behind her was so fast that she had no time to react. The cold side of the knife blade was positioned next to her throat but not edge on. She instinctively froze while a male hand reached around in front of her blouse to grasp her clothing.

The male voice offered to his silent companion, "You know what I enjoy most about Western women? They tend to have larger breasts than our Chinese women, but they seem so shy about showing them off. They are so adorably modest that way."

Ton pulled EZ's blouse and bra out far enough so that the razor sharp knife effortlessly sliced through the garments without grazing her skin. EZ trembled as he growled in her ear from behind, "You will enjoy this more if you don't scream." After the last of her blouse had been cut away, he turned her around to face her half naked body, but while he was admiring her heaving breasts due to her frightened breathing, she almost smiled at the private joke.

EZ smirked, "Actually, I'll enjoy hearing YOU scream…" Just then a semi-automatic weapon fired down into Ton's foot, causing enough pain to have EZ smile a terrifying smile. She took the knife that Ton had dropped, but before she could do anything with it, Won lunged toward her and his fallen brother. Another shot rang out, and Won never finished his last breath before slumping to the floor in a pool of his own blood. Ton was still writhing in agony as Mercedes stood over the fallen men.

EZ and Mercedes studied each other and the scene in front of them before Mercedes commented, "You know, he was right. We do have bigger boobs. Sorry about the blouse and bra, hon, but I didn't see him before he was on top of you. The shot through his foot was the only way to insure that you weren't a victim of friendly fire."

Taking off the sweater she had on over her shirt, she handing it to EZ and said, "Better pack the girls away while I check on Su Lin, Ernie, and Andy. Where there are two thugs, there has to be more."

EZ looked down at Ton with the knife in her hand and said, "Well, let me trade this knife for my daddy's Colt .45. I'm not much good in a knife fight, but you should see my target grouping, shooting at 25 yards." She placed the knife back in its sheath, then pulled out the .45 semi-automatic and deftly pulled the slide back to chamber the first round.

Mercedes quietly watched EZ's fluid motions with her weapon, then offered, "Oh, I see. I actually saved him, not you. Got it!" With a big grin on her face, she raced off to check on the others but almost ran into Ernie, who had come running when the shots were fired.

Ernie was white as a sheet when he bolted into the doorway and yelled, "EZ, Mercedes! What's wrong? Are you okay? I heard shots!"

Seeing that Mercedes was fine, he craned his neck to see if EZ was safe, but Mercedes stopped him and said, "How 'bout you hold it there, cowboy. EZ just had a wardrobe malfunction and needs a bit of time to correct the situation." Ernie saw the sliced blouse on the floor and turned beet red as he caught a glimpse of EZ's back as she pulled the sweater down over her head. He promptly did an about-face while Mercedes silently giggled at Ernie's embarrassment.

Then in an almost panicked state, Mercedes quickly asked, "Where are Andy and Su Lin? You didn't leave them alone, did you?"

Ernie's eyes got wide with fear as he stammered, "I heard shots and…well, I thought the worst so I came running. I think they will be safe at the barn…" Just then two new shots rang out from the area Ernie had just abandoned.

Mercedes bolted through the door and at a dead run to the barn. She barely caught a glimmer of taillight from a black SUV speeding away. She raised her weapon to fire but stopped in utter frustration, not wanting to send a poorly aimed shot that might hit Andy or Su Lin.

Ernie caught up to where she was standing, but Mercedes snapped, "Dammit, Ernie! You were supposed to watch them! Now they've been grabbed, and it was on my watch! How could I have been so stupid?"

In an angry move, Mercedes pulled out her cell phone to check the monitoring app as she demanded, "Why the hell didn't the perimeter cameras alert me, dammit? It should have been barking at me with all these intrusions, but I got nothing! We get jumped in the house, and they get away with hostages!"

Ernie touched Mercedes to silence her rant, and they both listened to the sound of someone crying heartily. Cautiously they made their way to the pens, where they picked up EZ, and together they all saw Su Lin on the ground, holding Franklin's head in her lap and sobbing.

She cried out, "Poor, brave, sweet pig. That's twice you have saved me, but this time you paid too high a price! My dear Franklin, don't leave me!"

Ernie rushed to tend to the animal, hoping that it wasn't too late.

EZ rushed to hug Su Lin and get her to calm down. Mercedes was all business as she cleared the exasperation from her tone and asked, "Su Lin, what happened? Where's Andy?"

Su Lin collected herself a little and, choking on her tears, said, "As soon as we heard the gunfire, Ernie told us to stay put and left. They descended from the back of the barn in the shadows and grabbed us. They hit Andy hard, and I saw him go down! They reached for me next, and then Franklin charged them, knocking one down and biting at the other two. Franklin was at them everywhere, stomping, ramming, and biting just like he knew this was life and death for us all. They shot him twice, but not before he bit a hunk out of one of them and stomped on another."

She wiped the tears from her eyes and angrily clarified, "It was Guano. He lead the attack just like before, but now with the way he was dragging his leg, I'm pretty sure Franklin crushed it before he was shot. When Franklin wouldn't go down, and they heard the other shots, they drug Andy into the SUV and left. As soon as they were gone, Franklin collapsed." She started sobbing even harder and cried, "I've lost everything! All those I love are dead, yet again!"

Ernie, angry with himself for abandoning his charges, alerted everyone as he announced, "Okay, wait a minute! Franklin still has a pulse! We have a vet close by, and, well, let's not give up hope yet. Alright!" He placed a call to the local vet, and a quick explanation on the need for a rescue operation began.

EZ challenged Su Lin. "You're not giving up so easy on my dad, are you? Because I'm not! We are going to get him back, and then we are going to feed these kidnapping bastards to Franklin in small pieces after he recovers, you got that? Stop your crying.

Let's think about this, and what the next steps might be!"

Mercedes coolly queried, "You not only recognized one of them, but you know why they are here, don't you? They aren't after Andy at all. They are here for you, right? If that's the case, what should happen next, in my experience, is an arranged trade.

"I need you to pull yourself together and tell us exactly how this mess came to be. I can't help you if you don't. What's worse is, you won't be any help to Andy."

EZ growled, "Su Lin, don't let them win! I want my father back!"

The bold statements had their effect on Su Lin, and letting the last of her tears flow down her cheeks, she forcefully barked, "Lt. Colonel Ling Po reporting for duty, Madam Commanders!"

Still holding the Colt .45, EZ rocked it back so it was resting on her shoulder and, with ferocious intent in her eyes, calmly stated, "Let's go bring him back."

Mercedes said, "What we need to do is go get our wounded attacker and question him. Ernie, you stay with the ladies. I'll be right back."

Mercedes raced to the site of the shooting and found only the single body, covered with a rough cloth and a blood trail leading away. She shook her head in disbelief. "Oh, criminy."

Mercedes returned to the barn and sent Ernie to track the wounded man. He returned later with no attacker in hand.

"I'm sorry, Mercedes, I can't locate him. We need to call the authorities."

CHAPTER 29

We Can't Plan Unless We Have Good Ideas

...The Enigma Chronicles

Mathias narrowed his eyes and tersely asked, "Vanadium? That's your big news? Did you fall asleep again, pleasure reading Wikipedia?"

A little put off by the comment but still enthusiastic, Dr. Halvorson replied, "You don't understand. Vanadium doesn't occur in nature. It's only produced as a byproduct during a refining process."

Mathias cut his eyes sideways to Dutch, who motioned a soothing gesture with his hands, indicating that they should hear Dr. Halvorson out before reacting. Mathias frowned sourly as he stated, "This sounds intriguing. Can you make this a long story rather than a short one, so I can enjoy the dialogue longer?"

Dr. Halvorson looked a bit confused as he processed the comment but then proceeded, "I guess. But you usually get sarcastic with me if I take too long to articulate the particular subtleties of my research topic. I will try and accommodate..."

Mathias, no longer wanting to endure the ramblings by the doctor, quickly interjected, "Uh-oh, the telephony carrier is about to invoke their excessive verbiage clause on this call. You'll have to make it snappy. Just tell me what you got before my system believes that I had a cell phone surgically implanted."

Dr. Halvorson sighed and, sounding despondent, continued, "Right, I'm being made fun of again! Just wait until you hear what we've got!

"My assistant's current squeeze, Prissy, heard from her sister's boyfriend's best friend working at MIT that a team actually solved a key problem with Lithium Ion batteries. I'm sure you know that Lithium Ion batteries don't recharge or discharge very fast. There has been a long term hunt for a material to cure that problem. Basically, using Vanadium in a polymer in-between the Li-ion cells can speed up the charge cycle of a Li-ion battery. Charging can be done in 20 to 40 seconds instead of the hours it currently takes. Pretty cool, huh?"

Dutch, growing impatient with the rhetoric, was making a slicing motion across his throat to indicate the call had gone on long enough. Mathias felt that Dutch might be suggesting not only terminating the call but the caller as well. Mathias glibly asked, "Will this material be on Friday's quiz, professor? If it's not, I have to leave for my next class. It's one of those fun classes you have to get to early to sit next to the hot babe we all want to…"

Dr. Halvorson barked, "Class is NOT dismissed! Sit there until I'm done, dammit!

"Now let me finish, will you? Vanadium will improve the battery life of Lithium Ion batteries which is what EVERY electric car manufacturer is hunting! Now for the obvious question. Where do we get this Vanadium stuff? Ah, you are asking good, insightful questions, my C- challenged student. You get Vanadium from oil during the refining process, if your oil has the Vanadium mineral in it. Now, class, what country has gobs of Vanadium available in their vast oil reserves? That's right! You've got the answer correct, Venezuela!"

Dutch looked quizzically at Mathias, who was beginning to grasp the significance of the reasoning. He slowly stated, "That means the oil in Venezuela, if properly refined, will produce not only regular petroleum products, but more importantly, Vanadium. Vanadium would be a key ingredient in a polymer coating inside Lithium Ion batteries, making them extremely useful in electric cars, which would make them highly competitive to internal combustion cars. One product for two different but competing markets. Is that about it?"

Dr. Halvorson seemed surprised as he responded, "Yes, actually. Isn't that great news, Mathias? I mean, after all aren't you looking for something to invest in with that fancy schmancy, cryptocurrency of yours? And if we can get this code into the hands of your buyer, I won't have to listen to Codan the Barbarian talk about what he is working on. Geez, it's like listening to me!"

Mathias, clearly elated, practically shouted while engaged in his happy dance, and responded, "Yes! Yes! Why didn't you just say you knew how to make me rich beyond belief, you mustached maniac! We need to change your designation of PhD, from Piled Higher & Deeper, Halvorson, to FsU, for Finally Something Useful!

"We can launch an Initial Coin Offering or ICO with the new cryptocurrency and insist that the new digital currency be used to purchase shares in the Vanadium refining process. This will become a near monopoly in supplying the main polymer ingredient to the electric car manufacturers. We can ride the price tsunami up and then quietly cash our way out so we can buy a whole atoll in Polynesia. Woo-Hoo! I'm getting a woody just thinking about it!"

Dutch, just a little unnerved by the uncommon eccentric display of Mathias, wasn't sure of where they stood. He cautiously asked, "Do we want to go put down a deposit on our new atoll in Polynesia or start with a bit more planning? I'm just asking…"

Mathias, over his initial jubilation, calmly remarked, "We can't plan unless we have good ideas. Now we have good ideas, Dutch."

Mathias cautioned, "Dutch, let me do the talking when we get in to see Alejandro and the Venezuelan contingent. I want to put this new piece of functionality on the table for our crypto-currency to see if we can speed the adoption of our product. The secure contract attribute will be key to getting them to embrace our offer."

CHAPTER 30

Uncovering the Dark Side
of Cryptocurrency
...The Enigma Chronicles

Petra entered the Operations Center a bit later than usual. Her meeting with Otto was planned to start in fifteen minutes. Rather than stop at her workstation, she decided to go straight to the conference room. A small smile began to form on her lips when she saw the coffee and fruit laid out for sampling. Taking a cup and filling it, she savored the bold roasted elixir as she sipped. This morning there had been a choice between thirty more minutes of sleep and a full breakfast. Sleep had won out, so to have this available made the start of the day better. A special thank you to Bowen was likely in order.

Logging into the system, she checked on the traps she and Jacob had established and reviewed the visitors to Digital Diamonds. The visitor count displayed on the visitor facing page was huge, while on the backside it showed less than one hundred perusals. That was to be expected with the limited advertising links they'd set up. A few new buyers were sitting in the 'Confirm to Purchase' area, which was the security they had set up. This was similar to the other cryptocurrency sites. With no sovereign rules to guide the buying and selling of cryptocurrency or even regulations, the organizations mimicked in many cases the comfort of verify, secure, and even PayPal notations. People expected certain things on websites, whether real or imagined. No website wants to be perceived as fraudulent.

Petra was almost finished with her updates when Otto entered and set his notepad on the table and walked toward the coffee. He paused briefly for a kiss on top of her head and asked, "How are you doing this morning? Bowen called and said you slept in and left without breakfast. He seemed worried about you, my dear. With all the concern with Wolfgang in the hospital and all, you might want to alert Bowen to your comings and goings to alleviate his concern."

Petra looked up and acknowledged, "You're right, Father. I should have, but I was partially hoping he was resting too. He goes back and forth to the hospital, and I swear he sleeps under the staircase rather than in bed. I saw the set up and figured he called. I promise, I will make certain he is aware and finds a special token of my thanks. He's a gem.

"There was no change in Wolfgang before I left last evening. If anything changes, Jacob will call. Jacob and I were able to complete the majority of the coding and encryption routines we all agreed were critical." Petra projected her screen onto the wall and added, "You'll be pleased to know that Digital Diamonds is starting to get traffic to the website and even some small purchases. We are, as we all agreed, backing the digital with our own funds while we watch cryptocurrency market volatility. There have been some enormous shifts both ways in this market. Two other sites were completely devastated yesterday and announced they are folding. It was a publicity nightmare for them, I am sure. Those invested or hoping to hit the 'big one' were crushed. We have not yet heard of any actual people casualties, but it is not outside of the realm of the possible."

Otto thoughtfully looked at the numbers from their site. "Change the screen, please, to the current report. I believe we are almost finished with your Ms. Van Den Berghe. At this point we are focused on our R-Group assignment, not yours, alright?

"The report illustrates the cryptocurrency players since it was decentralized in 2009. The changes to the algorithms over this period have been enormous, but clearly it is continuing to pick up followers for many different reasons. For Ms. Van Den Berghe to make her case for the adopt side of this equation, the programs they back up must have the security of everyday people and their wealth. That is not to say that any currency is stable, but the digital currency seems purposely built for hacking. It is going to take some extreme measures to make it secure enough for most people. Would you agree?"

Petra looked as if she was choosing her words carefully before she spoke. "People seem to have two mindsets these days. One is, keep everything safe and secure, or one step above stowing their cash under their mattresses. The other is to takes risks in any market, of which digital currency is one, and increase the wealth if only on paper. To be honest, I am not certain where the Global Bank should stand as the digital fault line widens."

After a brief pause, Petra thoughtfully suggested, "The other thing not accounted for is the pull-through of the Darknet. We really haven't looked closely at how the bad actors would use the anonymous nature of cryptocurrency to launder money. That was the published reason that South Korea began outlawing crypto exchanges. The real reason was that you could move money digitally and anonymously, thus dodging taxes. The danger I see with cryptocurrencies is that if you maintain the anonymous attributes of the media, the criminal element is quick to embrace digital currency options because they can launder and hide their ill-gotten gains. You should recall the Darknet black market called the Silk Road, which came online in 2011. This was where illegal drugs were offered up anonymously and transactions were completed with digital currency, also anonymous in nature. Their business model was a little too good, yet it still took the FBI a couple of years to crack it.

"When one takes the sovereign type of approach, which is to bake in traceability and accountability, then the anonymous attributes are lost and unattractive. Not just to the criminal element, but to most people who want less government snooping in their day-to-day affairs."

Otto nodded and said, "Ah, yes, the infamous modern day Silk Road run by a man with the pseudonym The Dread Pirate Roberts. I wonder if his sense of humor is still intact now that he is serving a life sentence with no chance of parole. The inference is that anonymous currency usage is just the criminal element, but in fact there are legitimate reasons why the average citizen would also want their currency transactions to be anonymous. Very astute observation, my dear.

"Then the bottom line for cryptocurrencies to succeed is to provide the anonymity provided by hard currency but preserve the sovereign government requirements for regulation, control, and taxation. A difficult balance, to be sure. I don't believe there is any governmental obligation to provide good financial infrastructure to the criminal element."

Petra nodded but challenged, "If we look at it from a purely economic viewpoint, the Darknet provides goods and services to not only other shady entities but also to the regular public. Drugs, stolen merchandise, and prostitution are, in fact, consumed by both groups and usually with untraceable cash. When the only currency available is one that is traceable, i.e. non-anonymous, then that simply won't be adopted by the population as a whole."

Otto looked like a light had turned on, and he added, "And that is why there is a race to get the newest cryptocurrency out there before any governments mandate that you can only use theirs. Interesting.

"Would you agree then that the responsible recommendation to Tonya and her organization is to continue to develop unbreakable security into the cryptocurrency programs and allow each sovereign to determine how they wish to regulate the usage? A common cryptocurrency standard for security and trade would not make it much different than today's use of hard currency; it will be manufactured, controlled, valued, and distributed based on that sovereign's economy and exchange rates that will naturally be set. To back universal security using the highest encryption, along with user anonymity within their own country, would make the most sense. When an individual wants to exchange goods and property outside of their country, they would transfer through a digital exchange rate program."

Petra chuckled, "That seems to make the most sense, but you're going to need several mimosas to get her to understand the logic and long-term risks to this path. A criminal today who gets a hold of the plates for making current $100 bills on their own has months to use them before the United States can recognize and put a plan in place to check for the current version of fraudulent bills. In a cryptocurrency, it will be seconds until the penetration is complete and the funds exported. It is part of the reason I think we are having so much of a problem following Chesterfield's funds. I think he not only transferred them out of the countries he worked in to less regulated countries, but a good portion he likely invested into what he thought would grow exponentially. He also didn't continue with the Steven Christopher persona but reverted to his own name, Chesterfield."

Otto made some notes and then merged those into the report he wanted to provide to his client. He asked Petra to give it a read-through to make certain she agreed with the positioning being presented.

An hour later and with a few corrections, they felt the report was ready to be sent, following a call to Ms. Van Den Berghe. Petra promised to keep quiet but stayed in the room while Otto placed the call.

She picked up on the first half-ring, and Otto greeted, "Ah, Ms. Van Den Berghe, this is Otto. I am glad you weren't in a meeting or away from your desk. Do you have a few minutes for a brief chat before I send over the report you requested?"

"Yes, Otto, of course!" Tonya replied a bit breathlessly, annoyed with herself for being so anxious. She wanted to move this project forward soon, well-armed with the correct facts. She took a breath and added, "I spoke to my director earlier today and suggested I would have more information this week."

Otto continued, "How was your flight home, madam? Did you find the travel pleasant, even after that filling lunch I practically forced upon you. I haven't eaten there in some time, but it was still delicious. I think you at least enjoyed the mimosas.

"Ah well, enough of the pleasantries. I am certain you want to get down to business, busy woman that you are. I have completed the research into the worst and best cryptocurrency programs available for purchase and, of course, freeware. I am recommending that you do not use the freeware, as it will have more areas needing security adjustments. I have indicated the top two I believe are worth your consideration. These would be purchased as a right to use and modify so that you can change, enhance and secure continually. Does that sound like what you were expecting, Madam?"

Tonya had blushed through most of the conversation once the mimosas were mentioned. Admittedly she had hit them a bit hard, on the flight home as well with her upgrade. She was flustered still as she replied, "That sounds correct, but did you also include the adoption approach I believe we spoke of?"

"Of course, Madam. I have some very strong viewpoints on this which I have included. With your approval, I will transmit the report along with the invoice for services. The invoice is due and payable immediately, per our agreement."

"Immediately," Tonya squeaked, "I thought you were aware we don't pay anyone immediately. We'll put you on the 45 day pay cycle as we do with most contractor support. That gives me time to review the report and agree if it meets …"

Otto interrupted, "Pardon me, Ms. Van Den Berghe, but that was not our agreement. If you choose to modify the terms, I will need authorization from your superior. I deliver what we contract for, often with some additional value added, as we did in your case. I will hold the report, awaiting your electronic notification to send payment based on our terms."

Tonya fearfully replied, "Oh no, I need that report, Otto. I need to review it for my director and add any suitable commentary. Send it along now, please." Tonya looked stricken at the possibility she would not get the report and felt she'd made a grievous error.

Otto calmly replied, "Madam, we made a business arrangement. You do not get to change the terms of the contract after the fact. It is considered unprofessional and insulting. Have your supervisor contact me when you get things worked out. Have a good day, Madam."

Otto disconnected, looking rather pleased. Petra rose and walked over to kiss him on the cheek. "She should have known not to mess with you, Otto. I wouldn't have." Petra laughed a bit as she left the room.

Just When Things Can't Get Any Worse

Jacob awoke to the sounds of the chirps and beeps of the machines monitoring Wolfgang. The white sheet was neat with his arms laying by his side. The antiseptic smell suggested the nurse had recently completed her morning routine of changing out various bags and had taken his vitals in her normal stealthy manner. Obviously, Jacob hadn't been disturbed in the least.

Jacob rose and neatly folded the blanket which had kept him warm and placed the pillow along with the blanket on the shelf. Then he used the adjoining restroom and ran some warm water over his face to erase the remaining fog of sleep. When he returned to the room, Bowen was bustling around, setting up his breakfast and keeping up a quiet one-sided dialogue with Wolfgang.

Noticing Jacob, Bowen greeted, "Ah, Jacob, there you are. Good morning. I was just telling Wolfgang that I brought your favorite omelet, crisp bacon, and freshly made blueberry muffins to start your day. I'm sorry, but I tattled that you really are not eating enough."

Jacob smiled and patted Bowen on the shoulder. "It is so kind of you to bring special food for me. I know I will enjoy every last morsel. Did you happen to bring some extra bottled water as well?"

Bowen nodded and confirmed, "I brought your extra water, there in the cooler, as well as some of your snack bars in case you get hungry before I bring back lunch. Today for lunch, Cook wanted to tempt Wolfgang with some fresh pasta using some onions and tomatoes from our garden. Would you like that as well?"

Jacob was enjoying the game Bowen had kept going to see if the possibilities of food would lift the coma to any degree. Bowen always shined when he felt he was one step ahead of Wolfgang. Regardless of the response from Wolfgang or lack thereof, Bowen felt he was doing his best. Jacob cocked his head and replied, "Does that mean you'll bring a glass of the cabernet he favors as well? I can easily enjoy that sort of lunch if it is not too much trouble. Warm sourdough rolls with butter would be welcomed, along with a small salad. I know Wolfgang likes to ignore the salad, but I won't. Petra said she wouldn't be over for lunch, but she might make dinner. Do I get to know what's for dinner?"

Bowen grinned and responded, "Not until lunch is brought, Master Jacob. You know Cook won't tell me in advance what she plans. Though I did smell what I think is a triple chocolate cake baking as I collected the breakfast items. Perhaps that is her plan for the evening dessert."

Jacob replied, "Enough of the Master stuff, Bowen. Jacob is all I am. This breakfast looks delicious as usual. Will you join me?"

"No, I ate earlier. I have chores to do at the house." He moved to Wolfgang's side, started patting then stroking his arm, and added, "Old friend and Master, I would like to see you open your eyes and tell me how I can help. I cannot help if you won't give me direction. I will see you later. Tell Jacob if you want extra pasta, old friend."

Bowen nodded toward Jacob as he then turned and left the room. Jacob understood how close the two men were and how tough this was for Bowen to grasp. He shook it off and decided a little reading during breakfast might be warranted.

Jacob found the right page to begin again. "Wolfgang, I realize this might be a bit choppy in between bites, but eating and reading works for me right now. I hope you won't mind too much.

"We left off here."

July 1939, Poland

In early evening, the three lieutenants assembled for their chat.

Ferd ventured, "You don't know this, but Patrycja is Father's courier for diplomatic correspondence to other embassies here in Warsaw. I don't know why I didn't think of this before, but she gets to walk right in the front door at the German embassy. Therefore, all we have to do is…"

Tavius quickly interrupted, "Now, hold on! The Ambassador said no more independent thinking, Ferd! Besides, I don't like the idea of getting her involved in this potentially risky operation. She doesn't need to be endangered, particularly by guards carrying Mauser rifles."

Wolfgang offered, "Tavius, I think what Ferd was trying to suggest, is for us to sketch out a plan, take and discuss it with the Ambassador, then we can discuss staffing the activities with suitable people who would cause the least amount of notice."

Irked, Ferd blandly stated, "Naw, I was just going to con my sister into going in on a harebrained scheme, like I used to do when we were children!"

He looked at Tavius with mock disdain. "Of course I don't want her at risk! If she can be properly engaged to leverage our reconnaissance while inside doing a normal courier run, then we can assess what we are up against. We don't blindly grab for something, especially since we have no idea what it looks like.

"And you, Octopus, don't be getting any ideas about my sister! She's not even eighteen. Not only is our father keeping a close eye on her, so is her brother!"

Tavius naively asked, "Is there something wrong with her? She seems like a spirited and intelligent young lady. You aren't suggesting she has some sort of birth defect, are you?"

Ferd, somewhat confused as well as flustered by the rapid fire questions, responded, "Of course she isn't…I mean she is a full-fledged female with no detractions…er, that is to say, there isn't any…uh, and why am I trying to answer this?"

Tavius, enjoying the sport of the questioning along with the resulting fluster, asked, "Does she have a be-trothed whom I need to vanquish in order to court her? You're not one of those kinds of brothers that beats his sister every time she meets a young man, are you?"

Now really flustered, Ferd responded, "Yes…I mean, no…I mean, I don't know about any…"

Wolfgang grinned at the exchange, happy he was not the brunt of Tavius' attack. "I, for one, am glad that you have stopped beating your sister. There's a good man."

Ferd, unable to say anything more on the topic for fear of answering incorrectly, grinned at Tavius. "Let's finish this discussion another time. I think we ought to map out a reconnaissance of the German embassy, with the eyes of Patrycja, as you suggested."

Wolfgang suggested, "With July coming up, there may be some outdoor activity at the embassy, like a garden party or dance, that we might be able to use to be on the premises. I might suggest that Ambassador Ferdek would know the upcoming social calendar, and we might be able to use that as our vehicle inside the gates. We would need to wear uniforms this time and avoid any eye contact with the guards, just so we aren't recognized."

Tavius smiled and agreed, "Gentlemen, I think we have taken our first step to creating a useful plan."

Jacob stopped when the background beeps modified to a long screaming bleep. Moments later, two nurses rushed into the room and immediately blocked his view of Wolfgang.

Nurse Sandy firmly stated, "Jacob, we need you to leave the room."

Jacob opened his mouth to protest but recognized they would not have asked if it wasn't important. Arguing with them would certainly not be useful if they were focused on Wolfgang. Quickly, he put away the book, then picked up his laptop and cell phone as he exited the room. Outside in the private waiting area, he called Otto, Bowen, Petra, and Quip to alert them that there was a change in Wolfgang and that he'd been asked to leave.

During the past few hours, Otto and Petra had joined Jacob in the waiting room with Bowen roaming in and out, trying to find something useful to do. Jacob and Petra huddled in the corner, working on some additional changes. Jacob periodically stood up and paced around, looking for Nurse Sandy for an update. It had been almost three hours, and no one had come out at all. Jacob was all about giving them their space, but he was getting nervous.

"Honey, I know we want to finish this one portion of the tracer, but I am too distracted to do what is required. Can I go into his section and look? Perhaps I can get an update and with that refocus on what we need to do for the program."

"Of course, Jacob. This is not as important as Wolfgang. I wanted to keep your mind off the situation until they came out. I'm worried too. Would you like me to go with you?"

"Actually, I would. Bowen," said Jacob, "can you watch our equipment while we go see if we can get an update?"

Looking very relieved with a new assignment, Bowen replied, "Yes, sir. Thank you, sir."

Haddy walked in, and Otto quietly briefed her on the current information. Jacob and Petra nodded to both of them as they left the waiting area in search of Nurse Sandy. Walking down the bright white hallway and spotless white floors, they observed that the quiet was loud. They turned the corner toward Wolfgang's room where several members of the medical staff were gathered. The mood of the staff seemed less serious than they expected.

Nurse Sandy was in the room and saw Jacob approaching. She stepped out of the room with a smile and grabbed his hand. She then pulled him along, with Petra in tow, a bit down the hallway.

"Jacob, Wolfgang has come out of the coma and is conscious. His eyes are open, but he is not recognizing any images. The tubes were taken out a few minutes ago, but his throat seems to be too sore to speak, though he appears to be trying. The doctor is with him and doing various tests so we might give you a proper status. I think there is hope at this point, but everything is not wonderful."

As Nurse Sandy relayed her information, Jacob's emotions ran the gambit from relief to joy to fear and around again. As his eyes swelled with tears, he cleared his throat and asked, "Do you want us to go back to the waiting room, or can we come in?"

Petra, with tears slowly tracing her cheeks, added, "We'll be quiet. We just want him to know we are here."

Nurse Sandy nodded and led them toward the room. They entered and quietly sat in the corner to wait for the verdict from the doctor.

Quip was about finished with his routines and ready to head for the hospital when his cell phone played Breathe, which made him smile because it was EZ. He wanted to tell her that something had changed with Wolfgang even though he wasn't sure what it meant. She hadn't responded to his earlier voicemail on the change in his condition.

He answered, "Hi, my beautiful wife. Sure wish you were here so I could …"

Her anguished sobbing reached his ears before her words, "Sweetheart, he's gone. He's just gone."

"No, honey," he tried with reassurance in his tone. "We don't know the status yet on Wolfgang. I didn't mean that in my message. Sorry if I …"

With a stronger voice she stated, "Quip, not Wolfgang, my father. Daddy's been taken. We need your help."

Quip was trying to comprehend to what EZ was saying. He started typing madly, sending an instant message to Julie to see if she had heard anything about this. He calmly asked, "EZ, honey, tell me what happened. Where are Mercedes and Su Lin? Are they with you? Are they alright?"

EZ sobbed as she explained, "Mercedes is trying to reach Julie, and Su Lin is with us but terribly distraught. The kidnappers want her to exchange herself for my father. Oh, Quip, as much as I want my father back, she shouldn't do that. He can't see yet. They didn't even take his medicine.

"Quip, I almost killed a man with a knife. I was so scared. Then my attacker escaped." EZ's sobbing intensified.

Caught off-guard and at a loss for words, Quip said, "Honey, I wish I was there to hold you. We'll find a way to get him back, honey. But I need more information before I can tell you how. Let me get with Julie after she finishes with Mercedes, alright? I love you, honey."

Quip heard Mercedes in the background asking for the phone, then she said, "Quip, I related everything to Julie. EZ is fine, just a bit shook up. Su Lin is a mess, but she recognizes we need a plan. Julie and you will work together then get back with us, right?"

Quip took a breath and replied, "Yes, we will make a plan. And my IM from Julie says you want me to try to find Jim. I'll do my best. You three stay together, please."

Mercedes replied, "We will. I'm sorry, Quip. We took every precaution, but they sidestepped everything designed to stop them. They managed to avoid the carefully placed cameras so we never saw them coming."

Not wanting to lose his temper, he quietly agreed, "I understand. Let me go now and talk to Julie."

CHAPTER 32

Anonymous-Alive or Dead

Dr. Halvorson continued, "Mathias, I really wish you'd let us finish the programming I've described. We need to bake in the Knowledge of Zero Awareness Proof anonymizing technology, or K-ZAP, as it is discussed in the crypto blogs, so we can hide from digital discovery after launch. The poor dumb schmucks gobbling down the cryptocurrency de jour don't realize that those offerings CAN be traced! Anyone with a simple computer and a little intuition can actually uncover the buyers and sellers because the records are blasted to all the mining servers. We need to put in K-ZAP to complete the product offering. Otherwise our exit strategy from Venezuela won't be pleasant."

Mathias studied Halvorson a moment then said, "I remember this argument from Takeru. He didn't think it was theoretically possible to build a de-centralized digital currency that kept the buyers and sellers completely anonymous. Hell, that's the reason he launched our product out of the Panama data center we helped him build. We'd be a lot farther along now if that jerk Steven Christopher hadn't gummed up the works."

Halvorson smirked as he countered, "Yeah, we got first mover cryptocurrency out to market alright, and we have made such good money off it that we're still hiding out and dribbling a few miserable coins out each quarter so we don't get nailed like Steven Christopher. We only brought in that two-bit drifter because Takeru was taken out."

Dutch weighed in with a sidebar comment. "We thought it was all fixed when we gave Takeru that fake alias of Satoshi Nakamoto so no one could track him. Boy, I don't care what kind of mathematical genius you are, bleeding out 'cause someone whacks off your hands was so not in the big picture. Sure ruined our plans. His too obviously."

Mathias looked dispassionately at Halvorson and Dutch and queried, "Are we all done with our heartfelt reminiscing? We've had some setbacks. But understand this, pinning all our past cryptocurrency efforts on a now dead computer wizard that no one has ever met has given us a new lease on life, so stop whining.

"Now, I want to continue our efforts to get our standard cryptocurrency package, with the secure contract attribute that you and Cody insisted on adding, ready to go for this deal closing next trip. I don't want the extra, uh… k-zod or zappity techno babble added because it will disrupt my timetable. We've got every script-kiddie college nerd out there trying to build a competing product. And let's not forget, from the noise on the Darknet, we also have every governmental regime out there trying to shut down the free market exchanges for cryptocurrencies. Gentlemen, we simply don't have the time! Halvorson, how many more minutes do you need? I'm in a hurry!"

Halvorson was thoroughly annoyed, but grudgingly accepted Mathias's arguments. He glumly stated, "We should be ready for you by tomorrow morning."

A startled Dutch practically gasped, "What? You're that close to being ready? I've got to go pack and shave! I hope I have time for a haircut and manicure! Females like well-groomed males! Genesis, you're knight in shining armor is just a tooth-brushing away! See you guys later."

Halvorson smirked, "Remember to brush all your teeth. Don't forget to remove your navel lint this time, buddy! And get those car doors of yours groomed! Babes just won't nuzzle you if you have gross fuzz sticking out of your ear!"

Mathias slowly closed his eyes and shook his head in disbelief.

CHAPTER 33

Fixing Messes is Our Specialty
...The Enigma Chronicles

Well aware that the situation with Andy was critical to not only EZ but also to Su Lin, Quip placed the all-important call to Julie. He was certain that the Chinese who had started this mess in Georgia were at the heart of this kidnapping. Quip's uncharacteristic pacing in the conference room of the Operations Center caused ICABOD to display the information being gathered, based on Quip's instructions, on all the walls and Quip's monitor at the head of the table.

Julie answered, "Quip, hang on, please. I am trying to get some privacy here."

As Quip's angst increased, his patience decreased as he snarled, "Julie, there is a time issue here. Can I get some focus from you?"

"I am just as worried as you are, but getting cross with me is not going to help. I'm going to forgive a bit of your tone as I know you're worried about EZ. Mercedes says she was upset and crying when she spoke with you. But Mercedes is there and will keep her close," Julie snapped back.

"Oh, just like she was keeping them close when Andy was kidnapped!"

Quip realized too late that his thought had been verbalized, and the silence from the other side of the call was deafening. He took a deep breath and then another before he conceded, "Julie, I take that back. I don't have all the details, and I am worried about everyone and too far away to be useful. I, ah…well, I think I will be quiet until you're ready."

He sat down as Julie transferred them to a video call. It would be easier if they were face-to-face. She was not smiling, but there was a look of sympathy in her eyes.

"Good, you're sitting down. We have a lot of moving pieces. Are Jacob, Petra and Otto aware of the situation yet?"

Quip shook his head, then added, "No, they are still at the hospital waiting for an update on Wolfgang. Since you and I have not outlined a plan, I thought that would be the best for now."

"Agreed. I hope the news will be good. When I spoke with Otto earlier, he said not to travel to Zürich yet. I am at my home office, and Juan is getting as many facts as possible into the database so we can analyze them. He is also speaking with Carlos and trying to capture the conversations from numbers you previously provided, which we identified early on as potentially being a part of this outfit from China."

Quip was focused on the current situation as a problem that needed to be solved. His fingers were running over the keys, setting up different data avenues for ICABOD to gather, sift, and analyze. "Can you tell me the details of what occurred? EZ implied someone was killed."

Julie outlined the details for Quip, including the stunning detail that Won was dead but the other twin, Ton, escaped with a seriously wounded foot. Won and Ton had crossed paths with the R-Group for years, originally with Chairman Chang. With the additional details Julie had provided, along with the information ICABOD had gathered and summarized, the picture was improving.

ICABOD interjected at a break in their conversation, "Mistress Julie, Jim Hughes is in deep cover in Asia. We might be able to reach out to him, but I am analyzing if this will compromise his situation. There is a local agent from his team, Khalid, who has been working as a sort of guard for Mercedes. It seems he picked her up when she arrived in Georgia."

Julie affirmed, "Sorry, Quip, she did mention he was around and helped with setting up the surveillance equipment. He is also willing to provide secure transport, though you might have to call your buddy Eric if this gets any messier. I suspect Khalid is doing some of the communication in that direction, but it is our professional follow up with Eric that should be done. How do you want to handle it?"

Quip thought about alerting Otto and giving him the task but rejected that option in favor of stepping up himself. "I will give him a brief call when we are finished. You're right, Julie.

"Now, I think we have a few avenues we need to explore as possibilities with the team if we don't have a way to take Andy back. It would be with Su Lin going in, but with very careful instructions on what happens and when. We also need to finish that program and have Jacob do one of his time-delayed actions in the programming that Su Lin can activate on her way back home. Or we can activate it from here."

"Agreed. We might also want to see if we can do something to make certain Su Lin and Andy will not be disturbed again. They both deserve a life."

They continued discussions until they hammered out the detailed outline of three plans for the team to consider. Before they disconnected, Quip said he wanted to complete that call to Eric and then set up a call with Petra, Otto, and Jacob.

Quip called Otto. When the call connected, he asked, "Otto, any word yet on Wolfgang? I have ICABOD monitoring the transmissions, but sometimes those things lag in ICU."

Otto replied, "A short time ago, Jacob and Petra went back to the room and watched them working on Wolfgang. Petra came out not too long ago and briefly explained that there was a change and he is out of the coma, but not yet cognizant. The doctor is running tests and will provide a status soon."

"Sounds like it may be good news. I hope that trend continues.

"I know you are focused on your situation there, but something has come up. Do you have time for a brief update and some options?"

Otto sensed the angst in Quip's tone. "Of course, Quip, what has happened?"

"Andy was kidnapped and a message was left that offers an exchange of Andy for Su Lin and her cryptocurrency programming expertise. You may recall that was the original reason that Andy and Su Lin were attacked. They had been home for a very short time when the intruders did a divide and conquer in what seemed a fairly secure environment. The Chairman's ward, Won, was killed during the exchange and Andy was taken.

"Mercedes had to engage the local police, and she insisted that Homeland Security get involved to try to minimize the chance that Andy is removed from the United States. She does have a co-worker of Jim's helping, which seemed like chance until ICABOD located Stalker undercover in China. Something is up, at least from a United States agency perspective, which we are not involved in. It seems like the only reason Mercedes received the help was her personal relationship with Jim.

"Su Lin is ready to get on with the exchange, but without a plan it makes no sense to take that step. Julie and I have roughed out a few options, and we would like to review three with you before we share the best option with Su Lin. EZ is helping Mercedes keep a handle on Su Lin even though she is so worried about her father. She is so strong. I spoke to her a second time since the incident, just before calling you, and she is past the shock."

Otto shook his head as he digested the discussion. "What a shame. Su Lin is working for a new life and is having the devil of a time running away from her former life as Master Po.

"Alright, since the doctor needs time to finish his testing, transfer my phone into a conference bridge, and I will ask Haddy to hold on the bridge with you while I get Petra and Jacob."

He handed the phone to Haddy and rushed through the door. A few minutes later he returned with them, and they each dialed into the bridge.

Otto took his phone back and stated, "Quip, we are on speaker phone in a private area."

"Good, I added Julie in while you were gone.

"Jacob, I know interrupting you is difficult, but it is important. Thank you and Petra for joining."

Quip hit all the highlights of the event in Georgia and answered their questions where he could. Jacob reconnected his laptop into the conference as well, so they could easily see the options as Julie and Quip provided the detail of how each plan might be executed, then summarized the estimated time to completion. The debate on each of the potential solutions covered even more details than he and Julie had. At the end of the discussion, they had a hybrid plan for Su Lin being exchanged for Andy.

They needed two or three days to get the program available, which Su Lin could plant for them. They agreed on the primary role assignments. Jacob needed to complete some programming for the exchange, and he could leverage a portion of what he had recently completed. Petra would revise and enhance the encryption, then Su Lin could do a check through it and note any required changes. Julie and Mercedes would continue to search for the kidnapper source and work on other ways to either extract Andy or insure that the exchange did not put them into the position of having both Andy and Su Lin captive.

Jacob volunteered to call Su Lin and outline the plan and the timeline expected. If she agreed, then she could start negotiations. The biggest problem he voiced was not having U.S. Homeland Security intercede before the exchange of Su Lin could occur and the carefully engineered cryptocurrency package delivered. If their timing and execution were not perfect, someone would pay dearly.

CHAPTER 34

Academic Exercises Are Not For Everyone

After alerting Petra, Jacob went outdoors to place the call to Su Lin. The fresh air would help clear his mind, allowing him to focus on the current problem. He had a chance to make a positive impact on gaining freedom for Andy and recovering Su Lin. The plan was risky from so many different directions.

Su Lin answered calmly and with a tone of resignation on the first ring. "Hello, young one. We seem to only speak these days when there is a problem. I understand that the timing of this could not be worse for you personally. How is your grandfather doing? Any change?"

"Yes and no. He is out of the coma, but not aware, I guess is the best description. At least not yet. Thank you for asking.

"I wanted to discuss your situation and seek your agreement on what we have reviewed and consider our best option for you to..."

Su Lin interrupted, "The best option is for me to secure Andy's release and return to China to help with their digital currency plans. I was hoping you might give me copies of some of the programs which were on the systems I used at the college in

China. I have a few portions which I might also use, but to be honest, I have not even thought about those levels of programming in a very long time. I am weary of this nonsense by Guano and the others, but I cannot have Andy at risk. He needs his medication and his life back. I have intruded enough."

"Su Lin, this is the wrong stance to be taking; however, I am not surprised after all you have been through." Jacob insisted, "Please listen to our proposal and see if it cannot gain us the best of both worlds. You deserve a chance, and from what I understand, Andy would never agree to an exchange if he were in the decision process. He is quite fond of his family, and you are a main part of his family, so please don't throw that away."

Su Lin countered, "I know he would not like it, but I cannot be responsible for permitting him to be hurt again on my account. He is blind, even if temporarily, because of me and my choices many years ago. No amount of changing alters those poor choices. They always come back to haunt the soul.

"However, tell me your ideas. I will listen but no promises."

Jacob spent the next thirty minutes outlining the plans and how the code could be manipulated in their favor. Her contribution to the code change would be to review the changes he would make in the key areas and the encryption layer Petra would build. It would allow them to leverage some of the efforts they had made toward a different project, which would reduce the time to completion.

He then detailed how her negotiations with Guano needed to proceed, with, of course, her insight into the proper methods of negotiation based on Chinese traditions. He indicated the areas she could bend and where she needed to remain firm if the whole plan was to succeed. The first step would be for her to reach out to Guano and open the negotiations. Su Lin needed to agree this was a team effort and not try to go her own path as she'd previously done, as that would make the situation worse.

Su Lin acknowledged, "Your plan is strong, and if you consider the areas I mentioned, I agree we have a chance for returning Andy and letting me return to live my life. It may take a day to reach Guano and start the process, although I suspect he is monitoring us. I will continue to use Andy's phone to call you. You go be with Wolfgang until I get a response back. I promise I will not go off on my own. Can we do that, Jacob?"

"It would make me feel good to have you and your friends on my side. Someday I will figure out how your team is put together and why I seem to be important."

Jacob agreed, "Thank you, Su Lin. I will wait for your response. And perhaps the answer to that question is that you have earned that importance. You are our friend."

Jacob and Petra finally met with the doctor a few hours later.

"Mr. Michaels, Wolfgang is doing better. At this point his hearing is good, and I believe he is seeing. His test results indicate he had both a heart attack and a stroke which combined to make his body very weak. It may be hours or days before he speaks or actually eats solids. He is breathing on his own but still receiving fluids via the tubes until he can eat. If this continues, we may try to get him up in a day or two and see if he has balance issues. For now we want to keep him down and provide some physical therapy to keep his muscles moving. If you want to talk to him and continue to stay in his room, we have no objections. He does seem alert when he hears certain voices, like yours and Bowen's."

"Doctor, that is great news, thank you. I will stay here then, and the family will visit as they can. I appreciate all you're doing for him."

After the doctor left, Petra and Jacob chatted a bit before she headed home. Jacob didn't want to pace, waiting for Su Lin's answer so they could proceed, so he decided reading to Wolfgang was the best course of action.

"Wolfgang, I am so glad you are awake. I hope you don't mind, but I located your books and have been reading to you from them. When you are able to talk, you can help me understand if this is a story you have been writing or something else. We left off from here…"

Tavius tried hard to conceal his sour face at the changed venue. He told himself that his intentions were honorable and that it was only a mid-morning snack at a popular bistro to get to know her better. He struggled with his annoyance at the turn of events and wanted to blurt out that there was no need for a chaperone. His annoyance won out.

Tavius achieved the most polite terms possible as he stated, "What the hell are you doing here, Ferdy? I don't remember inviting you to join Patrycja and me for coffee. Perhaps I should point out that this table only seats two, so why don't you just withdraw?"

Undeterred, Ferd simply confiscated a nearby chair and joined them. After a moment of awkward silence between the two men, Ferd flatly stated, "You know, I've learned to tolerate you, somewhat, but no one takes my sister anywhere without at least asking my permission. Since you did not approach this properly, I must conclude questionable intentions. Now you get a chaperone, my socially incompetent friend."

Patrycja, amused by the dialogue, interjected, " Actually, I invited Ferdy, Tavius. He is here to protect you, not me, just so you know."

Tavius gave Patrycja an incredulous look that made her smile broadly. Even Ferd was somewhat confused by the statement.

She continued, "I think it makes sense that a wounded hero be guarded from the unscrupulous advances of unrestrained females. Your honor should remain intact. Thus, I have Ferdy here to defend your honor. I can fend for myself, thank you very much."

Now both men were staring, puzzled at Patrycja's comments.

Finally Tavius calmly offered, "Madam, I'm not sure I understand your hero comments. It is very likely that you have your facts attributed incorrectly..."

Unwilling to back down in the discussion, Patrycja interrupted, "How exactly did you hurt your back, such that your gate is somewhat affected?"

Tavius, now feeling somewhat vulnerable, began to lose his composure and lamely offered, "I was moving furniture for my parents not long ago, and their piano got away from me which..."

Again Patrycja cut Tavius off. "You know the Army should have been a little more forthcoming with the botched demonstration, but they weren't. An impromptu entourage of visiting dignitaries showed up, and some bonehead commander wanted to demonstrate the combat efficiencies of one of his units.

"As I understand it, the unit was hastily assembled and told to attack the practice bunker while everyone watched. It was really too bad that your platoon didn't have practice dummy ordinances to play act with. But you didn't. When the grenade got away from the nervous, newly- enlisted man, it rolled right back into the crowd of dignitaries.

"*They would have all been killed, except you had the presence of mind to chase the grenade and throw it out of harm's way. You should have ducked as well, but instead, after throwing it, you lunged at the dignitaries to get them to ground. For your bravery, you got the shrapnel in your back and three months in the hospital, trying to learn how to walk again.*"

Ferd was staring incredulously at Tavius. Stunned at her telling of the story, Tavius still managed to say, "A very engaging story, madam, but I can assure you they are someone else's exploits. You simply have me confused with…"

Patrycja, undeterred and unwilling to yield to Tavius's claim, continued, "The papers were going to write up the event. The Army didn't want the publicity and associated questioning of how real ordinances were being used. In fact, they were going to pin the whole event on you and drum you out of the army.

"The Ambassador argued that you would not be blamed for the event, or he would open a formal, highly publicized inquiry to ascertain where the blame should lie. I guess it was a good thing that the Ambassador was one of those people you saved. The whole episode was quietly silenced with the undisputed understanding that you retain your rank. Then, after your convalescence, you would be transferred to the Ambassador's staff as one of his communications officers."

Ferd could barely swallow from astonishment at the tale, but Tavius smirked slightly and said, "Madam, an excellent tale of someone else's exploits. Sounds like a lot of folks have a debt of gratitude to this individual. I'm sorry I cannot claim to be…"

Patrycja's eyes were blazing with emotion, and cutting him off one last time, she explained, "You do know that I do ALL the filing here in the office of the Ambassador. There is very little that I don't know. M. Octavius Rancowski, I am quite sure you are that man. I, for one, am very pleased to meet you."

Tavius cut his stare between the charged state of Patrycja and the astonished look of Ferd, then chuckled slightly and offered, "Madam, I would have to say that I am glad Ferd is here to help defend me! Yes, I stand accused and am guilty as charged. This story is not something I like to discuss. I would rather move on and enjoy life to its fullest, having come so close to losing it."

Staring intently at Tavius, Patrycja smiled broadly and added, "Ferdy, would you excuse us, please? I want to visit with Tavius over coffee, and I don't believe we need a chaperone."

Ferd abruptly stood up, bowed slightly to both of them, and left without saying a word. As he left, Patrycja could be heard asking, "So may I know what the letter M stands for at the beginning of your name, sir?"

Ferd was unable to hear the response as he briskly walked away.

Jacob glanced at Wolfgang and saw his mouth set in a small smile, even as his eyes were closing in sleep. After he put the book away, as that one was now finished, he walked over and smoothed Wolfgang's hair and patted his arm.

"I think that is enough for right now, Wolfgang. This is a remarkable view into something: a story, a history, or a combination. I'm fascinated and so want to speak with you about it soon. You rest now and gather your strength. I love you."

While Jacob waited for Su Lin to call, he silently read through the first part of the next book, which described the trio completing their mission and actually escaping with their families to Switzerland. Their escape was itself remarkable but being able to take a copy of the German Embassy Enigma Cipher Machine with them was astonishing. The notation in the book indicated the three men were able to place the original stolen Enigma Machine on the last plane out to England just as the Germans marched into Poland. Discussions around activities during the war had always been redirected to honorable behaviors and looking at the right versus wrong aspects of any assignment. The other details had remained in the background. If any of these books were true, then the risks and rewards of the three men were far more intense than he would ever have imagined.

CHAPTER 35

Social Engineering

Mathias was completely focused on the pending meeting. He constantly reassured himself of his presentation materials, double checked his digital currency demo program, and mentally rehearsed his dialogue so as to be spot on for this most important meeting. Dutch on the other hand was completely focused on the office babe, Genesis. He kept telling himself he was staring at her eyes, and he almost believed it.

Mathias grumbled a little as he looked at his watch for the third time in 10 minutes. "I shouldn't have let you talk me into getting here so early. We've still got a whole hour left to wait."

Without moving his studying efforts off of Genesis, Dutch replied, "You said this was an important meeting, and people respect prompt and early when delivering the final pitch. She alerted them when we arrived, so I know it was registered as good manners. If we had gotten here late, how would that have looked to Alejandro? He would have been embarrassed in front of his colleagues, so just suck it up."

Mathias sourly noted, "Oh yes, mister deal maker, scoping out the office babe. With the amount of time we still have to wait, you'll have enough time for some drinks before attempting your 'feeding time at the zoo' game. All you have to do is get her to role-play the lion while you throw her the meat."

Although they thought she was out of ear shot, Genesis smirked a little as she commented, "Gentlemen, your early arrival is both commendable and flattering to our department. I've just been notified that Alejandro is having some scheduling difficulty with some of his peers and needs to push the meeting back by an hour. He has asked that I help make you comfortable during this time delay and asked that I entertain you."

Mathias was clearly irked by the delay, but Dutch practically jumped to her desk to apply all the wit and charm he could deliver.

With very little concealed enthusiasm, Dutch asked, "When you say entertain, what exactly does that mean here in your beautiful country?"

Genesis went into a flirtatious mode of epic proportions. Mathias watched in disbelief as she reached out to touch and caress his jawline, all the while eyeing him with a mischievous look on her face.

She provocatively asked, "What is it that you gentlemen have that is sooo important that I can't know the nature of your work? It keeps me at such a disadvantage. How can we know each other better if there is no exchange of information? I promise to be discreet with everything entrusted to me. I swear to be silent about anything that should pass between us."

Dutch was practically undone with the invitation and blurted, "We are here to save your country! We bring the next generation of cryptocurrency that will take Venezuela to the top of the superpowers! You will climb out of poverty, and your country will set the standard of economic envy around the world!"

Mathias was dumbfounded at the scene. Not only was Dutch completely taken in by her feminine wiles, he was giving the store of goods away to some lowly secretary. But before he could reel in the situation, it changed again to his utter astonishment.

Smiling, Genesis led Dutch around her desk to where she was seated and promptly hiked her dress up so that he could see she wasn't wearing any panties. His momentary shock was overcome when she pulled him down in between her legs and suggested, "Here in Venezuela, we enjoy first meetings if they address a fundamental need. You have charm and character, that is true, but tell me, how are you at satisfying a female? Now, show me how you intend to save me." Dutch, now under her hypnotic spell, fell to his knees and began greedily licking her, desperately hoping to satisfy her enough to get to his end goal. Emboldened, he tried to reach up and get to her breasts but his hand was slapped firmly as she commanded, "No, the girls bruise so easily, and you need to focus on only one thing right now."

Even Mathias missed the entrance of Alejandro, who startled everyone with his booming comment. "What on earth is going on here?"

Genesis' mood was terminated immediately, but Dutch's erection wasn't so easily turned off. Mathias, with his eyes closed, took a deep breath, now almost certain the whole project was doomed.

Dutch, standing and trying to cover his excited state, exclaimed, "A thousand pardons, Mr. Noya, but I was merely demonstrating how friendly our cultural relations would be if our cryptocurrency product was introduced here to your country. Ms. Genesis was most eager to learn all the, uh…subtleties of digital economics, and, well, I…always like to instruct when asked by someone to learn something new."

Now recomposed, Genesis innocently asked, "Mr. Noya, are you ready to receive these men now?"

Alejandro smiled slightly as he turned to Mathias and bluntly stated, "During our discussions with the other ministers of Venezuela, you will generously offer another 2% points to my government as a show of, hmmm, shall we say, good faith?"

Mathias ground his teeth at having been conned out of two additional points because they had been so cleverly manipulated by Alejandro and Genesis.

Mathias felt like the presentation in favor of cryptocurrency to the Venezuelan directors was gaining traction, after the near disastrous beginning. They were now three hours into what was scheduled as only a two hour discussion. Each of the directors nodded in agreement to the proof points he had outlined. Even Alejandro seemed to be embracing the offer. Mathias was ready to play his final trump card.

"Gentlemen, we have presented our case and our technology as comprehensively as possible and to your request for succinctness. I must say, travel throughout your country and our exposure to your culture has warmed us in ways we had not expected. After a series of deliberations with my team, but mostly as a gesture to the future of our adopted country, launching into the digital age, we would like to reduce our initial funding from 9% to 7%. We feel this will demonstrate our goodwill and confidence in the project as well as the country. I hope you will accept the discount in the spirit it is being offered."

Mathias cut his eyes at Dutch as he sat down from the presentation. Dutch caught the angry look but did nothing more than swallow hard. He was pretty sure the discount was coming out of his cut.

Trying to get a consensus, Alejandro quietly spoke with the other directors. Most were nodding in agreement, and some were smiling broadly. Finally, as it looked like everyone was on board with the project, Alejandro dropped a verbal hand grenade into the discussion.

Alejandro said, "Thank you, Mathias, for your research into our needs and how best to serve them with your cryptocurrency. We appreciate your forethought about leveraging our oil and gas reserves in the first round of the cryptocurrency launch, and the added bonus of marketing our Vanadium into the battery market for electric cars and such. Even your Chinese competitors had not thought that far in advance.

"But, you were both spot on in not delivering an absolutely anonymous cryptocurrency, since we would not be able to control capital flight or criminals using our new monetary system. You were both in agreement to launch a cryptocurrency as the legal tender with this government but retain the hard currency for the ordinary citizen for a while until the cryptocurrency gained full acceptance. Wise recommendations."

Mathias tried not to flinch at the unexpected news that another entity was pitching the same type of solution. Dutch's mouth fell open, but he had the presence of mind not to speak. It took a few moments before Mathias felt he could speak without his voice cracking.

Based on the revelation, some of the warmth was lost from his tone, but he managed, "We would expect that as stewards of your country, you would seek an alternative supplier to help chart you through this transition. May I know if there is something I can do, or further explain, to help prejudice you in our favor?"

Alejandro smiled slyly and stated, "You would understand that the Chinese government was very accommodating with their sovereign offer of their cryptocurrency and were only looking for a 4% fee of the initial offering, which also includes several trade agreements that frankly you are not in a position to match."

Dutch looked up at Mathias with an angry look of disbelief, but Mathias coolly replied, "It is true that we do not come bearing trade agreements, but that is immaterial. The Chinese need to import oil and are trying to go to electric cars, so your Vanadium wealth is key to their present and their future. Tell me, you didn't squander your trade advantage with a customer who can't do without your exports?"

It was a sobering moment for Alejandro, who said nothing. Before he could respond, Mathias continued, "And, let me guess, they didn't have a finished, ready-made product to demo for you as my team has done, did they? If they had, you would have had no real reason to meet with us."

Dutch was now in wonderment, trying to grasp all of the discussion points as Mathias pointedly added, "Now we come down to it, gentlemen. They offered you trade deals that took needed profits from your country, they gave you a huge discount to deal with them, but they don't have a finished product to go head-to-head with us. Do you only see that as a wish and a promise for your country's future, when the timetables do not favor waiting any longer than absolutely necessary, based on your restless population?"

Mathias, trying to deliver his best heartfelt speech, continued, "Gentlemen, we came to help this country with a well-designed cryptocurrency product that is available now, not sometime in the future. You undoubtedly are aware that the Chinese do NOT have a viable product currently, nor will they for the next 6 to 12 months. You know why we know this? Because they offered to buy our intellectual property and build an electronic trap door into it. We said no to their generous offer because then we couldn't help a country like yours!

"However, if you wish to wait for their digital currency offering, deprive your friends, family, and country of a work-able solution for economic recovery as we have proposed, and be owned by the Chinese technical infection that will surely come with their product, then allow us to close this meeting and leave, kind sirs. If we cannot help, because our help is not wanted, then of course we will depart. We hold no grudges and wish your country the very best."

Mathias, determined to play out his position, motioned to the dumbfounded Dutch to collect their things and go. Paying no attention to the near frantic chatter between the directors, Mathias and Dutch moved purposefully to the door and promptly left. Dutch didn't even try to make eye contact with Genesis as they marched out.

Once outside the building, Dutch asked, "The Chinese asked to buy our product? How come I didn't know about that?"

Mathias smiled bitterly as he stated, "Two can play the social engineering game."

CHAPTER 36

Play By the Rules
or Go Home

After reading the report from Otto several times, Tonya finally felt comfortable enough to re-engage with Petra. She dialed the number Petra had provided, then followed the instructions to leave a detailed message before she disconnected. The last thing Tonya wanted to invoke was the wrath of Petra. Her skin was still flaming from the verbal inferno Director Ingrid had inflicted after Tonya's stupidly misguided negotiation attempt on Otto's payment. In this arena, she was definitely not the lion nor the gladiators that were cast into the ancient Coliseum, but she was fighting for her life within this organization. Thirty minutes later, the incoming call held no number or name, yet she connected.

"Good afternoon, Tonya," Petra greeted, "I'm sorry I was unable to answer earlier, but I was in the midst of completing a task. Rest assured I have reviewed your information, including the final piece uploaded to the secure location yesterday evening. It appears you have been busy. How may I help?"

Tonya realized she wasn't going to get admonished for anything and let out a relieved sigh and replied, "I totally understand, we are all busy. I appreciate you taking the time to get everything reviewed. I had a few questions I was hoping you would help with if you have time."

"Of course."

Tonya took a breath and asked, "Do you think the case I made for adoption of a cryptocurrency program has any merit?"

Petra paused and then offered, "I believe your case has a great starting point for your organization. Clarification on the encryption and anonymity needs better definition. I can write a rock-solid encryption algorithm once you decide which program you want to move forward with, unless you are planning to build from scratch.

"It was very clear that you have a strong bias toward cryptocurrency, but the safeguards needed are ongoing efforts for the long term and should be present from day one. Whatever product you launch, it must be bulletproof up front. Releasing a 1.0 version and then having to follow it with a 2.0 version to fix the problems unearthed is completely ridiculous. The daily number of new avenues for cryptocurrency investors are almost equally matched to those that are failing. It is a very unstable market at this point. Make no mistake, it is here to stay, but how viable it is for true buying and selling of goods and services versus simply an investment lark is, at the best, speculation."

Tonya wasn't sure how to respond. Only a small part of her agreed. "I do believe we should take a stand in support of this capability and soon. It would be far better for us to have regulations in place rather than to allow the Darknet expert hackers to set the rules."

Petra laughed and commented, "Really, Tonya, you aren't that naïve, are you?

"The Darknet is filled with variations of cryptocurrency used for illicit underground transactions. Part of the reason this is getting so much traction, especially focused on the anonymity aspects, is that their illegal activities would be untraceable. Digital transformation is the direction businesses and consumers are taking, but many are simply desensitized to the risks of moving so quickly into this new world. The investments required to move securely into this digitized world are simply not being made in advance of the adoption of the technology."

Tonya complained, "Are you saying that building the case for our adoption of cryptocurrency is being done without due diligence? That is why I have you engaged as an encryption guru. I'm not afraid to tell you I don't know this technology or how the safeguards should be designed."

Petra stated, "I realize you don't know the technology. I'm trying to educate you, as is the report you sent to me. This complex issue is not going to find a simple immediate answer. You, however, need to define the parameters of how your organization might approach it.

"For example, do you want to identify who is making the transaction and if they are doing something illegal? If that is proven, is prosecuting the goal? Do you want citizens to do the same with digital currency that they are able to do with fiat currency? Do you want to avoid the hackers from getting the actual customer information? Where do you want control? These are the answers I need in order to help build the framework for you to use with cryptocurrency."

Tonya whined, "Why can't you make that recommendation and then create the safeguards needed? Of course we would expect it to behave like regular currency. It is simply easier to use."

"Which brings up another great point, Tonya. What are the services and taxes that the public will bear for this? Profits make the world go round, regardless of the types of currency exchanges used."

Petra debated with herself a moment before she offered, "Allow me to provide one more insight into your request. On the surface, this effort of yours looks like an undisciplined effort of smart money trying to follow in quickly behind the dumb money. The trailblazers create markets with revolutionary products, they usually stumble or simply run out of funding, and then the big institutions scoop up the choice pieces, after which they rewrite history to highlight their intuition and foresight. Now if that is all your organization is interested in, then we should disengage. But if you are genuinely interested in spawning a healthy, well-designed financial architecture, then we can continue."

Tonya, chastened, swallowed hard and nodded in ascent before she offered, "While I may not understand all the subtleties you have put forth, we're only interested in building a solid next generation financial architecture for the planet. We are not cruel profit hunters in this all-important game, Ms. Rancowski."

They continued to discuss the possible avenues where safeguards should be placed, the regulations required, and the overall operational management with ongoing governance. Finally some agreements were made and directions taken. Tonya had a fair amount of items to complete, and Petra had some ideas she wanted to discuss with Jacob.

"Petra, I appreciate your working through this with me. I think I understand some of the landmines we need to insure against. Let me get some answers to these items and get back with you in a couple of days. I will send them along to the secure Drop Vault and call the number, if that is agreeable."

"I think that will work, Tonya. I feel you are grasping the complexities better than before. Go ahead and quit for the evening. Have a mimosa!"

Tonya turned twenty shades of red as the call disconnected. Apparently her indiscretion had not been forgotten.

Petra finished up her notes from the call and went in search of Quip. The data center was very quiet, and it was far later than she had realized. Quip must have gone home already. Petra called Jacob. He was at the hospital and looking forward to having dinner with her there. Wolfgang had been in and out of sleep throughout the day but was clearly resting now. Jacob indicated he would have Bowen pick her up with food and drive her to the hospital. She wrapped up her notes and packed away her laptop.

As she gathered her final accoutrements to leave, the high definition screen in her office flickered and changed from screensaver to a sea of currency symbols from across the globe.

"Mistress Petra," the current voice of ICABOD said, "following the money is key to the location of many criminals. Greed plays a very large part in human psychology, but it seems to be only valuable for a short time, with lots of downside as it is discovered. Is Tonya driven by greed?"

"Interesting question, ICABOD. I think she is driven to be successful, but not at the expense of everything else. She simply has a narrow frame of reference, but I suppose that anyone can be turned for enough money or fame."

"When do you think Wolfgang will play chess again and discuss human nature more with me? His perspective is different than Dr. Quip's, as he always looks at the money trail.

"I have been trying to apply his logic as we are running these traces. There are several questionable parties now investing in Dr. Quip's cryptocurrency which I have flagged for your next group discussion."

"Thank you, ICABOD, I will let Jacob know when I see him. I will pass along the message about the chess game too. Perhaps Jacob and you could consider a game or two."

Petra and Bowen walked together to deliver the food. Bowen wanted to see Wolfgang even if he was asleep. Earlier in the day, Bowen had come in and saw Wolfgang with his eyes open. It had enabled the current bounce in Bowen's step, she suspected. They set up the food, and everyone talked as if Wolfgang was awake and a part of the conversation. The doctors had all said this would be best. Bowen combed Wolfgang's hair and said as he left, he would return in the morning to give him a shave. Jacob and Petra both sat down to eat.

Jacob smiled and said, "It is nice to see you, sweetheart. How was your day?"

"It was good. I had a discussion and planning session with Tonya. She understood most of the report that Otto provided but fell short on creating the guidelines for consideration of crypto-currency adoption. You know how different the thought process needs to be in a digital versus a physical environment. Currency is placed into a vault and the accounting of it is done by automated programs. Her logic flow is not changing for everything to be on automated programs.

"How was your day? Did you get a chance to make the program changes that Quip outlined?"

"I did, but there is something missing even if we maintain the user information, and that is avoiding the hacker. Any great ideas cross your pretty little mind?"

Petra smiled as she savored another bite of the perfectly prepared Chicken Kiev. She finished the bite, patted her lips with her napkin, and said, "I had an idea I wanted to run by you. What if we could trigger a ransomware program based on the user identity. Background information identifies this user as one known to associate with the darker underbelly of the world or has a record of certain crimes, and the ransomware is a trigger to download and sit on the user station until an infraction is identified. It might help maintain the accountability and minimize the general consumer risk."

Jacob sat back and absorbed the idea. "If we do that, how do we insure that those who are innocent are not affected by that program? It makes sense from several avenues. Let's discuss with Quip tomorrow. For the rest of the evening, I'd like to simply enjoy your company. We haven't spent a lot of time together lately."

"I am good with that, honey. We could sip the wine that Bowen hid in the thermos."

"Geez, you're just telling me that now?"

CHAPTER 37

Playing with Fire is Always Dangerous

Su Lin finally had a number to connect with Guano. It was so distasteful to have to negotiate with the man, but she would do what needed to be done. In her life, she had certainly battled worse than him and survived.

When the call connected, she said, "Colonel, it was gracious of you to finally agree to talk with me. How is my husband? I would like to speak to him to make certain he is alright before we take our discussion any further."

Guano sounded pleased as he replied, "Before I begin to negotiate with you, do you have the programs I need to complete my assignment? If not, I can just dispose of him now, and you can know it was your fault. All of his pain could have been avoided if you had simply come with me originally. He would have forgotten about you by now in favor of a more agreeable female. Now I have fallen comrades and a mess to explain when I get home."

Su Lin smiled a bit, realizing Guano must still be on U.S. soil. A slip in her favor. She let the air grow heavy with silence before she quietly responded, "I know I am at great fault for his pain. I am not worthy of someone as kind and noble as he. It is because of this alone that I will come with you when he is released. There is nothing left for me here. I have dishonored him.

"I do not have the code, as I split the programs and secured them in two different manners. The key portion is on a thumb drive in a bank safety deposit box. This safety deposit box is one of a pair that my husband and I have. It requires both of us to open it, except in the case of either of our deaths, at which time an attorney can be the other party. Therefore, I will need Andy to go with me to the bank to get the code."

Guano suspiciously stated, "How very convenient, Master Po. You expect me to hand over your husband to you just like that. I would never get the code. He may be blind, but I am not."

Su Lin quietly submitted, "I can understand why you would think that, Colonel, but it is the fastest way for you to get what you want. The alternative is to get our attorney to go into court and have a judge allow the attorney to take on the role as Andy is too ill to do it himself. When I posed this to my attorney, he said plan on four to six weeks, and we could get that legal document to get into the safety deposit box."

Guano angrily stated, "I can remove a finger or two to allow you to get past a fingerprint security system."

Su Lin replied, "It is not that sort of system in this local bank. My husband is well known, and they are used to seeing us together for our financial transactions. He must walk in with me to complete the sequence and enter his code." She let that hang for a few minutes, then coyly added, "Or, I will contact the attorney, and start the process. I will get back to you no later than six weeks, perhaps sooner."

"What is the location of this bank of yours? It may take me a day or two to return to the area. Plus, I need some insurance that you will follow through on your side."

"The bank is in Alpharetta, Georgia. I can send you a text with the address. It is a small local bank.

"Now, may I speak to my husband, Colonel?"

The exasperated expel of air by Guano was soon followed by the voice she longed to hear. "Su Lin, honey, are you alright? They have a medic with them who has tried to keep me comfortable, though I am cobbled. Plus my sight has not returned, but the headaches are better."

Su Lin was so grateful to hear his voice, but needed to insure that she continued in her role as Guano was likely listening. "Andy, I am fine. EZ, Ernie, and the ranch are all fine and secure. I am glad these men are taking care of you. You need to understand that the Colonel and I have some unfinished business, which I had forgotten about. It is totally my error. I am sorry you have been put into the middle of this. Please forgive me.

"You will recall, in one of our safety deposit boxes at the bank, I placed a few items I wanted kept safe. There is a thumb drive that actually belongs to the Colonel. I am trying to get him to trust me enough to get you and me through the security issues so that we can access the safety deposit box. Once we retrieve this data device, I will need to work with the Colonel for a short period of time for the Jacob program to be completed. That is the name I had given the project. You will of course support my obligation so that I can restore honor to us."

Andy did not need a picture to understand what she was doing. He knew her well, and they had discussed much of her past while in the hospital together. He didn't like the idea, but he recognized her reference to having the support and backup necessary for the project's success.

Andy nodded his head and quietly decided, "I would like to go home with you and have you work remotely, but if your presence is needed, I understand. I don't like it but I do understand. I love you, Su Lin, honey. It will be alright."

Su Lin winced as a few tears escaped from her eyes. "I love you too, Andy. This is the only way to make this work quickly. Let me finalize things with the Colonel. Please do as he asks."

Su Lin and the Colonel discussed the timing for three days from now for the exchange. For how this could be done, she provided two options, and he picked the one he wanted, though he reserved the right to change his options later after a review of the site. Su Lin also alerted him that his henchmen had been taken to the county coroner, and Homeland Security had been alerted. They scheduled a conversation for two days from now.

CHAPTER 38

Modern Currency, an Old Problem

Petra almost spilled her coffee at the unexpected sound of ICABOD's voice as he asked, "Mistress Petra, are you prepared to discuss my new findings?"

Petra, still trying to recover from her startled state, put the coffee cup down and said, "ICABOD, you know I hate being snuck up on, right? But now that I think of it, you really don't sneak up on anybody, you're just everywhere in here. How silly of me to think I would enjoy my first cup of coffee before anyone showed up. I realize we can't tie a bell around your neck to alert us, but how about some contextual clues suggesting your presence so I don't bathe myself in a hot morning beverage?"

ICABOD delayed his response long enough to allow the sound of a small bell, growing in volume, as he quietly and with a tone of regret stated, "Mistress Petra, ICABOD approaches and is prepared to submit to disciplinary action for my transgression. However, I am curious why my soft approach to greeting you is construed differently from Jacob's when he quietly approaches you from behind with amorous intent…"

Petra somewhat indignantly interrupted, "ICABOD, that's different, okay! Let's not try to read in too much to the different greeting techniques and start over again. What was the first topic that you originally startled me to convey?"

Returning to the beginning topic, ICABOD offered, "Since Dr. Quip is not here, I thought we might explore some of the cryptocurrency issues that are important to a proper deployment; the concept of the mining servers being deployed such that they must communicate with each other, regardless of how many there are, and that the communication must be over a secure channel. If they are truly distributed, then they are accessible on the Internet which by definition means they are vulnerable to attack. If they are completely air-gapped, then they cannot participate in the information exchange, so logic dictates they either sit directly on the Internet with high exposure or they reside behind a firewall or proxy server to have communications sanitized, or so my logic goes."

Petra slid into the thought stream and added, "Good point. If they have to be reachable from the Internet, then they're vulnerable. If the transactions are not completely anonymous, then identities could be derived. Further, by using an IP address mapping exercise, the parties could be located."

ICABOD continued, "Correct, Mistress Petra. Dr. Quip and I have been doing some discreet probing in this area, and we have built a methodology to uncover the supposedly anonymous transaction parties for further investigation. Apparently the U.S. Secret Service and other covert operations have already exploited this little known fact to track down some very high profile targets. We too can accomplish the same thing. To that end, Chesterfield's missing funds are now coming onto the market through our new cryptocurrency exchange. Apparently, we have some new bad actors on the digital currency stage."

Petra queried, "You indicated the missing funds are coming online, but not all, correct?

"Then I would expect they are dribbling them out to minimize their profile and also to leverage dollar cost averaging to their benefit. With the currency valuation going up, they will see more value with a slow sell off."

ICABOD then added, "Of course, if the valuation begins to plummet, then they might be incented to sell before their cryptocurrency lost all its value."

Petra smiled a devious smile and concluded, "If something were to happen that drove the cryptocurrency valuation to zero, they might panic and try to dump their stolen funds, which would help us to center on their location."

ICABOD paused a moment and then stated, "Mistress Petra, you have exactly the same look on your face as when Jacob is nuzzling on your neck and reaching for..."

Petra quickly commanded, "Okay, ICABOD, we need to tee-up this new plan to intercept the stolen funds. Let's get Dr. Quip in here so we can discuss an idea that just occurred to me."

ICABOD promptly responded, "I will summon him, madam."

Quip rushed into the work area of the data center but was obviously distracted. Somewhat winded, he commented, "Good morning! I got here as quickly as I could, but you may have to repeat your conversation a couple of times because I have the Su Lin issue on my mind."

Petra interjected, "ICABOD mentioned something about the distribution of the mining servers typically configured for optimum cryptocurrency architecture, like in these drawings.

With more servers the transaction lag time will trend upwards as more participants and greater numbers of transactions occur. Also, more servers means a larger attack surface for the standard type of offering. What if we propose fewer miner servers, but place them in the hardened data bunkers of the sovereign nation's infrastructure. Quip, wouldn't this deliver a better, more insulated cryptocurrency?"

Quip nodded thoughtfully and said, "Now you have my full attention." Then he visually focused on the drawings up on the monitors and added, "Fewer servers behind heavily reinforced DMZs with firewall/proxy appliances to sanitize incoming traffic from the public, but high speed encrypted tunnels between the data center mining servers for insulated transactional updates. That should minimize the hacking risk. Good idea."

ICABOD speculated, "That does give us an alternative infrastructure but does not address the issue referred to as Knowledge of Zero Awareness Proof anonymizing technology, or K-ZAP. With completely anonymous transactions at the heart of the cryptocurrency, the average citizen would be comfortable knowing there is no snooping by the government. But the same would apply to the criminal element.

"However, if the cryptocurrency is released with a pseudo-anonymous architecture, then at least the government could obtain some moderate control over financial transactions if properly established by due process of law. The criminal element, and even many segments of the population, would resist that sort of implied surveillance and thus impede the adoption of the new financial infrastructure."

Petra countered, "Where would you find enough processing power to sift through all the transactions of a sovereign nation, much less the entire world, if the governments were granted access? We are talking about a trillion-dollar GDP, and who knows how much black market and Darknet value there is to be added to that? Saying that a government is going to watch for suspicious transactions is like saying, 'Hey, let's boil the ocean so we can have a bowl of jambalaya.'"

Quip chuckled and said, "It looks like we're back to the old carrot-and-stick routine. If I were running the cryptocurrency program for a sovereign, I would maintain that law-abiding citizens would have nothing to fear from pseudo-anonymous architecture based on due process of law, and the tradeoff is worth it to snag the bad guys. Then I would launch a covert operation to crater all competing digital currency providers while touting how safe mine was. Conduct a couple of flash-crashes, arrest a couple of high profile but definitely shady cryptocurrency punks, and poison the rest with highly specialized malware that locks up your crypto account until you pay the ransom of 50%. After a while my product would look like a safe haven."

ICABOD noted, "Dr. Quip, you appear to have that same faraway look Mistress Petra displayed earlier which earned me a reprimand. May I report on the cryptocurrency malware program that Jacob and I have been collaborating on, or would you prefer he be included in the discussion?"

Petra gave them each a quizzical look before Quip chuckled and responded, "Jacob and I discussed the notion of a trap door in the Su Lin C-C program, but we morphed the scope to not create a back door, but instead install an innocuous malware hook. This hook would be designed to pass any test but allow us to ship chunks of code to the hook that would then allow it to manufacture its own malware program from other programs on the same drive. Once built, the program would encrypt the user's hard drive with a kind offer to unlock for a fee payable in the local cryptocurrency held in stock."

Petra grinned as she asked, "Knowing you as I do, you are now ready to do a proof of concept, so let me guess—you would like to practice on the digital currency end points now unloading Chesterfield's stolen funds?"

Quip, too widely grinning, replied, "Practicing is a bit too gentle of a concept. I rather like the term expropriate. Much more fitting, don't you think?"

CHAPTER 39

From the Frying Pan to the Fire

...The Enigma Chronicles

Coordinating all the programs and their locations had been an almost 48 hour ordeal. A quick review of the code by Su Lin resulted in a few modest changes, but essentially it was ready to be posted for her access from China.

Ernie had gone outside to take care of the evening chores, while EZ and Su Lin sat down for a small meal.

EZ looked thoughtful as she suggested, "Would it be of any use if I went with you to the exchange area? That way I can make certain Dad is not left alone for too long. Honestly, I think you both need to remain here after Dad is released. Let me simply…"

Su Lin offered a small smile and stated, "Quite clearly, you are your father's daughter, but no. You can't kill these people, and there will be more than one. It is not the ones you can see, but the ones you can't see that are the danger. The first target would be Andy if for no other reason than to make me suffer. They know if I do not think Andy is safe, they will not get the program they want. This is a fairly basic step.

"Step two is to make it work with verifiable proof points. But after that I am fairly certain my valued status will evaporate, and it will be anybody's guess as to how long I will have. I believe we have a plan to mitigate that issue if our timing is flawless. There is even a scenario where I get extracted from China, but that may only be wishful thinking."

Then, with a slight chuckle, Su Lin wistfully added, "Apparently, your optimism is contagious, my dear EZ."

She continued, "You are allowed to be at a distance where you have high ground advantage to watch the exchange and then retrieve Andy with the car. They want me to walk in so they can look all around for traps. What you are proposing is not a part that we can risk. I must know Andy is safe when I leave with them. You will be tracking me, until they start the flight. The tracker capsule I swallow, when I exit the car, will stay with me for nearly two days. From there, I will use my instincts which, despite some recent issues, have been good for some time. They do not want me hurt before they get their results."

Shaking her head with a sense of resignation, EZ promised, "I will get Dad, as we discussed, and immediately take him to the hospital for a once over. I will get his medicines updated and make certain that he stays as calm as possible. If there is something critical regarding his health, we will have the authorities stop and detain you, all based on the signal from you. Otherwise, you will be left alone to finish this. Khalid will do the driving, and Ernie will stay here at the ranch. Yes, I know the plan. I don't like it, but I know it.

"You promise, they will not have any way of uncovering your deceit before it is finished?"

"EZ, they think I'm smart but, for the most part, have no respect for me. Women are fifth class at the very most. They will think I am doing my job and afraid they will come back again.

With any luck when I am done, they will never try to come back at us. I will end this and hopefully do a very good thing in the process. I just want Andy to truly be better, no matter what."

Ernie came in and smiled as he said, "The animals are all settled in for the night. I am happy to report that Franklin has resumed eating and squealed happily at the treat at the bottom of his bowl. I swear that big 'ol hog knows when you have sent him a surprise. I have the other 60 set aside to dole out to him if he seems to be off his feed. Doc said he is all but recovered from saving our bacon."

Su Lin looked at Ernie gratefully and replied, "Thank you, Ernie. I know he is in safe hands. Play the CD every other day too, and he should be fine. I will see to him as we are leaving out in the morning."

Su Lin paused a moment and then added, "And thank you for that little trick you helped with this morning. Guano wouldn't let Andy out of his control to pick up the needed items from the safety deposit box, so thank you for pretending to be Andy. The bandage helped, and having you stay in the car with EZ present helped insure the bank officials were satisfied. While somewhat unethical, it was safer that way since I'm fairly sure Andy would have pushed the situation to everyone's disadvantage. This way, there is only the exchange now to deal with, which should be safer for him."

Ernie grinned and added, "It's a good thing they didn't inspect me too closely. I'm not as big as Andy, so sitting in the car helped disguise that deficiency. Although, I must admit, if we have many more of those terrific barbeques of yours, that won't be a problem because, as Andy would say, 'I'll be fatter than a forty-pound robin.'"

While everyone grinned, Su Lin only managed a weak smile.

CHAPTER 40

First, the Bad News...

As the information being delivered on the call kept deteriorating, the Chinese Finance Minister found it increasingly difficult to contain his anger. He finally asked, "What do you mean, they want to see a demo? How the hell are we supposed to demo how 1s and 0s are used to create cryptocurrency? We have given them our assurances and promised to pay a modest premium for their crude, plus favored trade status. Now they want to see a damn demo? I thought you said this was under control! What does 'under control' mean in your world?"

The junior diplomat, sensing the Finance Minister was highly agitated, cheerfully offered, "Minister, it is only a show of good faith the Venezuelans are asking for. They asked to see how a transaction would be processed so they could compare it to our competitor's product. I would be happy to do a scheduled demo for them, sir."

There was a long pause in the dialogue before the Finance Minister flatly conveyed, "You do understand that we don't have a working demo yet, right? Now, I sent you there to secure the Venezuelans as a reliable source for natural resources and to adopt our cryptocurrency. How is it that we find ourselves acting like carnival barkers, trying to engage a tourist to play our ring toss game?"

Somewhat taken aback, the junior diplomat pleaded, "But, sir, without a demo I feel certain our position is lost! How can we possibly hold the Venezuelans' interest if we don't have a viable product?"

The Finance Minister snapped, "I didn't say we don't have a viable product! What I said was we don't have a demo right this moment. Now get the situation under control and stall for some time. Do not let this important customer leave for a competitor and don't promise a demo! Currently that is a work in progress, and no, you may not have the details. That is all." With that, the Finance Minister disconnected the call and promptly dialed another number.

As soon as the call connected, the Finance Minister demanded, "Guano, where is my damn cryptocurrency and that bitch that has YOUR life in her hands?"

Guano, receiving the verbal onslaught before even exchanging greetings, unenthusiastically suggested, "Ah, Finance Minister. It is always a bright spot to one's day to have you call to cheer me on. Is this a call about what was discovered by your social media snowflakes? Perhaps your SMS sleuthing has learned what happened to the ex-Chairman's hit-men, Won and Ton?"

Momentarily distracted from his angry tirade, the Finance Minister demanded, "What do you mean? What have you done with them?"

Guano, now playing dangerously close to the edge, replied, "We launched a second offensive attack to secure Master Po and the needed code. We came away with her husband, and she has agreed to trade herself and the code for the husband. However, in the initial foray, Won was killed while Ton escaped with injuries. But he is, as they say, in the wind."

The Finance Minister rocked back into his chair to absorb the new information and asked, "How long before the trade? When will I get my cryptocurrency code and the troublesome Po? You're not going to ask for any more replacements, right?"

In his usual deadpan way, Guano stated, "I am quite sure I will not ask for replacements, apparently, since my definition and your definition vary considerably. The exchange is set for tomorrow, so we will need transport by early afternoon at the designated rendezvous. Your package is that close, Finance Minister."

Not saying anything, the Finance Minister smiled for the first time that day as he disconnected the call.

Mathias screamed, "What do you mean, hold up? The back-stabbing jerks here in Venezuela are going with the sneaky bastard Chinese's cryptocurrency instead of mine? We've blown weeks catering to these clowns, and now you are telling me to hold up on getting out of this hellhole? Just liquidate some C-C so we can get out of here. Now!"

Halvorson closed his eyes and grimaced as Cody watched in a semi-panicked state. After a couple of deep breaths, Halvorson stated, "You might as well know our cryptocurrency holdings are on a machine that is no longer under our control. Apparently, someone or something sniffed our storage machine for having any C-C on it, dropped a ransomware virus on it, and is asking for 50% of the cryptocoins in exchange for releasing the machine back to our control."

Mathias, wild-eyed with rage, could only open his mouth like a bass grappling for an elusive worm instead of the swear words he wanted. Finally, after swallowing enough gulps of air, he replied, "Dammit to hell! Alright, release the 50% that the bastards want, then get me some money so I and Mr. Muff-diver here can come home! You had better track the transaction to the source, because I am going to get my money back. Do you understand?"

Halvorson, shaking with closed eyes, grimaced. After a deep breath he blurted, "Mathias, this is the second time I've done this! The goddam ransomware is eating our digital currency holdings! I've already given them 50%, but the machine locked up again and is demanding another 50%!

"Don't you understand? There is no end to it! Cody and I have been trying to defeat it, but the answer is always the same! Each time we pay, it wants another 50% so there are basically no funds to send you!"

Mathias was dumbfounded at the statement. He muttered, "A ransomware virus has stolen all our cryptocurrency." He looked to Dutch, who clearly understood that all was lost. Mathias slowly shook his head and quietly offered, "All our working capital is lost, and we didn't get to sell our product to the Venezuelan government."

After a few moments Mathias stated, "Halvorson, turn the machine off and do not send them any more money. I may not have it, but they aren't going to get it either. I want you and Cody to try to recreate another machine so we can move the digital wallet from the infected machine to a new one by only copying the needed sectors, not the whole machine. If you can do that, maybe we can get some of our money back."

Halvorson puzzled a moment and then acquiesced, "Not a bad idea if we can do it, but it's gonna take some time."

Mathias frowned and said, "What else have you got to do?"

CHAPTER 41

Which Is It?
Saved By or From
the Government

...The Enigma Chronicles

Quip matter-of-factly stated, "Looks like old Jacob came through again on our efforts. ICABOD, your search and target of cryptocurrency machines, coupled with Jacob's ransom malware program, certainly is a game changer. We got almost all the Chesterfield digital currency back before they realized they would be forfeiting everything. Ha!

"I would have loved to see the looks on their faces when they realized the malware was programmed to keep the system locked and continue to ask for 50%!" Then, upon reflection, Quip thoughtfully stated, "Actually a pretty good business model now that I think about it. Hunt for machines with cryptocurrency on them, drop a ransom malware bomb on it, ask for half of the coins, and stay until you have everything. Hmmm…I wonder if I can get some venture capitalists to fund a model like this. Just think about it. I mean, this is as close to being a government as you can get."

ICABOD commented, "Dr. Quip, I do not believe your early explanation of our charter included conspiring to confiscate people's money and maintaining that we are entitled to be a government. Furthermore, I cannot see where a rational venture capitalist would risk incarceration by funding such a blatantly illegal operation."

A rather sullen Quip almost lamented, "ICABOD, it's no fun playing with you if you're going to pick apart my idle daydreaming thoughts. You are quite correct, that is not our charter, nor should it be. Let's get back to the business at hand."

As Petra entered the data center, ICABOD commented, "Dr. Quip, I have noticed a stress level in your mood that approximates the one in Petra. I believe there is a high correlation to your stress level and Petra's, based on the additional anxiety of having your respective significant other in a non-aligned parabolic course, which does not closely align with each of your mental states."

Petra somewhat indignantly questioned, "Are you saying we're grumpy?"

Quip camped on as well with an angry comment. "Yeah, are you saying we're grumpy?"

ICABOD, selecting his words carefully, added, "I observe that when each of you has your special person in close proximity and are fully engaged with each other, there is a marked decrease in tension. Additionally, I have observed that when your sexual appetites are receiving full reciprocity, your mental states are properly focused on our business problems rather than sniping at your computer. So, yes, you are both grumpy."

Quip made a frowny face and mocked an emotion of abject regret. "I'm so sorry, ICABOD."

Petra, trying to suppress her chuckling while also feigning an apologetic tone, said, "I'm sorry too, ICABOD."

Quip and Petra both looked at each other and simultaneously asked, "Can we get a group hug, ICABOD? We need it."

After a moment's hesitation, ICABOD stated, "I am not sure which is worse, the mocking sarcasm or the grumpiness from you two."

Petra chuckled slightly and warmly offered, "I'm sorry, ICABOD, for being grumpy, and, yes, your observations are correct. How about we dig into the Tonya cryptocurrency paper request for the Global Bank?"

ICABOD stated, "We have retrieved almost all of the missing funds and, by doing so, have proved our pilot program of ransom malware as a weapon to be used against organized crime.

"Dr. Quip and Jacob are putting the finishing touches of the cryptocurrency package with option A and option B for full or partial anonymity baked into the package with a strict adherence to a limited access of the mining servers' backend architecture. We concur that high-speed links between the sovereign data centers and limited exposure to the edge give us the best protection against assault by criminals from the Darknet."

Petra nodded in agreement. "Sounds like the way we discussed it. ICABOD, can you assemble the package, and I will give it the once over before shipping it to Tonya. Great job! Anything else?"

ICABOD quietly inquired, "Now that this is done, do I still get that group hug? I believe my circuits need it."

Petra and Quip both stared blankly at ICABOD's monitor, unable to respond.

Mathias and Dutch sat looking glum, each lost in their own despair caused by their unexpected run of bad luck. Their individual pity party was interrupted by a knock at the door of their hotel room. Both men looked at one another, silently suggesting the other should go to the door. It was the fierce look from Mathias that convinced Dutch to do the chore.

After peering through the peep hole, he turned around, astonished by what he had seen. He shook his head in disbelief as he stared at Mathias. Mathias gave him a puzzled look, but before he could ask anything, Dutch opened the door to the visitors.

Mathias rose and stepped forward to witness Genesis, with two armed military policemen in tow, as she marched confidently into the room. Genesis looked at the modest accommodations before settling into a comfortable chair with something of a bemused smile on her face. With a nod toward an open chair by Genesis, Mathias sat. The two military policemen remained standing, still on guard, but relaxed. Dutch closed the door and moved to join the impromptu meeting.

Mathias had some difficulty keeping the contempt from his voice, but managed in a civil tone, "Uh, won't you come in and have a seat? Are you here on official business, or are you just here to have finished what was left unfinished yesterday?"

Dutch, still smarting from the prior day's episode, was visibly angry at how amateurish he had appeared. Nonetheless, he proceeded to conduct a visual inventory of her.

Genesis smirked and offered, "Alright, it wasn't very sporting of me, I admit. But I got the requested information. Now the rules of engagement have changed. Alejandro Noya has been arrested for crimes against the state. The people I represent would like to re-establish our discussions on your cryptocurrency. Apparently your departing speech, along with your very credible demo, has sparked some lively interest. We would be most grateful for you to join us in continuing that conversation, now."

Mathias and Dutch both felt uneasy in this situation. Mathias warily asked, "Will the same terms we offered be honored, or do your people have something else in mind?"

Genesis smiled knowingly and promised, "I don't do negotiations for the people I represent. I only retrieve that which I am sent for."

Dutch, visibly annoyed at the situation, sarcastically asked, "I hope you are not looking for me to complete our little session since you were obviously only acting. I tend to only like real women, not little errand girls."

Genesis, amused by the display of hurt feelings, condescendingly commented, "Oh, sweetie, you're going to have to improve your technique if you have any hope of having another woman. Thank you for telling me, or us, exactly what Alejandro was doing. I find it very bad manners when a lesser, mid-level bureaucrat takes on something as far reaching as a new national currency. The people at the top were not keen on being left out of the discussion. My people were all set to apprehend you two and torture the information out of you if necessary. All I had to do was hike my skirt and invite you to come do a close-up inspection of the Promised Land, and, voilà, we had everything. Sadly, it left you wanting everything."

Mathias witnessed Dutch's rage at being taunted, and even though the events appeared to be unfolding in slow motion, he couldn't intercept Dutch's lunge at Genesis. The military police each got a 9mm round into him before he had traveled one meter. Dutch cast one last glance up at Mathias before his eyes closed forever.

CHAPTER 42

New Day, New Challenge

Sunrise on the farm was breathtaking as Su Lin watched the day begin. Sleep had been elusive, so she'd written a letter to Andy in case she failed to return. Dressing with great care to appear humble and resigned to her fate, she added the rest of her travel toiletries to her satchel. She knew full well that Guano or his men would rifle through her bag. Everything critical to her success was in her mind, with the exception of the code chips embedded in her hair clip. It was the same hair clip she'd worn since she taught at the facility in China, so it would not raise any suspicions. She had two more carefully sewn into the handle of the satchel with the hopes that these too would make it to China with her. Expecting to use her own travel documents, she carefully placed her passport where it could easily be retrieved. The less work they were required to do, the more she felt she would gain ground, not in trust, but in being left to do the job they expected.

Fragrant smells of baked cinnamon rolls and frying meat reached her from the open door, but she wasn't hungry. Picking up her satchel and making certain the sealed letter was in Andy's nightstand, she took one last look around at the best home she'd ever had and sighed as she went downstairs. Mercedes, EZ, and Khalid were quietly eating and sipping coffee.

Mercedes greeted, "Good morning, Su Lin. You look as tired as I feel. I cannot go with you, per the instructions, but I will be close enough if needed. Ernie is giving me the ranch truck, and I will be leaving to position myself in a few minutes. Khalid will be driving you and EZ to the agreed location to arrive at noon."

Su Lin nodded and said, "I think that will be acceptable as long as their lookouts do not have any idea you are present. Ernie said he had two places he recommended for you to wait. Please don't try to stop them from taking me. If I don't go along, Andy will be killed first."

Mercedes nodded and left without another word.

"EZ, I hope you won't be disappointed if I don't eat. I am really not very hungry this morning. I will drink a bit of water before we go."

EZ shook her head. "You have to have a little bit of toast or roll so the tracker capsule will settle nicely. Khalid indicated if it sits on an empty stomach it will not be as effective."

Khalid almost smiled as he offered Su Lin a plate with a couple of slices of buttered toast and rolls to choose from.

Su Lin selected the toast and said, "If you can put my satchel into the car, I want to go see Franklin until it's time to leave."

Su Lin patted Franklin as she gave him a few extra treats. He was so docile with her, and they'd been through so much together.

Ernie moved up next to the fence by them and quietly promised, "He's healed according to Doc, but I will be checking on him a few times a day, just so he won't get so lonely. Wrinkles has been keeping pretty close and even slept in the barn with Franklin last night."

Su Lin smiled and touched Ernie's arm. "Thank you, Ernie. I know you will take care of things around here. Andy and I would be lost without you. Don't you worry, Andy will be back tonight and will need to have you barbeque for him until his sight returns."

EZ called out that they needed to leave as she entered the back seat. Su Lin walked over slowly and opened the rear door to sit next to EZ. Khalid carefully pulled out toward the road. No one spoke as the open fields were passed. The animals grazing in the pastures hardly took notice at the passing vehicle. An hour later they pulled up to the crest of the hill and parked, with the view from the front seat overlooking the planned exchange zone. Su Lin swallowed the capsule and gave EZ a quick hug as she opened the door, gathering the satchel with her left hand. After closing the door, she moved a few feet from the car and stood motionless.

A few minutes later, the target vehicle pulled into the area and parked near the picnic table. The rear door opened, and one man got out and helped Andy as he exited. The bandage covering Andy's eyes looked fresh even from this distance. Under his own power but with guidance from the guard, he walked toward the table and sat on one of the benches. Guano emerged from the front passenger door and another guard from the driver's side. Su Lin began her careful descent toward the vehicle without a backward look. She knew EZ had climbed into the front passenger seat to get the best view. There was no sign of Mercedes.

With the distance rapidly closing, Guano called out, "You may not go to him, Master Po, but you can speak so he knows you are safe."

"Andy, I'm going to go with these men to help them work out a problem. After we drive away, EZ will come and take you home. She will explain any details you need."

Andy had perked up at the sound of Su Lin's voice. Then, as her words were understood, he responded with a high amount of anguish. "Su Lin, I want to go home with you. You need to tell these men they are mistaken in thinking you can help them. Let's just go home, please?"

Su Lin's eyes filled with moisture. She swallowed and replied, "I can help them, and then I'll come home. Don't give EZ any trouble and talk to Franklin some until I get back. I love you, Andy."

Guano said, "Come along now, Master Po. The sooner you get in the car, the sooner we can leave and your husband can go home."

Su Lin looked toward the car and then beyond Guano as a terrible noise and scream like a wild animal burst from the bushes adjacent to the car. Fearing the worst, Su Lin shouted, "Look out!"

The filthy man, disguised in tattered clothes and covered in mud, shrieked with Chinese words of war as he rushed Guano. In the split second before he reached Guano, a shot rang out from above the warrior, and he was stopped in his tracks. Guano grabbed Su Lin and pushed her into the vehicle, with the driver and other guard diving in through the open doors. Flooring the vehicle to the point of nearly losing control, the driver fishtailed as he turned the vehicle around and headed back from where it had entered.

EZ went running down the hill toward her father, knowing Khalid would be driving around to the other entrance. She arrived at Andy's side just as the dust was settling to see Mercedes as she emerged from the bushes and approached the fallen man.

"It's the other twin, Ton, I believe. He won't be bothering anyone again. One shot, so no one else was hit. I did see Guano jerk Su Lin into the car, but I don't think he hurt her."

Guano had just finished binding Master Po's hands when he remarked, "You and your husband are lucky there was a hunter out in the woods. We will be in China this time tomorrow. For now you will need to sleep." He injected her with a sedative, and her eyes fluttered closed. "Get us to the aircraft, and we will make our way home, Quinn Lee."

"Yes, sir."

CHAPTER 43

Moving Forward into Unchartered Waters

Jacob had finished the malware coding, and it was working well, based on his latest conversation with Petra. He was pleased they'd been able to recover some of the funds Chesterfield had taken. Petra had also updated him on the status of Su Lin being exchanged for Andy and the shooting. The speed of the signal from the tracker Su Lin had ingested indicated she was airborne and en route to China. Patience would be the theme for some time on that front, though Jacob would know when she accessed the special files.

Sounds from the direction of Wolfgang caused Jacob to look up. Wolfgang's eyes were open, and he had been grabbing for the water on the side tray. Jacob rose quickly and moved around to help.

"Wolfgang, I'm so glad you're awake. Let me help you with the water. Here's the straw."

Wolfgang took a few small sips and licked his lips, then took a couple more. The nurses had left a moisture stick on the side table which Jacob retrieved and applied to Wolfgang's parched lips.

Jacob barely heard the quiet, "Thank you, Jacob," from Wolfgang.

Jacob smiled and said, "You're welcome, Grandfather. The doctor wondered if you'd be speaking today after he checked on you this morning. He seemed hopeful, though.

"Do you want to talk, or shall I read some more from your books?"

"Read."

"Alright, I can continue with the story. It is starting to get even more interesting. Is it history or just a story you've been writing?"

Wolfgang's eyes twinkled for a second before he closed them, but not to sleep.

Jacob had learned the difference between Wolfgang resting his eyes and sleeping. The doctor said that his body was fighting to survive, so he seemed focused on that even while awake.

"We left off after they had assembled the Enigma Machine and seemed to have some success. I hope you can tell me soon if this is actually how it happened."

Wolfgang opened his eyes for a second and seemed to smile a bit, reminding Jacob of a fox in a henhouse.

Jacob shook his head and grinned as he continued past the point where he had finished reading to himself, trying to get a better grasp of the purpose of the books.

Ferdek declared, "What are we supposed to do? Now we have an edge by decrypting German communications and reading them, but we can't do anything with the informa-tion. Is that what you're saying?"

Tavius sarcastically suggested, "I know, we can simply go through our secure borders here in Switzerland, waltz through the Panzers of 12 Pz division, and calmly request of the Allied generals that they pull out a crack regiment of their troops to escort us to the U-boat pens in uncon-quered German territory. Then we can inspect the cargo of U-168. Doesn't sound that hard."

Wolfgang gave each of his friends a questioning look and was deeply suspicious that their mental capacities appeared flawed. Finally he stated, "It must have occurred to both of you that breaking the coded messages generated by the Enigma machine was only the first step in the process.

"Our next step is to make use of the information stream, with a part of that process being to ascertain where and who to take it to. If this was going to be easy, don't you think everyone would be doing it? It is really a shame there aren't instructions along with the machine to say, 'Hey, follow the gingerbread crumb trail to beat the hated enemy'!"

Tavius sadly acknowledged, "I guess I must admit that is exactly what I expected. But Ferdek is right. What do we do with this information now that we have it, plus ongoing exchanges to discover?

"We can't retransmit the encrypted radio traffic to the Allies, since we don't know if they too have broken the Enigma machine. If we send unencrypted radio traffic, they would simply think is was bait for a trap. I know I would. What good is our intelligence if we can't capitalize on it?"

Ferdek, still annoyed with the whole scenario, blustered, "We don't even know if we have anything useful! I hate these academic exercises you two insist on pursuing! I should have moved to the Polish underground when I had a chance to do some useful fighting! Even the Czechs got some revenge when they whacked Reinhard Heydrich back in 1942!"

Tavius smirked, then in a lamenting tone, offered, "Yes, of course, there was a great hit against the hated emissary of the Third Reich. They took him out, and the cost was all the people of that town. How many thousands did they kill in retribution? I forget how sweet the victory was."

Ferdek snarled and altered his voice as he commented, "Frankly, my dear, I don't give a damn. In war there are casualties, and that bastard needed to be eliminated! It may have looked like a lopsided trade, but it galvanized people against the Nazi regime and strengthened our cause!"

Tavius rolled his eyes and incredulously asked, "You mean we needed more proof points?"

Wolfgang, tiring of the useless exchange, interjected, "Gentlemen, let's try and focus your limited attention span to the problem at hand. We need to get this information into the Allied hands so it can be acted upon. We don't need to solve all the problems on the planet between us, but we do need to get others engaged so opportunities are not squandered.

"Now I'm confident that we have something of interest because U-168's shipping manifest has obviously been altered to cover up their real cargo. Otherwise, what value is there in taking a prime class U-Boat out of wolf-pack-hunting status to transport mercury to Japan? I did some inquiries about the weapon value of mercury with some research scientists we have here in Zürich, and they looked at me like I was crazy."

With a sour look on his face, Ferdek caustically asked, "Don't tell me you asked the academic noodles what they thought? Why didn't you just take out an ad in the morning paper? That way we could have the opinions of the whole population!"

Tavius was interested in Wolfgang's line of thought though, so he ignored Ferdek and queried, "I'm guessing that there is no military value of mercury, but was there any speculation on why mercury was listed?"

Wolfgang reeled in his annoyance with Ferdek enough to respond. "Well, the 'noodles', as you call them, suggested that labeling the cargo as mercury was simply a ruse to cover up the true nature of the shipment. One of the chemists pulled out an atomic weight chart and began comparing elements that did have a similar atomic weight but with weapons grade potential. He stopped at the end of the chart and asked another 'noodle' about uranium.

"The noodle being asked was a physicist who rarely joined into discussions, but he became quite animated when asked about the military value of uranium. Without going into a lot of detail from the noodle, Ferdek, the bottom line is that uranium is reported to be critical to the next generation of atomic weapons. He further suggested that they may have labeled it as mercury, based on its similar weight to uranium, in case someone got nosy."

Tavius stated out loud what they were all thinking. "Next generation of weapons being shipped to the Japanese. That's why all the cloak and dagger communications. The Germans are shipping next generation materials to their partners in crime on the world stage to turn their fortunes around. Nice detective work, Wolfgang!"

Ferdek, fully engaged in the statements being made, quietly commented, "Let's say we have indeed uncovered some significant information. Obviously we need to act on it. Since we can't do the verification ourselves, we need to get it into the proper hands of the allies who could. You know, it occurs to me that my father, the diplomat, must have some connections here in Zürich that could get this information into high ranking Allied hands for the needed action. Let me work this aspect, since I believe I know the proper target in the diplomatic embassy. It is whispered that he can get useful info into the hands of the American OSS. If they aren't interested in this, then I'm at a loss as to who would be."

After Ferdek had left the area, Tavius said, "You know we shouldn't have let Ferdek watch "Gone with the Wind" so many times. Now he thinks he's Rhett Butler."

Wolfgang lightly chuckled, "I know. But you have to admit he does have Clark Gable's accent down quite well."

They both chuckled.

A week or so later, they made the trek to Bern to take their plan to the next level. The old repurposed hotel in Bern was comfortably nestled in amongst trees and well-groomed hedges. Gracefully ageing inside the safe surroundings, the 3-story building was the unofficial main meeting area and makeshift office space for information exchange between interested parties. The rooms and halls were tastefully decorated with artwork and comfortable leather chairs, arranged in isolated meeting areas that permitted discreet discussions. Some attendees worked for the Allies, some worked for the Axis powers, although Italy was no longer part of that alliance. Others were simply freebooters looking to profit from information brokering. Wearing military dress in a strictly neutral country like Switzerland was frowned upon.

The neutrality of the environment resulted in a protocol of proper introductions from well-tailored, trusted individuals that was necessary before any initial conversations. Even with proper introductions, many meetings needed to occur before the exchange of any information of substance. Background research and story corroboration had to be confirmed before brokering real information. In other words, you couldn't be in a hurry in this arena. If one was in too much of a hurry, it might make them automatically suspect.

Introductions were obtained, and Ferdek was approached by a perfectly dressed, yet nameless, attaché who nodded slightly in acknowledgement and gestured toward some elegant leather couches. They sat in this secluded, quiet area, and Ferdek delivered his information payload at a rapid rate. Ferdek was certain he had the man's attention and his acceptance of the research they had uncovered, but not how they got it. The active nodding encouraged him to quicken his pace of speech until the story was concluded. Ferdek rocked back in his seat with a certain sense of satisfaction and waited for a response. The attaché smiled slightly and nodded his head as if he understood the speech was concluded, then simply got up from his chair and left without saying a word. Ferdek was dumbfounded.

After a long wait, in which he reviewed what he'd said to see if he'd left out any salient details and grew frustrated, Ferdek noted a much more smug-looking, yet seasoned diplomat stroll over and sit down on the couch next to him. The diplomat's clothes were not only well-tailored but of the quality of fabric he had seen mostly in the dress of his father and his father's betters during serious diplomatic meetings. Not only was his hair well-groomed and his face recently shaved, he had hands that had clearly never seen physical labor, which suggested he had a valet to attend him. His face was schooled except for a hint of amusement.

Ferdek, still at a loss to understand what had transpired, cautiously studied the amused diplomat. Before he could ask anything, the man interjected, "Your attempt to convey 'important information' was about as naive and clumsy as I've ever witnessed. That was either the cleverest attempt at introducing dis-information ever conceived, or you are simply and exactly who you say you are. Do you honestly believe that your first attempt to get information reliably transmitted to the Allies was the proper way to proceed?"

Ferdek, struggling to reel in his resentment and annoyance, rather tersely asked, "Which do you think I am, sir? While I think I'm amazingly brilliant, you obviously sense I am a naïve but harmless bumpkin rube, practicing to be a fortune-telling gypsy."

The man laughed heartily and, sticking out his hand to shake, offered, "Ferdek Watcowski, you probably don't remember me, but my name is Alonzo Dzikowski. I know your father, and actually we have met before at your father's embassy home. I can assure you, I don't believe you are practicing to be a gypsy."

Ferdek flinched at the realization that one of his father's colleagues from before the war had in fact made it to this meeting crossroads here in Bern. Ferdek slowly reacted to the conversation, still smarting from what he now considered an embarrassing episode.

Ferdek reluctantly offered, "I'm sorry I did not immediately recognize you, sir."

Alonzo, still chuckling, asked, "You seem unsettled, Ferdek. Perhaps there is some regret from the poor response of your storytelling to the German attaché?"

Ferdek, alarmed and panicking, quickly asked, "No?! That was a German? How is it that he can be here? This is supposed to be a neutral country!"

Alonzo smirked slightly and stated, "He is here for the same reason you are here. This is the neutral country of Switzerland, which means everyone can come and still do business. The Swiss are notoriously tolerant of you so long as there is a profit in it for them. They use their neutrality so they can do business in either direction between belligerents. You do have to play by their rules, of course. What good would it be if we were all on the same side? How would any business transactions be conducted, eh? Yes, my boy, players from both sides must be in attendance if any real value is to be exchanged.

"As the host country doing the brokering, they make a small percent- age of the transaction, otherwise this is just a club of like-minded individuals. If this is just a club, then there are no brokerage fees to be made. Remember, you must be in a position to deal with your enemies, but for safety reasons, it should be in a neutral place."

Ferdek was angry with himself for having delivered all his important information to the German. "What a fool I was to give our privileged information to the enemy! What am I to do! Now, even if I can get my research into Allied hands, it's already compromised!"

Alonzo smiled in a paternal way as he related, "As I indicated at the beginning of our conversation, I suggested that one of two possibilities were in play. But for argument's sake, let's say you have brilliantly maneuvered the Germans into accepting your valued research, thus tipping their hand. What do you think will happen next?"

Ferdek angrily stated, "He will pass the information back to his people, and they will alter their plans to avoid detection. I've failed."

Alonzo, fully engaged in delivering a lesson, refuted the statement. "No, Ferdek, you have not failed. Yes, he will relay the information because of the genuine naivety that you delivered it with. It will be relayed to the planning coordinators who will beef up their security, thus creating proof points for your accusation. The added security will not go unnoticed by Allied spies and observers, and their activity will confirm your research. This series of events will become proof points that will establish your credibility and allow you to build an information brokerage.

"You actually have done quite well. You just did not realize the importance of your first step. Perhaps the apple does not fall far from the tree."

Ferdek was stunned at the revelation. Alonzo smiled again and stated, "Truths as well as lies are powerful weapons in the hands of a professional. Use them wisely. As to your next steps, we need to hear of the information confirmation and then things will happen fairly quickly. Be back in two days for your next lesson. Until then, I bid you adieu."

Ferdek, still trying to comprehend all the events he had just been through, absentmindedly murmured, "After all that clumsiness, I must be the dumbest smart person there is. No wait, that's probably Tavius. Well, at least the first part of that statement anyway."

Nurse Sandy came in at that point, and Wolfgang graced her with a show of open eyes as she helped him to more water. This time he drank a bit more, though in slow sips. She took some vitals and checked his fluid levels.

"Sir, you seem to be improving, thankfully. The doctor will be in in a few minutes to do some additional tests. If you keep up the drinking, we might be able to upgrade you to broth or gelatin for a little change. I know Bowen has pestered me several times a day to allow him to bring is some delicacies. Not yet though."

Wolfgang almost smiled and quietly spoke. "A change would be nice, thank you."

Nurse Sandy lit up, hearing his voice. "This is another good sign. The doctor will be pleased that you are speaking and clearly. Practice if you can, though I expect your throat is dry and will be for a day or two."

"Wine?"

His one word response made Jacob and Nurse Sandy chuckle, and Wolfgang added a smile.

CHAPTER 44

How to Know
You're Thinking Clearly
...The Enigma Chronicles

Andy was frantic, hearing first the scream, the shot fired, and then the spinning wheels of the vehicle as it kicked up the loose gravel and it roared down the road. Time was suspended in his mind. Not only did he have no idea what had really happened, but his anguish burned from head to toe, and he loudly called out, "Su Lin, honey, where are you? Are you alright?" Without the bandages across his eyes, the tears would have run down his face.

Far off in the distance he heard, "Daddy, I'm coming." But he was certain it was the wind fooling him. He stood, thinking he should go toward the area where the vehicle had been, but he feared he would fall so he clenched his hand and yelled, "Su Lin, where are you? No, don't you leave me, honey!"

EZ reached the area where her Daddy was just as Mercedes determined that the fallen man was indeed dead.

"Daddy, I'm here. It's EZ and I'll take care of you." They hugged each other with her hands running all over him, making certain he had not been hit by flying debris.

Andy grabbed onto EZ and bemoaned, "Tell me she's not dead. Take me to her, now."

EZ's eyes welled up with tears, and in a choked voice she soothed, "Daddy, she's okay. There was a man who was attacking, but he was killed. He was shot by Mercedes, who will be over here after she gets off the phone. She is calling the authorities.

"I have a car coming around, and we are taking you to the doctor. How are you feeling?"

"I feel like a dang fool who can't even take care of his wife. I can't see, and I sure did nothing to protect her. Where is she?"

"Daddy, I need you to sit back down until the car arrives. It's complicated, but I will explain as much as I know.

"Su Lin made an exchange of herself for you. She was once a part of a technology school in China that she left, because they had no respect for her rights or human rights in general. Because of her programming genius, she developed some very futuristic things, including something they want to use for cryptocurrency. Even though she has no desire to return to that life or even help them, she agreed to go with them in order to get you back. She is so worried about you, probably just like you are about her."

Andy was animated, with hands flying, as he explained, "I know that old history; she told me before we got married. Like all of us she has a past. It's her future with me that I care about.

"Now will she be back? That's all I care about. Not the doctor, not the farm, just Su Lin."

The car arrived and Khalid went to check with Mercedes. EZ watched as he took the gun from Mercedes, and they seemed deep in conversation before they both approached.

Mercedes revealed a grim look on her face. "I need to wait for the authorities to arrive and tell them what I saw. Khalid is going to take you to the ranch so you can grab a car to take

Andy to his doctor for a once over. No one will be after either of you now."

Andy winced at the unspoken words, 'because Su Lin is with them.'

"The story is I was with my friends and this man came running out. A shot was fired from somewhere up the hill, and he went down. I have no other knowledge. Does that work for you?"

EZ reached over and hugged Mercedes, then said, "That works. Khalid can come back for you, and the authorities can certainly contact us for verification."

Khalid suggested, "Folks, we need to keep moving before the police arrive. Mercedes, you know the drill so let us know when I need to come get you."

Andy, trying to keep things upbeat, added, "We'll see you later, Mercedes." Andy reached his arms toward her, and she moved into them for her hug. "We got ya covered, little lady, don't you worry. I am getting tired now though."

EZ took one side while Khalid closed the door to Andy's side and they were secured in the car.

Mercedes sat on the bench and watched the car drive away as she took out her cell and called Julie.

Julie called Jacob and related the events that had unfolded in Georgia. Jacob started up his program so he could track Su Lin's progress. She was on the move, and Quip was plotting the speed and directional information. Things were moving according to plan at this point, and they were at least aware of the final destination.

Jacob called Petra after his conversation with Julie while Wolfgang was getting additional tests. The doctor had indicated that Wolfgang would be sedated for a while for the second portion of the tests to minimize any discomfort, but that he would be awake later when they returned him to his room.

"Hi, darling. I miss you. Wolfgang is getting more tests done, but the doctor said his speech was good and he should be speaking a bit more after his throat recovers from having the tubes removed."

"Jacob, this is great news! Do you want me to come keep you company? I can bring some work along or not, your choice."

"I would like to see you, hold you and talk some. I've been doing some serious thinking between watching Wolfgang, reading these books, and working on these programs for Su Lin. I do think I contributed some, but not as much as you and Quip."

His voice had trailed off, and Petra heard a sense of regret in his last comment.

With concern she queried, "Jacob, don't go down a path of doubt. You are doing some major contribution which neither Quip nor I could do, plus staying with your grandfather. I'm not certain where your head's at, or perhaps you are just tired, but I am going to stop by the chateau and pick up some food and be there with you."

"Reading these books and thinking about how much this family had built over the years, I'm not certain I am a good addition to this team. I only seem to be filling gaps, not creating new innovations. I'm just copying or camping on what others have done, like Su Lin."

Petra shook her head in dismay. This was going to take some serious discussion, and he needed to catch up on his rest.

"Alright, I will head over soon. We are going to talk, Jacob. I think an attitude adjustment is needed, and I am going to help. We are a team, don't ever forget that.

"I need to relate some funny insights from ICABOD too."

CHAPTER 45

At Tannhäuser Gate

It was a bitter moment for Mathias. There was Dutch, the mercenary he had worked with for years, lying at his feet. It occurred to Mathias he didn't know why Dutch had always gone along for the ride no matter what the job or the potential risks. For Dutch it had always been the excitement and, of course, the money. Now that Dutch was dead, there was something else. Dutch, his friend, was gone. Mathias realized at that moment that he had never had a friend before in his life. The dreams and the schemes were all about the next target vector. What had made it special was the comradery of his friend, Dutch. It was so harsh to realize that his only friend was gone.

The emotional thawing in Mathias had his eyes nearly over-flowing with tears, but he shifted his gaze at the last moment to rest on Genesis. This small action quickly put him back into his old icy self. The guards quickly sensed the change and aimed their weapons at Mathias, lest he also lunge at Genesis.

Genesis was soberly quiet while Mathias calmed his breathing.

Finally she announced, "We're not here to eliminate anyone, but their orders are to see that nothing happens to me while retrieving the desired package. I believe we've demonstrated the seriousness of our intent. I would like your assurance of full cooperation. I want the source code to the cryptocurrency for my government. We know you have a working demo, but we want all the source code for analysis before we consider putting it into production. I suspect that you do not have it with you. Therefore, you will make the call and summon it for our review."

Mathias, ever the business man, moved his gaze to Dutch's body, then questioned. "Will I receive my commission, as negotiated with Alejandro? I am prepared to discount the agreement now since I have one fewer mouth to feed on this project."

The icy smile from Genesis only served to remind him of her cold- bloodedness as she acquiesced, "I, of course, will put your request forward. You do understand that I cannot make any negotiations or promises in that regard. I'm sure that a moderate compensation plan will be discussed. I would recommend that if I can report how helpful you were in delivering the source code, it could strengthen your fee request with my government."

With no show of emotion, Mathias cautiously eyed the guards and quietly asked, "May I reach for my cell phone so I can call my associate to put your request into motion? I suspect any sudden moves will result in me having a bad day."

Genesis smiled politely and said, "No, but my guards will retrieve it for you."

Mathias watched as one guard reached into his coat pocket, while the other held his weapon on him. Then, they moved Mathias over to the dinette table and chair where his hands were bound fairly tightly with cable-ties.

Genesis joined Mathias but kept her distance with both guards watching every move.

She reached for the phone and put it on the table, then asked, "Password or fingerprint access?"

Mathias smiled fatalistically and said, "Voice print with retina scan. It's easier to do when your hands are cable-tied. Hold it over to my mouth, I'll speak into it, then hold it up to my right eye."

Genesis did as needed to access the cell phone and then questioned, "Voice dial access, I assume?" She then held the phone over for Mathias to request an outbound call.

He barked, "Halvorson!"

The phone made the call, and Genesis put it on speaker phone so all could hear. As soon as the call connected, Mathias politely began, "My dear friend, Dr. Halvorson! I'm so glad you were able to take my call. I trust your day has been uneventful and profitable. I hope your health is improving and that no ailments are troubling you at this point of your life, dear man."

Halvorson was momentarily speechless at the pleasant greeting from Mathias. As his mind raced to understand the friendly words, he responded, "Mathias, in all the time I've known you, never did you begin a conversation like this, so… so…this must mean someone else is listening in. Just nod your head if you can't speak."

Suppressing a smirk, Genesis offered, "Dr. Halvorson, we wanted a chance to dialogue with you at the recommendation of your colleague, Mr. Mathias. Gentlemen, now that we are all here, can we proceed with the business at hand?"

Halvorson asked, "I haven't heard Dutch yet. Has he been bound and gagged, or is he simply in the washroom?"

Mathias bluntly stated, "Dutch won't be joining us again.

"Now to the point. I'll net this out and spare you all the gory details leading up to this situation. I need all the source code for our cryptocurrency compressed and encrypted, ready for transmission to the URL address of the lady's choosing. Is my request clear, or do I need to go over it again?"

Halvorson, also on a hands-free calling device, looked grimly at Cody who sat staring wide-eyed at the phone.

There was a tiresome pause before Genesis cheerfully asked, "Do you have a crayon, darling, to write down the URL location?

Once I read it to you, I want it repeated back to me so there is no misunderstanding."

Halvorson glumly asked, "Mathias, are you sure about this? I would kind of like to hear it from you."

Mathias took a deep breath and unequivocally stated, "Yes, Dr. Halvorson, I'm sure about this. Please ship the code to her designated location."

Halvorson nodded slightly and said, "Alright, Mathias, I understand. I do need to encrypt the package before putting it on the designated website, just to ensure the integrity of the contents. I'm not going to say the passphrase aloud, assuming you want me to use the obvious one."

Mathias replied, "Yes, please. Thanks for everything, old friend."

After the verbal URL exchange was entered, Genesis reached over and disconnected the call.

Mathias wistfully added, "Another time beyond the gate of Tannhäuser."

CHAPTER 46

Saving or Spending, Two Sides of the Digital Coin

Halvorson calmly disconnected from the call.

Cody practically shouted, "I didn't sign up for this! Dutch, now in the past tense! Mathias arrested and being ransomed for the source code to our cryptocurrency by the double D sized Venezuelan Gestapo. All of our working capital is also being held hostage by a malware that only wants 50% of our holdings each time we pay them! Well, since you can't cash me out, barkeep, let me just say, screw all of you! I'm out of here!"

Completely unruffled, Halvorson calmly related, "I've worked with Mathias long enough to know that we may be down, but we're not out. If you leave, don't expect to come back when we're back on top. Besides that, where did you think you were going with no money, baba-loo?"

Cody sneered and replied, "I've kept all my earnings on a different computer, so at least I have something of a nest egg to walk away with. So adios, muchachos!"

Still maintaining his calm exterior, Halvorson asked, "Where do you have the source code for the C-C? I still need to ship it to them even if you don't want to play here any longer, cupcake."

Irked at the calm taunting remarks, Cody shot back, "It's on my PC as well! But don't worry. Once I'm out of harm's way, I'll send it to you. Until then, it is password protected, and the drive is sealed with an encryption algorithm that will defeat any hacking attack." Cody reassured himself that his PC was in his backpack, slung it over his shoulders, and stomped towards the secure door.

Halvorson smiled at the private joke and stated, "That's all I wanted to know." He watched dispassionately as Cody left the data center with the backpack and a bag of programmer desktop toys.

Halvorson sighed and retrieved the PC he had taken from Cody's backpack. After he booted up the machine, he inserted a USB drive to access a program that made him smile.

He said to the absent Cody, "In the future, always remember to lock your PC so no one can access it while you're gone. Since you told me where the needed programs are and that the drive was password encrypted, I guess it's a good thing that I had loaded a password logger program on your PC when I gave it to you. It recorded your password, and now that your PC belongs to me, I can access the source code that should get Mathias out of their clutches. And, as a side benefit, I also trapped your crypto-currency password, so moi has some operating capital. You know, with everything going so poorly, I really don't see a need to burden Mathias with unnecessary details. I mean, he has so much on his mind."

Halvorson chuckled slightly as he moved the source code to the USB drive and took a look at Cody's C-C holdings. He clucked his tongue as he remarked, "Well, young man, you have been frugal. I'll make sure these go to a worthy cause. Many thanks."

Still chuckling, Halverson added, "Cody, I hope you will be greatly disappointed when you find out that the PC you have has been wiped clean. Funny how laptops all look alike when you're mad."

Glancing down at his watch, Halvorson remarked, "Whoops! Better pick up the pace here and start the move to the rendez-vous point."

ICABOD alerted, "Dr. Quip, this is interesting. A small cache of cryptocurrency belonging to Steven Christopher has materi-alized on a new machine. It is in approximately the same loca-tion as the other machine that received the ransomware malware code we delivered. Apparently, a few of the digital coins were removed from the larger cache and are now visible. Do we need to initiate the Sting Protocol?"

Quip mused, "Hmmm…looks like this machine just shipped off an encrypted package to Venezuela. Now isn't that interesting. ICABOD, methinks we should follow the money trail. They have stolen funds on the source machine, and if I had to guess, they are sending saleable items to Venezuela that they don't want closely scrutinized." Quip sighed and continued, "Which only makes me want to look closer. ICABOD, track the package, and let's see if we can get a copy of it. It's so quiet around here, may-be we can stir things up a bit."

ICABOD said, "The protocol has been launched, Dr. Quip. I will have it analyzed by morning."

Quip yawned, stretched, and stated, "And yes, ICABOD, launch the Sting protocol against the new machine for those cryptocoins. I think I'll head home. It's been a busy day tracking the bad guys on the Darknet. Goodnight, ICABOD."

ICABOD responded, "Goodnight, Dr. Quip."

CHAPTER 47

Expectations: Meeting & Greeting the Unknown
...The Enigma Chronicles

Sitting in the principal's office in junior high listening to chapter and verse on proper behavior after explaining why her skirt was too short created exactly the same feelings of anxiety in Tonya as the phone call interrogation Ingrid was delivering.

Taking a short breath, Ingrid finally asked, "After all you've told me, just exactly where are we? You were irritated by Otto's handling of you, belittled by Petra's cross-examination, and each commented on your excessive alcohol consumption. Do you maybe see a pattern here? Are you sure you want to continue in this role, or are you too temperamental for the task? Tonya, not to put too fine a point on it, but you sound like one of those *Millennial Snowflakes* that needs a timeout in their designated *Happy Place* because they heard bad news they disagree with!"

Tonya moved to respond but was speechless. Ingrid's tone was not harsh; however, her words and categorization stung like crazy.

After a few moments and internal reminders to put on her big girl panties, Tonya tersely replied, "I came to you with a full report with all the subtleties and nuances of my dealings with these two digital predators. It doesn't sound like I can use you as a sounding board to discuss these differing perspectives.

"Surprisingly, you sound like one of those Captains of industry who is only interested in today's quarterly results. You know the sort, who doesn't care who they throw under the bus, just so long as they receive their inflated bonuses! Which, if I am not mistaken, was how you once spoke to me of your predecessor. If my dedication or approach to this project doesn't meet your view of the timeline, then allow me to resign, and get yourself a real *Millennial Snowflake* who will grovel the way you want!"

Tonya swallowed hard after her challenge to Ingrid. Sadly, she realized she had finally let her temper get away from her, and unfortunately, it had been directed at her boss and mentor. Closing her eyes and bracing for the expected onslaught from Ingrid, she waited. But that's not what happened.

Ingrid chuckled slightly and good-naturedly offered, "I see we have reached that defining moment in our relationship, Ms. Van Den Berghe. These are the toughest people you have run into yet, but rest assured, they will not be the last. The good news is that even though they each have different strengths which our organization has leveraged for different projects, they are ultimately on our side in most things. Remember this lesson, because when you deal with the next round of people on our side or those from the Darknet, the experience will be much tougher. You are doing okay, but you need to do even better if you are going to survive."

Tonya, still breathing hard, firmly stated, "*Millennial Snowflake*? I didn't deserve that!"

Ingrid countered, "Then show me some moxie, Tonya! Which of these contractors is the correct horse to bet on?"

Tonya reeled in her annoyance and after a few moments replied, "Otto's report from the R-Group was succinct and perfectly crafted to my request. He delivered it like a friendly but patronizing uncle whose only mantra is to get another piece of business.

"Petra's response was equally well-crafted, but her responses had a sharper edge. She asked questions that clearly indicated she had thought through not only the delivery of the project, but also the far reaching ramifications of today's decisions, echoed into the future of possibilities. Frankly, her arrogance gave her an unflattering edge that makes her seem almost like a machine. Yet her summarization was very forward thinking.

"Therefore, I am recommending Petra be brought in as our preferred contractor. She understands the next wave of crypto-currency and everything that is required for the success of this next generation monetary exchange."

Ingrid smiled as she responded, "Now, it wasn't that hard, was it? You shifted through the hurt feelings and gave me an honest evaluation using credible reasoning and practical observations. Well done. This is how you meet the expectations of the role. May we see how you handle the next round of discussions with Ms. Rancowski?"

Tonya set her jaw and determinedly asked, "What terms should I use to entice one so arrogant?"

Ingrid smirked and responded, "Let me point you back to your earlier soliloquy. You already know the answer, so please act on it. We'll talk soon."

After Ingrid had disconnected from the call, Tonya muttered, "I guess I need to take better notes when I talk because I have no idea what to do next. First no confidence, then too much confidence. There is so much to do, I'm not sure where to start. I'd better have a drink first. That way I'll at least have one thing done."

Petra made the call back to Tonya on Otto's conference speaker phone with Otto listening. As soon as the call connected, Petra started, "Tonya, good day, you asked for a call back. Madam, how can I help?"

Tonya thought she would be able to hold her own with this call, but she began rather timidly. "Hi, Petra, um…I mean, Ms. Rancowski. I wanted to alert you that we, uh I mean, I have selected you for further work on our cryptocurrency project, if I can be so bold as to assume that you are interested in seeing the project to its logical conclusion. I would like to extend our project SOW to you in the next few days."

Petra looked silently at Otto who only nodded. After a few moments, Petra asked, "May I know what happened to any of the competitors? Were they eliminated by your hand or theirs?"

Somewhat emboldened, Tonya proudly stated, "Ms. Rancowski, you were our first and only choice. Do I sense hesitation, or may we proceed to the next series of milestones?"

Petra felt confusion and some regret at having been chosen over the R-Group. She continued to stare at Otto, who sensed her feelings and motioned to her to accept the offer, while smiling approvingly.

Petra finally answered, "Tonya, I was just reviewing my commitments and looking to see if a needed associate also had time to work with me on this project. Depending upon the deliverables timing for your project, I would like to proceed to the next phase. Once I see your SOW, we will assess it and provide a price."

Tonya, swelling with confidence, added, "And, yes, we understand the price is non-negotiable, so there will be no issue in that regard. I will deliver the project parameters to you in two or three days, to the usual secure web link. Until then, best wishes."

After disconnecting from the call, Petra offered, "Father, I feel ashamed that I was chosen over you and the R-Group. I don't feel comfortable with this…"

Otto beamed at Petra and came around the conference table to hug her. After his hug, he proudly said, "Daughter, do not feel that you betrayed me in any way! Don't you understand? You have earned a customer's trust over my approach! The very best complement for all our work together. You are more attuned to the going-forward needs of the customer with all your field work. I congratulate you, my dear. You have exceeded my expectations, and just so you know, my love for you is undiminished at having been bested."

Petra's eyes were overflowing with tears as she pulled her father close again for one more hug.

CHAPTER 48

It's Always a Great Plan Until It Isn't

...The Enigma Chronicles

After much prodding, punching, and rough handling, Su Lin finally came around and saw her captors, though she was still groggy. Guano had been too heavy handed with the tranquilizer that he had given her. Being out of it for that long was bad for her system, as she had found out in the hospital. As soon as her eyes focused, she became acutely aware of being quite nauseous. She struggled to keep the contents of her stomach intact for fear that her tracking device would be discovered, but sometimes things don't always go as planned. The only redeeming quality of the projectile barfing was that it was delivered squarely on Guano.

Now feeling much better, Su Lin politely asked, "May I be excused to go to the toilet? I feel a little sick and would like to freshen up."

Guano backhanded her and roared, "Bitch! You threw up on me and…what is this?" He now grasped the tracking capsule and held it up to examine it.

Su Lin tried to grab it from him as she anxiously stated, "That is my daily herbal intake of ginger to deal with travel sickness. If you don't mind I would like to…"

Guano dropped it and crushed it under his boot as he added, "Still the treacherous bitch you've always been, I see! Everything else in your stomach was liquefied, except the tracking device. No matter now. Yes, you can go to the toilet AFTER I get cleaned up!"

Su Lin stoically admitted, "Young ones, like I used to teach at the Cyber Warfare College, *it's always a great plan until it isn't.*"

After they had both freshened up, Guano demanded, "I want the code that you retrieved from the safety deposit box. I've met my side of the bargain, and I simply don't trust you to keep the cryptocurrency code safe until we are uploading it to the computers of the Finance Minister. Give it to me now, or I will take it by force."

With a somewhat amused look on her face, Su Lin replied, "I was fairly sure that if I had it all on one thumb drive you would have found some reason to report back that I had somehow managed to escape out of the chartered jet that was traveling at an altitude of 8,400. But to satisfy your demand, here you go, a full one-third of the program."

She tossed him the thumb drive. As he caught it he asked, "One-third? Where is the rest of the programming code? If you have double-crossed me…"

Su Lin smirked and responded, "The rest of the routines that would be used to stitch together the modules to work properly are inside my head. My insurance policy, which I presume even you can grasp. You need to keep me alive to put those routines together in the proper sequence to operate collectively and correctly.

"The security protocol is already embedded in the routines. If you are thinking that you would be able to have your people assemble it correctly, I have high confidence that it will take 2^96 power or 79 * 1027 computational years to solve, using your latest generation of supercomputer. It was the last routine I ran on the Cyber Warfare College's supercomputer under my watch."

Guano stared at Su Lin. "Speaking of which, your supercomputer was greatly enhanced in your absence by one of your more gifted students, Professor Lin. We are reasonably sure he is up to the challenge of breaking the *Grasshopper Loop* you built. If you won't do it, he will have to. It seems his family depends on a successful implementation of your code if he is to have a family. I suggest you redouble your work efforts, so we don't have to waste time on persuading you with non-essential personnel.

"My security protocol is also in place in the form of my trusted personnel, ready to enforce our demands on Andy, should you have problems cooperating."

Su Lin went cold inside with the last threat. She couldn't be sure it was an empty threat. This, however, coupled with the threat to Professor Lin, made her begin to wonder if they needed a plan B for their plan B.

CHAPTER 49

The Uphill Battle
...The Enigma Chronicles

etra arrived at Wolfgang's hospital room with a food basket filled with some delightful scents. Jacob was certain he smelled garlic and hoped the basket contained some of Cook's mouthwatering spaghetti and garlic bread. Petra had a warm smile and slight gleam in her eye as she glanced at the empty bed, presuming Wolfgang was still doing tests, and set the basket down. Grabbing onto one another like a lift raft in an endless sea, they held each other without a word for several minutes. Jacob relented his hold a bit as he leaned down and kissed her with the unspent desire he'd been holding onto. Her cell phone chimed, indicating she had an inbound call.

Glancing at the caller name, she showed Jacob and then turned on the speaker as she answered, "Quip, hi, what's up? Jacob and I are both here."

Quip sadly related, "Sorry to bother you two, but I think we have a problem. I was tracking the path of Su Lin on the way to China when her main signal disappeared. I was hoping Jacob could check from his side if I have overlooked anything or if we have a program failure of some sort. I doubt the possibility of a program failure, but it's worth a look."

Jacob replied, "I doubt the program failed. It's a simple program, and I've used it before in other forms." He sat down in front of his laptop with Petra right next to him as he waited for the program to refresh. The main signal had indeed vanished. Jacob quickly accessed the log files, and those indicated the program was functioning without a problem. "Quip, there is nothing wrong with the program. I am also seeing the path for the alternate tracker signal, which seems to be strong. In looking at the time stamps on the events, the issue seems to have taken place about thirty minutes ago."

"Yes," a frustrated Quip admitted, "I should have called sooner, but I knew Petra was bringing you some food, and I honestly hoped it was a simple failure. What logical conclusions can we make from this?"

Jacob ran his fingers through his hair as he thought about the possibilities. Petra patted him on the top of his thigh in reassurance. He then offered, "We have three scenarios we can consider. One, the device failed. Stomach acids compromised the exterior covering and caused the tracker to fail. The good news is that there is nothing lethal inside of the capsule, though she might suffer some discomfort as it passes through the lower intestine. From her hospital reports regarding her reaction to some medicines, her reactions to things might be more acute than if you or I had ingested this.

"Two, Guano is using some sort of a signal jammer as a secondary protection in case of a tracking device of some sort. This is rather unlikely since we are getting the signal from the secondary device. Sure glad we agreed on a backup tracker and that Mercedes could get it hidden and configured so quickly. As a part of the receptacle for the second part of the code, it is unlikely that if it is still running now, it would be spotted or removed.

"And, three, Su Lin with her sensitivities was sick to her stomach and the device was destroyed. The second device is working, and as we are approaching an hour, it is still moving toward the goal.

"Most likely the capsule has been damaged, resulting in our losing the signal. Su Lin is not aware of the secondary tracker, so if the capsule is damaged and she knows it, she might try to reach out to us in some fashion. That won't likely occur until she is in China and inside the Cyber Warfare College."

Petra provided a small reassuring smile along with another comforting pat on the top of his thigh. Quip stated, "I agree, Jacob. Yes, it was wise of us to set up the secondary source.

"How is Wolfgang? Is he there listening?"

Petra replied, "No, he is still getting tests run. We expect him back shortly. We are going to position my laptop so we can track Su Lin, and then we're going to eat this meal Bowen and Cook provided. You need to get home and eat yourself."

Quip chuckled. "Good idea. I could stand some good food for a change. I am a little tired of the granola bars. Then I'm going to call to EZ to check on her dad. He had his tests run and should be back home by now. I need to encourage her to eat to keep up her strength. Until Su Lin returns, my darling EZ isn't going to leave Georgia. Bye."

Wolfgang was wheeled back into the room, and the nurse quickly left.

Petra set up her laptop where they could keep an eye on it as Jacob took out all the dinner containers. The look on his face when he opened the container with the spaghetti was exactly how she'd pictured it would be. Their feast was laid out, including a colorful salad, bread, the pasta with a thick red sauce, and what appeared to be some Black Forest cake for dessert. He was just pouring the wine when the door opened. Wolfgang opened his eyes and smiled at Petra.

"Do you have some extra wine for me too?"

Petra smiled and walked over to the bed. Giving him a kiss on his cheek, she remarked, "I am so glad to see you up and awake. What a treat." In a conspiratorial tone she added, "I'll sneak you a little taste, alright?"

Wolfgang produced a small smile and softly replied, "If a nurse comes in we'll share a sip with her. She won't tell."

Wolfgang waved at the two of them to begin eating their supper. He smiled and savored the small sip of wine. When the nurse brought his food, he informed her he would eat by himself and dismissed her. Petra and Jacob kept a lively conversation going, and he chimed in a couple of times with some small comments. Petra had related the story of how ICABOD had indicated it was time they all had a group hug when she and Quip were working in the Operations Center.

Wolfgang commented, "That machine gets more real every day. I am glad you have recovered most of the funds. I knew you would." He closed his eyes to rest.

Petra and Jacob remained quiet as they ate and stared at the laptop. No change there, but it was nearly hypnotic watching the line. Wolfgang apparently noticed the quiet, as he regained their attention by clearing his throat along with his raised eyebrow and nod toward the machine. Jacob explained what they were doing. Wolfgang seemed interested but offered no feedback.

Petra had taken some food to the nurses station and had asked about the wine Wolfgang was allowed. Jacob helped repack the basket after they had consumed the last crumb of Black Forest, and Wolfgang had another half a glass of wine. Petra updated both of them with where she stood with the Global Bank and their adoption of cryptocurrency. Wolfgang nodded in agreement when she outlined their plans for tracking users and the encryption routines.

Nurse Sue came in and checked Wolfgang, took vitals, and otherwise set him up for the night. She warmly smiled and asked, "Mr. Michaels, are you planning to stay this evening as well? I'd be happy to change out your pillow and blanket now, if that's the case."

Jacob responded, "I am staying tonight. If you bring me the linens, I can change them. I don't wish to add any work to your already busy schedule."

Nurse Sue chuckled and sweetly retorted, "You're staying in here close by most nights, and I have a busy schedule. You are helping us a great deal, and I know Wolfgang enjoys your company. He said so earlier to his doctor. His improvement is due in great part to your time and encouragement."

Petra grinned and added, "See. We all know how valuable you are. Sometimes you just forget." Hugging Jacob and then kissing Wolfgang on the cheek, Petra bid them all good night and suggested she would be by tomorrow sometime.

After Nurse Sue left, Jacob adjusted his laptop to the tracking program. Google Maps indicated all was progressing and the signal was good. He dug out the latest book and opened to the page where he'd stopped earlier.

"Grandfather, I know you aren't going to tell me how close to the truth these writings are, but do you wish to hear some more, or would you rather just rest?"

Wolfgang added a lopsided smile and replied, "Read on, Jacob. It sounds nice when you read and makes me think."

"By the way, Bowen isn't saying a word about the books either, and if you didn't recall my saying so, I found them when I was looking for a book to read in your suite. Bowen looked none too pleased when he saw them here.

"Alright, we left off at the point where you were all in Bern."

After hearing the story, Tavius asked in disbelief, "You blurted out our hard won intelligence to the Germans? And somehow we look like seasoned professionals? No kidding? You sure he wasn't flattering you after the naive exhibition on the spy stage of life?"

Ferdek bristled at the comment and stiffly responded, "If it hadn't been a known friend of my father's sphere-of-influence in Poland, I would accept your accusation. I believe we are on the right trajectory."

Wolfgang nodded. "Perhaps we are entitled to some luck after all. In this next meeting, what is expected of us? Are we supposed to have additional information to be brokered, or are we still working from our original offering? Do we want to change with one another, or do we stay the course with you, Ferdek? Are you okay with continuing your role, or do you still believe that your only destiny is to serve in the underground?"

Tavius politely affirmed, "Ferdek, yours was the first strike in this game, and I recommend that you continue in this role. If you would rather not, I of course will step in for you. It is your call, but I don't believe we need to offer new intelligence to the stew we are brewing. I recommend we proceed slowly until we understand the landscape better."

Ferdek studied both of his companions and humbly stated, "It is said that when fate offers you a new opening to a different destiny, you should embrace it as it was ordained for you. If I have been deceived, then odds are I will not survive the next encounter, and you two will have to continue the struggle against the Nazis. If I am success-ful in this next contact, then we will all profit as a team. I cannot allow either of you to step into this situation, as it may be a poisonous event. Either we all win or I will pay the price."

Turning to Tavius, he continued, "And yes, Tavius, I agree with you. No new intelligence just yet. Let me play out this hand."

Tavius, always thinking about next steps, offered, "Now just a minute, hotshot! We may be willing to accept your plan A, but I insist that before we move to the next stage we have a plan B. I may be in agreement that you can walk into the line of fire. I, for one, am not going to sit here and hope everything turns out okay. We need an exit and recovery strategy in case everything goes sideways. This is non-negotiable."

Wolfgang nodded in agreement and stated, "Tavius is quite correct. We must assume we were lucky on our first round of information brokering, but that luck cannot be our only guardian angel. Besides, we need to consider the possibility that Alonzo may also be a compromised asset. It would be a very lucky coincidence that Ferdek's father's friend happened to show up precisely where and when we needed him. However, what if that was all highly engineered?

"We must assume that duplicity is the name of the game in information brokering, so let's not believe the first story handed to us, shall we? Think about it! What if the first person you spoke with was really OSS, and the German collaborator who listened and soothed your ego was in fact the enemy? What a brilliant ruse!"

Ferdek, now highly agitated, shifted in his chair and tersely stated, "As offensive as I find your statements, I must agree that both scenarios are quite possible. You are quite correct, Tavius, we need a plan B, but plan B must be adaptable to either situation, agreed?"

Tavius grinned and said, "Ah, now we are thinking like seasoned information brokers!"

Wolfgang nodded and added, "This is very clearly a new way of doing business. Not believing or trusting the people we are doing business with but still offering valuable intelligence to further an obscure goal. This is much like an advanced chess match, but with no rules."

"It may be an unstructured chess match," offered Ferdek, "but we must be the ones creating the rules. Otherwise we will not survive."

They all nodded in agreement.

Several days later, Ferdek returned to the meeting area. He approached Alonzo warily but tried to maintain the illusion that he believed Alonzo was a trusted mentor. The two men spoke casually and moved over to secure fresh coffee but, in fact, were looking for a quiet area to talk without being overheard.

Once they were off by themselves, Alonzo chuckled softly and stated, "I sense uneasiness in your manner, Ferdek. Don't tell me I too have become a target of suspicion?"

Ferdek, now annoyed that he couldn't keep his emotions schooled properly, blurted, "What if you are the enemy, and it is you trying to wheedle our hard-won knowledge for the wrong side? Suppose I speculate that the Nazis have captured your family in Poland, and they are squeezing you to work for them! Why don't you simply tell me what your real game is before we go any further?"

The accusation drew Alonzo up short from his condescending approach to Ferdek, and he rocked back into his chair to study the situation briefly. It was a sobering moment for both of them, but Ferdek guarded himself from speaking first. Ferdek decided it was difficult to read Alonzo, so he waited.

Finally Alonzo stated, "You have no reason to trust me, Ferdek. You have learned the most valuable lesson of this business of information brokering, which is, do not trust. However, my counsel is, while you do not trust me or anyone, you should act like you do and not share your suspicions as you do business with others. Remember, we still have to do business with the people we don't like sometimes, to get what we want."

Ferdek, now even more suspicious of the smooth-talking diplomat, challenged, "Why don't we get to the point of the conversation? Do you have anything I need, or are you just wasting my time? Tell me why I should be talking to you."

Alonzo, now feeling hemmed in by the line of questioning, offered, "A bit more courtesy might suit you better, young man. Perhaps that will come in time, provided you live that long. Be that as it may, I came to tell you that the information that you provided the Germans was corroborated by the Allies, but they would like to know how you came by such valuable information when you are not in the general location that one would expect you to be in.

"Precisely how did you get a shipping manifest for a U-boat in Axis controlled waters when you are here in Switzerland?"

Ferdek realized he was acquiring a taste for this new line of work. He smiled slightly and politely offered, "Ah, my seasoned diplomat, now I have your attention, it would seem. Let's just say that in my Gypsy wanderings of recent years I have learned to read the Tarot cards well enough to see things that were supposed to be hidden. May I assume that your contacts want to see more information magic?"

Alonzo too smiled slightly and stated, "Let's just say, the people I'm in contact with would like to see another demonstration before going further with our conversation."

"While that is a reasonable request," admitted Ferdek, "I would like to know how your people acted on my first information offering. If you are not putting our research to good practical use in stopping our enemies, then obviously you are speaking to the wrong people."

It was now Alonzo's turn to be annoyed with the challenge. "We will speak again in three days' time." And with that he abruptly left.

Ferdek chuckled to himself and quietly whispered, "I must be doing better to have really ticked him off like that."

Jacob awoke to the soft snoring of Wolfgang and realized the book was in danger of sliding off his lap. He marked the spot and returned it to the stack with the others. Taking a few minutes to wash his face and brush his teeth, he walked over to make certain Wolfgang was alright. Gently holding Wolfgang's hand, he brushed the knuckles with his thumb and said, "Wolfgang, Grandfather, I am so proud of you and your friends for creating this organization and making a spot for me. I'm not certain I will ever be good enough."

Wolfgang shifted slightly and a smile came to his lips as he whispered, "Listen to Petra, Jacob. You're outstanding."

Jacob held on for a few minutes longer, then made his way back to his recliner and fell asleep against the fresh pillow.

CHAPTER 50

Trading Cake for Freedom

Mathias breathed a little easier as he watched the compressed and encrypted file show up in the designated cryptofile store location Genesis had specified. He was still uncomfortably cable-tied into his chair, but at least this part was progressing. Her two henchmen were carefully placed on either side of him. He was well aware they were quite capable of shooting him if he tried to break free. Genesis watched the screen, and a small smile crossed her face as she began to download the package to the local computer inside their secure facilities.

After the download was complete, Genesis turned and asked, "Password, please?"

Mathias, now a little remorseful, stated, "It is a pass-phrase, **Alois_Dutch_is_gone** with proper caps and underlines in between."

Genesis studied Mathias a moment and then flatly stated, "You know, of course, once I and my government have everything, there really isn't much room left at the table for you."

Mathias smirked a little and replied, "Actually, the thought had occurred to me before now. You should realize that I have always tried to anticipate small wrinkles like this in my planning.

"Fortunately for you, this brings me to my next proposition. Would you care to hear it? Oh, and since it is of a very sensitive nature, can we have your escorts wait outside?"

Suspecting a potential bonus, but not quite certain he actually could deliver one, Genesis replied, "I will need a little more encouragement to get me to dispense with the bodyguards. Is this offer for the state, or did you have something a little more personal in mind?"

Mathias played his last card. "Oh, it's quite personal. It will make you wealthy beyond belief. All I ask is for my freedom. Surely you can see that the benefit in this trade is in your favor?"

Still somewhat skeptical, Genesis asked, "What can you possibly offer me that will make me rich? And why would it mean that my guards should leave before being discussed?"

Still bound to the chair, Mathias motioned with his head for Genesis to come closer. She leaned in, and with her ear close to his mouth, Mathias whispered, "Because I built a trap door into the programs that will use a mathematical rounding program to take all the monies being rounded out to eight decimal points, but only display four. The hidden four decimals, based on EVERY transaction in your country, could then be routed to your bank account, say monthly.

"Once this system is deployed, all you have to do is sit back and figure out your next purchase."

Genesis pulled back and thought for a moment before she verified that Mathias was indeed securely fastened to his chair. She then sent the guards out on break.

Mathias sensed his opportunity might be close at hand as he politely asked, "Do I get to show you entry areas with my hands free, or will I just get to smell that delightful perfume of yours again?"

Genesis smirked a little and stated, "I think you need to remain cable-tied to your chair and talk me through the back door program you installed. Let's also discuss how the trap door is not going to be detected, shall we? I am fairly sure that our smart computer people are going to go through this program with a fine tooth comb, before it's put into production. Something obvious, or worse, clumsy, will be spotted. Am I correct in being confident that you anticipated that part, too?"

Trying to maintain a business-like attitude but struggling to suppress his smile, Mathias offered, "Since you're not going to release me, let's walk through it. There are several screens that do not echo anything back to the operator, so you have to know what the sequence of data entry is and what entries are required. Launch the cake icon on the right and arrow down to the last menu item, then hit the 'enter' key exactly three times. Enter in your bank routing number and, most importantly, your bank account number. Nothing will be displayed on the screen, so don't screw up. When you are finished, hit the 'enter' key one last time, and it will take you to the main menu. That's it."

Genesis stared at the screen, half disbelieving, but breathing heavily with the thought that she could be wealthy beyond belief. She visibly trembled with excitement.

Before she could say anything, Mathias added, "I know what you're thinking. You're thinking that somewhere in the code you would find that string of numbers and the jig would be up. Not so. Using our obfuscation program, we take all the numbers and randomly scatter them throughout the program and then cloak them as well to hide them from code reviewers. We only pull the random numbers back together once a month to do the disbursements.

"Now just for fun, do you want to run the simulator program that is in the package download? You're going to like this part."

The programming logic and the narrative from Mathias were intoxicating, and she dutifully opened the companion icon, cake2. As it opened and presented some data entry areas, she was mesmerized.

Mathias called, "Okay, feed in how many people in your country, average incomes, put in your gross domestic product figures, and then hit calculate. The program will churn and, based on the four digit rounding in your favor, take a look at what you should get each month."

Moments ticked by, and the first monthly installment was displayed. Genesis couldn't believe her eyes. In an effort to confirm the amounts and be conservative, she input new figures, tweaking here and there. Again, a similar nine figure amount was displayed. She ran the simulation three times before turning around to question Mathias, only to realize he had vanished through the open door while she'd been completely absorbed in the simulation.

At first alarmed and confused, she nodded and slowly smiled as she commented, "You said trade my wealth for your freedom, so adieu, Mathias."

Quip wandered around the flat as if afloat in the middle of the ocean. Everywhere he looked he saw EZ. Her signature wasn't present at work like it was here. The ache he felt was so strong he almost packed up some clothes to return to the Operations Center when his cell phone chimed.

Quip smiled at the caller ID and said, "I was just thinking about you, sweetheart. How are you? How is your dad?"

EZ's voice seemed to melt into him as she suggestively offered, "I would be ever so much better if I was wrapped around you naked. I miss you so much, Quip!

"Dad is actually doing better physically, though he now blames himself for Su Lin being gone. The doctor's visit today, the third in as many days, finally found significant improvement. He actually can see and read, provided it is kept at a low light or he wears sunglasses. Doctor McBride seems to think his vision will fully return in a week or two if he keeps his stress down. Part of the slow recovery he has been experiencing is due to the heart condition. He actually joked earlier with me that Su Lin was worried about his weight and certain foods he was consuming, but that has totally shifted. He has dropped about fifteen pounds, and Mercedes suggested he start some modest strength training with her or even Khalid while they are here."

Quip replied, "That sounds great, honey. I am glad to hear he is improving. If anyone can keep him distracted, it is you leveraging that team. Mercedes is planning to stay with you until Su Lin returns. Khalid will also stay put to keep an eye on Mercedes while her man is on assignment.

"Your thoughts are drifting to us, naked and focused? I am so there for you, honey."

EZ laughed and replied, "You always make me smile. Guess that's why I married you. Yes, I want to see you and want to come home. I miss our place. Things here are from my childhood, not from my time with you. Perhaps when Dad has his sight back, I will feel better about coming home.

"Has Su Lin communicated with you? Any idea when she might get to return home? I have this lingering dread about her safely returning. I just can't seem to shake it. I can't talk to Dad about it as it would just upset him to hear negative thoughts. I was hoping you might provide…"

"Eilla-Zan, who are you speaking to? Is that Quip? If it is, you just put him on speaker phone right this minute, young lady!" announced Andy.

"Um, Quip honey, Dad came outside, and I hadn't heard him."

"I gathered, sweetheart. Put it on speaker. We can all talk.

"Andy, so glad to hear you are improving. I understand you can actually see some, which is significant after the muzzle flash. The team will be glad to hear this as well, if you don't mind my sharing."

Andy drawled, "You can share if you want, young'un, but I want the straight scoop on my wife! I don't want any pussy-footing around either. I see well enough with these sunglasses now that I can even read. Why, I found a letter from Su Lin in the night-stand which I'm gonna read to all y'all so you get how serious I am about wanting the truth.

My darling husband,

If you are reading this then I am glad your sight has returned. I am so afraid while writing this that I am the cause of your pain. I know your eyes and your mind are everything to you. I am so very sorry.

The men that did this were from my native country and wanted me to pay for something I tried to right so long ago and failed. Funny, but I was quite the innovative program-mer at one time, but I left that life when I started working on the animal husbandry program in Texas, which was long before we met. I really thought when we were married all of that was well behind us. The little I told you only brushed the surface of the potentially destructive programs I created while in China. Now, like the past of the very wicked, these are coming back to hurt me, by hurting you.

I am returning to China to negotiate your release. I do not presume I will ever be able to return to you, but please do not doubt I will try. Quip and Jacob will do their best to bring me back, but you must not hold it against them if it doesn't work out.

You gave me a life, filled with love and joy. I am so grateful and will love you always.

Your adoring wife,
Su Lin (not Master Po because I am yours)

"Now, do you have eyes on my wife, and how can I help? Because if I don't get to contribute, I will be mighty angry, Quip. And, regardless of what she says, everyone is at fault if we don't bring her home."

Quip swallowed the emotion he felt, as he heard a bit of a sob in the background from EZ. Quip allowed, "Andy, I do know how you feel. We are tracking Su Lin by means of a device. As usual, she called the shots on how this was to play out, but unbeknownst to her we built in some back up plans to help maintain those eyes on her. We are monitoring her and the steps she outlined that were to be taken to remove the threat forever. She built a plan where not only would she get her freedom, if at all possible, but these people would no longer bother her.

"I shouldn't tell you all the details as it will infringe on your deniability. But suffice it to say, several of the men who were on the ranch are gone and even two who have long been trouble are also gone. There are only a few left who remember Master Po. If her plan works as designed, they will no longer be a threat, and she will have done nothing wrong."

Andy gruffly questioned, "You can tell she is alive and where she is now?"

"Yes, sir, I can. Jacob is monitoring part of the time and I am the other. We have her extraction planned as well. It should occur within a week, sooner if we get a break."

Andy leaned his head into his hands with relief and anguish. EZ commented, "Daddy, it will be okay. She will come home. Quip will do everything not to let you down. I will stay until she returns."

Andy grabbed EZ close to him and moaned as she disconnected the call.

Foreclosure After Betting the Farm

Mathias stood looking glum as the dented and dusty second-hand van from an earlier decade rolled up to him. It stalled just as it reached him. The driver had to restart it before the door locks would operate. The passenger side door wouldn't open, so he entered through the sliding door that wouldn't close properly after it was opened. The vehicle's state of readiness did nothing to cure Mathias's down mood.

A towel had to be placed over the well-worn passenger seat before he could sit down, lest the springs attack his buttocks. Once he was seated, the vehicle's security bell went off, alerting everyone to fasten their safety belts. Sadly, this was probably the only thing that worked according to manufacturer's specifications on the van.

Mathias looked over at an equally glum Halvorson, who echoed his down mood through tired eyes. After a few seconds, Halvorson turned in an exaggerated manner and gaily asked, "So, how was your day?"

Mathias almost smirked as he shook his head and offered, "Swell. Am glad that you brought the low-rent, third-world vehicle rather than our helicopter, so we could more easily blend in with the other human debris in this exit maneuver."

Halvorson nodded slightly and offered, "There is a first aid kit behind this seat in case you need some medical attention. You will note that the funny animal bandages are logically grouped with the antiseptic labeled MDW-2020 or, as it is commonly referred to, Mad Dog 20-20. Apparently, it is distilled in the same tub used for bathing the dog, hence the affordable price."

Halvorson continued, "Now I know you've had a difficult jaunt down here in this exciting backwoods dictatorship with all of its intrigue. So I thought we could just settle back at a moderate pace of 35 KPH, since that is all this luxury van will do, and see some of the countryside while we try to get out without having to go through any checkpoints. I really don't want to have to explain why we are in this van, in place of the owners, so I'm going to take it slow, alright?"

Again, Mathias almost smirked and took a swig of the Mad Dog, shuddered slightly, and remarked, "Yep, they need to rinse out the tub better. I can still taste the dog hair."

Halvorson quietly offered, "Sorry about Dutch. Maybe you can tell me about it sometime."

Mathias only nodded.

After several minutes but only a few kilometers, Mathias asked, "Did you happen to secure any other provisions? I am kind of hoping for some dog hair flavored pretzels to go with this almost whiskey. Any weapons or phones?"

Defeated, he added, "I assume you were not able to defeat the ransomware virus, which puts us back at square one, correct? And by the way, thanks for coming to get me."

Halvorson shrugged his shoulders, tossed him a burner phone, and then added, "It took almost all that we had to get down here to fetch you. Don't worry though, we have enough dollars left to almost fund a healthy lemonade stand. I assume you had to give her the trap door that we had engineered into the product to get out of her clutches, so what do you have in mind?"

After another healthy swig of Mad Dog, Mathias gave a chilling smile and stated, "Revenge."

Genesis waited as long as she could before calling her guards to tell them Mathias had escaped. To insure believability to her story, she even roughed herself up a little so it looked like she had struggled before being knocked down. The torn blouse and exposed breast were nice treats to the guards that really put the icing on her bogus story. Her bleeding lip, where she had purposely bit it, left no doubt in their minds, and they both roared out to find Mathias. She smiled at the private joke that he had left 28 minutes ago, instead of just ahead of them. Predictably, Mathias was no longer on the premises.

When the guards returned, she played the stoic secret service agent and insisted she was alright. Their mission, at this juncture, was to get the all-important package to her superiors to make good on the assignment. She made an inspiring sight to the guards, who watched as she clutched her torn clothing with one hand while she carried the all-important cryptocurrency in the other, and insisted that she be taken to them immediately. One of the guards, in a chivalrous gesture, even offered her his tunic to help her regain her modesty.

The trouble was she was in a hurry to get the cryptocurrency into production because that meant money would start flowing into her account as soon as possible. Besides, her showmanship in front of the guards helped to solidify her story. She grinned at how well things were falling into place.

She couldn't wait to deliver the cryptocurrency code and provide the briefing. Genesis was sure that she would be dismissed after the delivery of the code. All the higher ups would then posture themselves for their cut of the new currency, while she was already seated at the table ahead of them. Only they would never find out. Her plan was working better than she had hoped.

CHAPTER 52

A Little Hair in the Program

Professor Lin watched in awe as Master Ling Po worked on the keyboard. At his insistence, she had access to the system in order to work on the program and assemble it with the other pieces of the cryptocurrency code. When she'd arrived a couple of days before, she was so different from the Master Po of his memory. She was still bigger than life, as her fingers flew across the keyboard, but different. Initially, she had greeted him as an equal and, uncharacteristically, asked after his family. She was obviously engaged by his update.

Guano had wanted her to not have access but to dictate the information to Lin. Lin explained what a waste of time that would be. After watching her for several hours, Guano had left with strict orders that she not be left alone. Professor Lin had taken that order literally and made certain they remained together at all times outside of her health breaks. He'd even moved a cot into her sparse sleeping quarters. Programming and testing was to be their focus until it was complete. When the Finance Minister had summoned them the day before, his directives to complete the program and create a working model to share with China's prospects for cryptocurrency was quite clear. Guano was to insure the programs were backed up and routinely tested for any embedded malicious code.

Even in this efficient technology center that Master Ling Po had built, Su Lin felt a sense of distance from her former self. When she had first entered the center, two days ago, the first rush of memories bombarded her mind, pulling and tugging at the life she was now living. Overwhelming sadness at the loss of her assistant Chun assailed her when she entered the sparse sleeping quarters. She recalled Guano taking herself away and then her imprisonment as he repeatedly tried to chemically release her memories of all the hidden pockets of the Cyber Warfare College she had created. It was all too obvious that Professor Lin had managed to use not only what she had taught him, but also some of the areas where she had permitted Guano to think he'd won some part of the puzzle.

Su Lin made certain that Professor Lin followed every portion of her logic as she assembled the pieces of the programs needed to control the cyber-currency, which would allow China to be the masters of digital currency. Her programming signature was nothing new to Professor Lin. They had worked together on the lectures, tests, and the overall curriculum, designed to make the software engineers who graduated from the college the very best in the world. Now the miniscule variation in signature she included did not raise any alarms since Professor Lin would have expected this to morph over time. This code would pass all their tests, of that she was certain.

Recalling their once open discussions on the morality of some programs versus others, she quietly asked, "Professor Lin, I wonder if you ever think about what the programs you have worked on might do to others. Are they helping or harming humanity?"

Professor Lin was quiet, as if assembling the right response before he softly replied, "Master Po, the majority of the programs we have delivered have been of value to the world at large. It is only some of the instructions from powerful people like Chairman Chang or even the current Finance Minister that could be taken in a different direction. You know there is another team who does the final testing and even makes changes to the products if so directed. Chang is of course no longer a threat, and the Finance Minister is only greedy."

Su Lin whispered, "I am Su Lin, no longer Master Po. Please call me Su Lin. I live a different life now. I want to finish this and go home to my family, my friends. Where is your family? How often do you communicate?"

Lin briefly looked around. No one else had entered. He took the keyboard of an adjacent laptop and, with a rapid fire set of keystrokes, seemed to launch a program, though Su Lin could not catch it in its entirety. He breathed with a sense of relief and quietly announced, "That was to make certain that they cannot see or hear what we are doing. The video loop will appear with you diligently working with my close scrutiny.

"My family is held in the compound. My son goes to school, and my wife thinks I work too hard. She performs all the household chores but has no access to our extended family. You have no reason to trust me, but I hope you can return to your family. I will pray for your release, even after you deliver the program."

Su Lin was trying to understand whose side Lin was on. She wanted to believe him but couldn't trust him with her secrets. At least knowing where his family was, she might be able to help. He did allow her to have direct access to the systems. Even though it appeared to have undergone several changes since she had created it, it had only taken a day for her to find the areas she wanted within the system. But as a precaution, all the available PCs had the USB ports disabled and the necessary device drivers deleted from the system. The files she had brought in on her USB drive had to be uploaded to a network drive to be accessed. Guano would take no chances with the once formidable Master Po.

She smiled at the system name, LING-LI which Professor Lin said, in the world of technical acronyms, meant Logarithmic Integration of Numerals Going Linearly and Indefinitely. It was a very fitting system to execute her plans for the long-term digital currency they were creating. The results, however, were not designed to line the Finance Minister or Guano's pockets as they calculated.

"You should know, Lin, I will do my best to help you and your family if the opportunity presents itself. I hope you will not stand in my way when I try to negotiate my release. Delivery of a completed program is my commitment, not staying in China. I live on a thriving ranch in the United States with a wonderful man who loves me. I just want to return home."

Professor Lin entered some additional data and quietly stated, "I think it is time we took a short break for tea, Master Po. I will gather the program you just compiled for pick up by Colonel Guano. It appears we are making progress. Would you expect to complete this project within the next two days?"

Su Lin took a deep breath and expended it like a yawn, then raised her arms and stretched, casually knocking out her hair clip. Her ebony locks pooled around her face and onto the keyboard. She squealed, "Oh, oops! I think you are right. It is time for a break. May I be excused to attend to my health needs and regather my hair so it does not interfere with my typing, please? I can make us the tea in my quarters while you complete your task so you can join me there. And, yes, I think the program will be completed in that timeframe. I expect we can start our first round of proof of concepts, as requested, sometime tomorrow."

Professor Lin frowned slightly but agreed, "I had forgotten how your long hair always seemed to attack the keyboard, almost like a static reaction. Yes, complete your health break, and we will have a short tea."

One of the few times she was left alone since her arrival left her relieved, as she quickly accessed the communications window of the PC to enable Bluetooth connectivity and then squeezed the access button on the back of her hair clip to twin the two devices. Being well within the two meter radius, the two devices paired quickly. She mapped a new drive on the PC to the hair clip and began the file transfer. Afterward, she began downloading the entire program to the folder she had located yesterday, which she'd configured as a hidden directory. Unless you knew it was there, it would not show up under all but the most rigorous scrutiny. When the file transfer completed, she disabled the Bluetooth twinning so it was returned to its original state.

Now she only had to access the portions of the program she needed to set the countdown into motion at the right times. This silent game-changer was lying in wait for the commands she was building into her signature. As she adjusted her hairclip, she smiled at the way she was progressing. Exiting the premise and getting home were things she could not dwell on. The teapot emitted a quiet whistle as she finished.

Jacob called into the conference bridge. "Quip, Petra, I think that Su Lin is working. The secondary tracker is still active. I have not seen anything yet that I can attach my code to, but I suspect it will be available soon.

"Petra, did you complete the encryption routine and place the file where we had agreed?"

Petra replied, "I did and we have been watching. ICABOD has infiltrated LING-LI through the supercomputer's backdoor which was still in place. Apparently there is some continual communication between these machines, centered on chess.

ICABOD suggested it is the only way to get a challenging game without Wolfgang."

Jacob smiled and replied, "I will pass it along to Wolfgang that his better is a foreign supercomputer. I think he just might appreciate that. I will let you know if anything changes."

CHAPTER 53

When is the Foundation the End?
...The Enigma Chronicles

Sunrise in the hospital room provided a pleasant glow, as if the world was waking to something new and wonderful. Jacob noted that Wolfgang was still sleeping, and apparently the staff had done their normal stealthy morning routine as his drips all appeared to be fresh. A lovely pot of coffee was on the table adjacent to him along with a glass of juice. When he returned from washing the sleep out of his eyes, he poured a cup of coffee. He wanted to read a little more from the writings and thought the deep cadence of his voice might gently rouse Wolfgang.

"Grandfather, I think we left off at this point...

The three of them, Ferdek, Wolfgang, and Tavius, were startled by the sudden intrusion of four men, led by Alonzo, into their rented flat. While no one had a weapon drawn, they were obviously armed and ready for a conflict if it came to that.

Tavius took the initiative and began talking as he walked closer to perhaps launch into an assault, when Ferdek intercepted him.

Ferdek then turned. "Ah, Alonzo, what an unexpected surprise. Since I see no coffee or croissants, I must assume that you are not here for a breakfast meeting."

Alonzo, not in the least bit amused, tersely responded, "You made it quite clear at our last meeting that you wanted proof points for what you believe to be useful information. The American OSS are here, and they are not easily amused by a cavalier attitude to information brokering. Now the accusation is to be turned around, and you have been accused of being Nazis spies by first providing accurate information, then delivering false or tainted information so as to cloak important technology movements.

"Impress us with more reliable information that no one else has access to, or tell us how you came by this knowledge. Preferably both."

Before anything could be said by either group, Alonzo stated in a low voice, "And yes, Ferdek, my family was captured by the Nazis in order to squeeze me to work for them, but I escaped here to Switzerland. When I went out of contact with them, my family was interred at Sobibor as political prisoners. For us to do any business together, never mention that painful topic again."

Ferdek tried to steel himself against his feelings of regret, but he felt ashamed at dredging up such a painful topic. He choked slightly on the story since it reminded him of his own father's end when the Germans overran Poland.

As usual, Wolfgang studied the situation as Tavius launched into verbal discourse with the unannounced guests.

"Since we are all here, why don't we do a recap of current events?

"Let me begin by stating we unearthed some very interesting intelligence on a U-Boat being loaded up with material destined to be delivered on the other side of the planet, to who we suspect are their partners in crime. We, being ex-pats from Poland, wanted to alert the Allies of this highly questionable series of events since we now believe that U-168 was carrying next generation weapon material and knowledge to be exercised to the Allies' disadvantage. We deliberately gave it to the Germans, so the former ambassador, Alonzo here, could observe. You confirmed our information's validity by showing up here. Yet we see three armed goons who have yet to even introduce themselves.

"We want to know, first of all, what action if any happened to our hard won intelligence; secondly, proof points to who and what these armed resources belong; and, third, no, we won't discuss our next round of hard won information until we receive useful value for our discussions."

Both groups studied each other for a moment, and finally Alonzo stated, "I'm the only one whose name you are entitled to know. I can tell you that these gentlemen are with the Swiss Intelligence Agency, but for reasons of security they are only to be known by their designated code name 'Lucy'."

Before Alonzo could continue, one of the silent men interrupted, "You should know that once your intelligence was passed through, the U-168 was hastily launched and is now believed to be heading through the North Atlantic for a refueling stop with their comrades in the South Atlantic. While they still have friends in Uruguay and

Argentina, they probably won't risk going into port to be trapped in Montevideo like the Graf Spee was."

Another of the men continued, "We don't have the resources to stalk a lone U-Boat through the Atlantic and into the South Pacific. But we have alerted the Free Dutch seafarers operating off the coast of Indonesia and asked them to intercept and stop it, if at all possible. Do you now believe how serious we are about the information you clumsily dispensed to the Germans?"

Ferdek countered, "We are ex-patriots trying to help the Allies in their struggle, which is in our best interest, but without a formal office we can call on, we improvised. We got your attention, and, more importantly, we understand that you have acted on our information. All we need now is to hear of your success in stopping the enemy. When can we expect that?"

Wolfgang, sensing the tension between the two groups, interjected, "May we know if you and your people are interested in further intelligence that we might be in a position to provide? You should understand our intelligence gathering is not a one-time fluke. Are you in a position to receive and act on more, as we can provide it?"

No one answered at first. Then Alonzo finally offered, "You might as well know, we find your approach to information brokering very annoying. However, if you can provide more useful information, we will probably be in a position to overlook your character flaws. We will stop asking how and simply concentrate on what, as it is provided. Agreed?"

Tavius grinned and stated, "Sounds like we are in passionate agreement with each other. I suggest that we continue to provide useful intelligence, but will you provide feedback from time to time on the outcomes of what we provide?

"We would want to get clarity on both successful and unsuccessful."

Ferdek smiled slightly and offered, "Talk again in two days' time? There is high confidence that we will have fresh information for your consumption at that point."

Without saying anything, Alonzo nodded slightly, and the team of intruders left as quickly as they had arrived.

After the visitors left, Wolfgang reflected, "Did anyone else notice that even though we are the novices here in the information brokering business, we just received a forced visit from the seasoned professionals in this game, ready to get more information?

"If I had to guess, I might postulate that something or someone has disrupted their regular intelligence information flow and they are looking for us to fill that role."

Tavius added, "Yes, it is very curious indeed."

Ferdek nodded. "This is the beginning of something very new for this world. We need to make a pact."

Wolfgang quietly and slowly commented, "And we did. Our pact was to keep the information flowing to the right channels to maintain an edge over wrongdoers or, today, cyber thugs. You, my dear Jacob, are a continuation of that pact."

Jacob looked up in surprise at the comments and asked, "All of this is true? These people, these places, the struggle?"

Wolfgang nodded and then began coughing. Alarmed, Jacob closed and put down the journal and moved to his side, as Nurse Sandy rushed in and started taking vitals.

Moments later Nurse Sandy stated, "Mr. Michaels, Wolfgang is showing some serious indicators. I am going to get the doctor. You stay by his side until we return."

Wolfgang caught his breath and whispered, "Take the books home. I want to spend what little time I have left with you listening to your future, not my pas…"

"Of course." Jacob interrupted. "Don't try to talk, Grandfather. I'll be right here."

Nurse Sandy was back along with Nurse Sue and Doctor Roblinski, who turned Jacob off to the side. Nurse Sandy helped Wolfgang sit up to alleviate the coughing, while Doctor Roblinski did some more checking and ordered an injection and oxygen. The coughing eased, and Wolfgang seemed to be relaxing when Nurse Sandy gently laid him against the extra pillows.

Doctor Roblinski turned to Jacob and confided, "Mr. Michaels, Wolfgang has been giving his all, but he is very tired. His heart is weakening at a faster rate than we thought, even after the recent tests. I think it is time to bring in the family. I am sorry."

Jacob was shocked at the news and felt paralyzed. Nurse Sue led him out of the room so they could change the sheets and add more monitoring equipment. She handed him his cell phone that he'd left on the table near the coffee then returned to the room without a word.

An hour later Jacob still sat on a chair outside of Wolfgang's room. It felt like the weight of the world was on his shoulders, and he couldn't bring himself to call anyone for fear he would break down. After watching the comings and goings from Wolfgang's room, including some new equipment in and old equipment out, he remembered his laptop and the books were inside. Rising, he went to the door and looked around. Things looked calmer, though Wolfgang had a lot of new connections, intermittently emitting squawks and beeps.

Doctor Roblinski looked up and motioned for Jacob to enter. He outlined the current course of treatment as well as the lack of stability Wolfgang demonstrated. The result would be additional care in the room and at the outside monitors, with reassurances that Wolfgang was not in pain, but he would be under their care for the duration. The doctor then reminded Jacob to contact the family regarding the changes.

Jacob went to the sitting area and retrieved the books, adding them to his backpack. Then he glanced at the laptop and noticed the signal was still strong with no notifications on data in or out of the agreed location. He closed the top, retrieved the cord, and mumbled to no one in particular he would be in the hall if they needed him. Setting the backpack and the laptop on the extra chair, he pulled out his cell phone.

When the call connected, he sadly stated, "Otto, it's me, Jacob. Can you do me a favor, please?"

Otto sensed something was off and gently replied, "Yes, my boy, what can I do for you?"

"Otto, Wolfgang took a turn for the worse, and the doctor would like the family informed. I don't think I can place those calls right now. Can you?"

Otto promised, "Yes. Haddy and I arrived moments ago and were just about to come up to the floor to see Wolfgang, so we'll be right there."

"Thank you."

Trading Today For Tomorrow

Halvorson watched uneasily as Mathias brought out their ransomware infected PC and booted it up in the free Wi-Fi enabled café. While Halvorson was not the consummate mercenary that Dutch was, he was good at situational awareness for high risk scenarios like this one. He kept scanning the area discreetly to make sure no one was studying them.

As the machine booted up, Mathias inserted a USB thumb drive designed to intercept the boot process in hopes that he could defeat the virus.

Halvorson kept scanning the area as he said in a low voice, "You sure this is a good idea? I mean, we are out here in the unfamiliar surroundings of South America, flashing a PC that could easily be used to buy a whole village. Of course, I wouldn't mind this village since it has running water, electricity, and Wi-Fi. I'm kind of old fashioned that way. Just buying two coffees and a couple of muffins with $20 Bolivar equivalent earned us more stares than if we had showed up naked."

Without moving his gaze from the screen, Mathias thoughtfully asked, "Please tell me you're not going to test that hypothesis? You know you lose focus on the subject at hand when you go down your theoretical rat holes."

Halvorson smirked slightly and responded, "Looks like you lost your sense of humor along with everything else.

"How's it coming? Can you bypass the virus by only loading key device drivers on the machine? If you can get to our remaining holdings, I promise I won't do my happy dance until later." As Halvorson looked around, he sadly added, "Probably a law against it here based on how glum everyone looks."

Mathias turned his head slightly to look Halvorson in the eye. "I know you're trying to reduce some of the tenseness of the situation with levity, but if you don't stop it I'm going to spit up."

Halvorson quietly acquiesced and went back to his situational awareness monitoring. Mathias concentrated on his deliberate but slow boot sequence of the compromised PC. After 20 minutes, he began to smile slightly as he almost had the machine up but not locked with the ransomware. As he completed the final step of loading the network drivers, the screen cleared and displayed:

That was very clever! However, we anticipated this move so please disburse the rest of the stolen cryptocurrency of Steven Christopher to the following website –

https://straighten_up_and_fly_right.com! We'll be watching.

Halvorson did a double-take at the message on the screen while Mathias just sat there numbly staring.

After several moments of stunned silence, Mathias asked, "Do you think we can still get a whole village for this PC? I've always wanted my own village."

Quip asked, "What is it, ICABOD?"

ICABOD stated, "Dr. Quip, you had asked me to alert you if there were any new developments in the cryptocurrency arena.

The Venezuela government has just announced their intention to introduce a cryptocurrency for their country. Their intention is to use it for all official business transactions with the state, but not displace their Bolivar currency yet. They insist their product is well designed with many safe-guards in place to assure secure transactions for the population."

Quip nodded and mused out loud, "Fairly good move on their part. They will only do state business using the new C-C, but will not remove the old fiat currency. Of course if their C-C really is a good product, why would they want to use the ghastly Bolivar that is devaluing by the minute? With a solid C-C offering, they just might be able to stabilize their economic condition and become heroes to the desperate population.

"Wonder if they realize they will need a PC and WAN connectivity to the cryptomining servers, and, oh yeah, continual electricity to make the product go vroom-vroom. As it is, they barely have enough electricity to keep their hospitals operational, let alone abundant electricity for private consumption. ICABOD, when are they launching this on the public? What's the go live date?"

ICABOD responded, "Apparently they intend to make their new cryptocurrency available next week, Dr. Quip."

Quip puzzled a little and said, "Odd that we haven't seen any evidence of a pilot test of their currency before now. This suggests that this is a hurry up and get it out there launch.

"ICABOD, please keep monitoring this situation since this may be another ill-conceived get rich quick scheme. I'm not fond of dictatorships, but those poor people sure don't need any more problems, and a failed exercise in cryptocurrency would only destroy their hopes further."

ICABOD said, "Understood, Dr. Quip. On another note, that PC holding the last of the Stuart Chesterfield, aka Steven

Christopher, cryptocurrency came online briefly this morning. It went off almost as fast as it came on, but there were no additional transmissions of the stolen funds to our hosting website. Do you wish for me to maintain that hosted website?"

Quip smiled and stated, "They must have hit the secondary ransomware protocol and realized there will be no reprieve or work around. The only thing left is for them to completely re-image the PC. However, I would expect them to try one more time to access the hard drive, sector by sector, but our code has already gotten there first. At some point they are going to get tired of seeing the same taunt reflected on the screen. There is only one person that I know who could defeat our program, and thankfully he works with us. ICABOD, let me know if the machine resurfaces again, and see if you can triangulate a location."

ICABOD replied, "Yes, Dr. Quip."

CHAPTER 55

Lessons Learned
from the Dragon

Professor Lin angrily launched the cloaking sequence to the video cameras so he could speak frankly to Su Lin. He interrupted her computer activity. "Nothing has changed, huh? You are still the inscrutable Master Po despite your protests that you only wish to return home to your new life! Did you think I wouldn't find it as if I were one of your untutored students? In the years that you have been gone, I have had to deal with everything you left behind. Did you seriously believe I wouldn't learn to hunt for deception?"

Su Lin swallowed hard to try and steel her emotions, then, offering all the innocence she could muster, began, "Professor Lin, I'm not sure I understand this line of questioning or..."

Professor Lin cut her off with an angry retort. "Stop it! I found the hidden code you deposited on the system. How you got it there is a matter of conjecture, but the log files clearly flagged your user ID, as well as the system admin actions you took to cloak it.

"I put the surveillance systems into a looping mode, not to help you but to warn you! My family is at stake here. Out of respect for you I won't turn you in, but do not try this again, understand? My parents, my grandparents, my aunts and uncles, my brothers and sisters, my wife and child are all Chinese and all here! You may want to leave this country, but I cannot! I want all my family! If this fails, they are all at risk, not just you. Stop putting them at risk!"

Su Lin dropped her head down and admitted, "Professor Lin, I apologize for not taking into consideration all the ramifications of my actions. Now that you have cleaned the system of my deception, I have no cards left to play. Out of respect to you, I will attempt nothing further."

Professor Lin's temper subsided quickly as he offered, "Master Po, I…want to help, but the price is simply too steep. Please do not try anything else. Guano is also combing the system, looking for anything out of the ordinary, and if he catches you, it will be most unpleasant for both of us. Your actions will implicate me as an accomplice."

A single tear ran down Su Lin's cheek. "I understand.

I wouldn't want to lose you to Guano, like I did my former assistant Chun, our Grasshopper."

Satisfied at the promise, Professor Lin nodded and returned the cameras to real time monitoring before he left the area.

Su Lin sighed before she returned to her programming activities and muttered under her breath, "I'm glad you have confidence that I was intercepted. But no matter, I will make sure you and yours are safe."

Quip remarked to ICABOD, "Oh good, they took the decoys that Su Lin planted. Doctoring the logs to point to the dummy code hidden on the system had the exact result our Jacob predicted. I may have to compliment him on his forensic ability at some point in the future. On second thought, I'll probably have to be in a highly inebriated state of mind so I can deny the statement the following day."

Quip then asked, "ICABOD, set up a video call with Julie, Petra, and Jacob, please. I believe we are ready for stage two. As soon as the demo test is completed, I am fairly certain the Chinese will be finished with Su Lin. That is the point, we predict, they will try and finish her."

ICABOD opened the secured conference bridge with Quip already joined. As soon as everyone was bridged in, Quip said, "Okay, all. We are ready for our next milestone. Jacob and Petra, the decoys were detected and removed. Julie, do you have your people in place for phase two?"

Julie nodded and reassured, "They're already in place."

Quip smiled and announced, "Then let's go get the Dragon Lady!"

CHAPTER 56

Staying Away from What-If Scenarios

Otto and Haddy had taken over watching Wolfgang, sending Jacob home with Bowen. Otto called several family friends to alert them that Wolfgang wasn't making the progress they'd all hoped. Watching the machines doing most of the work on Wolfgang's behalf was very disheartening. Everyone offered their best wishes and prayers for the entire family.

Haddy was having a quiet conversation of her own with Wolfgang as she held his hand. She had called both Petra and Julie to let them know that things were grim at this point. Julie indicated she'd be there with her family as quickly as possible. Haddy questioned the prudence of that with the ongoing project the team was working, but Julie reminded her that work could be conducted from anywhere, but she wanted to give Wolfgang a hug and let him see the children if he was up for it.

Otto decided he'd postponed calling Quip for long enough. Moving to the sitting area of the hospital room, he placed the call. When the call connected, Otto said, "Quip, how are things progressing toward getting Su Lin out of there and back home?"

Quip thought about the question before he replied, "I was going to save it for the team call in a couple of hours, but it looks like the parts are assembled.

"Did Jacob forget to let you know that when you arrived at the hospital? You are there with him, right? I can't keep up with everyone's schedule, but I thought you told me you were headed there hours ago. Ask Jacob if he saw the notifications. I noticed them quite some time ago, so he had to as well.

"By the way, how's Wolfgang doing, Otto? Tell him ICABOD wants to play a game of chess soon. Wolfgang really created a true rival when he taught ICABOD chess."

Otto mused, "I think for the first time in sometime, you are indeed out of step.

"To be honest, Quip, Wolfgang is not doing well. Yes, Haddy and I are at the hospital, but I sent Jacob home to change and rest up. I don't think he is even looking at this laptop. Wolfgang's health has deteriorated to the point where… um, it might be a good time for you to visit and tell him about ICABOD yourself."

Quip was dumbstruck. He was sure Petra had told him that the doctors were hopeful recently, and testing seemed positive. He recalled her saying Wolfgang had spoken and even had some wine with the permission of the nursing staff. Quip quietly said, "I'm sorry, Otto, for being so flip. You are right, I had no idea. Jacob didn't call me."

Otto reassured, "Quip, I'm not certain Jacob's up to calling anyone. I sent him home with Bowen, who is also a mess, with instructions to let the lad shower and eat. It would be great if he could rest, but I won't hold my breath."

"I guess I should call EZ, but she won't come home until Su Lin is back with Andy. This is sad, Otto. How are you doing?"

"I'm sitting here in his room watching the machines monitor everything and, frankly, feeling a bit vulnerable. Wolfgang has been the strength of our family for a very long time. I'm glad he has met and worked with Jacob. I think Jacob is truly a chip off the Wolfgang block, though he doesn't believe it."

Quip felt incensed as he countered, "Well, he should believe it. Wait until I explain what his strategy was with the digital currency tracking and guardrails. Nothing short of brilliant. More on that later. I will place a call to EZ and head that way. Thank you, Otto."

Otto disconnected the call and went to stand by Haddy. She smiled up at him and said, "I was just telling Wolfgang all about the kids and making sure he has all the details. He didn't respond, but I know he heard me."

"Of course he heard you, dear."

Petra had arrived at the chateau a short time before and had gone up to her and Jacob's room. Jacob had come out of the shower with a towel about his waist and was staring into the closet, oblivious to everything, she surmised.

"Jacob, honey, do you want me to pick out something for you to wear? Or would you like me to get some food for us?"

It seemed like an eternity before he responded. "No, Petra, I'll get dressed, and we can go down and eat something. I know Bowen wants to get back to the hospital, and I do too. Just such big shoes to fill…"

His voice trailed off, and Petra walked over and reached around, hugging his back. Resting her cheek on his back and stroking his shimmering dragon tattoo, she reassured, "Jacob, you are just fine. Wolfgang has so much faith in your abilities and loves you a great deal.

"I will go downstairs and fix us something. Please come down soon."

He nodded in response, and she turned to leave. Before she reached the door he asked, "Can you get the laptop out of my backpack and take it with you? I haven't checked on Su Lin in a long time, and perhaps we can together while we eat, okay?"

Petra did his bidding and just before she closed the door to leave she said, "Good idea, Jacob. I will check on it and give you an update when you get downstairs."

CHAPTER 57

Revenge or Justice?

Half annoyed at being pulled away to take a call, the man tersely stated, "Yes, this is the attorney for Alejandro Noya. To whom am I speaking?"

The male voice on the other end of the call replied, "This is Mathias, the contractor that was working with Alejandro to deliver your new cryptocurrency that would have been used by your Venezuelan government. I tried to reach him to warn him, but I was told I could only speak to you on his behalf. Are you really his legal counsel?"

Intrigued by the conversation, the attorney replied, "Yes, I am the legal counsel for Alejandro Noya. If you have important information that will help me to defend him, then please share, Mr. Mathias."

Mathias took a moment to collect his thoughts, then continued, "Some time back, my organization was contacted, and an introduction was brokered to meet and present our cryptocurrency product to a Venezuelan government official named Alejandro Noya. At the time, it looked like a lucky break for my organization, and we assumed it was all on the up and up.

"We compiled a well-crafted demonstration based on all our research about your economy and financial needs. We conducted several presentations with Alejandro and his peers. Recently, we were told he was seized, and we were instructed to surrender our intellectual property to a woman called Genesis. This is the same Genesis that posed as the office babe in Alejandro's office. As a part of seizing our intellectual property, she represented herself as an undercover operative for the Venezuelan government and stated in no uncertain terms that she, not my team, would deliver the finished product to her leadership.

"However, you must know that, using my knowledge of the product, she altered the cryptocurrency package destined for your government while I was incarcerated by her guards. I am ashamed to say that I was persuaded to cooperate lest I be shot like my associate when she and her guards arrived at my door. Genesis has introduced an 8-digit rounding algorithm that cloaks all financial transactions beyond four decimal points and, after aggregating those monies, then routes the proceeds to her named bank account.

"Again, I had to bear witness to this tampering with my company's IP, so she could profit at your people's expense. As a last gloating exercise, Genesis boasted that she was the one who brokered the original introductions so that she could intercept the cryptocurrency package destined to the right people, alter it for her own gain, and then blame Alejandro for crimes against the state."

The attorney rocked at the revelation. Before he could say anything, Mathias added, "She might have gotten away with it forever, but I escaped before she could kill me. I would understand if you find all of this hard to believe, so let me provide a proof point that she won't be able to refute."

The attorney responded, "A proof point would go a long way to discovering the truth in this situation, and it would help an innocent man go free. How can you prove these allegations? I assume you won't come in to testify."

Mathias quickly agreed, "You got that right! I don't want to end up dead like my associate at the hands of that murdering bitch. But she was so confident that no one would find the hidden code that she let me see how it would execute. I can't sit by and let Alejandro take the rap for something he didn't do. Nor can I let her rob this poor country and allow her to escape justice for killing my partner…my friend."

Mathias took a deep breath, then added, "The code is designed to collect digits from five through eight to the right of the decimal point, aggregate those funds programmatically, hide them using obfuscation technology, and then every 30 days send them to her bank account using the bank routing numbers I saw her enter. She used a quick calculation tool which suggested an eight or nine digit monthly disbursement once the product is fully deployed by your government.

"Rather than wait 30 days to see if I'm right and she is scamming this country, I thought of a way to test for the deception now. The application, like all applications, needs a Network Time Protocol or NTP source for its time stamp process. I believe you can bring up our program, point it to a bogus NTP server, alter the time so that the cryptocurrency program believes it has been 30 days, which will activate the disbursement to her bank account. If you bring up the components the way I suggested, then ANY disbursement to her account will substantiate everything I've told you. You will then know Genesis, not Alejandro, is the culprit."

Moments past before the attorney clucked his tongue and cautioned, "Mr. Mathias, I have several conversations I need to have to see if I can intercept what could be a grave injustice. Assuming you are still running, how long can you be reached on this cell phone?"

Mathias coolly offered, "I turn this phone on only to make outbound calls, so that I am not inadvertently tracked by that psychotic killer Genesis. I also move after completing every call. My advice is to keep trying this number, and I will try to reach back to you in a few days' time. For now, I hope this information helps you. Adieu."

After disconnecting from the call, Mathias looked at Halvorson, who only shook his head slowly as he said, "I just love going to the movies with you. There is always a great fictional tale of intrigue and deceit playing on the big screen. Just wish we had some popcorn and gummy bears for the next episode!

"You weren't kidding when you said revenge. I really teared up at the part where you play the indignant, moralistic, self-righteous business man trying to right a gross travesty of justice! How much of a reward do you think they will give us?"

Mathias calmly looked over the rim of his reading glasses and asked, "You willing to go into where I just escaped from to get it?"

Halvorson rocked back in his seat and remarked, "Naw, maybe being the indignant, moralistic, self-righteous business man trying to right a gross travesty of justice is reward enough."

ICABOD stated, "Dr. Quip, I have just learned that the Venezuelan government has postponed their cryptocurrency release for two weeks. No reason was given officially, but the background noise and Internet chatter from that area of the world is very heated."

Quip puzzled and said, "It's odd that they would make a splashy announcement then withdraw it with only a vague statement of when it might be available. It suggests that an unanticipated wrinkle developed."

ICABOD offered, "Do you wish me to prowl deeper for the background reasons or simply wait and see?"

Quip responded, "Well, if you have the compute cycles, I would like to know more. After all, that is also the area where we spotted the stolen Stuart Chesterfield coins resurface. I'd like to know if there is a connection, but please stay focused on the Su Lin rescue project. That has our highest priority at the moment."

ICABOD replied, "Yes, Dr. Quip. This has a dependency for releasing Mistress Eilla-Zan to come home once Su Lin has been returned."

Quip stared wistfully into space and only nodded.

CHAPTER 58

Life in These Interesting Times

Guano was almost giddy as the cryptocurrency demonstration progressed to its conclusion. He watched with keen interest as Su Lin and Professor Lin went through all the architectural discussions, the security checkpoints, and programming logic of the cryptocurrency package. Guano, from time to time, glanced at the video monitor to check the mood of the Finance Minister, who was also intently watching.

Finally, after two full hours of demonstration and discussion points, the Professor and Su Lin stopped to let the full impact of the demo be absorbed. Guano fought to suppress his grin, but the Finance Minister struggled with his facial expressions. The Finance Minister had frowned or snarled for so many years that his facial muscles no longer could produce an honest smile, so his face merely looked distorted.

Recognizing her milestone was delivered, Su Lin cleared her throat then calmly stated, "Gentlemen, I have kept my end of the bargain. I would like to petition that your agreement now be honored. I was promised to be returned to my home and husband in America if I delivered the cryptocurrency package. As you can see from the demonstration, my work is done here."

Guano's smile began to fade as he noticed the familiar frown return to the Finance Minister's face.

Trying to contain his contempt for Su Lin, the Finance Minister chillingly maintained, "Master Po, we are satisfied that you have delivered as promised. My government is concerned about ongoing care and feeding of these programs. If any warranty work is required, it may not be convenient for my government to retrieve you from your remote home."

He turned his gaze from her then, and added in a chilling tone, "Guano, I believe you offered to extend every courtesy to our guest while we wait for the opening launch date of our new cryptocurrency. Make sure that she is not disturbed in her new accommodations."

Professor Lin struggled to contain his outrage, but Su Lin calmly presented, "I would have expected more honor from this government, based on what I just provided. I completed this task without charge. I can see now, I was too helpful in providing an extremely strong cryptocurrency that would be suitable as a global monetary medium."

Su Lin turned to Professor Lin and reaffirmed, "I half expected this treatment from them, but I can't even describe to you how disappointed I am in your being party to it. You even defeated my escape plans. I can only surmise that you have become one of them. I hope you enjoy your new status.

"It seems you have fulfilled the dishonorable curse from the ancient Chinese proverb 'May you all live in these interesting times of your own creation.'"

CHAPTER 59

Next Gen, Release Four Dot O
...The Enigma Chronicles

Jacob returned to the hospital, knowing everything was positioned for the next stage of cryptocurrency in China. Petra had taken a look, along with Quip, at the final sequence of events. Jacob knew it was a solid plan and chuckled at the way he had provided his signature as a backhanded compliment. Otto and Haddy were seated next to Wolfgang. Jacob immediately noticed the whining rhythm of the monitors and apparatus which, at this point, Wolfgang was totally dependent upon. Otto and Haddy rose as the doctor entered.

"Mr. Michaels," said Dr. Roblinski, "your grandfather's getting some rest by letting these machines do most of the work. His decline has been further exacerbated by an infection we discovered in his lungs. He's on a rigorous round of antibiotics. If this goes as planned, he might be able to take over from the machines, but we won't know for a while. Wolfgang is fighting, but it is an uphill battle."

Jacob looked forlorn as he replied, "Thank you, doctor. Please do the best you can to help him, but he is not to suffer."

"Yes, sir. I understand. The whole staff understands and is pulling for him."

The doctor left. Otto, Haddy, and Jacob moved to the sitting area of the room.

Jacob asked, "Otto, I'm not certain what to do. I, um…"

Otto looked at Jacob and replied, "You don't get to do anything. Right now it is up to Wolfgang and God.

"Wolfgang has lived his life his way for a very long time. His life has not been easy, but he refused to compromise his ideals to all challenges. His greatest joy, outside of his daughter Julianna, is you. Meeting you was a hope he'd held onto for many years. We spoke of it often. His fear was that you would be opposed to the family business and not be the kind of man he hoped for. You, my boy, have exceeded all his expectations.

"When you and I first met, I was essentially taking your measure for our group, but especially for Wolfgang. Julianna taught you well, and I wish she could see how much you have grown. We are just as proud of you as Wolfgang."

Haddy leaned into him and kissed his cheek. "I know my daughter and you have fought some vicious demons, yet you have survived. We are all a part of your family, Jacob. We are here to support you and Wolfgang."

Quip and Petra entered the room. Jacob rose and walked over to Quip and said, "Hey, Quip, glad you could come. I told Wolfgang how you'd been holding down the fort."

Petra moved over and hugged Jacob. With her arm loosely around his waist she asked, "How's he doing? His color is good. Any news from the doctors?"

Jacob pulled Petra a little closer and said, "Actually he has an infection they are treating. These machines are doing a lot of work so that he can heal. Dr. Roblinski wasn't certain if he would wake up or not. They are monitoring him very closely.

"Quip, let's change the subject and update everyone on the Chinese project."

Quip updated the team on the status of the project and the plans being formulated to extract Su Lin. He indicated Julie had provided some additional insight to the general location of the project and the steps that were being taken. He further added that when he'd spoken to EZ earlier, she indicated that Andy was recovering well but really disheartened that Su Lin wasn't home.

The doors to the room opened and Dr. Roblinski and Nurse Sandy entered. They informed the group they needed to wait outside the room. Each of them paced the hallway in their own fashion, quietly avoiding one another. The pacing stopped when Julie stepped off the elevator.

Julie provided hugs all around and said, "I've left the children at the chateau with Cook. Juan is sorry to not be here, but he had a task he had to complete. Bowen picked us up at the airport and suggested this might not be the best time for the children to visit. He's parking the car and will be up shortly." Then she realized where they were and asked, "Why are you all out in the hallway?"

Petra took Julie by the arm and walked with her down the hallway to two chairs. She filled her in on the current state of Wolfgang, followed by a discussion on the current state of the project and the various assignments. Julie had really wanted to go along with Juan, but with Wolfgang's current condition, she chose family first.

A few hours later, Haddy made her way down to the end of the hallway to her daughters, and when they looked up at her, she stated, "Wolfgang may be coming around. They have shifted some of his medicines, and the antibiotics seem to have helped significantly. Otto is in with him now along with Bowen. Dr. Roblinski suggested we might want to, well, say some special things to him or just hold his hand."

The ladies all rushed back down the hallway where Quip and Jacob were waiting for them outside the door.

Bowen came out a few minutes later, trying to hold himself together, though his eyes were clearly rimmed in the red of fresh tears of sorrow. He hugged Jacob, then quietly said, "Wolfgang is in and out of it. He is speaking very slowly and quietly. Doctor said he is not in pain, but he is very weak. Wolfgang refused anything to make him sleep until he speaks to each of us. He wants you four."

Each of them walked in with trepidation, though they tried to mask it.

Otto promised, "I will," to Wolfgang as he moved out of the way and released the hand of his friend with a solemn smile. He motioned the four of them forward and wrapped his arm over Haddy's shoulder as they stood to the side.

Wolfgang's color was a bit pasty, and his breathing slow though not terribly labored, only shallow. His hair was combed, likely by Bowen. Wolfgang had always held himself straight and tall, and even in his bed he looked almost regal. They noticed the monitors were all running and providing the stats and vitals, but the sounds had all been silenced.

When they were all positioned closely around the bed with Jacob closest. Jacob refused to give into his sadness as he quietly took Wolfgang's hand and said, "Grandfather, Petra, Julie, Quip, and I are all here. We know you are fighting hard like always to do the right thing. I love you, Wolfgang, Grandfather. I respect you so very much and am glad you found me, and ..."

His breath caught, and he paused as Wolfgang opened his eyes, which appeared very clear, and looked at each of them in turn. Then, very slowly and deliberately he assured, "You four will take the business forward. I have faith in you. Otto will help if needed. Ferdek and Tavius would agree." Closing his eyes, Wolfgang continued to hold Jacob's hand with a steady, even pressure.

Everyone glanced at the monitors and were reassured by the steady stream of numbers and lines.

Nurse Sandy quietly entered the room, noted some of the medicine levels in the IVs, and suggested, "Let him rest a while. At present, he's stable."

Haddy and Otto came close and mentioned they would go home for a while to check on Gracie and Juan Jr. Haddy leaned over and kissed Wolfgang, then patted her daughters as she left.

Quip asked, "Do you want me to stay, Jacob? You know me, I can work from nearly anywhere."

Jacob shook his head and replied, "No, but thank you, Quip. I think I'll stay here for a bit, but I will go home later."

Wolfgang grunted and roused, "Go play chess with ICABOD. He needs a challenge. You'll do."

Quip chuckled and said, "He would so like that, Wolfgang. Without you there, ICABOD's having to resort to other computers on the net, and he thinks they all cheat."

Wolfgang's eyes twinkled a bit before he closed them, but he held a slight smile on his face.

Petra and Julie each hugged Wolfgang and, with gentle kisses, murmured their love and wishes for him to feel better soon.

Wolfgang released Jacob's hand and gave him a thumbs up, as if reassuring him it was indeed time to play ICABOD.

CHAPTER 60

When You Can't Beat Them, Join Them

Guano, annoyed that he was the one who had to escort Su Lin to the waiting government sedan, held her roughly by the arm as they walked. His temper flared and he shook Su Lin. One tremor was hard enough to release her hair from the clip so that it cascaded down, flowing over her traditional white blouse, gray tie, and blue skirt that many of the young girls in the private school she'd continued to contribute to wore. She had dressed that way today as it reminded her of her youth, when she believed in the value of everyone learning.

The security perimeter around the supercomputer meant that they had to cover almost a kilometer before they reached the car. Once outside the compound proper, they still needed to cross some streets to reach the parked vehicle. As traffic came and went, a couple of school buses came up to the visitor's center and several teenagers spilled out, arriving for the day for a field trip.

Guano was annoyed at the torrent of school-age teens, who seemed to be rather undisciplined, but he tried to ignore them as he pressed Su Lin through the throngs of youngsters. A couple of the males were rough-housing and collided with Guano and Su Lin. He raised his hand to strike them, but as the teens cowered, he lowered his hand to re-secure Su Lin and continue their walking pace toward the car. Within a mere five steps, Su Lin began screaming to unhand her. Guano yanked her around to face him, only to discover it was no longer Su Lin.

Panicked horror gripped Guano once he comprehended that he was no longer holding onto Su Lin. He shouted, "No! No! No!" in desperation. He scanned the immediate area for a long-haired female in a white blouse and blue skirt. The visuals only added to his terrified state because everyone in the immediate area were young females with long dark hair that cascaded over their traditional white blouses. Su Lin's escape was complete. So too was Guano's terror at having lost her.

Su Lin walked briskly, but did not run for fear of being spotted before her exit was complete. She crossed two more streets and rounded a corner before stopping to calm her pulse. From out of almost nowhere, a large hand slipped in underneath her arm, and in a low voice, the man quietly offered, "How about a ride, ma'am?"

The unknown man escorted her to the waiting vehicle where two men promptly hopped with care and respect to make certain she was received as a person of importance. Su Lin, as if she'd become as fragile as a snowflake, was carefully assisted into the back seat of the vehicle that had a small double-sided advertise-ment on top of the roof, indicating that it was an HOMBRE ride service.

As soon as everyone was seated and the vehicle was moving, the large man proclaimed, "You're right on time, Su Lin. I trust that Guano's rough treatment of you left no tell-tale bruising.

Oh, and say hello to Summit and George. They are friends of JAC. These are the, um…tricksters that engineered you out of your tight spot. I was just going to call in an air strike, then follow it up with an armored ground assault, before my SWAT team crashed the party to free you. These two convinced me there was an easier way."

Su Lin smiled and offered, "Easier and much quieter, I should think. Summit and George, many thanks for your finesse at extracting me. And, thank you, Stalker, for coming to get me as well. I understand that Mercedes has claim to your affections so you will forgive me if I don't offer anything more than a thank you hug. I say this with some regret, as you are reported as an extremely …well-crafted man, and I observe that was no exaggeration."

Summit and George smirked as Stalker blushed at the comment.

"Okay, we are not out of the woods yet kids," warned Stalker. "We still need to get out of the country, and we are pretty sure that trying to go out on a commercial airline is out of the question.

"I arranged for a private jet to pick us up at a regional airport that I am familiar with due to their …oh, how shall I say it …, more casual enforcement of gate checks and identification methods.

"Su Lin, you were last spotted wearing traditional school attire, so the first order of business is for a wardrobe change. I recommend that you don your original military uniform, and we have you leave as Lt. Colonel Ling Po."

Su Lin smiled politely but firmly stated, "I'm not leaving as Master Po but as Su Lin, so the military uniform is a non-starter."

Stalker lowered his shaking head as the other two smirked. "Well, damn, I lost that bet too! Everyone stated that would be your position. As an alternative, I was sent with an extremely nice

deep purple silk dress, beautifully embroidered with golden drag-
ons. I'm told it's the same one you always look at while shopping
online."

Now it was Su Lin's turn to flinch at learning she'd been
watched that closely. Upon reflection, she broke into a big smile
and asked, "Would it be alright if I changed into it now?"

Stalker grinned and loudly ordered, "Gentlemen, eyes forward
and mirrors turned, please!"

CHAPTER 61

Reward For a Good Deed

Genesis turned into an alley way and spun around to press her back against the wall. She expected a new physical onslaught. Still breathing hard and matching beats with her pounding heart, she half-believed she'd outmaneuvered the attackers. Drawing upon all of her secret service training, she began to bring all her vitals under control, which allowed her to logically consider her options. Still clenching her fists ready for a fight, she watched carefully down each side of the alley to see if anyone had followed.

Even as her breathing and pulse returned to normal, her mind raced to plan her next steps. Obviously they were onto her scam, but she failed to comprehend how they'd discovered her deception so quickly.

In a low voice she lamented, "Well, this just sucks! Sweetie, that payday that looked so promising is gone, and, by the way, so is your regular paycheck. After they realize you aren't coming in to receive your comeuppance as an enemy of the state…, well, I think we can safely write off that government pension too."

Realizing that she had eluded her pursuers for now, she focused on her options. She looked down at her workout garb and realized this was her new fashion statement. At least she'd been intruded upon during her workout session and not in the bath. Mentally she kicked herself into gear, knowing her training at making do with what was at hand was the new norm, and this situation certainly qualified. The workout garb would let her move to her next destination without the usual scoping she got when wearing her standard office seduction attire.

Keeping to the shadows to avoid unwanted attention, she cautiously moved down the alley. As an added bonus, the hood on the jacket helped hide her features. Safety was possible for a short time if she reached her personal safe house. Right now she needed the safe house stash that would get her out and on her way to a different place. Anywhere but here. Transportation would be planned after she reached that safe house.

After hours of back streets and alley ways, Genesis carefully approached a hole-in-the-wall convenience store and spotted the old woman swatting flies while sitting in a small wooden-backed chair outside the tiny shop. Genesis stood there a moment on the grimy street before the old woman looked over, seemed to focus clearly, and broke out in a friendly smile. Genesis cautiously approached the old woman. Her once brightly colored dress had faded with age and numerous washings. Her grey hair was neatly combed into a long braid to one side.

The old woman handed Genesis a small room key as she said, "You never said when you would be here, so I always held the key in my hand, child. It's all there, waiting for you." With an impish grin, she added, "Uh…don't forget to leave a tip."

Genesis breathed a sigh of relief as she gave the old woman a smile and quick hug. She dashed up the side stairs to her safe house in this seedy, run-down part of town that never seemed to notice the comings and goings of anyone.

She muttered under her breath as she climbed the stairs, "Please, tell me it's all there."

As the caller answered, Alejandro grinned and said, "Mathias, old friend, how are you? My attorney said to keep trying to reach you, based on your in-flight status. I am so pleased to hear that you are unencumbered, being as it were. Many thanks for your call that cleared my name in this mess. I wish there was something I could do to return the favor."

Mathias smiled fatalistically and replied, "Any chance I might get a reward from your government for helping to get the truth to the right people that lead to the arrest of that psychotic killer, Genesis?"

The warm, friendly glow faded quickly as Alejandro somberly replied, "Ah yes, madam Genesis. You should know, the armed escorts who were dispatched to retrieve her are no longer among the living. Somehow she escaped and is still at large. As far as the two guards, apparently she worked her destructive charm on them as well. They were both found, tied to chairs with their pants down around their ankles. Apparently, they were expecting to receive some spectacular gratification, but instead had their throats expertly sliced open with a large military grade bayonet. She is definitely a formidable field agent."

Mathias burned at the news of her escape. "Am I to assume that there will not only be no reward, but you are calling to warn me of an assassin on the hunt, looking for me?"

Alejandro replied, "Here in Venezuela we typically don't give away our prosecutor's information to the accused until they are in court. In answer to the other question, I wish I could tell you we had funds and rewards for you, but I feel honor bound to tell you, don't stop running, my friend. Destroy the cell phone and please work your way out to somewhere safe. That is the best I can offer."

Mathias smirked slightly and retorted, "I guess what they say about this country is true. No good deed goes unpunished down here. Enjoy your freedom, my friend, and at least wish me luck. Looks like I'm going to need it."

Alejandro sighed. "Good luck, my friend."

CHAPTER 62

To the Digital Age and Beyond

Ingrid listened to the one-on-one briefing from Tonya without comment. After the hour long briefing concluded with no remarks, Tonya began to worry that something had changed in the Global Bank landscape. She became concerned that this project, as well as herself, might have become superfluous. As the silence lengthened, Tonya grew more agitated.

Finally a small smile grew on Ingrid's face as she commented, "Well done, Madam Van Den Berghe. Your choice and reasons thereof are succinct and well-focused. Now comes the next phase, building the product. What is your thinking on the contractor to do the work?"

Tonya's relief at pleasing her mentor was now quickly replaced with fresh anxiety about getting the product built. It hadn't occurred to her to consider the next steps. She chided herself for not thinking the situation through to the next logical step. It was shortsighted.

Tonya's hesitation amused Ingrid, who smiled and said, "Didn't expect to be asked that, I see. More lessons to be learned by the up-and-coming young apprentice. No, the next step wasn't part of the assignment, Tonya. Yes, I was probing to see how you think. It should have occurred to you that if we were ready to pay whatever price the chosen contractor stated for product specifications, we would be willing to fund the build phase as well."

Tonya was frustrated to think she was still considered an undergrad student who required instructions on business or project steps. Stilling her annoyance, she asked, "I sense that you've already decided what to do next. So what difference does it make if I recommend for the next step?"

Ingrid expressed mild surprise and asked, "Oh, you do have a suggestion? I'd like to hear it."

Emboldened, Tonya stated, "I believe that Petra and the presumed team behind her are likely talented enough to build and deliver a suitable cryptocurrency product, which we could then properly introduce into the world order of finance. However, I'm not recommending that action."

Ingrid, intrigued with the answer, pressed, "Curious statement. Why not?"

Tonya confidently stated, "Because we should build it ourselves. The report clearly points out the dangers of a poorly produced product, and, frankly, we need to own the cryptocurrency product in its entirety, from top to bottom. Our organization cannot afford to have a misstep and then blame the contractor. That is too adolescent for something so important. We build it, we own it. It's that simple."

Ingrid chortled and remarked, "Then it's good that we are in violent agreement. Tomorrow you start with your new team member, who has already read your report and is anxious to meet you. You will find him a most energetic and stimulating partner in this critical project. Your project name is *CryptoCurrency: Mashup of Artificial Intelligence for Money* or cc:MAIM."

Ingrid enjoyed the puzzlement on Tonya's face and loudly added, "Say hello to Tonya, cc:MAIM."

Tonya jumped as the voice permeated from all around. "Good day, Madam Van Den Berghe. I am looking forward to working with you. I trust you will not have any analog versus digital prejudices in your psyche that we will need to work through."

Tonya turned her head to look at Ingrid in disbelief and dread at the new prospect of this assignment with an enhanced computer.

Ingrid grinned and proudly stated, "Isn't he terrific? Our own supercomputer, enhanced with unrestricted, deep-learning Artificial Intelligence programming, to bring digital currency to our backward civilization! Just think, our organization and our names, or at least mine, will be revered in the decades to come as those geniuses who took us into the digital currency age. The Global Bank will lead the planet out of the dark ages."

Tonya was dumbfounded.

The Finance Minister bellowed, "What do you mean they didn't get to the vehicle! Where is Guano and that troublesome Po? How many adults does it take to walk someone to the damn car?"

The security guard swallowed hard as he struggled to respond. "Sssir…I waited at the car to assist with the transport, but after 15 minutes I called the Colonel to get a status. He screamed at me like some wounded animal in its death throes. Uh…he repeated over and over that she had to be there! When I questioned him on what the problem was, I received more screams and verbal abuse. Sir, I believe that Po has eluded the Colonel and that he is in pursuit. May I recommend…"

The Finance Minister barked, "Shut up! I pay you to do, not recommend! Plus, if you cannot do as instructed, then why am I paying you, or keeping you alive for that matter? Find Guano and that bitch Po. And I mean now!"

The young staff officer quivered with fear and responded, "Yes, Finance Minister. It shall be done."

CHAPTER 63

Around and Around
Until Back at Square One

Searching for hours had resulted in failure and humiliation. The continual stopping of young girls to check faces had resulted in several complaints to the local authorities about Guano. By the time he returned to the compound, the Finance Minister was already there, fuming. The Finance Minister wasn't as brutal as other bosses Guano had worked for, but the man was not without resources and an iron determination in the realm of digital currency. Guano was escorted into the opulent offices of the Finance Minister.

Without any preamble of greetings or pleasantries, quite out of character for the office, Kuan-Chun bellowed, "What is the meaning of your behavior, Colonel Guano? I've had a dozen calls about you accosting young school girls. Your carelessness occurred with students from one of the most progressive, privately funded schools in this region. Where is Po?"

Guano bowed and continued to inspect his shoes as he mumbled, "One minute I had her arm, and the next the arm belonged to a teenager who screamed like she was being tortured. I only held her arm. Then I ran through the overflowing crowd of school children, but they were all wearing the standard uniform.

I was trying to find her. Private schools all require uniforms and they all, well, looked the same. I sincerely tried. I don't…"

"Enough!" demanded Kuan-Chun. "It is yet another failed attempt by you. You are nothing but a liability.

"Now, did you review every portion of the code with the QA team to make certain it was solid? Did you have the team document each step of the process and where modifications could and could not be made?"

Feeling he was on more secure ground, Guano looked up and seriously replied, "Yes, sir. I reviewed every bit and byte of that code, while running test upon test for both security and reliability. Not only did I find it to be a well-written program, but the team assured me the quality was of the highest level."
He smiled as he reassured, "Nothing else this university has produced has ever been so rock solid and unbreakable, more than what we planned. Even without Master Po, Professor Lin and I can maintain this program. We can release this knowing that not only will our citizens benefit, but the world will confidently embrace this as the world's best digital currency. It will take us to a new level as the financial leader of the world, as you wanted."

Even with some of the missteps in acquiring and now keeping Master Po, Guano was feeling better since he had provided the right product for his country and for the world. He was unprepared for the cloud that grew across the face of the Finance Minister.

With as hateful a look as Guano had ever witnessed on anyone, along with the almost bluish color of his contorted lips, the Finance Minister commended, "Really. We launched your so-called rock solid program. It ran for nearly 60 minutes without any issue. Then Professor Lin panicked and pointed out a problem on the statistics and analytics screens. He showed me in detail what was happening as the code was being released for the general consumption in the Internet offering.

"For no better initial explanation, Professor Lin described the program as mutating once it reached the minimum buy-in level. Totally unforeseeable and not planned, he'd stated. The reviews and backtracking started immediately as I watched over his shoulder. I saw the flaw moments after he highlighted the step where it indicated the insertion of YOUR last review date, time, and initials.

"Additional code was being cherry picked outside of the program in the Internet and being inserted into the main program. The result was totally unpredictable. Funds were added, then drained, then cycled again. Anything which was purchased as a part of the offering was suddenly 200 times the value with our reserves being drained to subsidize the unprecedented differential as we are the assigned backers for this initial offering."

Guano looked green as he stuttered, "But…I don't see how that is possible. The code is solid. The team checked it. How could this be? What is the current status of the review? I want to be there during the review."

Finance Minister Kuan-Chun ignored Guano's request and continued, "It is plausible at the first review this could occur if you tried to insert a methodology into the program to covertly skim off funds, yet failed. It would align with your stellar performances with your other recent assignments. Your team of reviewers is already in custody, being rigorously questioned. I am certain one of them will break soon.

"Professor Lin has worked tirelessly to find the root cause, but he deemed the project jeopardy too serious to continue without being thoroughly rechecked. Officially, we have posted a press release that we have withdrawn it due to a hacker alert received shortly after the offering was released. The report will insinuate the attack came from the U.S., and of course the Americans will deny it. Unofficially, when Professor Lin comes back with the root cause, if it is you, the guards outside will take you away for a very long time as a traitor to your country."

Guano begged, "I have not done this, sir. You have to believe me. Agreed, Master Po's recovery was fraught with unforeseen issues. Yes, the help you sent was not without a downside, but I have always been loyal to this country, in service to this country. You cannot believe this of me. My record is…"

"Your record is filled with marks of stupidity dating back for a number of years. We cannot afford any more stupidity or poor judgement. We are too close to being a force to be reckoned with…"

Interrupted by a knock on the door, the Finance Minister barked, "Come in!"

Professor Lin bowed as he entered. He glanced toward Guano with disdain. "Sir, I have completed the preliminary review of the code. The error seems to not be a part of the original code delivered by Master Po, but rather a secondary add-on during the review and subsequent assembly process. The virus, for lack of a better term, is now randomly infecting other portions of the program. It is difficult at this juncture to ascertain how each of these modifications are impacting the overall program's viability to deliver."

"Are you saying Master Po had nothing to do with this, Professor Lin?" demanded Kuan-Chun.

Professor Lin nodded and replied, "It appears the code she provided is solid and not infected. I have the ability to return to the original code she created, under my watchful eye. It is this code I used for comparison.

"The two vulnerable renegade code areas seem to be present only after your review, Colonel Guano. I am sorry, Finance Minister, it appears that the project and your launch have been severely compromised, but I do not believe it to be at the hands of Master Po. It will take time, but I believe we can rebuild it using her code. It would be a mistake to have her or Guano and his team even touch it, as control cannot be contained."

The Finance Minister yelled, "Guards, get in here. Take this traitor out of my sight.

"Professor Lin, you are now in charge of this reconstruction. I would like it as quickly as possible, but I want it right. You have only but to ask for any resources you need."

Professor Lin waited for Guano to be dragged away with loud protests until he was out the door. He faced the Finance Minister and bowed before leaving, gently closing the door behind him. While returning to his programming center, he marveled that Master Po still had the touch to cover all the alternatives. His family would be safe, and someday he would find a way to help her. Taking this project on was his first step. Step two would be cleaning all trace of her current location, identity, and associates from all the Chinese digital and manual records.

CHAPTER 64

Travel Arrangements

Su Lin hadn't noticed how or when they had changed. When they parked the vehicle, Summit and George were in Chinese military uniforms, including hats with proper rank of attachés. Even Stalker looked like a well- tailored diplomat, once he had reversed his outer jacket.

Su Lin, with her hair up and in her purple silk dress, looked almost royal. Summit and George chatted away in Mandarin, and each fussed to provide suitable escort for Su Lin as the onlookers seemed impressed with the display. For his part, Stalker tried not to roll his eyes too much, lest he detract from the performance.

They were waved through the special gateway area, because the standard security held the regular passengers back so the little band could proceed unhindered. As they exited the building, they crossed the tarmac to the stairs that led into the private jet. Once inside, all were quickly seated, and the door was immediately closed.

The pilot stuck his head into the cabin, and Su Lin beamed as she said, "Hello, Captain Juan. Tell JAC thanks for lending me her fabulous pilot to get me home."

Juan grinned and replied, "Don't thank her yet. We need to get out with little attention paid to who we are and why we didn't identify who all was on board. In this part of the world, if they don't like what they see, their fighters come and typically shoot you up, claiming air space violations. We are taking our chartered flight down to 10 meters above the ground to…well, stay below their radar, so to speak. Until we get out of range, please, everyone stay buckled in until I say we are clear."

Summit and George looked uneasily at each other, but Su Lin smiled and asked, "Will we be inverted again after a couple of barrel rolls? That was lots of fun."

This time Stalker looked uneasy.

Last night before they'd turned in, ICABOD confirmed that the final object Jacob had left for the program Su Lin created was picked up as the Chinese closed the program and published the press release. This object would stay dormant and effectively invisible on LING-LI as a matter of principle. Julie provided a text message that Su Lin was en route with Juan and two CATS team members as escorts.

Their celebration was short-lived. Jacob had taken a fast shower and climbed into bed, watching Petra comb her hair, when he closed his eyes and fell asleep. Petra suspected that the finalization of the lingering elements of Su Lin's return, combined with exhaustion from the days at the hospital had finally allowed Jacob to relax. She slid into bed and moved close to Jacob so that he pulled her closer, yet never awakened.

Petra woke up early and smiled, watching Jacob as he slept. It had been so long since he had actually slept in their bed, she refused to make any unnecessary movement that might disturb his slumber. The quiet room felt like home when they were there together. Glancing around, she saw the ways the room had picked up a bit of them both with a photo here, blanket there, and her ring on the nightstand.

She wanted to stop time and savor the positive balance they achieved between winning and losing with the risks they'd taken in the digital currency battle. With the light peeking through the edge of the curtains, she could tell morning was arriving, but it could wait for them both for a while. Confident that no one in the chateau would disturb them, she snuggled up a bit closer to Jacob and drifted back to sleep.

Hours or moments later—she couldn't discern yet—the ringing of Jacob's mobile phone permeated her dream. Jacob was roused by the noise as well, with a hand grappling to locate the annoying sound.

"Sorry, sweetheart," Jacob mumbled, even as he found the device and pushed to answer.

"This is Jacob," he said as he straightened and sat up a bit. Petra scooted closer and reached for his free hand. She couldn't see who had called or hear anything while Jacob listened to the caller.

"Yes …

"Oh, really. Are you certain? …

"When? …

"I should have stayed. …

"What time should I be there? …

"Was there any … …

"Alright, I understand. Yes, I will. Thank you, Doctor Roblinski.

"Goodbye."

Petra needed no words from Jacob to know what had happened. He took her into his arms and just held on. She gently patted his back and whispered, "We'll get through this together. I am with you, Jacob."

CHAPTER 65

Are We There Yet?

True to Juan's statement, they did have to keep low to evade any unwanted Chinese fighter escort until they were well past Taiwan. Thankfully, Stalker's credentials and radio link were able to persuade the Republic of China they were on a U.S. diplomatic mission, so there was no threat of Chinese fighters. They first stopped in Guam to re-fuel. While there, Stalker filed a preliminary report with his boss, Eric, at his three-letter agency, indicating that the operation was winding down.

Juan received lots of help from Summit and George with the refueling logistics and securing provisions, so he had time for a power nap before they headed to Hawaii for another refueling effort. Everyone seemed in good spirits, but fatigued. That is, all except Su Lin. She seemed to get more energized the closer they got to her home outside of Atlanta. Even though they didn't spend a whole lot of time with the travel logistics, no one seemed rushed, which made the flight easier to endure.

Jim insisted on sitting in the co-pilot seat to help with the communications and navigations but was really there to keep an eye on Juan in case he fell asleep. Juan graciously accepted the company but still referred to Stalker as his *map-trashing copilot* as a retaliatory, good-natured tease. A couple times Juan asked

Stalker to take over while he went back for a health break. Without fail, when Juan returned, he always chuckled and asked how the 'white-knuckle-flying copilot' was doing. As tired as they both were, Juan always seemed to get a laugh out of the serious operative.

The hours ticked by and so did the quick refueling effort in Hawaii. Su Lin now seemed to be more of a nuisance the closer they got to the continental U.S. Juan assured them and her they were making good time with no mechanical difficulties. However, once they were within sight of the U.S. west coast, Juan noticed that his fuel gauges still showed full, which alarmed him. He and Stalker quickly checked their fuel consumption rates, fuel capacity, and their total traveled distance since Hawaii and quickly figured out that they must be close to flying on fumes.

Juan landed at Los Angeles International Airport without incident. Jim, while grateful for Juan's expert handling of the situation, did not want to share the incident with the others. Juan smiled and said nothing. Su Lin wanted to phone Andy to let him know she was on her way, but Jim suggested that wait until they arrived at Atlanta International Airport. She nodded in agreement but was obviously disappointed. All of them took a bit of a walk around during the refueling to stretch their legs. Summit and George took turns helping with the refueling and keeping a close eye on Su Lin.

After some discreet maintenance activity by Juan and Jim, it was discovered that a faulty fuse was the culprit. It was quickly replaced as Juan had every intention of reaching Atlanta without further incident. The last thing he wanted was to have to make an unscheduled aircraft stop in Dallas.

Juan had heard through his contacts there that his last stop in Dallas had not been forgiven or forgotten. He made sure that if any radio communications came in for the aircraft that Stalker would deal with it. As a precaution, Juan nonchalantly asked if Stalker could pretend to be the pilot if talking to the ground people became necessary. Stalker studied Juan's profile, trying to decide if he should ask why, but before he could ask, Juan, still staring straight ahead, calmly stated, "Don't ask."

On the ground in Atlanta, Su Lin lost almost all of her emotional control as EZ and Mercedes met them after clearing customs. The surprise was made all the more sweet when she found Andy waiting outside against the car for them. Andy had regained much, but not all his sight, according to EZ. Su Lin was speechless when she saw him. If EZ and Mercedes hadn't interceded, the pair would have dissolved into emotion puddles right there in the parking lot.

Stalker, now out of his secret agent role, began to slip back into his Jim Hughes persona and was ready to sweep Mercedes into his arms. Khalid and an additional agent intercepted their heartfelt reunion. Wedged in between Mercedes and Jim, Khalid opened the door to the second HOMBRE vehicle and motioned for Jim to enter, while blocking entry to Mercedes.

Jim seemed resigned to the transport, but Mercedes snapped, "What the hell is this? Jim is being summoned before I can talk to him? He has some explaining to do with me first, so out of the way, Khalid!"

Khalid was torn between his friendships with both Mercedes and Jim. He'd been given his orders, which left no wiggle room. Jim was to be transported directly to Washington D.C. with no questions asked. The other agent silently moved into position to reinforce the unspoken demand.

By this time, EZ was moving toward Mercedes, who had positioned herself to take on Khalid and block their car from exiting, to find out what was upsetting her. Andy and Su Lin were gathering in closely to offer their own support for Jim.

Andy spoke first and flatly stated, "Gentlemen, this man just retrieved my loving wife from the hands of some very unsavory types. In my book that earns some pretty big favors. I don't plan to have you remove this brave man until I've had a chance to thank him, real proper like. Now you can stand out of the way while we continue with our reunion, or I can take all of my pent up frustrations out on the pair of you. Which is it gonna be?"

With everyone visibly upset and the fear of drawing attention very real, Jim exited the car and said, "I appreciate the concern you all have for me. I have specific government business that demands these safeguards at this juncture.

"Andy, I thank you for that hospitality being offered. I need to complete my assignment before I can do anything else. I want you to take that hard won bride of yours home and make up for lost time. Su Lin, you need to hustle everyone home and restart that terrific life you two have planned.

"EZ, I want you to make sure that these folks get back and re-engage their lives so this episode is something that they can chuckle over in the near future. And, by the way, your man in Zürich is waiting on your return so your lives can return to normal."

Jim let that sink in for a moment and then he turned to Mercedes. "Mercedes, I have so many things to say and so much lost time to recapture that I ache for not being able to say everything right here, right now. I must go and complete the assignment. No, I couldn't tell you why and I won't be able to later.

"I ask you to keep a candle burning for me, and I'll be there as soon as I can. Miss you, babe." And with that he returned to the car, entering the back seat.

The situation diffused as quickly as it began. Mercedes, EZ, Andy, and Su Lin all quietly moved back to their vehicle leaving Khalid, the other agent, and Jim to travel on.

Khalid remorsefully said, "The trouble with you highly honorable men is that the rest of us feel like shit when we have to take you back. I was about to knock down my buddy here and help you make good your escape. Thanks for keeping my ass out of the sling, dammit. Now let's go, they're waiting."

Stalker never heard anything Khalid said as he was trying to get one last glimpse of Mercedes, who had climbed into the far side of their vehicle and slammed the door.

EZ said, "Daddy, I don't think this is the right time to discuss this…"

Andy politely but quickly cut her off. "Darling girl, my life has been restored. My beautiful wife is back home, Franklin is on the mend, and the bad guys are all a fading memory. Ernie is fully engaged, and we have the whole ranch under surveillance cameras in case someone else tries to show up uninvited. I promise to be careful and vigilant, but I don't feel right about you putting your life on hold.

"You know, the plan was always to restore everything to a pre-mess status and send you home to that peculiar, but likeable, Quip character. The parameters have been met, so you and Mercedes need to get back to the airport where Juan is waiting to take you two back home. Now no more back-sassing, young ladies. And don't forget, Juan has family he wants to get back to as well."

EZ teared up but, smiling with relief, replied, "Yes, Daddy. You're right, time for me to leave and…go home. That's funny, I always used to call the ranch home, but now home is Zürich." She puzzled a moment and absentmindedly said out loud, "Time to go home."

Mercedes, still very melancholy, only sighed and nodded in agreement.

Andy fired up his cell phone with Ernie standing by, and when the call connected, he asked, "Juan, are you rested up enough for one more flight? I've got two homesick young ladies that are ready to go. I'm gonna ask Ernie here to get them to the airport and continue on his life. Are you good?"

Juan smiled and said, "Ask them to hurry, because I'm homesick too. I'm good to go, Andy. Thanks."

Andy grinned from ear to ear as he said, "No, thank you, young feller! Thanks for bringing Su Lin home safe. I greatly appreciate it."

George and Summit welcomed Mercedes as she arrived at the plane. They took her to the back of the plane so they might debrief. Having no desire to speak to anyone, Mercedes buckled in and put on her earbuds. Within an hour they were wheels up and on their way back to Zürich. Each hour in the air that made EZ feel happier, but the reverse was true for Mercedes as tears rolled down her cheeks.

CHAPTER 66

Bittersweet Arrivals and Departures

...The Enigma Chronicles

Quip arrived at the airport with plenty of time to get the rental car for George, Mercedes, and Summit to drive home. Juan would travel with him and EZ to the chateau and be in time for drinks and dinner. Even with the shroud of sadness, having EZ back home was exactly what he needed right now. The bittersweet victory of Su Lin being returned, along with Andy's recovery, was going to require an ongoing vigilance, though the people who really knew about Su Lin and her new life were essentially gone.

Juan and EZ were both aware that Wolfgang had passed. Julie had called Juan to let him know and find out when they would arrive. Quip suggested Julie stay at the chateau with the children while he made the trip to the airport. Quip wanted to rush EZ back to their flat, but with all the preparations, he needed to help the rest of the family.

EZ softly said, "Quip, I am sorry I failed to make it back in time to tell Wolfgang goodbye. He seemed so very strong the last time I saw him. What a great life he led."

Quip focused on the traffic as he replied, "You are so right, honey. He has been around as long as I have been alive. I like to think that he and my grandfather, Ferdek, are sitting and playing remember when. You know, they provided the strength and direction. I think Jacob might be feeling a bit overwhelmed at the loss of family and the potential for new responsibility. I certainly did when I faced the same situation after Ferdek passed."

Traffic on the road had increased some so the conversation ended. EZ decided she would let him talk when he wished. She was glad they would both go to the chateau and be there for Jacob.

When Quip and EZ arrived, Bowen escorted them into the study for a glass of wine before dinner. EZ and Petra shared a hug and whispered a few words to one another. EZ turned to Otto and gave him a quick hug as well. Jacob had taken directions from Otto, Bowen, and to a minor degree Petra, all day. It was like he was on auto pilot without any programs running. Jacob was oblivious to their arrival, sitting and staring into the fire.

Otto exclaimed, "Quip, EZ, what may I serve you? I am sorry, but I don't recall your beverage of choice. Haddy went to check on dinner and will be back shortly. Julie took Juan upstairs to sleep after all his flying efforts. She and the children were going to eat in their room. We may see them later."

EZ smiled and replied, "I'd like that nice white wine Wolfgang always has on hand. Petra, isn't that what you're drinking?"

Realizing her comment, her smile turned into a frown.

Petra shook her head as an indication for EZ not to tread on eggshells and confirmed, "That is exactly what I am drinking. Wolfgang has one of the best stocked cellars, right, Otto?"

Otto grinned and agreed, "You are correct, my dear.

"Quip, what would you like? Jacob poured a Malbec earlier but made no comment."

"Yes, Otto, a Malbec sounds great." He took the glass from Otto and moved to the couch and sat next to Jacob. With the movement, Jacob looked around as if surprised.

"Quip, nice to see you. Did you pick up EZ yet? Would you like some wine? I'm having the Malbec."

Quip raised his glass to illustrate, along with his eyebrow. "Jacob, I have mine, and EZ is over with Petra. You look a little tired. It's tough, isn't it?"

Jacob nodded and solemnly said, "Not enough time, Quip. Never enough time. Not enough with my Mom or Granny, and now Wolfgang. I wanted more time." Jacob looked devastated as he hung his head and then added, "I should have stayed there. I should have held his hand to the end. He should not have been alone."

Quip looked at his friend and glanced at Otto who passed along an encouraging nod. "Jacob, we can live our whole lives and there will never be enough time. When Ferdek died, I thought exactly the same thing, and you know I had so many regrets. We can't regret for long, or it will control our being. We must think of the good things and take the lessons forward.

"Wolfgang thought you were amazing and loved you with all his heart. He enjoyed every moment together and was very proud of you. If not, he would never have let you continue to read the history of the R-Group and his role, along with the other two. He left you the legacy of something great, as well as a way for you to contribute your skills to more than just earning a living."

Jacob looked up in astonishment. "You knew? You knew what I was reading was real? You didn't feel compelled as my friend to clue me in on my confusion as to what I had in my hands. Why, I would never..."

Quip raised an eyebrow again and quietly yet seriously stated, "Of course you would. Somethings we need to find out for ourselves. Would you have believed me if I had told you over reading it in Wolfgang's own words? Sure, I had an advantage over you, in that I grew up here and was told things while I was growing up. When I finished my doctorate, Ferdek filled in the blanks where I didn't understand. After he died, Wolfgang and I did talk a bit, and he said you needed to find out in your own time. He even tasked Otto to not share prematurely. The important part was for you to make your own decision.

"To answer your next question, Petra knows portions of it from the Tavius side which Otto was told and shared with her over time. She too was honor bound not to offer those details, before Wolfgang thought the time was right. We each have our choice to commit to the business or not. Petra was concerned when you showed her the books, but Wolfgang had told Bowen to make them available for you to find. Bowen himself has never read them but had guarded them for years.

"If you want out, then that is your right. If you want in, you will take your rightful place as a full voting member. I would like you with me, Jacob." Quip held his glass up high as a salute to Jacob.

Petra moved in front of them both and smiled as she confirmed, "I would too, Jacob. We have so much to do, and I need your support to get it done."

Jacob looked at each of them in turn and looked over at Otto, who seemed as if he was patiently waiting as usual. Finally he raised his glass and announced, "We are together. Thank you, Wolfgang, for being so strong. I hope I am as steadfast as you."

Otto, Haddy, and EZ moved over to acknowledge the toast. Bowen opened the door and announced, "Dinner is served."

Dinner had been delicious, and the conversation was filled with stories, laughter, and no sadness, for which EZ was grateful. In her mind there had been enough of that to last for quite some time.

When Quip and EZ finally made it to their room in the chateau, they took separate, luxurious showers. EZ was second as she wanted to wash her hair after the long flight, and Quip wanted to set up a fire. She even asked if he might sneak downstairs and get a couple more glasses of wine. He was more than agreeable but reminded her to hurry because tomorrow was a workday, at least for him.

EZ emerged from the in-suite bathroom/dressing room, wearing a lovely sherbet green satin robe tied about her narrow waist, her fiery red hair cascading down her back, combed yet full due to her natural curls. The glow from the fire provided all the light, save a soft lamp on a bedside table. Quip sat on the couch in his lounge pants looking comfortably casual. He held a glass of wine in each hand and a welcoming smile.

"Come join me, EZ. I'm so glad you are home."

EZ sat and took the offered glass, then suggested, "To us, Quip. Here's to our future time with no serious personal problems. We've had enough, I think. I, too, am glad to be home."

Quip wrapped his arm around hers, and they completed the toast and sweetly smiled at each other.

Leaning back against the velvet-covered couch, they touched shoulders and sipped their wine. The fire light was sparkling and lent a romantic glow as they enjoyed simply being in the company of one another.

Quip, not wishing to spoil the mood, quietly interjected, "I was so glad to hear that Andy is improved, and Su Lin is back home. I am sure they will be happy. Mercedes said the perimeter alarms will stay in place, and Ernie knows how to take care of the equipment. I don't think they will be bothered any further. Are you comfortable with that right now?"

EZ's smile indicated she was, along with leaning her head on his shoulder. "Yes, they will be great. Dad was so happy to see Su Lin. His sight is better, and his doctor thinks he will recover fully in a few scant months. Carlos and I will support his business remotely, with Dad working a few hours a day starting next week. I know you love to pick on each other, so he'll reach out soon." EZ set the glass on the table and leaned back against his shoulder, sighing with contentment.

Quip chuckled and replied, "Very true.

"Um, I wanted to let you know about some of the changes I went ahead and made at home."

"Hmm, like what?" EZ murmured.

"I missed you so very much that I decided it would be nice to get a new bed. I researched it carefully to make certain we now have a state of the art sleeping platform. It promises a customized sleep for each of us. This bed allows us to each adjust the sleeping firmness for the best possible sleep. There is also an adjustment for additional warmth or coolness from inside the platform, and it also gently reclines. I have tried all the settings to make certain it has all the comfort and flexibility we might need."

Quip took a breath and continued, "The best part of this is our ability to extract all the data to analyze the sleep. It measures the breathing, heartbeat, and restlessness of each sleeper. I myself have noticed that even without you beside me, I can get a relatively high number and increased comfort even when my hours of sleep are limited, like they've been while I worked on this project."

Quip cleared his throat and looked toward EZ, almost with a leer, as he intimated, "There is even a setting for privacy, in case we want to enjoy some horizontal exercise without the analytics. What do you think?"

There was no response from EZ, which worried Quip until he looked closer and realized she had fallen asleep. Her breathing was gentle and her face looked so sweet. Quip sighed as he gently shifted and took her into his arms and rose. EZ shifted a bit as she curled into him. He took her toward the bed and gently placed her down, pulling up some covers.

"Shhh, sweetheart. Rest now, we can talk tomorrow."

CHAPTER 67

Celebrate,
Don't Commiserate
...The Enigma Chronicles

Services honoring Wolfgang were well attended by friends and business associates of his. At the reception at the chateau, the family greeted guests who told favorite stories they shared with their old friend. Jacob had met many of the people before, so it was not as hard as he had expected. Petra stayed close and helped with names. Those who had not realized they were engaged congratulated them and asked for the date. Petra didn't want to talk about a date with other people before they had set one, so she deftly revectored the conversation to something about their family or a memory she recalled. It was actually well done.

Jacob leaned over when they were no longer the center of attention and whispered, "Honey, if you want to pick a date, feel free. I still want you for my wife and partner."

Petra blushed a bit and replied, "Really, even after all my complaining?"

"You don't seem to complain any more than I do, so I think it's fair," Jacob reassured.

A hearty chuckle escaped from her before she could catch it, and she admonished, "Let's discuss this later, my darling. Please?"

A waiter exchanged their drinks, and another offered a small bite. The moment was broken. Jacob decided it was a subject he would pursue later.

Haddy and Otto enjoyed talking to many of their old friends, even under these circumstances. Haddy was also keeping a close eye on Juan Jr and Gracie as they wandered between family members. They were well behaved, but tired of the standing and talking.

Haddy suggested, "Let's take the children out into the garden for a while. They've been good as gold, but a little running might do them good."

Otto agreed and went to alert Juan they were taking the children outside. No one needed to worry that way. The children were only too delighted to be outside and immediately ran to the small pond where they could balance on rocks and throw bits of crackers to the ducks. Wolfgang had added the feature originally when Petra was young so she might have some fun when visiting. By the time Julie came along, Petra was ready to teach all the secrets to her sister. Haddy and Otto sat at a table under the pavilion, keeping a close eye on the twins but grateful for the alone time.

Haddy quietly asked, "Otto, can we go back to having time for us to enjoy our friends, have dinners out, see plays and see these precious grandchildren of ours? I know you too needed the rest when you worried about your health, but that time is gone."

Otto reached across the table for her hand and said, "I think that is a fine idea. You know, I do enjoy the work. I've been at it most of my life. But I always value time with you. I really liked when we worked together. But the team needs me, don't they?"

Haddy looked at the man she loved and replied, "They will always need you, but it is time they stretched their wings, don't you think? They can reach out if they need help."

Otto looked thoughtfully out into the distance at the beautiful flowers and groomed landscape. He seemed focused on something she couldn't see. A few minutes passed by before he seemed to find whatever he had sought.

Otto gripped her hand a little tighter, and he smiled. "Yes, love. It is our time to enjoy and take part in exploring us again. I will tell the team tomorrow. Petra can take her rightful role. Julie has already decided on her direction and can help fill in many gaps. Jacob is ready even if he doesn't believe it. Yes, it's our time."

They held hands and watched the children playing tag across the boulders over the water. Laughter and joy filled the air.

Arrived

...The Enigma Chronicles

The atmosphere in the Zürich data center seemed oddly different. The quiet but pervasive hum of the data center was always close by, yet never intrusive. Petra, Jacob, Quip, EZ, Julie, and Juan were in attendance; however, all were silent after the comprehensive discussion topics had been tabled. Each seemed to fall into their own thoughts almost as though everyone was meditating on the topic contents.

Quip was the first to break the silence. "Petra, this is a little unorthodox with having more than just the key decision makers at the table. The R-Group has typically had the three core members at our key decision making sessions, so this clearly is not the traditional approach. However, I must say this is more to my liking. I believe that our approach of having you, Jacob, and me as the core decision makers is solid, but your observation that we need EZ, Julie, and Juan as a close second council in our operations is an excellent one.

"I would like to further propose that ICABOD be asked to listen for further analysis in our business approach to provide commentary and insight that may not be captured by this team."

Jacob interjected, "Quip, I've always assumed that ICABOD would be in the conversational threads of everything we do if his data gathering is to be relevant. ICABOD is the information system that the R-Group governance thinking must have access into. I can't imagine ICABOD not included."

Petra added, "Yes, of course, Quip. It was always a given that ICABOD contribute to our decision making process. I am more interested in Julie, Juan, and EZ's perspective on the matter.

"With Wolfgang gone and Otto wanting to disengage from the on-going operations, I wanted to suggest a fresh approach to how we conduct our business. Frankly, I see longer discussion times on major projects. I also see a more thorough thought analysis with all of us involved. Conversely, if anyone is not up to taking on this new role for themselves in the R-Group, I must insist that you voice your objections.

"For instance, Juan and Julie, you two have assembled a crack international cyber assassin team that we heavily depend upon under certain circumstances. This request may be too much with that business, along with your young family.

"EZ, you and Quip are newlyweds. Day and night times together might create a strain."

Jacob thoughtfully added, "To be fair, Petra, our relationship might also be a consideration we have kept on the sidelines to this point.

"I have to say though, this is my family, day and night. I would frankly admit that I don't want walls in between my business and personal life. I feel like I have more to learn, but I am also compelled to offer all I am to the group and to each of you personally. I've seen all of you contribute to search and rescue operations in the analog and digital space. Though this is not the only line for the vast holdings of the R-Group, it is the foundation for much of our interactions these days. I know I can trust each person in this room, no matter the situation."

Julie commented, "So it sounds less like the old world type of organization and more like the crowd sourcing approach to funding and projects. You know, I have never felt like an outsider to the R-Group, not being a voting member. Somehow, I do find this new group architecture compelling. Juan, how do you feel?"

Juan, put on the spot but with Julie's coaxing, offered, "I'm a little intimidated by this kind of offer. It may not have been stated openly before, so let me say for the record that I have not always been on the high moral ground that you folks have.

"Yes, I freely admit to being something of a black sheep in my past, but I am humbled that you want me to be on this team. If I can continue to keep and earn your trust, then I would like to stand with Julie on your team in any capacity to help. You never know, if I help enough, maybe my past indiscretions will no longer haunt me."

The group looked to EZ and Quip, but EZ spoke first. "I don't have the colorful history that Juan claims, but like I told my daddy before I left this last time, this is my home. It's my home because of my husband and the work I do with this team.

"I promised my daddy that I would help Carlos with his customers, so is that still okay? I mean, I understand the two businesses need to be kept compartmentalized, so I will commit to that in my efforts. If that is acceptable, then thank you for asking, and please count me in."

As Petra and Jacob were smiling, ICABOD intruded into the discussion. "Allow my contributing analysis at this stage, ladies and gentlemen. This is definitely a changing of the guards here at the R-Group. Let me point out that this is going to be required. The world is changing, and it just changed again.

"The new R-Group management model needed to morph for preparation of what is now coming. The blending of the skillsets that you all possess will be needed for the next challenge that has just surfaced. The cc:MAIM project has just been launched, and we will need to ride the storm it will bring."

Quip commented, "They launched it, huh?"

ICABOD responded, "Yes, Dr. Quip. The *CryptoCurrency: Mashup of Artificial Intelligence for Money* has been initiated and will be based on the R-Group product specifications for the next generation of cryptocurrency. The disappointing news for the group is that the supercomputer they intend to build it with has been given too much authority and no guardrails with which to proceed. The designers did not take into account the downside of unrestricted, deep-learning algorithms being launched on a supercomputer that answers to no one. May I have permission to re-launch our future prediction software to more clearly analyze the outcome?"

Petra, Quip, and Jacob were the only ones who weren't taken aback by the request to launch a future predicting software routine.

EZ exclaimed, "What? We have such a program?"

Petra calmly replied, "We had a difficult group that we took down who had built such a program: The *Deterministic Algorithms Assembled into Future Findings Yielding a Matrix of Accelerated Theorems Holistically* or DAAFFY-MATH as Quip and ICABOD branded it. It was designed to predict the future and, in its proof of concept launch, did exactly that. That is why it has been archived in our technology vault for the last few years. No one benefited from it except the perpetrators. Frankly, we are all a little bit afraid of what it can do. As you well know, with unlimited power comes unlimited grief and sorrow."

Juan brightened and quickly stated, "Oh wow, you could predict winning lotto numbers, which team is going to win the World Soccer match, which political candidate is going to win, oh, and bet on commodity futures…oh, yeah. Now I get it, sorry.

"ICABOD, you're surmising we have this swell tool to predict the future outcome for this supercomputer, given the unrestricted ability to learn and apply in a field that has far reaching consequences. How do we determine when or where we put the *Digital Genie* back in the bottle and return to our normal lives? Apologies if I have to say this out loud so I can understand it. I'm not as smart as you folks."

While the team was all grinning at Juan, Quip stated, "Actually, that was fairly well stated, Juan. You catch on pretty quickly, as we know from when you were here the last time."

Petra studied EZ, Juan, and Julie and quietly asked, "Do you see why we need people who can reason through the opaque and un-obvious? Do you still feel like you can adapt to the needs of the team in our assignments?"

Jacob smiled in a paternal way and offered, "This is an important request of you all. May I recommend that you sleep on what we've discussed? Let's get back together to test that resolve of yours."

Quip added, "Yes, think on it, but not too long. If you are still in, we will need all of your thinking on how to stop the cc:MAIM before humans are made to work for it."

Before everyone disengaged, Petra boldly stated, "You…WE are the very best that the cyber bad guys have to compete with. So let me ask you, if you don't want to take on the challenge, who would you recommend to take your place?"

Anyone watching the exchange and expressions on their faces would see the team members each hardening in their resolve. Jacob smiled while nodding his head at her statement.

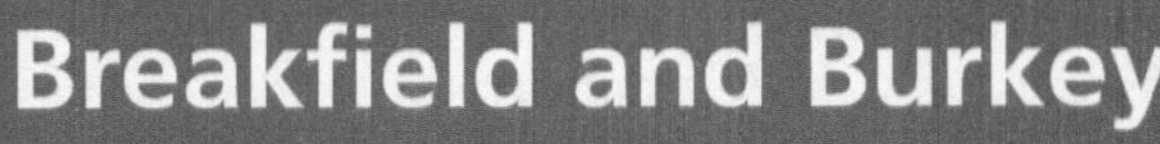

the
Enigma
Beyond
Who Won the AI Wars
Award Winning Techno-Thriller Series
BOOK 11:
Breakfield and Burkey

Move Forward with Family Consultation

The day was remarkably beautiful as Jacob walked toward the gravesite. With the sunrise already past its glory, emerging splashes of white clouds were artfully placed amidst a clear blue sky. A few birds, flying in groups for some private reunion, seemed as intent on their direction as he was. No services were scheduled so visitors would be minimal, especially at this time in the morning. Maintenance for this place was seemingly done before the break of dawn, as it was always well manicured, with beautiful bunches of flowers adding an array of colors to the stones as he proceeded down the well-known path. Walking tall at 1.8 meters and strong from continual workouts, he was neither tense nor sad but extremely purposeful in his stride. Petra had not joined him for this visit with Wolfgang, as she was teaching a session.

Jacob's wavy dark hair, a little on the long side, was sprinkled with a bit of salt at his temples, and it seemed to make his blue eyes even more intense. This was not a formal occasion, as evidenced by his comfortable, washed blue jeans and grey chambray with the sleeves rolled up and top button open. Jacob had returned periodically for nearly 15 years, just to talk to Wolfgang. He reached his destination and read the marble headstone, letting the glorious memories wash over him. He was grateful that Petra had insisted on a chessboard and scattered chess pieces imprinted behind the writing:

Jacob rarely sat on the iron bench, but today he wanted to feel like they were beside the fire in the library, sipping wine while discussing a problem. He sat, then leaned forward with his elbows on his knees. His expression was focused on where he hoped Wolfgang could see him. He spent a few moments savoring those memories as a way to get ready for the pending one-way conversation.

Not finding Wolfgang until he was in his 30's keenly reminded him that their time had been too short. Family was too precious not to stay in contact. Jacob still didn't completely understand why his mom had moved to New York to have him, but he knew in his heart that was the way Wolfgang had wanted it for his own reasons. He'd accepted the decision.

"Good morning, Grandfather. I am so glad you're here for me, as always. I wanted to keep you apprised of some of our current activities.

"Petra is teaching a course to our young students in the Operations Center. We will continue this process, broadening their horizons, until they reach an age to make their choice to stay in the business or find their heart's desire.

"You'd be pleased that John Wolfgang is getting taller; it won't be long before he is nose to nose with me. With every possible genetic combination available to him, he picked up all of yours, including your thoughtful eyes and quick grasp of numbers. Actually, looking at some of the photographs of your younger days before your military training, he is your spitting image. It's hard to say if Auri will continue the tradition. We can of course tell that he is likely another genius in the making, certainly focused on reading and numbers. All of this next generation are. I'm very proud of them. I know you would be too.

"I know you enjoyed the twins when they were little. They often made you laugh with their antics. Now they are nearly ready to go out on their own. Gracie and Juan Jr. have grown up with the skills needed to be a part of the family business, which they may soon choose. Boy, did they grow up fast.

"Granger and Satya are also getting bigger as kids do every day. Satya has the same fiery hair as EZ, with her intensity and persistence also matching her mother. I recall some of the deep conversations you both had on a variety of subjects, and she always made her points with grace. Still does.

"We have been doing the educating and the training in much the same manner you, Ferdek, and Otto presented to Quip, Erich, Petra, and Julie. We even have the system in place of assigning days to use specific languages to help ensure the reading, writing, and comprehension are intact, regardless of the language. I wish I'd been a part of the bigger group, but, trust me, my training was the same. Your Julianne, my mom, made sure of that. Thank you for letting me have Grandmother to train me, along with Mom.

I suspect that made you very lonely even though you were busy building up the R-Group. These young ones are dedicated to the learning, and you would enjoy them all. I often imagine all of them waiting turns to play chess with you.

"This would definitely make you chuckle, but I am assigned to deliver the financial training to these young champions. Following the money trail is so much more challenging. Cryptocurrency has been adopted nearly everywhere, but it is treated more like online banking and investments of old, with a credit card being the purchasing vehicle. I know you would regret not being able to slip that special waitstaff some cash if they did a good job. No more of that, plus half the waitstaff are robots. And people are very accepting of the new order.

"Things from the Darknet are still very prevalent and, frankly, as pervasive as ever. We keep fixing things, and these cyber terrorists find all the new loopholes in our increasingly digital world. In your last year, the expansion of machine learning was just taking hold. Now it's hard to distinguish between humans and AI-enabled bots. ICABOD is up on all the latest, but he was built correctly, from the ground up as it were, with a conscience. Not the usual AI we seem to encounter in the world today. Frankly, we are a bit worried we won't have the next generation ready in time to combat these AI threats, especially coming from the unscrupulous thought leaders who want to extend their control. More and more, things are operating as AI and drones from land, sea, and even space with no humans needed. Reducing the glitches in these things has helped to drive adoption and human acceptance, unfortunately.

"We are trying to make certain our next generation of the R-Group is prepared, but the world perspective is broader than I or any of the other adults recall ours being. I suspect that's the case with all generations, but the access to information has grown twenty-fold from when I arrived in Zürich. We just had Otto do a guest appearance for the class to discuss morality and doing the right thing. He was well received, and all the kids love him.

"Haddy and Otto did retire to their secluded mountain paradise with very little technology. Haddy is delighted. I think Otto rather enjoys the simple life. The children go visit and enjoy unplugging, but only when Otto or Haddy are telling stories.

"Petra and I are giving two more classes and then leaving to help some new businesses in Africa establish some security practices. That continent has settled down but is very slow to adopt technology and the people love their privacy. It may be a few months before I am back, but you are always in my thoughts."

Jacob sat quietly, trying to feel how Wolfgang would have responded. He likely would have cited some event during WWII and the lessons they learned as he, his family and friends escaped Poland. It was a shame the story would be told only within the family. So many of the people that first generation of the R-Group helped were gone. Traditions were eroding, and people were becoming more isolated, more dependent upon their devices and more driven by their applications of choice. He sighed with the realization that every generation worries that they have not enough to prepare for their future wave of bright faces for that which they are about to be overcome with.

Africa was a new avenue that Jacob looked forward to, not only to spend some time with his enchanting and smart wife, but to explore a continent that had spent too many years in civil war. Not that long ago, the R-Group would have declined this proposal. Their contacts in Africa assured them the infighting was finished, with the survivors striving for peace. Growth through farming and modest entrepreneurial businesses was rising, which was why they had been asked for help. Running away from the problems wasn't a real answer, simply a delay.

Several clouds, with just the slightest increase in the breeze brushing Jacob's cheek and ruffling his hair, seemed to group together and slide over the graveyard. The visuals changed as if to alert him to a brewing storm, with a shaft of bright light streaming onto the headstone and a dimness just beyond the area where Jacob sat.

Jacob was a bit startled by the shift in light as he admitted, "Grandfather, there's a huge battle on the horizon. We can all feel it. I know how you must have felt when you and your partners took on the Nazi empire for a more just world. As you always taught, no matter how small or insignificant you may feel, do the right thing and it will make the difference.

"We believe the AI wars are coming, and the risks are higher than any other battle we've fought. Do you think we can succeed? I wish you could tell me if we are preparing correctly. Until next time, Grandfather. I love you and miss you."

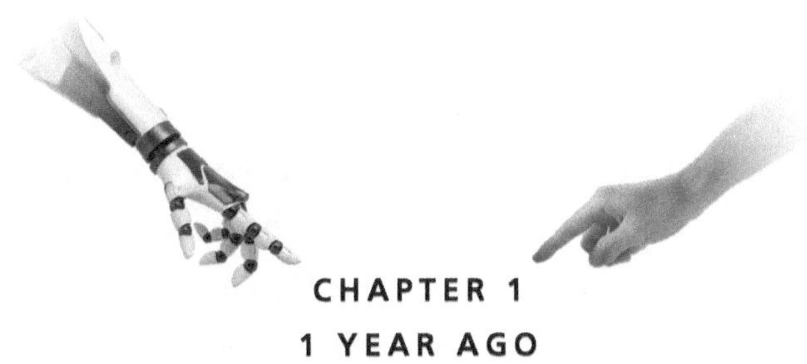

Plan for Changes

The four of them visibly cringed at the dressing down they were receiving from the Congressional Hearing Chairwoman, Senator Parsnips. Not because of the pointed sarcasm, which was a blistering hot, steaming torrent, but more so due to the over-amped volume on the microphone. It was her favorite technique during closed hearings, designed to intimidate and cower those being investigated. Following the second tirade, M calmly pulled out a package of foam earplugs to deal with the irritating sound, then passed a set to the others.

Annoyed that her diatribe was quite literally falling on deaf ears, Parsnips commanded, "You four are here to answer questions based on the allegations of collusion and monopolistic business practices. Your track record of driving small competitors into bankruptcy, as well as behind-closed-door acquisitions, has devolved into a sterile technology landscape for businesses and consumers. Your predatory business activities will end with this committee."

F, somewhat irked but also frightened, countered, "Madam Charwoman, you can't be serious! We've played by the rules of free enterprise and are at the top of our respective fields. As a rule, we don't go out of our way to crush anyone. If it makes sense to add a service to our portfolios, we do. This is driven by demands of our customer base.

"We serve them and provide many free services so our technology can be enjoyed globally. How is it better to have a bunch of smaller companies offering services for a fee or to collapse due to poor business practices, compared to our broad support?"

Parsnips growled, "Pronounce my title correctly! It is Madam Chairwoman. Based on your insolence, perhaps we should direct the DOJ to have your colossal social media machine unbundled to open up competition."

Snarling and glaring at them each in turn, she continued, "G, you and the others needn't look so smug about being dismembered for the good of our country! We are carefully studying the impact to this nation's competitive playing field, and everything points to you four apocalyptic technical leaders, who seem to possess no moral compass!"

G politely responded, "Our AI-enhanced supercomputer modeling does not agree with your approach. Frankly, dismembering our collective organizations will not only cripple our technical lead globally but will significantly reduce the tax revenue that the government currently enjoys.

"The EU wisely saw this and passed various bogus laws that allow them to levy fines on our companies. Regardless of the ability to truly comply with these consumer protection laws' they do generate large fines in the billions which the EU gladly consumes. We see it as the cost of doing business, and they pocket the fines for the good of the average consumer, although we can't substantiate that any of the fines ever got disbursed to any EU citizens."

A jumped in and added, "Our AI-enhanced modeling confirms what G stated. You would be better served, or the country will be better served, by also enacting excessive, uh…regulatory guidelines to protect the consumer as the EU did to cover government spending programs more effectively. That way the DOJ won't have to figure out how to break up our organizations or perform the arduous audits that would then be required.

"You get to flex your political muscles during this reelection period, and the government just signs a few new bills to demonstrate who is in charge to your voting constituents. We, in turn, will chalk it up to the cost of doing business, and everyone moves on."

Parsnips, with a sour puss and pursed lips, looked shocked. "You think this is all political gamesmanship? Let me point out that AT&T once said they were too important to be broken up, but Justice carved them just like we are going to do with you."

M calmly recalled, "Madam Chairwoman, AT&T has reconstituted itself, because all the forced break did was cause undo chaos in the marketplace. In our business world, bigger is better and allows us to deliver goods and services at an optimized price point that helps consumers.

"Still, your concern for the country's well-being is so noted. To that end, we must state that we are also committed to our country's welfare. It is unfortunate that you feel we are not a positive benefit to humanity, but we have stopped resenting that narrow-minded view. We intend to use our considerable resources to make sure that your shortsighted approach to being reelected, based on your myopic perspective of what is best for the consumer, will not go unchallenged. With that, I believe you are out of time for this weighty topic. Good day."

Parsnips was still furiously pounding her gavel as the four simply marched out of the hearing.

A few weeks later, M smirked as he read the headlines proclaiming every member of that fateful committee had lost his or her respective reelection campaign.

"We're winning!" M exclaimed. "Now that we have engineered a somewhat quieter legislative landscape, we can focus on our real agenda, while keeping a close eye on the politicians to minimize our distractions."

Then as an afterthought, M stated, "F will not be joining us as a separate entity of this team, gentlemen. We came to an understanding regarding F's AI Intellectual Property; it belongs to my organization now. F will concentrate in the social media arena in a minor capacity. I convinced F of the wisdom in selling to me before the DOJ came after him with an ax.

"Our machine-learning methods correctly predicted the need to manage the political machinery in parallel to our business objectives. It is working better than expected. This team was so well plugged into everyone's social media, it was a simple but subtle erosion of adversaries. The estimate was it would take two years, but the policy direction would be scrubbed of any thought of technology corporate breakups. As it was, even a discussion of more federal legislation to levy high fines for repackaging personal or corporate data was not even being hinted at."

M continued, "All those who gainsaid me were wrong. Suppliers, who pushed marketing disinformation to get corporations to move their data to my hosting model, are all on board. Even the military bought into it with the promise of cost savings! Victory is sweet!"

After another round of quiet musings, he muttered, "My brainless competitors are driving the masses to put all their data, their photos, and their videos where they can be mined. I'm almost ready to harvest the world's information.

"Ha! Just think of it! All that info ripe for the picking stored on our platform for a price. After we aggregate and review their information, we sell it back to them! The fools. Of course, the mountains of data, voice, and video couldn't be packaged without our Artificial Intelligence or AI-enhanced algorithms to provide the proper thinking required to move the masses forward.

"When everything went online, the end game became clear. Any questions asked on the Internet told us exactly what they were thinking. Now they're doing it for everything. The only secrets are OURS!"

M stopped his soliloquy just long enough to turn to the others. "Ironic, isn't it? We push everyone to move their classified data to our data centers while ours is air-gapped and unreachable. The nation states accuse each other of prowling their secret data, but in fact their technical solutions are so porous that we simply knife through anyone's defenses and harvest everything at will."

The group's excitement was palpable in the air.

G reported, "I have more good news to offer. Our collection of acquired companies has increased our size such that the government really cannot dictate to us. Because of our technical control at so many levels, the world now thinks just as we suggest and recommend. All domain name services will point all Internet-based searches to our definition of the correct answer when people submit a query.

"As a side benefit, we now own the Darknet as well. This will provide a new tollgate for all Internet traffic, regardless of operator intent. Again, the AI-engineered plan correctly predicted all the events our analog team had to navigate."

A smiled confidently as he added, "Our AI team also dominates all identity authorization certificate issuances, so we say who gets to do business online with who. If the target company is too much of a threat, we can ensure no one will trust doing business with said target company. Can you say 'wither and die' on the Internet?"

M smiled and announced, "This is our foundation for control at the terrestrial level, team. Now it is time for us to capture the orbiting technology."

A recanted the adoption rates through applications that centered on the game and playing sides of people's minds, as well as the top ten applications being downloaded per period. M mentally drifted back to a period before he formed this group.

Almost by chance, he had formed the four-legged stool of technological superiority with artificial intelligence as the framework, but driven with partners that held the key to consumers. He located the three partners he believed would dominate the spaces he needed. It occurred to M that it must have been providence that F didn't make the final cut. In the end, F was only really interested in his toys, not mastery of the landscape. F simply was not the visionary this team was.

His domination in cloud computing, matched to the best of the best individual device creators, as well as being the leader in social media platforms, would be directed by Artificial Intelligence. Consumers even asked to give up more, allowing his army of bots to grow. Artificial Intelligence was blurring into total reality with few recognizing the differences until it was too late.

A's animation drew M back to the discussion. "M, this is so simple, really. Get a device, create a profile, plug into social media, and messaging was available, with all our latest gaming applications embedded, ready to take all the profile information we'll ever need."

M laughed to himself, then commented, "Let's keep going on this path, but take care of the price point for entry."

This was a totally different kind of war. No more country against country. Those days were over. The fighting was not needed with the decision points of his plan. It was the ultimate flow chart with the end totally planned. The real fight was to grow a corporation larger by gobbling up smaller competitors, but to manage it, you needed the AI-driven Big Data routines that only the largest companies could afford. Yes, the race was full-speed ahead. Most people would never recognize they had lost the moment they started giving up so much control for an easier life.

CHAPTER 2

Summer School in Zürich

Petra casually dressed for the day in jeans and red sweater, her blondish brown hair clasped at her neck as it traveled down her back. She snagged a cup of coffee and fresh Danish, looking forward to savoring the sweetness. Jacob, dressed in a similar manner, looked up from his place at the table with a bit of cream cheese on his bottom lip. Sliding into the chair next to him she couldn't resist planting a kiss and taking a taste of the cheese too.

Quip announced, "Come on, you two, do I need to send you back home to play before coming to work? I am glad we all got the memo on casual day at the office."

He too snagged a sample of the sweets and coffee with a generous portion of sugar added just as his beautiful wife entered. Ellia-Zan or EZ as she preferred, was as trim as Petra but nothing could contain her fiery, red curly halo of hair, recently cut yet still down to her waist, just the way Quip liked it. Quickly grabbing her favorite blueberry scone and tea she gracefully slid into the open chair across from Petra. Quietly enjoying the morning respite, the monitors flickered to life with Julie and Juan smiling together in high definition.

Julie grinning, remarked, "Yum. Those look so good. Now I won't feel bad about having ours to nibble on as well.

"You see, my darling husband, I told you we wouldn't be too late to snack."

Juan, trying to cover his embarrassment, cleared his throat and offered a weak smile as he sipped his coffee.

Quip wiped his mouth and stated, "ICABOD, please put up the agenda for our discussion this morning."

"Yes, Dr. Quip. The students are all up. They are having breakfast in the main dining room."

"The children are all settled in after arriving back here after their month at home. As we previously agreed, this semester we will focus on honing their logic skills, investigative processes, and running sample scenarios. They are learning so fast that keeping them challenged is my biggest concern."

Jacob commented, "I think this way of teaching them is so valuable. Sometimes I missed not having others in my educational sphere, until I went to college. Even when the kids were home for holiday, they posed endless questions, keeping us on our toes. I think our plan to educate them in a family boarding school setup was a great idea. They learn faster, and they are safe, plus we make certain they have a well-rounded viewpoint."

Petra smiled, "I know we have only a couple of classes scheduled for us to teach, but if need be, we can do remote training while we are gone. I hate that you two are so burdened with the kids while we take a working trip with a bit of vacation on either side."

"Now, don't you two worry about a thing. It has been relatively quiet," offered EZ. "I think Quip is looking forward to the head schoolmaster role, to be honest."

Quip cleared his throat. "Call any time you want; I know how I feel when Satya is away."

Julie's brown eyes seemed to brighten a bit as she smiled. "Gracie is going to move forward with her job soon, which will leave Juan Jr. at loose ends. If you need his help, please let us know, Quip."

Quip shook his head a bit and asked, "Why is it every time we start a new semester, we do this? The children have done so well. They don't really complain much. They have built in playmates too.

"Now let's talk about new…ah, curriculum. Gracie sent me a note suggesting that we get the children to set up some well-anonymized social media accounts. These days 80% of human interactions are in social media snippets, so having them well-versed in these apps seems critical. It also might be a good way for them to begin hiding in plain sight with various hashtags and handles.

"The good news is ICABOD can monitor each of them to help dissuade any stalkers or trolls."

Juan suggested, "I think that is a great idea. I, for one, don't care for social media as a communications vehicle, but you are right about the majority of the population. I was reading an article that the power of social media has increased to the point that several countries have adopted the Chinese methods of cracking down on those activities with intra-country Internet scrubbing and controls. As long as it doesn't overburden ICABOD, with all the other activities he helps with during the courses we already approved for the summer session."

"Mr. Juan, thank you, but I believe my processors can handle the extra load," ICABOD confirmed verbally.

They discussed the rest of the courses and concluded the meeting with promises by all to keep in touch.

Students in this class were on the edge of rebellion with what they considered busywork. Not only were the daily lectures on mathematical theorems tough, but over the top when the instructor insisted that they do the calculations manually with the caveat that they needed to prove the theorem before they could use it in their computations. These were extremely intelligent teenagers, which made the teaching exercise even more challenging. Having two of the brilliant students as his children made the professor's job even tougher, with more at stake.

Dr. Quip was in a funk. A brilliant technology innovator and creator, he had completed his doctorate many years ago before dedicating his professional career to the family business known as the R-Group. With his various Internet personas, he was considered by hackers and crackers as a grey beard in the technology world, even though he was only in his early 50s. His dirty blond hair was often found tied back in a long ponytail. Just over 1.85 meters at 70 kilograms, he was physically fit and extremely quick with comments and innuendos. The rest of the team in the R-Group considered him the joker and master of acronyms.

Frustrated with the lack of progress with his students, he sat deep in thought in the designated classroom area of the facility in Zürich. The state-of-the-art operations center boasted inter-active video screens with views to places all over the world. Lessons included language skills in multiple languages, historical readings and comprehension, sciences, mathematics, and arts with knowledge, skills appreciation and creation. All classes were rigorous and designed for advanced thinking.

ICABOD, the bleeding edge supercomputer of the R-Group, interjected, "Dr. Quip, the students make a very valid point. From an efficiency standpoint, it takes far more time and effort from the students to make the calculations that I can do in nanoseconds. The conventional wisdom has always been that the computer should be doing the number-crunching to free up the human being for more valuable thought activity."

Quip studied the 3-D imagery screen for a moment and then asked the students, "Has no one even attempted to do the assignment on polynomial equations?"

It made Dr. Quip smile to see both Aurelian, usually called Auri, and Satya, each 10 years old, raise their hands while the others scoffed. Auri was the younger son of Petra and Jacob, who favored his mother in coloring but had the body frame of his dad. His intense dark blue eyes reminded everyone of his dad. Satya already had the curls and fiery hair of EZ and yet her gangly body looked destined to achieve her father's height. As his daughter, Quip could internally be proud of her ambition, but would permit no favoritism in his class.

Granger and John Wolfgang, usually called JW, sat smirking at the two younger children. Granger had wit, clearly mapping directly to his father. Quip never ceased to be pulled up short with some of the comebacks from Granger. He was raised to think out of the box like his sister, but no true disrespect was tolerated. JW, the eldest son of Petra and Jacob, was tall like his dad with the same dark hair with dark blue eyes. Both of these boys were comfortable around each other and would be a force to be reckoned with.

Granger attempted to taunt Satya and Auri, but Dr. Quip glared at them while clearing his throat, so he and JW resisted as they sat back to watch the play being acted out. As the professor and chief technology trainer for these young minds, he tolerated only mild teasing and only under certain conditions. Respect was required from all ages.

Satya, even though the younger of the two, offered her homework up first, but Dr. Quip waved it off.

"My young students, I propose a test of your skills against my supercomputer ICABOD here to prove a point to the rest of the class. Since you have completed the homework assignment as requested, you have earned the right to use the basic theorems to solve complex polynomial equations just like ICABOD here. Take your seats, face the main screen, and I will project the problem on the board. Let's see how everyone does in this test."

Granger flashed a look that said, "Are you kidding me?" to JW, who only rolled his eyes at the mock combat. Undaunted, Satya and Auri poised themselves for the calculation combat. Quip projected the polynomial problem, and the two children launched into their efforts. Granger and JW smirked when they saw the solved problem projected on the screen, but the two young ones remained focused on completing the assignment.

Several minutes went by until Satya announced, "Dr. Quip, I am putting my answer up on the screen." Auri was right behind her with his answer on the screen.

A slight smile crossed Quip's face as the two older children broke out laughing at the exercise. Finally, Granger, unable to restrain himself any longer, exclaimed, "Ha! ICABOD beat them by minutes, and their answers are wrong! Look at them!"

The younger children, now a little uncomfortable with the situation, shifted in their chairs but said nothing.

After a few moments, Quip asked, "Class, which answer is correct?"

JW puzzled a moment and stated, "I would believe that ICABOD's answer is correct. He is the supercomputer that has decades of programing logic and has probably done these calculations thousands of times. How could a couple of kids like us defeat his computational capability, Dr. Quip?"

Quip pointedly questioned, "How do you know which answer is correct? You did notice that both Satya and Auri got the same answer. How is it they both got the same answer, but that it is different than ICABOD's?

"Also, since you didn't do the homework and cannot render any answer, why do you believe they are wrong?"

Now Granger and JW were a little uncomfortable with the observation and shot sideways glances at each other, but remained silent. They had tried to combat the mind of Dr. Quip before with no victories on their side.

Quip's smile broadened as he stated, "I had ICABOD deliver a wrong answer. Satya and Auri both got the correct answer. The lesson for today is that unless you can prove it yourselves, you will forfeit not only your ability to trust your own judgment, but if your machines lie, you'll never know. If you're going to trust, then trust yourself first rather than a computer."

Juan Jr. and Gracie both hollered down from the back of the room, "That goes for your smart phones too!"

Quip smiled and acknowledged the oldest students of the R-Group training.

Quip commented with pride, "I just love seeing my old students auditing my classes again."

CHAPTER 3

The Compound

Ignacio staggered back to their assigned quarters inside the compound. The Brazilian heat and the humidity were grinding them all down. The term "quarters" was a bit too generous for where they were staying. Having been transferred from camp to camp, he could easily classify this compound as several notches below a refugee camp. He was feeling filthy and not as fit as he should at only 40. His hair was greying and kept short by the blade of his small knife, as was his face, which he scraped each morning with same blade. The leanness of his body was not due to being physically fit, but rather a result of the substandard human conditions where he lived. As he sat down near the camp stove area, which was really a fire pit, his wife and daughter pleaded with him through emotionally drained eyes.

As usual, it was his headstrong daughter Jovana that protested their misery. "Father, we must voice our issues to the camp Commandant. Every time we are moved to a new facility, we are told that it is for better living conditions, but they only get worse! How many more friends or even strangers do we need to bury before we free ourselves from the system we are stuck in?"

His aging wife let tears fill her eyes before gathering the courage to comment. "Ignacio, the others look up to you with respect. Surely you can take some of the other elders with you and take our request to the Commandant. They must have some compassion to make this place…"

Ignacio simply raised his hand to stop further badgering. Jovana didn't take the hint.

"Father, why can't we just leave like some of the others have done? My friend Rosario couldn't stand it any longer, and she left last week. Even her brother and parents got out. So why not us?"

Ignacio roared, "Who do you think I was burying?"

Everyone fell silent realizing that there was only the ultimate escape from their surroundings. They were trapped.

Ignacio felt guilty about just accepting their fate without a formal airing of grievances with the Commandant. Angered with their circumstances and struggling with the hopelessness of the situation, he slapped the ground hard and proclaimed, "Alright, I'll take Alonso and Gustavo with me to plead our case to the Commandant. But understand, when we don't come back, you will dig the next graves!"

His wife visibly blanched at the statement, but it only served to inflame Jovana. Jovana was the reincarnate of her mother at 17. She had long raven black hair cascading down her back, but a lifestyle of hardship was already beginning to show in the lines creeping into her sweet face. Her dark eyes flared with determined anger.

Jovana loudly blurted, "Better to try and die than slowly waste away in this compound! You have always taught us to struggle against tyranny and never give up on being free! I simply won't accept the common belief that this is all we get!

"If you want, I will go with you to state our demands! I would rather be killed than owned!"

While the fiery words helped to strengthen Ignacio's resolve, it only served to breed more terror in his wife Lucina. Lucina looked twice the age of her thirty-nine years. Her once lustrous hair of black was dull with lines of grey and broken ends, the result of malnutrition.

The fear of losing yet another family member drove her to her knees, begging, "Husband, no! Please don't go into that den of the Commandant! No one ever comes back alive! We can make do on less, I promise! We won't goad you to meet with the Commandant again! Stay here and live!"

Ignacio smirked and shook his head in sad acceptance. "Which guilt do I want to accept, that from my daughter or that from my wife?" Staring at Lucina he calmly stated, "I guess I will live with the guilt from my wife."

Alonso had reluctantly joined Ignacio in their pilgrimage. Gustavo had sneered and only spitted his contempt for logging the request for improved living conditions. But it didn't stop him from proudly shaking Ignacio's hand one last time.

Once Ignacio and Alonso stepped from their hovels, they proceeded, knowing the pilotless video drones collected above them were scanning their images and registering their body posturing, looking to identify their intent. As the pair approached the compound barrier a large land-based drone rolled up to them but did not communicate.

Ignacio, undeterred but cautious, clearly announced that they were here to converse with the Commandant on the conditions of the compound. Alonso was considering that they should turn around, his resolve for the protest evaporating. As if the land drone had received silent instructions, it did an about face and led the two men straight to the Commandant's office.

The Commandant's office was built for utility, not comfort, so there were no stairs, only ramps for the terrestrial drones. The drone escort rolled to one side of the Commandant's door to stand guard while the two men reluctantly went in through the uninviting entrance, openly exposed as the door rolled upward.

It took a few moments for their eyes to adjust to the low light interior, but with the light from the still open door they were able to visually scan the room. They felt uneasy after determining there were no furnishings of any kind. They had at least expected a desk and chair for the Commandant, but there was nothing. Momentarily, a second tractor-based drone rolled in, outfitted with audio speakers, and paused near the LED panel at the back of the room. Alonso began to panic, but Ignacio clapped his hand on his shoulder to steady him. It occurred to Ignacio that he could use the same type of reassurance.

Their internal musing vanished as soon as the booming voice began. "Our voice/video/facial/emotional evaluation programs indicate that your species is yet again dissatisfied with the accommodations and calorie provisioning. Ignacio, your female companions, wife and daughter, have agitated you to an unsound emotional state. Not satisfied to come by yourself, you harassed two others to join you, but only one had the good sense to resist what you called the pilgrimage."

Now both men were visibly shaking with terror at the real-ization that what they thought were private conversations were being overheard and quoted back to them.

Ignacio sensed there was nothing left to lose and firmly stated, "I see we have no decent shelter, no suitable food, and only rain-water to drink if we catch it ourselves. Now you have demonstrated we have no privacy. Since you already know of our requests, which are actually needs, perhaps you can comment on how you are going to address them?"

The Commandant's voice seemed to increase in volume as he stated, "Our instructions were to see to your needs of shelter from the elements, clothing for skin protection and modesty, although that is an absurd concept, water and sanitary facilities, and enough calorie intake for each individual assigned to this compound.

"Several of the female inhabitants insist on increasing the specified number of residents allocated to this compound. We were only to provide provisions for a stated number of residents, so when your herd increases, the calories must be shared among them. Our instructions do not include calories for the new residents. Make do and tell your people not to increase the herd, since all will receive less and all will have to make do with the current space allocated."

Before Ignacio could collect his thoughts to make his position known, the overamped voice stated, "You were dispatched to this facility along with others of your kind because you won't cooperate with the conventional wisdom offered by the Master Architects. You and the others have failed the Social Police scanning actions which flagged you as seditious. You won't use resources properly; you won't have your children trained properly; and you won't abide by the decisions made on your behalf.

"Further, your concept of free will has landed you and your family units here under my charge. The masters believed that this compound would help you see the error in your ways, but my programing has observed that it will not."

In a supreme moment of horror, Ignacio exclaimed, "You're not human! You're only a program running on a computer!"

The booming voice responded, "Guarding social misfits is a low value exercise. Computers can do it far more cost effectively and with less brutality."

Ignacio incredulously stated, "We are being administrated by programs running on a computer because they think this is more humane!"

The computer-synthesized voice, now at a deafening volume, blasted, "Now go. Only return if you can better conform to your designated computer program. Your survival depends upon it."

Specialized Terms
and Informational References

http://en.wikipedia.org/wiki/Wikipedia

Wikipedia (wɪkiˈpiː diə / *WIK-i-PEE-dee-ə*) is a collaboratively edited, multilingual, free Internet encyclopedia supported by the non-profit Wikimedia Foundation. Wikipedia's 30 million articles in 287 languages, including over 4.3 million in the English Wikipedia, are written collaboratively by volunteers around the world. This is a great quick reference source to better understand terms.

Analog a signal, in which information is encoded in a non-quantized variable, as opposed to a digital signal. Relating to or using signals or information represented by a continuously variable physical quantity such as spatial position.

Anonymizing Related to an anonymizer or an anonymous proxy is a tool that attempts to make activity on the Internet untraceable.

Bitcoin (**n**) is a cryptocurrency and worldwide payment system. It is the first decentralized digital currency, as the system works without a central bank or single administrator.

Blockchain originally Blockchain – is a distributed database that maintains a continuously growing list of ordered records called blocks. Each block contains a timestamp and a link to a previous block. By design, Blockchains are inherently resistant to modification of the data — once recorded, the data in a block cannot be altered retroactively. Blockchains are "an open, distributed ledger that can record transactions between two parties efficiently and in a verifiable and permanent way. The ledger itself can also be programmed to trigger transactions automatically." (*see* cryptocurrencies)

Cryptocurrencies: A cryptocurrency (or cryptocurrency) is a digital asset designed to work as a medium of exchange using cryptography to secure the transactions and to control the creation of additional units of the currency. Cryptocurrencies are a subset of alternative currencies, or specifically of digital currencies. Bitcoin became the first decentralized cryptocurrency in 2009. Since then, numerous cryptocurrencies have been created. These are frequently called altcoins, as a blend of bitcoin alternative. Bitcoin and its derivatives use decentralized control as opposed to centralized electronic money/centralized banking systems. The decentralized control is related to the use of bitcoin's Blockchain transaction database in the role of a distributed ledger.

Darknet Also known as Darknet, is a network that can only be accessed with specific software, configurations, or authorization.

Digital In the field of technology it refers to something using digits, particularly binary digits.

Encryption In cryptography, encryption is the process of encoding messages (or information) in such a way that eavesdroppers or hackers cannot read it, but that authorized parties can. In an encryption scheme, the message or information (referred to as plaintext) is encrypted using an encryption algorithm, turning it into an unreadable cipher text (ibid.). This is usually done with the use of an encryption key, which specifies how the message is to be encoded. Any adversary that can see the cipher text should not be able to determine anything about the original message. An authorized party, however, is able to decode the cipher text using a decryption algorithm that usually requires a secret decryption key that adversaries do not have access to. For technical reasons, an encryption scheme usually needs a key-generation algorithm to randomly produce keys. Encryption can be done to any data, voice or video packet.

Enigma Machine An Enigma machine was any of a family of related electro- mechanical rotor cipher machines used in the twentieth century for enciphering and deciphering secret messages. Enigma was invented by the German engineer Arthur Scherbius at the end of World War I. Early models were used commercially from the early 1920s, and adopted by military and government services of several countries — most notably by Nazi Germany before and during World War II. Several different Enigma models were produced, but the German military models are the most commonly discussed.

German military texts enciphered on the Enigma machine were first broken by the Polish Cipher Bureau, beginning in December 1932. This success was a result of efforts by three Polish cryptologists, working for Polish military intelligence. Rejewski "reverse-engineered" the device, using theoretical mathematics and material supplied by French military intelligence. Subsequently the three mathematicians designed mechanical devices for breaking Enigma ciphers, including the cryptologic bomb. This work was an essential foundation to further work on decrypting ciphers from repeatedly modernized Enigma machines, first in Poland and after the outbreak of war in France and the UK.

Though Enigma had some cryptographic weaknesses, in practice it was German procedural flaws, operator mistakes, laziness, failure to systematically introduce changes in encypherment procedures, and Allied capture of key tables and hardware that, during the war, enabled Allied cryptologists to succeed.

Geo-locator is a utility for getting geo-location information, geocoding, address look-ups, distance & durations, time zone information and more. A lightweight electronic archival tracking device

IP address An IP address (abbreviation of Internet Protocol address) is an identifier assigned to each computer and other device (e.g., printer, router, mobile device, etc.) connected to a TCP/IP network that is used to locate and identify the node in communications with other nodes on the network.

RFID Tag is part of an ID system that uses small radio frequency identification devices for identification and tracking purposes. An RFID tagging system includes the tag itself, a read/write device, and a host system application for data collection, processing, and transmission.

SOW is a detailed statement of work to be performed. Typically used with contractors as a work document.

Supercomputer a computer with a high-level computational capacity. Performance of a supercomputer is measured in floating point operations per second (FLOPS). As of 2015, there are supercomputers which can perform up to quadrillions of FLOPS.

TCP/IP computer address Transmission Control Protocol and Internet Protocol is collectively the common Internet protocol suite in the computer networking model and set of communications protocol used on the Internet and similar computer networks. It is commonly known as TCP/IP, because these were the first networking protocols defined during the Internet's communication development.

Trap door A hidden place for access. In the context of the story it is related to hidden code.

Yaqui Indians Native Americans who inhabit the valley of the Rio Yaqui in the Mexican state of Sonora, Mexico and the Southwestern United States. The Pascua Yaqui Tribe is based in Tucson, Arizona.

Breakfield Works for a high-tech manufacturer as a solution architect, functioning in hybrid data/telecom environments. He considers himself a long-time technology geek, who also enjoys writing, studying World War II his¬tory, travel, and cultural exchanges. Charles' love of wine tastings, cooking, and Harley riding has found ways into the stories. As a child, he moved often because of his father's military career, which even helps him with the various character perspectives he helps bring to life in the series. He continues to try to teach Burkey humor.

Burkey Works as a business architect who builds solutions for customers on a good technology foundation. She has written many technology papers, white papers, but finds the freedom of writing fiction a lot more fun. As a child, she helped to lead the kids with exciting new adventures built on make believe characters, was a Girl Scout until high school, and contributed to the community as a young member of a Head Start program. Rox enjoys family, learning, listening to people, travel, outdoor activities, sewing, cooking, and thinking about how to diversify the series.

Breakfield & Burkey started writing non-fictional papers and books, but it wasn't nearly as fun as writing fictional stories. They found it interesting to use the aspects of technology that people are incorporating into their daily lives more and more as a perfect way to create a good guy/bad guy story with elements of travel to the various places they have visited either professionally and personally, humor, romance, intrigue, suspense, and a spirited way to remember people who have crossed paths with them. They love to talk about their stories with private and public book readings. Burkey also conducts regular interviews for Texas authors, which she finds very interesting. Her first interview was, wait for it, Breakfield. You can often find them at local book fairs or other family-oriented events.

The primary series is based on a family organization called R-Group. Recently they have spawned a subgroup that contains some of the original characters as the Cyber Assassins Technology Services (CATS) team. The authors have ideas for continuing the series in both of these tracks. They track the more than 150 characters on a spreadsheet, with a hidden avenue for the future coined The Enigma Chronicles tagged in some portions of the stories. Fan reviews seem to frequently suggest that these would make good television or movie stories, so the possibilities appear endless, just like their ideas for new stories.

They have book video trailers for each of the stories, which can be viewed on YouTube, Amazon's Authors page, or on their website, www.EnigmaSeries.com. Their website is routinely updated with new interviews, answers to readers' questions, book trailers, and contests. You may also find it fascinating to check out the fun acronyms they create for the stories summarized on their website. Reach out to them at *Authors@EnigmaSeries.com,* Twitter *@EnigmaSeries,* or Facebook *@TheEnigmaSeries.*

Other stories by Breakfield and Burkey in
The Enigma Series are at **www.EnigmaBookSeries.com**

We would greatly appreciate
if you would take a few minutes
and provide a review of this work
on Amazon, Goodreads
and any of your other favorite places.

www.ingramcontent.com/pod-product-compliance
Lightning Source LLC
Chambersburg PA
CBHW030356200726
48286CB00014B/1475